BADASS

BAD

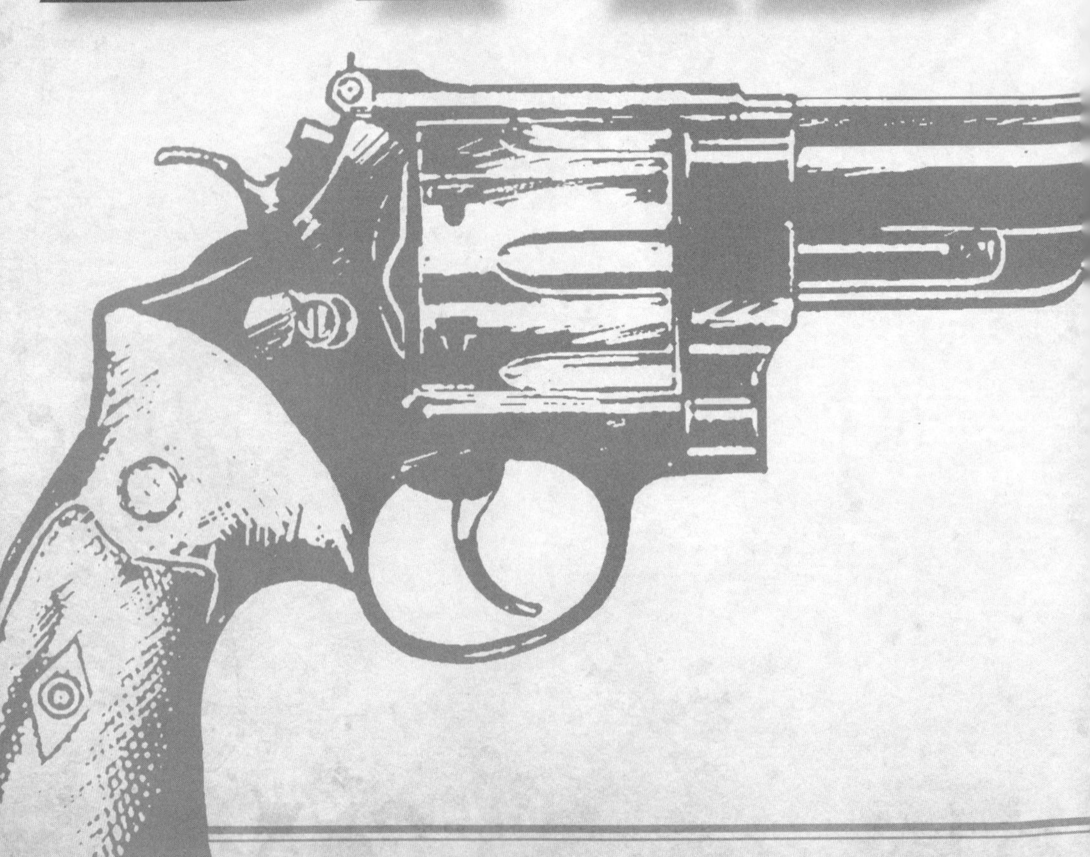

[BADASS]

BEN THOMPSON

A Relentless Onslaught of the Toughest Warlords, Vikings, Samurai, Pirates, Gunfighters, and Military Commanders to Ever Live

HARPER

NEW YORK . LONDON . TORONTO . SYDNEY

FIRST EDITION

Designed by Lorie Pagnozzi

Library of Congress Cataloging-in-Publication Data

Thompson, Ben.

Badass: a relentless onslaught of the toughest warlords, vikings, samurai, pirates, gunfighters, and military commanders to ever live/Ben Thompson.—1st ed.

p. cm.

Includes bibliographical references.

ISBN 978-0-06-174944-5

1. Heroes—Biography. 2. Outlaws—Biography. 3. Courage. 4. Fortitude. I. Title.

CT105.T57 2009

920.02—dc22

2009011502

09 10 11 12 13 OV/RRD 10 9 8 7 6 5 4 3 2 1

Let me not then die ingloriously and without a struggle,
But let me first do some great thing that
shall be told among men hereafter.

—HECTOR OF TROY, *ILIAD* XVII, LINES 304-5

CONTENTS

There's no one that can match me.
My style is impetuous.
My defense is impregnable, and
I'm just ferocious.
I want your heart.
I want to eat his children.

—MIKE TYSON

BADASS

THE BONE-CRUSHING PRINCIPLES OF COMPLETE AND UTTER BADASSITUDE

The difference between a successful person and
others is not a lack of strength,
not a lack of knowledge, but rather a lack of will.

—VINCE LOMBARDI

THIS BOOK FEATURES THE GREAT ASS-KICKERS OF WORLD DOMINATION. From those who rule the textbooks, such as Alexander the Great, William the Conqueror, and George S. Patton, to more mysterious and obscure characters including Wolf the Quarrelsome, Bass Reeves, and Irina Sebrova, these men and women routinely overcame seemingly insurmountable obstacles, wrecked the asses of their enemies in an exceedingly violent manner, and ultimately altered the course of history through their actions. While vicious conquerors such as Genghis Khan and Vlad the Impaler took great satisfaction in parading around the severed heads of their vanquished enemies, others, including Leonidas and Horatio Nelson, were noble heroes who fought to defend their homelands from tyranny and oppression at the hands of foreign invaders.

The historical figures in this book span every era of history, every corner of the globe, and every spectrum of human morality, but they all share certain qualities that define them as "badasses," and there are many lessons to be learned from them:

1. DESTROY ALL WHO OPPOSE YOU

At some point, all aspiring badasses come across some complete raging dickbrain who stands in the way of your manifest destiny. It is your moral obligation to destroy that person and everything he cares about.

There are several methods of properly obliterating the enemy, and you really should be familiar with as many as possible. For ranged weaponry, you should learn to use a handgun, reload a howitzer, accurately throw a tomahawk, work a two-man T-shirt cannon, and operate a sixteenth-century English crossbow. You'll also want to familiarize yourself with a wide variety of hand-to-hand combat implements such as broken bottles, baseball bats, chair legs, frying pans, circular saws, fire extinguishers, Phillips-head screwdrivers, pruning shears, weed whackers, nunchucks, ice picks, and dental drills. There's no way to know what will be available in a critical situation, so it's always best to be prepared. If it helps, just think of badasses as Boy Scouts with switchblades and assault rifles who can knock someone's head off with a flying side kick and send it bouncing down the street into a drainage ditch.

Badasses also have no time for telemarketers, cooking shows, or micromanaging bosses. For instance, when your boss goes off on you to do some actual work and stop wasting company resources on endless rounds of computer solitaire, if you're a true bone crusher, you'll grab your stapler, smash your boss in the forehead, and inform him (in a loud and threatening manner) that nothing can stand in the way of your epic quest to uncover the elusive ace of spades. To drive home the point, leave work fifteen minutes early (ostensibly out of protest), go out to the parking lot, and torch his stupid expensive midlife-crisis sports car with a homemade flamethrower.

2. DRIVE IT LIKE IT'S STOLEN

Whether it's Jason Bourne, Ellen Ripley, or Han Solo behind the wheel, almost every action movie hero out there is proficient in the operation and maintenance of most types of motor vehicle. In order to escape from zany anarcho-terrorist cyborg genetic clone scumbags that may attempt to kidnap and/or assassinate you and steal your identity, you'll need to utilize all of the resources at your disposal. This means being able to drive the hell out of a wide variety of automobiles, motorcycles, airplanes, spacecraft, jetpacks, hovercraft, and speedboats. If you want to take this one step further in the direction of being completely gonzo Xtreme to the max, you should also learn how to ride animals such as horses, camels, llamas, and zebras, as well as how to parachute out of a cargo plane, perform an ollie on a skateboard, properly harness yourself into a rickshaw, and hit a ramp in a rocket-powered wheelchair doing at least sixty miles per hour.

3. CONQUER THE ELEMENTS

Nothing screams "I am awesome" quite like camping in the wilderness for a week without dying of exposure or getting eaten by angry bears. This really kicks Mother Nature in the ovaries with a steel-toed boot. Outdoor skills like mountaineering, starting a fire with sticks, digging an ice cave with your bare hands, and eating a vast assortment of disgusting forest creatures will help you evade capture and survive when you're stranded deep behind enemy lines. Plus, your ability to club a yeti unconscious by hitting it in the face with a broken-off tree branch could someday prove to be the difference between life and death. In the unforgiving wilderness you must constantly struggle to survive, no matter what the situation, because coming home intact is always the first part of living for revenge.

4. LIVE FOR REVENGE

From Shaolin temples to your own death, there are tons of things out there that need to be avenged, and a true badass should never think twice about serving up a piping hot vengeance omelet to anyone who even halfheartedly tries to dick him over. While the desire for revenge is pretty much the oldest emotion humankind has ever experienced, it is important to remember that the vengeance does not necessarily need to be proportional to the crime committed. For instance, when some Mafia jerk had Frank Castle's family whacked, Frank turned himself into the Punisher and spent the next twenty years shooting criminals in the face with a gigantic bazooka. Whereas the ancient Babylonians might have suggested some kind of middle-of-the-road, eye-for-an-eye crap, Mr. Castle understood that every ass-kicking vigilante worthy of his aviator sunglasses always pushes everything well beyond the limits of logic and reason and goes full throttle all the damn time—no matter what the police or any other authority figures/rational human beings might say.

5. NEVER GIVE UP, NEVER SURRENDER

Badasses, much like Goonies, never say die. To that end, they also never say diet, and their color recognition vocabulary is limited to just six words. They don't flinch, cry, hesitate, show fear, or act like they notice when it's raining. Even if it's raining really, really hard. Nothing bothers them, nobody stands in their way, and they refuse to yield even when the situation seems ten light-years beyond hopeless. No matter what the odds are, they won't accept anything less than victory at all costs.

While all of the other principles in this list may be negotiable, this axiom is the single most important rule of ultimate face-beatery. In fact, steadfast, unwavering determination is the one thing that all of the characters in this book have in common. These men and women were all aspiring to different things, but every character highlighted in these pages went balls-out after what they wanted, never backed down, and didn't stop until they'd achieved their goals, however honorable or nefarious they may have been. In the end, that kind of determination, drive, and will is what really forges true badasses.

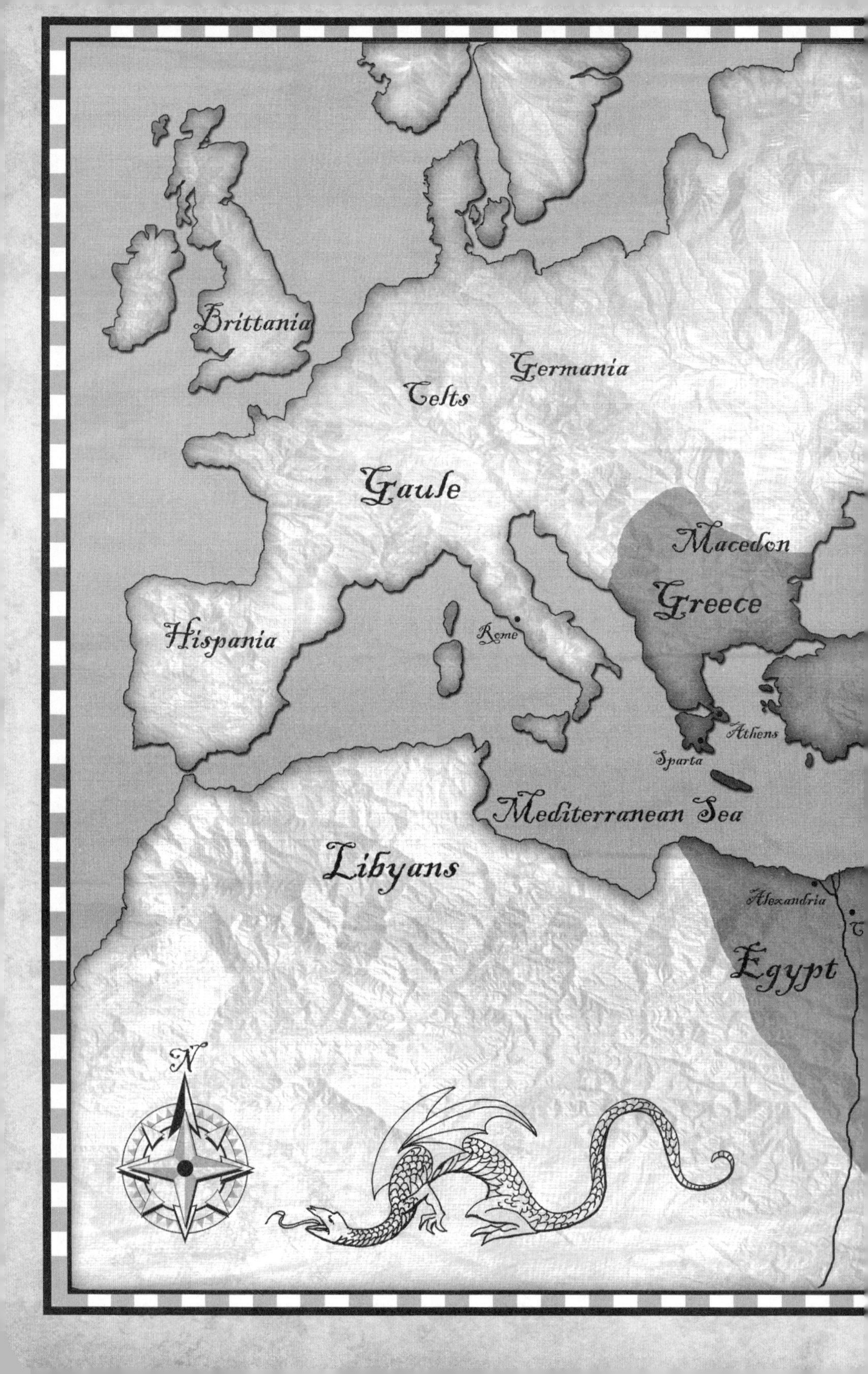
Brittania
Germania
Celts
Gaule
Macedon
Greece
Hispania
Rome
Athens
Sparta
Mediterranean Sea
Libyans
Alexandria
Egypt
N

Section I
Antiquity

2008

1

RAMSES II

(1303–1213 BCE)

My name is Ozymandias, King of Kings: Look upon my works, ye mighty, and despair!

—PERCY BYSSHE SHELLEY, *OZYMANDIAS*

RAMSES II ASCENDED TO THE THRONE OF EGYPT AT THE AGE OF TWENTY AND WOULD GO ON TO RULE THE NEW KINGDOM AS ITS MOST EFFICIENT AND POWERFUL PHARAOH FOR SIXTY-SIX YEARS, BY FAR THE LONGEST REIGN OF ANY OF THE GOD-KINGS. The guy was blessed with such longevity that he actually outlived his twelve eldest sons, which is pretty damn impressive considering that most people don't even produce twelve potential heirs. Ramses ushered in a golden age of prosperity, commissioned restoration projects on the Great Pyramids, and was worshiped as a living god who righteously kicked the asses of anyone who crossed his mighty empire. He also sired more than a hundred children from his endless harem of superhot nubile wives, including the beautiful Nefertari, a woman who was so fly that the Egyptian priests actually declared that she was a living goddess. This chick was allegedly so smoking that any man within twenty miles of her immediately popped a boner for no reason at all, and if you looked directly at her, your eyes melted right out of your face.

Ramses, who is also known as Ozymandias for some bizarre reason I'll never understand, was more than just the husband of a ten-megaton superbabe—he was also a genuine military ass whipper as well. As a young heir to the throne, Prince Ramses was commissioned to take down a group of jerkweed pirates that had been terrorizing the high seas with their bloody hijinks and murderous rampages. Ramses put an end to that nonsense quickly by sailing out with a small detachment of the elite Egyptian Royal Guard, hacking the arms off the scurvy bastards with a razor-sharp sickle sword and conscripting any survivors to serve as part of a mercenary army devoted to blindly carrying out his bidding.

As ruler of Egypt's New Kingdom, the largest and most powerful empire in the world at this time, Ramses the Great led numerous campaigns against the Libyans, Syrians, Philistines, Hittites, Hatti, Nubians, and a bunch of other obscure ancient civilizations, all of which featured at least one *i*. He managed to conquer lands as far as Lebanon, and successfully defended his borders from hostile raids by building a vast network of impenetrable forts across the outskirts of the empire, many of which would remain unconquered for centuries. After crushing a rival civilization, Ramses's favorite way to celebrate a victory was by cutting off the right hands and penises of his defeated foes and placing towering piles of severed hands and dongs in the center of town to serve as a testament to his godlike military might. (Seriously.)

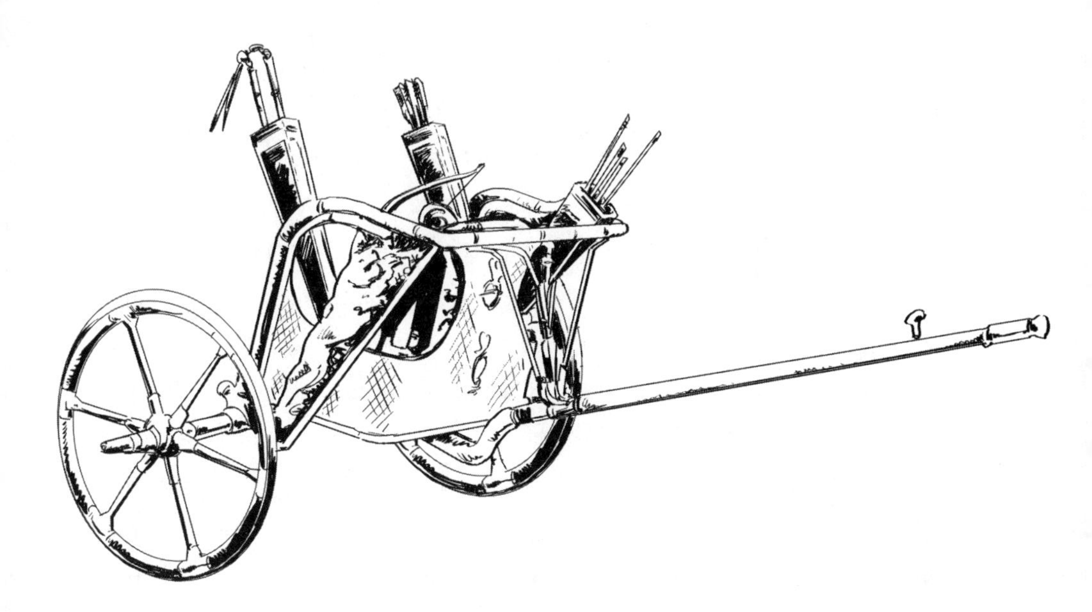

On top of his prowess as a military leader and conqueror who used his war chariots to mash the spleens of any barbarian ass-clowns dumb enough to mess with his people, Ramses also possessed the ability to run a propaganda machine that made Joseph Stalin look like the assistant editor of a semiannual middle school newsletter in suburban Iowa. In the uncommon event that his mighty armies lost a battle (gasp), Ramses would still go out and have his artisans carve huge reliefs depicting the mighty pharaoh riding alone on a chariot, firing lightning-bolt arrows out of his eyes, and caving in people's skulls with a meat-normous skull-obliterating club. If these blatantly self-aggrandizing carvings are any indication, Ramses also liked to wash down his victories by forcing his pathetic vanquished foes to grovel at his feet like dogs while he kicked back and got lap dances from large-breasted Egyptian fertility goddesses.

Ramses's raging egomania also manifested itself in the form of some totally sweet government-sponsored vandalism. In addition to building more structures than any other Egyptian pharaoh, this guy would go around to temples that had been built by previous pharaohs, cross out their names, and write his own on top. At the time of his death, nearly every monument in the New Kingdom bore Ramses's name, and you couldn't throw a discus without hitting a towering depiction of his scowling visage—the capital city alone had more than fifty different statues of the pharaoh, and every one was life-sized or larger (usually larger). What's more, since Ramses was a god-king, all of his citizens were required to worship him by prostrating themselves before the feet of these towering, angry monoliths.

The rule of Ramses the Great was a golden age in Egyptian history, and his name was passed on for generations, much like that of Julius Caesar in Rome, except there's no such thing as a Ramses salad (but there really should be—it would be romaine lettuce, dates, and goat cheese, and when you order it the cashier punches you in the face). After Ramses II, ten other rulers took his name, each one unsuccessfully trying to capitalize on his success and fame. He was such a baller that after his death the Egyptian priests actually went back and rewrote their entire mythology to incorporate Ramses as one of their foremost gods. Despite all of this awesome crap, perhaps the greatest testament to his sweeping badassitude is this: before the Europeans were able to decipher hieroglyphics, the only pharaoh's name known to Egyptologists was that of Ramses.

Everything I attempted I succeeded. . . . I found the enemy chariots scattering before my horses. Not one of them could fight me. Their hearts quaked with fear when they saw me and their arms went limp so that they could not shoot. They did not have the heart to hold their spears. They fell on their faces, one on top of the other. . . . I slaughtered them at my will.

—RELIEF CARVING DESCRIBING RAMSES SINGLE-HANDEDLY WINNING THE BATTLE OF KADESH. ARCHAEOLOGICAL EVIDENCE SUGGESTS THAT THIS BATTLE WAS ACTUALLY A CRUSHING DEFEAT FOR THE EGYPTIAN ARMY, OR AT BEST A DRAW.

Ramses's capital city was named Pi-Ramses Aa-nakhtu, meaning "The Domain of Ramses, Great of Victories."

During his reign, Ramses commissioned restoration work on the Great Pyramid of Giza. The pyramid now holds the honor of being the only one of the Seven Wonders of the Ancient World still standing. The other, pussier wonders all got their asses kicked by stupid garbage like catapults, fires, earthquakes, conquerors, and giant carnivorous sea monsters.

To make mummies, Egyptian royal undertakers would cut open the dead pharaoh with a piece of sharpened glass and take out his stomach, lungs, intestines, and liver. These organs were then dried, placed into individual jars, and neatly arranged in the tomb by an interior designer. What was left of the body was dusted with salt, embalmed, wrapped up in cloth, accessorized with gold, and then entombed.

The name Ozymandias is actually just the Greek bastardization of Ramses's throne name, User-maat-ra-setep-en-ra. How the Greeks got Ozymandias out of that is beyond me.

HATSHEPSUT

Another kick-ass Egyptian ruler was the female pharaoh Hatshepsut, who reigned from 1508 to 1458 BCE. This grim woman seized control of the throne in the name of her infant son and exerted her dominance over Egypt for more than twenty years. Her greatest exploit was a campaign into the land of Punt, where she drop-kicked her cowering enemies into the ocean and returned up the Nile with everything from perfume bottles filled with myrrh to an entire grove of frankincense trees she simply pulled out of the ground with her bare hands and transplanted to her palace.

2

LEONIDAS

(540–480 BCE)

They made it evident to every man, and to the king himself not least of all, that human beings are many but men are few.

—HERODOTUS, HISTORIES

ONCE UPON A TIME THERE WAS THIS PLACE CALLED SPARTA, AND EVERYONE WHO LIVED THERE WAS A TOTAL BADASS. They were so hardcore that whenever one of their citizens said some stupid nonsense like, "Hey, man, democracy kicks ass . . . I like reading books, petting small puppies, and not violently killing people with pointy sticks that are also on fire," they shipped his ass off to Athens to pick daisies and philosophize about a bunch of asinine drivel that nobody really cares about. Spartan men were all trained from birth to be highly disciplined, explosive killing machines, and the women were taught to raise strong children and encourage their husbands to die honorably in battle with another warrior's spear through their heart. Anybody who wasn't down with that way of life was sent into exile, where they were eaten by wolves.

Well, one day some jackass named Emperor Xerxes I of Persia got all pissed at Greece for some reason and sent his two-hundred-thousand-man army over there with explicit orders to incinerate everything they could find. Obviously this didn't sit well with the Spartans. They hate it when jerks burn down their cities.

Xerxes's army created an impractically large pontoon bridge across the Hellespont and arrived in Greece in 480 BCE with the intention of kicking everyone's ass and possibly even taking names while doing so. However, in order to get through the countryside and sack Athens and Sparta, they needed to march through a narrow mountain pass known as Thermopylae. The Spartans knew this, and they had every intention of using this unforgiving terrain to their advantage.

The Spartan king Leonidas hand-selected a force of three hundred of the most subatomically kick-ass warriors in Sparta to defend the pass at Thermopylae. Knowing that it was pretty much a suicide mission, all the men he chose to accompany him had sons who were old enough to take over as the heads of their families. When Leonidas's wife was like, "What shall I do while you're gone?" Leonidas just tipped his helmet and said, "Marry a good man and have good children," before draining his wine bowl and riding off into the sunset like the Clint Eastwood–style badass that he was.

The Spartans arrived at the pass, which was already being held by a force of about four thousand other Greek troops. The Spartans were like, "Go home, hippies," and sent them back to organize the defense of Athens. Everybody took off out of there, except for a contingent of about seven hundred Thespian citizen-soldiers, most of whom weren't very experienced in the ways of war but were still pretty stoked about the prospect of stabbing Persian people in the throat with their javelins.

Eventually Xerxes showed up and was like, "What the hell is this crap?" He opened a parlay with the Spartan king.

Xerxes: What the hell is this crap?

Leonidas: Eat me.

Xerxes: There are two hundred thousand dudes here and you've only got a couple of hundred pussies guarding this pass. You're so boned. Just lay down your weapons.
Leonidas: Why don't you come and get them, bitch? We'll see who's a pussy when I shove all two hundred thousand of those knuckleheads up your ass.
Xerxes: Screw you.
Leonidas: Good one, loser. I've heard better insults from sock puppets.
Xerxes: That's it.

Xerxes flipped out and assaulted the Greek defenses, but the Persian light infantry was ill-equipped and way too lame to dislodge the battle-hardened, heavily armored Spartan warriors. They were torn to shreds by the huge spears of the Greek phalanx and then put into a giant three-man water balloon launcher and catapulted into the Aegean Sea. Xerxes ordered the light infantry to pull back and moved his archers to the front to fire a couple of volleys at the Greeks. According to the account of the battle provided by the Greek historian Herodotus, one Spartan remarked that this was all good because there were so many arrows it was almost like they got to fight in the shade for a while. The Spartans were just hard like that. Seeing that his nice, relaxing arrow shower was unsuccessful, Xerxes brought in his elite bodyguard contingent of ten thousand Immortals, a unit world-renowned for its incomparable beatdown skills. The Spartans and Immortals clashed in fierce combat, and Xerxes pretty much crapped a brick when he saw his most disciplined and experienced troops getting seriously worked over by Leonidas and his men.

At the end of the second day of battle, the Greeks still held the pass and the Persians had lost a buttload of their toughest soldiers. Unfortunately for King Leonidas, a Greek traitor named Epialtes defected to the Persians and told Emperor Xerxes about a secret path around the mountain. During the night, Xerxes sent what remained of his Immortals to the other side of the pass, and when the Spartans got ready to resume the fight in the morning they noticed that there were now Persians on both sides of them.

> ***Xerxes:*** All right, bro. Nice try, but now you're toast.
> ***Leonidas:*** Come on down here, then. I've got a present for you.
> ***Xerxes:*** Dude, you have no chance to survive. Just give up.
> ***Leonidas:*** I've got a better idea. How about you shut up and bite my dick? Does that sound like a good plan?

Surrounded on both sides, Leonidas then did the last thing the Persian king expected—he lined up his men and launched a balls-out charge right into the face of the overwhelming enemy forces. The Spartans fought bravely against ridiculous odds and held out for far longer than they should have, hurling themselves into the fray and battling with whatever they had—spears, swords, fists, teeth, sticks, knees to the crotch . . . you name it. Eventually, the last of the Greeks fell while defending the body of his fallen king. The Persians found the corpse of Leonidas, beheaded it, and crucified him outside the pass.

It takes a special kind of person to volunteer for a suicide mission and battle to the end against impossible odds. Leonidas found three hundred men willing to do just that. They did not fail the honor of their city or their people, willingly and unflinchingly facing an entire army to defend their homeland. The three hundred Spartans held the mountain pass for three days, being slain to the man but inflicting a tremendously high number of casualties on the Persian army's most capable units. They dealt a serious blow to Xerxes's forces and managed to hold back the Persian advance long enough for the Greeks in Athens to prepare for a major military engagement at Salamis, where they would crush the Persians and effectively end the invasion of Greece.

The Immortals were the elite heavy infantry of the Persian army and one of the most terrifying military organizations of the classical era. Formed under Cyrus the Great, this unit always consisted of ten thousand men, and for every warrior who died another was immediately promoted to his place. Since the regiment never appeared to suffer any lasting casualties, many of Persia's enemies believed these royal bodyguards were literally invincible.

Epialtes—the spineless ass-helmet who led the Persians around the mountain pass—fled to the land of Thessaly, where he was killed a few years later in a drunken bar fight by a dude named Athenades. Even though the reasons behind the killing were completely unrelated to the betrayal at Thermopylae, the Spartan government bestowed a massive reward on Athenades anyway.

Xerxes's first attempt to cross the Hellespont was unsuccessful due to inordinately choppy waters. When the emperor of Persia heard about this, he ordered the ocean whipped for daring to defy him. So some dude went out on the beach and smacked the water with a cat-o'-nine-tails a couple of times, and everybody called it a day. I'm pretty certain that this idea sounded a lot better in Xerxes's head.

FAMOUS LAST STANDS

Magellan's Douchery (1521)

The Portuguese conquistador Ferdinand Magellan landed a force of fifty men on the Philippine island of Visayas with the intention of teaching the natives a lesson in Catholicism and whup-ass, with an emphasis on the latter. His syllabus included things like randomly firing crossbow bolts at the natives and burning their villages to the ground, so fifteen hundred pissed-off Filipino stick fighters, led by their chieftain Lapu-Lapu, responded by charging into the surf and bludgeoning Magellan into a thin red paste. His body was never recovered.

The Sack of Rome (1527)

The jerkwad soldiers of the Holy Roman Empire proved themselves to be neither holy nor Roman when they plundered the Eternal City in 1527, torching it to the ground and using its citizens for crossbow target practice. During the destruction of the city, 189 members of the Swiss Guards fought a desperate last stand outside the gates of the Vatican in a valiant effort to buy the Pope time to escape through his secret Pope passage. His Holiness evaded the rampaging army, but only forty-two guardsmen survived the melee.

Miracle at Myeongnyang (1597)

Legendary Korean admiral Yi Sun-sin and his battle group of just thirteen warships went up against an armada of three hundred Japanese cruisers, all bearing down on him and filled to the brim with angry, screaming, *katana*-wielding samurai warriors. Yi positioned his tiny force in a narrow strait with cliffs on either side; the Japanese poured into the gap at top speed, and ran head-on into a powerful current that slowed them down considerably and left them exposed to withering cannon fire from the Korean battleships. During the course of the battle, Yi's tiny fleet relentlessly bombarded the enemy, and when the smoke cleared, he had sunk 123 Japanese ships and killed more than twelve thousand enemy sailors, including the admiral in command of the entire Japanese navy. Yi's losses totaled three wounded and two killed.

The Legion Dies but Does Not Surrender (1863)

Captain Jean Danjou of the French Foreign Legion, a lights-out ass-kicker with a wooden hand and a badass Rollie Fingers–style handlebar moustache, led a detachment of sixty-five Legionnaires in the desperate defense of a small hacienda at Cameron against two thousand Mexican troops. The Legion tenaciously fought to the end—the final five survivors, completely out of bullets, mounted a balls-out bayonet charge against an entire battalion of enemy riflemen.

Rorke's Drift (1879)

The 139 men of 2nd Battalion, 24th Regiment of the British Army found their small makeshift fort completely surrounded by an almost endless throng of spear-toting, face-stabbing Zulu warriors. The natives charged and broke through the outer defenses, and fierce hand-to-hand fighting ensued. Remarkably, the British somehow repelled the tribesmen, killing more than four hundred of the enemy during the bloody carnage. Eleven Victoria Crosses were awarded for actions during the battle, the most ever issued to one regiment in a single battle.

The Battle of the Saragarhi (1897)

A small garrison of just twenty-one Sikh warriors was sneak-attacked by a throng of more than ten thousand well-armed Orakzai tribesmen in the mountains of India. Unable to receive reinforcements in time and unwilling to surrender their strategically critical mountain fortress, these valiant men vowed to fight to the death. They withstood several determined assaults by the fierce Orakzai (not to be confused with Uruk-Hai) warriors, even fending off the invaders in hand-to-hand combat on a couple of occasions. The entire garrison was eventually killed to the man, but these ass-wrecking Sikhs managed to take six hundred enemy troops with them and checked the enemy advance long enough for the main body of the British Army to arrive and smash the tribal forces.

The Stalingrad of the East (1944)

At the Battle of Kohima a small, undersupplied garrison of fifteen hundred British and Indian soldiers fought in desperate defense of a tiny country club situated high in the forested mountains of Burma, holding out for thirteen days against a massive, continuous onslaught of more than twenty thousand Japanese troops. At one point during the battle, the two armies were dug in on opposite sides of a tennis court, taking potshots at each other from thirty feet away and making Federer and Nadal look like total pussies. When the garrison was finally relieved by Allied reinforcements, its defensive perimeter occupied a mere 350 square yards.

2008

3

XENOPHON

(431–355 BCE)

Whoever among you desires to return to his family, let him remember to fight bravely, for that is the only means to affect it. Whoever has a mind to live, let him endeavor to conquer; for the part of the conqueror is to inflict death, that of the conquered to receive it. If any of you covet riches, let him endeavor to overcome; for the victorious not only preserve their own possessions, but acquire those of the enemy.

I'M GOING TO GO OUT ON A LIMB HERE AND SAY THAT XENOPHON IS PROBABLY THE MOST BADASS GREEK HERO YOU'VE NEVER HEARD OF. This stalwart Athenian military commander fearlessly led a tough-as-hell group of ten thousand mercenaries on an odyssey so monumentally epic that it would make Homer crap his pants, traveling the entire length of the known world in pursuit of adventure, wealth, and jerkwads who needed to get their faces smashed, and then fighting his way home when all the odds were stacked up against him.

The saga begins with young Xenophon serving in a battle-hardened mercenary outfit of ten thousand Greek heavy infantrymen led by the noble Prince Cyrus of Persia. Cyrus's brother Artaxerxes was the king, and Prince Cyrus was pretty convinced that his bro was a giant raging moron unfit to run a PTA meeting, let alone govern the most powerful empire in the entire known world, so the fratricidal prince put together a ginormous army and set out to drown his brother in a sea of blood. For six months a mixed Greek and Persian army marched from the Mediterranean Sea into the heart of Persia, covering nearly a thousand miles before arriving outside the gates of Babylon itself—the farthest any Greek military force had ever ventured. To put the trip into perspective, this is roughly the equivalent of traveling from New York City to Des Moines, Iowa. On foot. Through the desert. With heavy armor, a shield, a full backpack, a sword, a canteen, and a six-foot-long spear strapped to your body. Basically, this mission wasn't for whiny schoolgirls who complained about blisters, deadlines, or bad hair days.

On the battlefield at Cunaxa in 401 BCE, King Artaxerxes showed up with an army nearly four times the size of Cyrus's. But Xenophon and his fellow Greek hardasses didn't even blink. They calmly marched forward, presenting a single line of sharpened spear points and impenetrable shields to their lightly armed adversaries. The Persian regiment opposite them took one look at this massive bulldozer of pointy death and wisely turned tail and fled without a fight.

Unfortunately, that was the end of the good news. Cyrus launched an all-out assault on his brother, but the king stabbed the Prince of Persia in the brain with a scimitar. After seeing their leader slain in an astonishingly gruesome manner, Cyrus's forces immediately laid down their arms and threw themselves at the mercy of their once and future king. The Greeks, who had chased their fleeing adversaries half a mile into the

woods, returned to the field to find their commander dead, their supply train plundered, and their onetime allies now aligned against them.

The Persian general Tissaphernes approached the Greek mercenaries under a flag of truce, convinced them there were no hard feelings, and invited them to send a delegation to negotiate their safe passage home. All of the Greek generals and captains went to Tissaphernes's camp to figure out what the goat cheese they were going to do, and were promptly double-crossed the hell out of. Those Greeks who were not slain on the spot were brought back to the capital and publicly tortured to death at a later date.

When the Greek soldiers heard what happened they realized that they were completely boned in more ways than an amateur porn actress. Our heroes were a thousand miles from home, deep in unfamiliar territory with no commanders, no food, no cavalry, no archers, and no medical supplies, and things were looking pretty bleak. It also didn't help that they were completely surrounded by people actively seeking to kill them.

It was at this point that Xenophon polished off his pair of gigantic brass balls and put them to good use. He woke the Greeks up, slapped them around, and said something to the effect of, "All right, are you going to die like bitches or are you going to be soldiers? Seriously, screw those assholes; we're going to fight our way home or die trying!" (He was obviously a little more eloquent than this, but you get the idea.) He appointed officers, recruited men from the ranks to serve as slingers, peltasts, and archers, and led his troops on a daring march toward freedom.

Xenophon's troops charged forward, broke through the Persian lines, and followed the Tigris River north, never knowing what lay behind the next rise. They were harassed the entire time by relentless day-and-night attacks from Tissaphernes's cavalry and archers, and in order to survive Xenophon had to resort to ruthless tactics—villages were plundered for food, natives were tortured for information, and dead bodies were mutilated to instill fear in the warriors that were following the Greek column. This was not a time for good manners. It was a time for survival.

Unable to find a good place to safely ford the Tigris, the Greeks continued north, leaving Persia and making their way into the mountains of Kurdistan. Here, they faced unrelenting attacks from the natives, who rolled gigantic *Raiders of the Lost Ark*–style boulders down on them and chucked arrows, spears, water balloons, and horrific insults down from the mountaintops. Xenophon maneuvered his troops through the treacherous enemy-controlled mountains, kicking ass at every turn and tenaciously fighting for every inch of desolate, inhospitable wasteland.

Next they passed into the highlands of Armenia, where a new enemy awaited them—winter. For those of you who have never been there, the Armenian winter is freezing-ass cold, especially when your uniform consists of a knee-length tunic, a pair of sandals, and a suit of metal armor, and the Greeks were getting their asses handed to them by hypothermia, snow blindness, frostbite, and starvation. They somehow managed to push through and gave that bitch Mother Nature the finger, Xenophon tirelessly pushing his men forward, until finally his warriors had arrived at the distant city of Trapezus, a Greek-controlled township on the coast of the Black Sea. From there, they restocked food and medical supplies before sailing off to Byzantium and, eventually, home.

All told, the March of the Ten Thousand covered four thousand miles in 215 days. This is the equivalent of walking from Miami, Florida, to Juneau, Alaska, in under a year. Six thousand men survived the perilous journey, an amazing number considering that they were constantly being wiped out by enemy soldiers, harsh climates, and unforgiving terrain. Xenophon returned home, jotted down his memoirs, composed a couple of books on tactics and philosophy, and penned the definitive history of the late fifth-century BCE. He died peacefully in his bed at age ninety, one of the greatest unsung heroes of the classical age.

Peltasts might sound like a group of guys who got busted for selling candy to kids out of the back of their windowless conversion vans, but they were actually face-puncturing Greek javelin chuckers. These light infantrymen would run right up to the enemy lines, hurl their javelins in their enemies' eyes, and retreat before the more heavily armed infantry could catch them.

Hoplite armor consisted of bronze greaves, a bronze helmet, a breastplate made from either metal or leather, and a three-foot-diameter circular shield known as a *hoplon* (this is where the word *hoplite* comes from—it has nothing to do with either hopping or being light). The whole getup weighed in at about sixty-five pounds.

Nowadays the phrase *balls-out* is just an expression, but back before the invention of Under Armour the ancient Greek Olympic Games were all contested by a bunch of big sweaty naked guys. The games featured naked boxing, naked footraces, and even naked wrestling. Things are different today, thankfully.

4

ALEXANDER THE GREAT

(356–323 BCE)

There is nothing impossible to him who will try.

ALEXANDER III OF MACEDONIA WAS A HARDCORE BASTARD WHO ACCOMPLISHED MORE TOWERING DEEDS OF HEROIC AWESOMENESS IN THIRTY-THREE YEARS THAN MOST PEOPLE COULD EVER HOPE TO DREAM OF IN THEIR ENTIRE LIFETIMES, EVEN IF THEY USED 100 PERCENT OF THEIR BRAINS. He was undefeated in battle, conquered most of the known world, and is remembered to this day as one of the greatest and most successful generals in the history of warfare, thanks mostly to his impeccable ability to annihilate faces and make the greatest military leaders of his era look like rejects who couldn't fight their way out of a convent.

Alexander was the son of King Philip II of Macedon, though he often claimed that his mother was actually sneaking around in cheap motel rooms with Zeus himself and that he was related to the classical heroes Hercules and Perseus. (After he conquered Egypt, Alexander also said that he was descended from the sun god Amun. That must have been one hell of a threesome.) I guess if your mom is going to screw around and have an affair, you could do a lot worse than the god of thunder.

As a young man Alexander was tutored by Aristotle, which is kind of like having Stephen Hawking as your algebra TA or getting batting tips from the ghost of Honus Wagner. Aristotle taught him the cryptic art of philosophizing, introduced him to all the joys of adventurous ass-whipping in Homer's *Iliad,* and when the time came to put that knowledge into practical application at the Battle of Chaeronea in 338 BCE, Alexander led King Philip's cavalry against the legendary Sacred Band of Thebes and made them look like the Sacred Band of Pussies, kicking their asses across Greece and wiping the fabled cavalry regiment out of historical records forever.

Two years later King Philip was assassinated, leaving Alexander to take over as the sole ruler of Macedonia. As you can probably imagine, most of Alex's neighbors thought they could screw with the new twenty-year-old king—barbarians from the north threatened Macedonia's borders, while the city-states of Athens and Thebes took up arms and sent Alexander engraved invitations to bite their collective asses. At a time when most twenty-year-old aristocrats would have crapped their pants and run off to get wasted on malt liquor and sleep with drunk coeds, Alexander raised an army and set about restoring order by delivering *Judge Dredd*-style death-vengeance to anyone stupid enough to cross him. His military maneuvers were so decisive, effective, and rapid that he had already destroyed the barbarian armies and completely surrounded the city of Thebes before the bureaucracy there had even decided upon a plan of action. Alexander vanquished the Theban army, executed everyone in the government, burned the city to the ground, and sold any surviving citizens into slavery. The next day, he received word that Athens had surrendered peacefully and was willing to bend to his iron will. They didn't want anything to do with that party.

Simply unifying the Greek city-states wasn't nearly enough to satisfy

Alexander's giant Ramses-sized ego, however, as he had his sights set on something much more ginormous—namely, the Persian Empire. As we've seen, the Persians had been screwing with the Greeks for a while now, and Alexander finally decided it was time to stick it to the folks who had spent the better part of two centuries battering his countrymen to death with red-hot waffle irons. As any good ruler did in those days, he consulted the Oracle at Delphi before marching forty-two thousand men into Persia. Her response: "My son, you are invincible!" You can't get a more emphatic answer than that.

Of course, the most powerful empire in the world wasn't going to start dry-heaving into a garbage can just because some punk-ass twenty-year-old kid thought he was the baddest mofo of all time, so the armies of the Persian king Darius III came out and met Alexander near the Granicus River in 334. It was here that the Persians finally realized what they were up against—the young Macedonian king led his heavy cavalry on a balls-out charge over the river, up a steep hill, and directly into the center of the Persian formation. Alexander himself spearheaded the assault, hacking up everything in his line of sight, and the Greek troops carried the battle.

Darius tried to stick it to Alexander outside the city of Issus, but the Greeks put their dicks in the proverbial mashed potatoes once again. Despite having overwhelming numerical superiority, the Persian lines were smashed by the unstoppable Greek phalanxes and heavy cavalry formations. The ass-kicking was so complete, and Darius peeled out of there in such a rush that he forgot to take his family with him—Alexander captured them and took Darius's daughter as his second wife.

The Greeks continued to move down the coast of Asia Minor, "liberating" the ethnically Greek villages they came across, and eventually entered Egypt, where Alexander founded the city of Alexandria—one of seventeen cities he would name after himself—and was received as a conquering hero delivering the Egyptians from the fetters of Persian tyranny. The only real resistance he faced en route to North Africa was from the heavily defended island fortress of Tyre, but something as insignificantly puny as impenetrable stone walls, unfavorable geography, and a complete lack of naval superiority wasn't going to stop Alexander from popping his enemies in the esophagus with a pipe wrench. He simply built a massive wooden bridge from the coast out to the island, loaded it up with catapults, busted down the walls, killed every man inside, and sold the women and children into slavery. Awesomely enough, over time the causeway he built was covered over with sand and has now become a permanent geographic feature, proving that Alexander the Great was so badass that he was even capable of making the earth itself his bitch.

Not even life-threatening wounds could slow down this human torture rack, and no amount of physical pain or suffering could keep him from personally leading his men on balls-out cavalry charges all over the Middle East. During his adventures slicing dudes up across the entire continent of Asia, Alexander was shot with arrows in both thighs, the ankle, the shoulder, and the lung, stabbed in the head and thigh, clubbed in the neck, smashed in the skull with a battle-axe, bitten by a lion, and nailed with a rock that was launched out of a catapult. He also once dislocated his shoulder leaping off his horse onto one of his dismounted enemies. Hell, not even explosive diarrhea put a halt to his quest for ass-kicking; he once pursued a routed Scythian army for twelve miles while suffering from severe dysentery.

Once the coast was secure and all opposition was mercilessly crushed under his sandaled feet, Alexander set out to bust Darius in the mouth and end the war once and for all. Outside Gaugamela in 331 BCE, the two armies squared off in the ultimate battle for Persia. Darius picked the battlefield, fielded a force three times the size of Alexander's, and launched a massive attack spearheaded by several thousand scythed war chariots, but he was completely outclassed. The Macedonians metaphorically de-pantsed him right there on the battlefield, destroying the

Persian army, annihilating the infamous Immortals, and seizing control of their empire.

Alexander hung out in Persia for a while, chilling with his three wives (and countless mistresses), getting wasted, throwing gigantor parties, and accidentally burning the city of Persepolis into smoldering cinders in a drunken rage. Eventually he got bored of living a life of inebriated luxury and headed east to India, where he faced off against armies of crazy war elephants and skilled Punjabi swordsmen. He donkey-punched all opposition he encountered, and once he had carved out an empire stretching from the Mediterranean to the Indian Ocean, Alexander realized his work was done. So, just like that, the greatest conqueror in ancient history died randomly of a fever in 323 BCE at the age of thirty-three.

One apocryphal story has the Amazonian queen Thalestris bringing three hundred hot sex-crazed warrior babes to Alexander's camp in the hopes that he would impregnate them and create a new race of supermen. There's no mention of whether or not this primitive eugenics program ever took hold, but that certainly seems like it would be a difficult proposition to pass up.

The fabled Gordian knot was a snarl of rope so absurdly convoluted that no human being could ever possibly hope to untangle it ever. There was a legend in that the man who unraveled the knot would be destined to be the greatest king to ever live, so of course Alexander decided to take a look at the accursed thing. He glanced at the unholy mass of cordage, drew his sword, and hacked the knot in half with one swing.

Alexander's mother, Olympias, was a crazy nut job. She was a member of the cult of Dionysus, which was like an over-the-top old-school swingers' club—their meetings usually consisted of getting high, drinking a ton of wine, worshiping snakes, and having extreme all-night orgies.

She ran the show in Macedon while Alexander was out campaigning, usually busying herself by boiling people alive and executing anyone she considered a rival to her power in the most brutal ways you could imagine.

Alexander rebuilt the Temple of Artemis at Ephesus, one of the Seven Wonders of the Ancient World, which was originally burned down in 356 BCE. It was torched once again by German barbarians in 409, and nobody has had the heart to build it a third time.

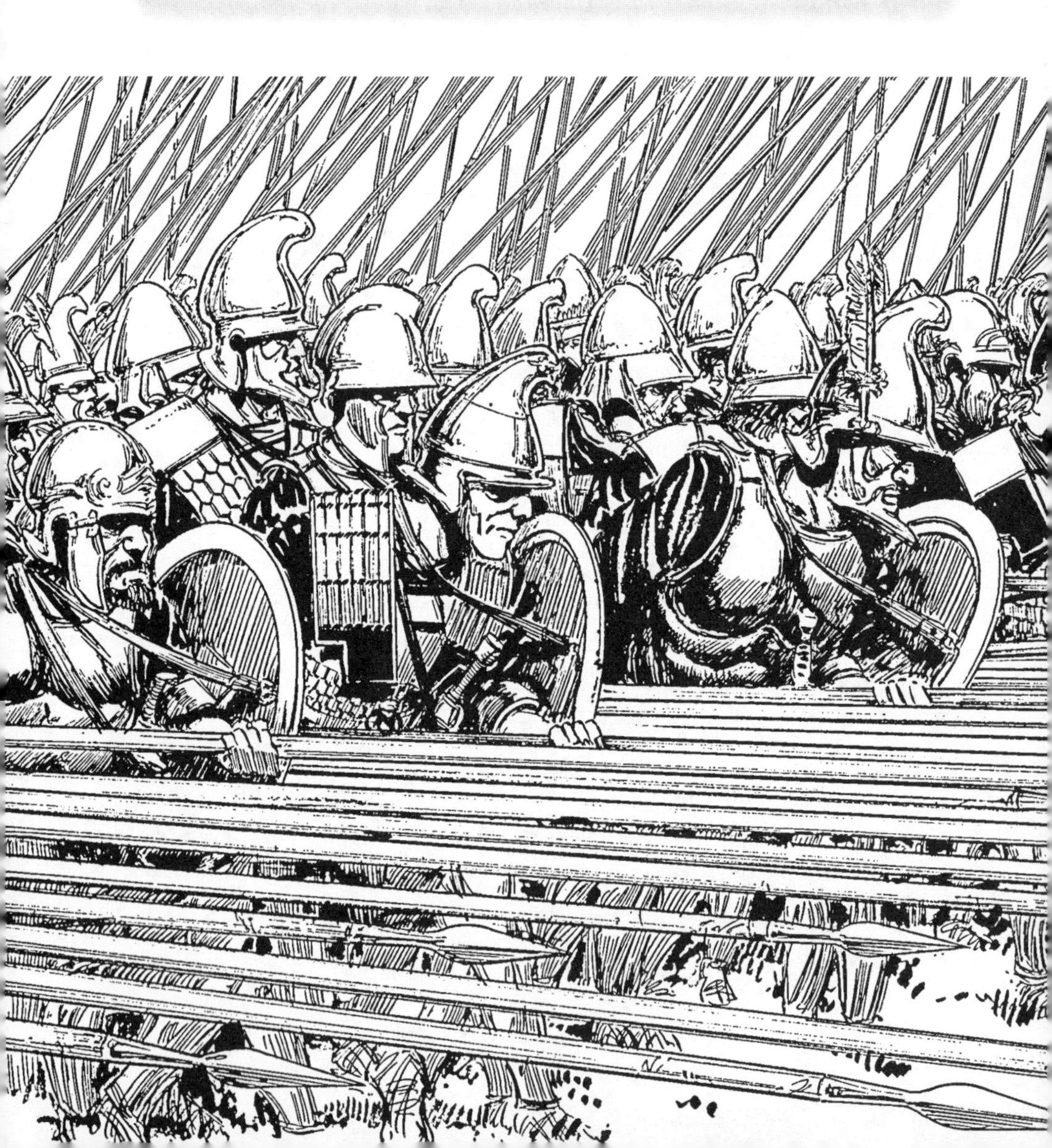

THE MACEDONIAN PHALANX

There wasn't a whole lot out there more effective at delivering ultimate face-stabbings than the Macedonian phalanx—a massive, immovable wall of bronze shields and pointy death. The basic unit of the phalanx was a 256-man formation known as a *syntagma,* which was 16 men wide by 16 men deep. When it came time to skewer d-bags, the soldiers stood shoulder to shoulder, brandishing their massive sixteen-foot-long spears at their enemies and slowly pushing their way forward. Five ranks' worth of spears protruded from the front of the formation, meaning that the poor bastards standing in front of this behemoth were looking at sixteen men and eighty spear tips. The spikes were sharpened on both ends to make it easier to stab wounded and dying men as troops walked over the top of them, and the spearmen also had a short sword they could bust out for close combat if the enemy somehow miraculously wasn't impaled by the inexorable push of the relentless spike wall.

2008

5

CHANDRAGUPTA MAURYA

(340–289 BCE)

A man is great by deeds, not by birth.

—CHANKAYA, CHIEF ADVISOR TO CHANDRAGUPTA MAURYA

IT WASN'T JUST THAT CHANDRAGUPTA MAURYA WAS ONE OF THE MOST POWERFUL MEN IN THE WORLD. It wasn't just that this orphaned commoner clawed his way up from nothing to carve out the most expansive empire in India's history, rule more than fifty million people, and command an army of six hundred thousand infantrymen, thirty thousand cavalrymen, and nine thousand war elephants. It wasn't just that he came from nothing to sit on a golden, jewel-encrusted throne, or that his capital city was eight miles wide, with five hundred guard towers and a nine-hundred-foot-wide moat. No, Chandragupta Maurya's badassitude stems from the fact that he knew how to use his power in the most awesome way possible—by constantly surrounding himself with a highly trained, hyperelite, well-armed personal bodyguard of more than five hundred Greek and Indian warrior women. These superhot babes followed him around day and night, just looking for one good reason to jam their blades into someone's cranial cavity, choke-slam them down a flight of stairs, or shred on their sitars.

We don't know much about our hero before 325 BCE—he just sort of materialized out of thin air like a face-melting UFO or a vengeful, homicidal rainbow, but apparently he had some serious beef with the people in charge of India at that time—the Nanda Empire. Unfortunately, there aren't many primary sources out there that give us any idea of who the Nanda were or what they did, but for our purposes it's probably safe to assume that they were all total dickheads who needed to be killed as violently as possible.

Chandragupta was evidentially so fired up that he attempted a daring coup d'état in the capital city, storming the palace and single-handedly attempting to overthrow the government with nothing more than a bronze sword and an unquenchable desire for human blood. As you can imagine, this went over like a lead balloon carrying a hippo across the gravity-rich surface of the planet Jupiter. Chandragupta was captured, beaten up, exiled, condemned to death, and thrown in prison in some godforsaken part of the Indian subcontinent. It takes more than a serious beating to keep a good megalomaniac down, and a paragon of insubordination like Chandragupta wasn't just going to sit in the clink and rot like a chump. He busted out almost immediately, probably by punching a hole in the stone wall with his skull and nonchalantly walking off into the sunset.

It was at this point that Chandragupta Maurya realized that charging into the throne room of the palace and trying to personally wrench power from the hands of the emperor, while awesome, probably wasn't the most face-searingly brilliant plan he'd ever had. He determined that it probably made more sense to gain the support of the outlying provinces before going after the emperor himself, so he put together a small army of people from his native tribe, won battles against the armies of rival Punjabi rulers, recruited throngs of pitchfork-toting disgruntled peasants, and eventually assembled an army capable of crushing serious balls.

At the head of a now-massive military force, Chandragupta Maurya defeated the Nanda army, marched on the capital, stormed the palace, and personally seized control of the government. He spared the life of the Nanda emperor, telling him that he could leave the palace in peace but was only allowed to bring that which he was capable of carrying with his own two hands. I assume that he just chose to carry his wife out, but you never really know with emperors.

Seated in his angular throne deep in the heart of the wealthiest city in the world, protected by his warrior women and surrounded by remote-operated trapdoors leading into cages of untamed, man-eating beasts, Chandragupta marched his stampeding hordes against the disorganized tribes of India. Before long, the twenty-year-old emperor had forged a kingdom stretching from the Bay of Bengal to the Arabian Sea, and as far north as the Hindu Kush in Afghanistan.

Much of Chandragupta's military might came from his strategic use of specially trained gigantic freaking war elephants. His men would feed the elephants vast amounts of booze before sending them out onto the battlefield, making them drunk and pissed, and no amount of stabbing could prevent anyone from getting their small intestines stomped flatter than a soda can being run over by a caravan of tour buses carrying the Japanese men's sumo wrestling team back from an all-you-can-eat dinner buffet. The elephants would either kick people harder than a genetic fusion of Jet Li and a donkey—causing enemy soldiers to explode like giant disgusting human-shaped water balloons filled with V8 juice—or gore them with their tusks and do their best impression of those psychotic orcas that hurl seals into the air for no reason at all. If that didn't work, the dudes riding on the backs of the elephants would just shoot you in the face with an arrow, a tactic that Chandragupta himself personally excelled at. After seeing their buddies get tossed around all over the place, most of the enemy just pooped their armor and ran as fast as they could to the nearest place that didn't have intoxicated elephants destroying everything in sight.

This tactic proved especially useful when a Greek provincial ruler named Seleucus Nikator attempted to wrest part of the Punjab region from Chandragupta's control. Marching a phalanx into a formation of war elephants is kind of like the military equivalent of smashing yourself in the face with a claw hammer until you die from it, and Seleucus succeeded only in getting several thousand of his men trampled to death. After getting his ass handed to him a couple of times, Seleucus decided to sit down at the bargaining table with our fearless emperor. The ensuing deal sent five hundred war elephants over to Seleucus in exchange

for all the Greek holdings in Afghanistan, cash considerations, a minor-league shortstop, and Seleucus sending his own daughter to serve in Chandragupta's private army of face-destroying dominatrices. Sure, it was a bit of a one-sided deal, but then again Chandragupta pretty much had the Greek commander's nuts in a vise. It ended up working out all right for Seleucus, however—he took those five hundred elephants and used them to smash armies across Persia and Greece, besting his foes with just a fraction of the Indian army's unbelievable trample power. It probably worked out pretty well for Seleucus's daughter, too—I'm sure that serving as a sword-swinging asskicker was a hell of a lot more exciting than whatever boring crap she was doing back in Greece.

In addition to being a destroyer of armies, a ruler of men, and a conqueror of cities, Chandragupta was also awesome because he was more paranoid than a crazy pothead conspiracy theorist on a guided tour of the Pentagon. I've already discussed the hot chick bodyguards who surrounded him day and night, but I should also mention that he never slept in the same room of his massive palace twice, actually going so far as to have additional bedrooms built on to his citadel as he needed them. He had food tasters try everything before he ate it, he probably installed a laser trip wire system in his throne room, and he actually put together what is believed to be the world's first secret police force—a hardcore organization of spies, secret agents, and government assassins so insanely all-powerful that it makes the Patriot Act look like the United Nations' Universal Declaration of Human Rights.

Eventually, Chandragupta got bored of being the most powerful man in the known world, so he abdicated the throne to his son, moved out to the desert, lived as a Jain monk, and became so hardcore Xtreme (capital *X*) that he fasted himself to death. He had laid the foundation for the first great empire in India's history, and his grandson, Asoka the Great, would be remembered as one of his country's most successful and benevolent rulers.

Chandragupta was a tireless administrator, often times presiding over court business from dawn until dusk. Of course, it's good to be the king—he usually had a team of four servants massaging his back and shoulders while he sat on his throne and arbitrated over disputes.

Chandragupta founded the Mauryan Dynasty in 320 BCE. He is not to be confused with Chandra Gupta, who founded the Gupta Dynasty in 320 CE.

While pretty much everybody enjoys talking about "thug life" and "busting caps in some punk asses," few people realize that the word *thug* is actually derived from a supersecret organization of Indian highwaymen known as the Thuggee. This loose association of brigands and murderers devoted to the worship of the Hindu death goddess Kali terrorized the countryside for centuries, killing unsuspecting dumbasses and stealing all their stuff. These dudes would pose as travelers or merchants wandering the countryside, and when you least expected it they would choke you out with a silk scarf and then ritualistically disfigure your body and toss it in a ditch. An estimated two million people "disappeared" in this manner over the course of several centuries. The British finally exterminated the cult in the 1830s.

Shield Maidens

Viking women didn't take crap from anybody, especially their husbands, and they enjoyed more rights than women pretty much anywhere else in the world during the Middle Ages. Numerous Viking sagas and histories mention savage bands of sea-roving chicks going into battle and performing prostate-bashing acts of bravery in hand-to-hand combat. Wives were known to go on raids with their husbands, dressing up in full chain mail and stuffing spears into people's faces alongside the men, and many women soldiers fought tenaciously in numerous military engagements across Scandinavia. Some particularly liberated shield maidens

were known to have forsaken married life altogether in order to pursue a life of adventure and ass-kicking on the high seas.

Kunoichi

In feudal Japan, female ninjas known as *kunoichi* were just as highly valued as the most smoke-bomb-dropping, *shuriken*-flinging, flying-sidekicking male shadow warriors. Trained in hand-to-hand combat, infiltration, evasion, and espionage skills, these women entered enemy camps disguised as everything from servants and nurses to geishas and cosplay Final Fantasy characters. Once they secured the trust of a rival lord, they would sabotage key strategic points, report troop movements to their superiors, poison food supplies, and assassinate high-ranking officials. After completing their mission these subversive chicks would simply vanish into the night without a trace, and anybody who tried to stop them usually ended up with a stiletto lodged in his trachea.

The Dahomey Amazons

Patriarchal European dumbasses really got a taste of girl power with multiple *r*'s when they faced the Dahomey Amazons of West Africa in the 1800s. An elite unit of pitiless warrior women armed with muskets, three-foot-long machetes, and remarkably bad attitudes, the Amazons had long been considered the most dominant fighting force in Africa, winning countless battles for their kingdom and collecting the severed heads of their slain enemies. Despite being heavily outgunned by superior European firepower, these fearless warriors threw down with the French Foreign Legion on multiple occasions; fighting fiercely with rifles, knives, fists, and whatever else they had available at the time. One account exists of how a French soldier disarmed one of the warriors only to have her take him down with a judo shoulder throw and tear out his jugular with her teeth.

Las Soldaderas

Brave *Chicanas* played a major role on the front lines of Central American warfare from the time of the conquistadors up until the twentieth century. Many of these women served primarily as camp followers, traveling with their loved ones and functioning as nurses, cooks, and quartermasters, but they didn't hesitate to drop whatever they were doing and bust caps in people's dumb asses when the opportunity presented itself. Many women courageously fought in the Mexican revolutionary army in 1910, battling for their freedom against the corrupt and tyrannical rule of *presidente por vida* Porfirio Díaz. *Soldaderas* not only fought with distinction on the battlefield but also served as officers and commanders of revolutionary military forces as well.

6

LIU JI

(247–195 BCE)

It was while dressed in rough cloth and wielding a three-foot sword that I conquered the empire.

BACK IN WHAT HISTORIANS LIKE TO CALL "THE DAY," THERE WAS A BAD, BAD MAN BY THE NAME OF QIN SHIN HUANGDI. Qin dedicated his entire life to burying Confucian scholars alive, torching monasteries, subjugating the countryside, and crushing his enemies like insignificant bugs beneath his heel. He put together a massive army, conquered everything before him, pillaged, plundered, et cetera, and united the people of China under one ruler for the first time in history. He then forced everyone to bow to his evil will and ruled as a brutal tyrant until he inadvertently killed himself by drinking mercury, a practice that he thought would bring him eternal life. It didn't.

After the emperor unwittingly poisoned himself to death like a dumbass, his son took over. Just as Qin was a bastard, his kid was the son of a bastard, and was so utterly incompetent and powerless that the Chinese nobility eventually forced him to do the world a favor by following in his father's footsteps and having the good sense to die a premature and unpleasant death. China fell into a period of brutal warlordism, where everybody basically started beating the bejesus out of each other in an effort to grab small, insignificant chunks of land for themselves.

Liu Ji—also known as Liu Bang, Liu Pang, Gaozu, Han Kao-Ti, Taizu, Liu Chi, Kao-Tsu, Gao Di, and probably half a dozen other crazy-ass names (none of which even contain any of the same letters), wasn't your typical scrotum-demolishing conqueror. He didn't push orphans headfirst over cliffs, he didn't construct evil armies of cybernetic killbots with buzz saws for hands, and his muscles weren't so freakishly jacked that he could crack a Brazil nut by putting it between his bicep and forearm and flexing really hard—he was just a jovial, charismatic, broke-as-hell Chinese peasant with a habit of spending his evenings sitting at the bar in the local pub drinking bowl after bowl of cheap wine, telling tall tales, singing bad karaoke, and running up a massive tab that he had absolutely no chance of ever being able to pay off. He worked as a local police officer in charge of transporting prisoners across his home province of Kiangsu, and, as it is with most crappy jobs, he was pretty much at the point where he would rather have jammed large pointy objects into his eyes than gotten out of bed most mornings.

One day, Liu Ji was in the middle of one of his much-hated cross-province prisoner transports when all of a sudden a bunch of his convicts broke free and escaped into the countryside. Liu, fearful that this failure would cost him his job, just decided to say, "Screw it." He popped open a flask of wine and used his charismatic charm to organize the ex-cons into a goddamned bandit outfit, and under his command they started launching raids on unsuspecting travelers and government officials across the province. This crew of merry men became so popular that poor peasants flocked to join up with him and pillage the rich imperial stores of all the wealth and booze they could carry. The band of brigands grew so powerful that they actually began to morph from a roving troop of plundering thieves into an organized cadre of freedom fighters battling against the corrupt empire on behalf of the underrepresented populace, kind of like a weird mix between *Oz* and *Red Dawn*.

Liu Ji eventually decided to attach his misfit merry men to the revolutionary army of a hardcore military warlord named Xiang Yu. Xiang was everything a good classical-age ass-beater was supposed to be—tough, cruel, and unscrupulous. For years, the X-Man had been shredding faces up and down the countryside, forging a kingdom out of unrelenting cold steel and arterial blood spray, and fighting his way toward the recently vacated throne. He executed prisoners of war, showed no mercy to his enemies, and maliciously gutted any man who deserted his army or showed cowardice in battle.

In contrast to Xiang's inflexible, blood-and-guts attitude, Liu Ji was totally chill; he spent his time hanging out with his motley crew of rejects, convicts, and peasants, traveling the land preaching revolution, earning the support of the people, eradicating the armies of tyrannical local warlords, and uniting the peasants against the despotism of

the corrupt nobility. When people surrendered to him, Liu gave them a sword and let them fight alongside his own troops, and everywhere he went he was warmly received by the cheering populace.

The rebels handily crushed the imperial army, and in 207 BCE, Liu Ji and his dashing band of rogues sauntered into the fortress city of Chang'an (also known as Sian, Shensi, Hsi-An, Xi'an, Ch'ang-an, etc.) despite being strictly forbidden from doing so by General Xiang. It wasn't exactly Liu Ji's fault, however—when the people of Chang'an saw Liu's army camped outside their gates and realized that the legendary peasant/drunkard/hero was approaching the city, they lowered their drawbridge, greeted him with open arms, and bought him a round at the local tavern.

Xiang Yu heard what was going on and immediately marched his conquering juggernaut of an army toward the capital, destroying and ransacking everything in his path like an unstoppable ball-crushing steamroller. He busted through the iron gates of the city, plundered it for three months, massacred the entire population, and burned every building down to the ground. He then appointed himself lord protector of China, divided the empire into several kingdoms, and immediately went to work mercilessly assassinating and executing his chief political rivals.

Liu Ji wasn't about to trade one tyrannical jackass for another, so he decided to put together a coalition of tribal leaders and revolt against this new government. He recruited thousands of eager peasants to assist him in his noble cause, and triumphantly marched his army out to face the battle-hardened, highly organized, well-equipped forces of the mighty lord protector.

He got his face wrecked. Badly.

Liu regrouped and attacked Xiang again, and even though he outnumbered Xiang's forces nearly three to one, his peeps were completely mowed down with the realness. The über-surly, ultrapowerful Xiang then wiped out what was left of Liu Ji's army and trapped our hero in his own castle, but Liu somehow managed to narrowly escape through a secret passage and run for his life.

Well, Liu Ji is the ultimate proof that badassitude doesn't always come from supreme ass-kickings—sometimes it's just about being totally awesome and uniting people in a common cause. For every victory that Xiang Yu achieved, every village he torched, and every prisoner he bitch-slapped, more and more people began to flock to Liu's banner. The guy was like the pied piper of disgruntled, pissed-off peasants who weren't going to take it anymore. As a laid-back, charismatic guy, Liu just kept on recruiting people who didn't want to put up with Xiang's bullcrap anymore, and finally at the Battle of Gaixia in 202 Liu fielded an overwhelmingly massive force and won a decisive military victory against the armies of Xiang Yu, defeating them and wiping out the battle-hardened core of the lord protector's army. General Xiang felt so disgraced that he'd been defeated by a damn hippie that he committed suicide right there on the battlefield by decapitating himself with a machete.

This was like the ancient Chinese equivalent of the 1980 U.S. Olympic hockey team taking out the Soviet Union. Peasants were cheering, everybody was going nuts, Al Michaels was asking people whether or not they believe in miracles, and the forty-four-year-old peasant-turned-outlaw was anointed Emperor Gaozu of Han in 202 BCE. In the span of five years he had gone from a friendly drunk at the local bar to ruler of the world's most populous empire—one of only two members of the peasant class to ever be crowned emperor of China.

As emperor, Liu Ji never forgot his roots. Sure, he took advantage of some of the perks the office of emperor provided—he took seven concubines, slept on the finest silks, and tasted the world's most expensive wines—but it was much more common to find him sitting in the palace barracks drinking cheap beer, telling dirty jokes, and playing poker with enlisted soldiers. He looked out for the peasants, was beloved by the people, and built the foundation for a golden age in Chinese history—the Han Dynasty would last for four centuries after his death, and would be one of the most powerful and richest civilizations ever established.

The Han Dynasty is considered the first golden age of Chinese history. Lasting 414 years and encompassing more than fifty-five million people, the Han saw flourishing trade, agriculture, and arts. The famous Silk Road was also constructed during this time, and the Mandarin word for "Chinese" literally translates to the phrase "the people of Han."

One of Liu Ji's favorite tactics was to send a diplomatic envoy to personally insult the enemy commander in an effort to get him so cheesed off that he would make a tactical error and send his troops directly into an ambush.

Qin Shi Huang was buried in a massive tomb filled with life-sized terra-cotta warriors and rivers of flowing mercury. The men who constructed the tomb were buried alive within it so that nobody would know the secret location of the emperor's final resting place. Qin's tomb remained hidden until a Chinese Jed Clampett accidentally stumbled across it in 1974 while drilling for oil.

7

GAIUS JULIUS CAESAR

(100–44 BCE)

The cohorts which Caesar had posted behind him ran forward and, instead of hurling their javelins, as they usually did, or even thrusting at the legs and thighs of the enemy, aimed at their eyes and stabbed upward at their faces. Caesar had instructed them to do this because he believed that these young men, who had not much experience of battle and the wounds of battle but who particularly plumed themselves on their good looks, would dislike more than anything the idea of being attacked in this way and, fearing both the danger of the moment and the possibility of disfigurement for the future, would not be able to stand up to it. And this in fact was exactly what happened.

—PLUTARCH, *LIFE OF CAESAR*

GAIUS JULIUS CAESAR WAS BORN IN ROME, THE NEPHEW OF A WILDLY SUCCESSFUL AND POPULAR GENERAL NAMED MARIUS. Young Julius's uncle was so well liked, in fact, that the entire Roman Republic was embroiled in a vicious, brutal war for three years, with half of Italy supporting Marius and the other half supporting a dude called Sulla. Sulla won by default when Marius fell ill and was diagnosed with a pretty terminal case of death, but since the war had such a boring, anticlimactic ending, Sulla decided that it would be cool to satiate his ravenous thirst for bloody vengeance by marching his legions into Rome, declaring himself dictator, and executing everybody who had ever opposed him for any reason ever. Since this guy was a crazy bastard initiating more purges than a bulimic supermodel, Julius decided he should make like a leaf and get the hell out of there before he ended up having his severed head used as decorative ornamentation adorning the gates of Rome.

Once Sulla retired and the streets were no longer running red with blood, Caesar caught the first ship back to his hometown. Unfortunately, his boat was attacked by pirates, who took him prisoner and decided to hold him for ransom. When Caesar asked them how much they were going to try to get for him and they told him twenty talents (I have no idea how much money this comes out to in real American dollar bills, but I am under the impression that it is a lot), Julius laughed right in their faces and told them that it was insulting for them to demand less than fifty for a person of his stature. He just didn't give a crap.

Caesar rocked out with the pirates for a while, drinking rum, sailing around, camping out on remote islands, and singing hilarious sea chanteys about boobs and sword fights, and everybody thought he was more awesome than a fully loaded baked potato with sour cream and bacon. One night around the campfire Julius said something to the effect of, "You guys are pretty cool. It's a shame that I'm going to have to execute you all when I get back to town." Then he raised his wineglass, shouted "Cheers!" and everybody laughed at this hilarious joke, even though some people didn't really get it. (Two weeks later, Caesar returned home, put together a fleet of warships, hunted down the pirates, and had them all crucified.)

Once he had satisfied his quest for vengeance, Caesar began to campaign for political office in Rome. His popularity and his oratorical skills got him elected tribune, quaestor, praetor, and half a dozen other cool-sounding political offices that nobody really knows what they actually did. He was also elected pontifex maximus, which was the office of head priest of Rome. Nowadays we call this person the Pope, only I guess back in antiquity instead of performing marriages, wearing fashionable hats, and living a life of celibacy, most clergymen spent their time secretly plotting world domination and bribing city officials to throw giant buckets of animal crap on their political rivals.

Eventually, J-Dog was appointed governor of Spain. As soon as he showed up, Caesar raised a couple of legions and got his conquer on, subjugating the uncivilized tribes of Hispania and acquiring territory stretching as far as the Atlantic Ocean. While everybody was pretty pumped up that Julius was such an unstoppable military genius, the Senate decided that he wasn't being a very good governor because he was killing all of his subjects, so they called him back to Rome.

Caesar didn't care. He formed a political alliance with Crassus, the wealthiest man in Rome, and Pompey, the republic's most successful military commander. These guys called themselves the triumvirate, which is the official term for a group of three classical-age diabolical madmen working together to control the government until such time as they all decide to backstab and kill each other. This group flexed its nuts and got Caesar elected consul and governor of a place called Gaul.

Gaul is what historians like to call France when they want it to sound tough. Sure, technically the two lands occupy the same geographic location, but there are some subtle differences when you observe them from an empirical standpoint. Gaul is the home of beer-chugging, pelt-wearing barbarians who eat meat off the bone, throw axes at people they don't like, and spend their time punching trees into lumber or playing bocce ball with severed heads. France, on the other hand, is where you can find baguettes, flowery cursive script, and movies that make about as much sense as a bad salvia trip.

In Gaul, Caesar proved himself to be one of history's most brilliant military tacticians, inspiring his men to victory against rebellious barbarian tribes on numerous occasions. In his ten years as governor, he conquered eight hundred cities, killed more than a million barbarian warriors, and captured another million enemy combatants. Despite being almost constantly outnumbered, sometimes by ratios of over three to one, and fighting in a hostile, unfamiliar land, Caesar's legions reached down their enemies' throats and pulled out a clenched fist holding an inverted nut sack, using divide-and-conquer tactics to whip up on the Belgae, Nervii, Helvetii, Lusitanians, Britons, Catuvellauni, Eburones, Suebi, Rauraci, Boii, Tulingi, Germans, and a bunch of other tribes you've probably never heard of before because Julius effing Caesar stomped their colons into oblivion over two thousand years ago.

Julius Caesar was a fighting general who observed the action from the front, running up and down the battle lines yelling words of encouragement to psych his soldiers up. On one particular occasion, the Romans were getting their asses handed to them and started to run away like sissies, so Julius grabbed a sword and launched a one-man assault right into the middle of a horde of charging, axe-swinging Gallic barbarians. His men were so inspired by this action (and afraid that their commander would be killed as a result of their sniveling cowardice) that they sacked up, turned around, and liquefied nearly the entire force of sixty thousand warriors. The city of Rome celebrated Caesar's victory for nearly two weeks.

Gaul eventually got sick of having all of its cities burned down and its people slaughtered, so they organized a revolt under a barbarian warlord named Vercingetorix. Caesar refused to be defeated by a guy whose name was reminiscent of an evil video game dragon, so he marched four full legions across the entire length of Gaul in the dead of winter and

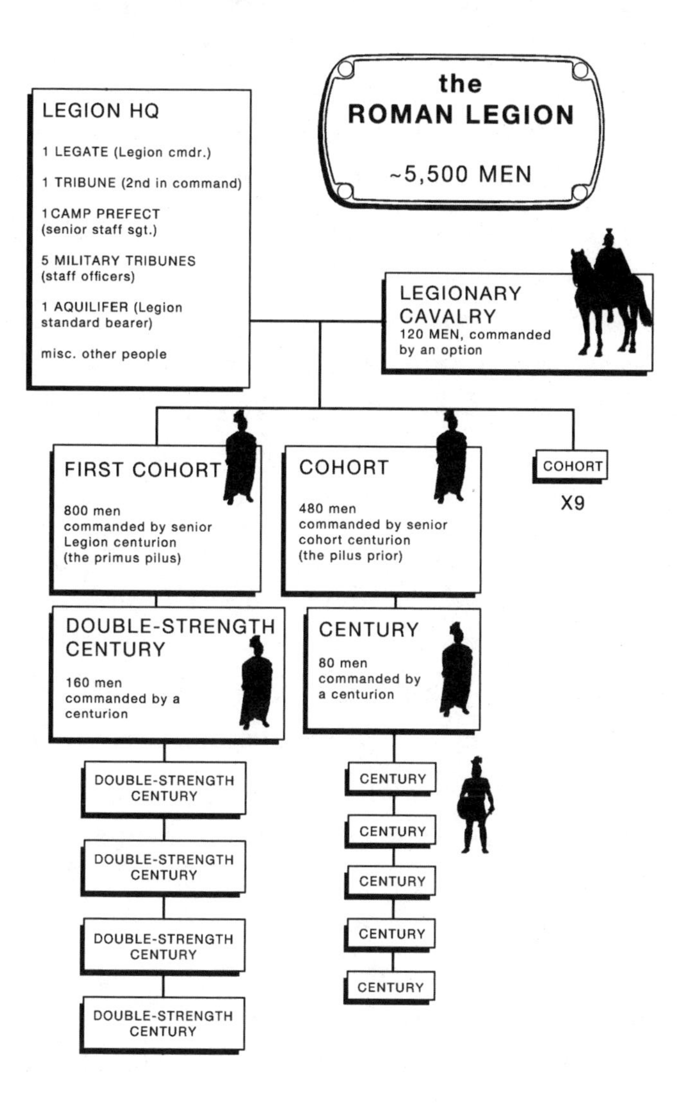

besieged the main body of the rebel force outside the city of Alesia. Even though a surprise Gallic counterattack left Caesar completely surrounded and outnumbered almost six to one, he completely destroyed the rebel armies, plundered their camp, captured the city, and had Vercingetorix dragged through the streets of Rome in chains. Gaul didn't attempt to organize another revolt for nearly three hundred years.

Caesar was also a master of manipulating the system to fit his own evil plans. Classical armies didn't fight during the winter, so as soon as it was time to bust out the Old Navy performance fleece Caesar simply took all the money he'd looted from Gaul back to Rome and used it to bribe government officials and citizens to support him. Eventually Pompey got a little unsettled by Julius's incredible popularity, so he tried to strip Caesar of his power. Caesar responded to this insult by assembling his army and marching across the Rubicon River toward Rome. Pompey was like, "Holy crap, I better get out of here before this dude rocks my face off!" and fled for Greece. Caesar marched through the gates of Rome, seized power over the republic, and immediately set out after his adversary.

At the Battle of Pharsalus in 48 BCE, Caesar's hardcore grizzled veterans stabbed Pompey's weak-willed troops in their pretty-boy faces. The soldiers who weren't killed in this manner were so horrified at the idea that they could mess up their hair or get nasty scars and ruin their supermodel good looks that they immediately ran for the hills like gutless prima donnas. Caesar's legionnaires flanked Pompey's forces, and that was the end of the Roman civil war.

Pompey was an expert at running for it like a bitch, however, and this time he fled to Egypt. Caesar chased after him, but a couple of days before he arrived in town some dude shivved Pompey in a dark alley. Julius decided he'd already come all the way out to Egypt, so he might as well hang out for a bit and help adjudicate a dispute over who should be the next pharaoh. On one hand was a stodgy uptight dickwad named Ptolemy, and on the other hand was the hottest woman in all of Egypt, Cleopatra, who was carried to him by her servants completely naked except for a bedsheet. Now, having hot, nubile Egyptian princesses delivered to your door like Chinese takeout may sound pretty far-fetched to you and me, but that's just how Julius Caesar rolled. For some strange reason Ptolemy was actually surprised when Caesar sided with Cleopatra in the dispute, so he put an army together. Caesar immediately emasculated him and all of his friends, got it on repeatedly with Cleopatra, and slam-dunked the hell out of a basketball for no reason at all.

After vanquishing his enemies in Egypt, Julius dominated Pompey's supporters up and down the Mediterranean, winning victories in Africa, the Middle East, and Spain. Then he returned to Rome and appointed himself *presidente por vida*, seizing sole power in the republic in a way that many other power-hungry megalomaniacs had previously failed to achieve. Eventually, some dudes were like, "Caesar is too awesome. It's not good for humanity to have such a total badass running around killing everyone," so they stabbed him in the back twenty-three times. Sometimes that's the price you pay for being awesome.

Part of the reason Brutus (of "Et tu, Brute" fame) was so eager to assassinate Caesar was because J. C. was banging his mom—they had an affair that lasted nearly twenty years!

After besieging and capturing the Gallic stronghold of Uxellodunum, Caesar cut off the hands of the surviving warriors and dispersed them across Gaul as a means of making sure they didn't *raise arms* against him again.

At one point Julius heard rumors about a possibly mythical land across the channel from Gaul, known as Britannia. Caesar, being the adventurous guy he was, became the first Roman to set foot on the island of Britain. He then immediately became the first Roman to slay a British person, as his legions started killing everyone they found and burning their cities. He eventually decided to head home when he realized that the British didn't have anything worth plundering.

During the Battle of Massilia, a brave centurion known as Gaius Acilius boarded an enemy vessel and immediately starting killing everything in sight. When the enemy lopped off Acilius's right hand, he single-handedly captured the ship by bashing everyone's skulls in with his shield.

8

THE SURENA

(84–52 BCE)

Nor was this Surena an ordinary person, but in wealth, family, and reputation the second man in the kingdom, and in courage and prowess the first, and for bodily stature and beauty no man like him.

—PLUTARCH, *LIFE OF CRASSUS*

CAESAR AND POMPEY EACH MET THEIR RESPECTIVE ENDS ON THE POINTY PARTS OF A COUPLE DOZEN WELL-SHARPENED KNIVES, BUT WHAT ABOUT THIRD MEMBER OF THE TRIUMVIRATE, THE ROMAN STATESMAN MARCUS LICINIUS CRASSUS? Well, in the year 53 BCE, Crassus was a complete raging dumbass. When most rich old white guys go spiraling into their midlife crises they're content to buy sports cars and nail strippers with giant plastic boobs, but for some bizarre reason the richest man in Rome decided it would be wise to put a huge army together and invade Iran. I should mention at this point that Crassus didn't really know the first thing about leading armies to glory on the battlefield, but he didn't give a damn, either—dudes like Caesar and Pompey were kicking ass all over the place, and he didn't want his subjects to think that he had a tiny dong or something.

Now, during this time period the Middle East was inhabited by a group of steel-toed hardasses known as the Parthians. These natural-born warriors were unparalleled horsemen, deadly archers, and almost completely impervious to all forms of conventional weapons. They had made a career out of kneeing the Romans in the groin every time some half-witted general tried to invade their homeland, and they certainly weren't going to make an exception for a douche-flavored taco like Marcus Licinius Crassus.

The bravest, strongest, and most crotch-clubbingly masculine of the Parthians was a dude known only as the Surena. This guy was a high-ranking noble, and his family served for generations as the defenders of the crown—members of his clan were responsible for protecting the king of Parthia at all costs, and it was their personal honor to place the crown on the king's head during coronation ceremonies. So he was kind of a big deal.

The Surena had already demonstrated that he was harder than a railroad spike; when King Hydrodes was overthrown and expelled from Parthia, it was the Surena who led the mission to recapture the kingdom. He personally assaulted the walls of the capital city, climbed up the siege ramps, crushed the defenders to death by swinging his ball sack around like a pillowcase full of bricks, and almost single-handedly cleared out the parapets with a fiery scimitar of neck-slashing death and dismemberment.

The Surena was also more attractive to the ladies than a going-out-of-business sale at a designer shoe store. The Romans, who aren't particularly known for heaping praise on people they considered to be "dirty subhuman barbarians," made especially sure to mention how good-looking this dude was, so you have to assume they weren't just blowing smoke up his ass for the sake of preserving cordial international relations. Of course, you can probably draw your own conclusions regarding his virility when you realize that it took two hundred wagons to carry his harem of sizzling-hot concubines. Interestingly, the

Surena never left home without his hoochie train—he even took them on military campaigns with him. Wouldn't you?

Crassus arrived in Parthia with a force of roughly forty thousand Roman legionnaires, and it was the Surena who rode out to meet him. Now, the Parthian hero's force was composed of just ten thousand horse archers and a thousand heavy cavalrymen, so he wasn't going to be able to get away with just hurling wave after wave of his own men at the Romans. Instead, he took advantage of the fact that Crassus was an arrogant douchebag who was so incompetent that he had to hire a guy to make sure he didn't pass out face-first into his Cheerios and drown in two pints of milk. The Surena baited him, hid the main force of his army, and drew the Romans out into the middle of the damn desert. Crassus,

being the inept toolshed that he was, was so pumped up about getting to watch his soldiers kill stuff that he marched his army full speed into the middle of the burning-hot wasteland and didn't even let the troops stop for water breaks.

While a small group of Parthians continually harassed the Romans, getting Crassus to chase them deeper and deeper into the desert, the Surena and his bodyguard of heavily armored lancers simply rode up behind Crassus's force and picked off the heat-exhausted stragglers, taking them out like a lioness weeding out the sick and the wounded from a herd of unsuspecting caribou on the Discovery Channel. When Crassus's men could finally venture no farther, the Surena made his move. The Parthians rode up en masse to the deafening sound of war drums, and the Romans all pretty much suffered myocardial infarctions right there on the spot. Crassus had his legions form into an anti-cavalry formation when they saw the Parthian horsemen arrive, but the Surena had no intention of charging face-first into the Roman lines like an overconfident idiot. His tactic was painfully simple—the horse archers just rode around the massed group of Romans in circles, indiscriminately firing arrows into the teeming throng of exhausted troops.

Not only were the Parthians ultra-elite snipers, but the fact that they were all mounted and capable of penetrating even the heaviest metal armor with their superstrong composite bows made this battle roughly the equivalent of a convoy of Humvees with .50 caliber machine guns circle-strafing a unit of Revolutionary War militiamen. The Romans, frustrated that they couldn't catch the Parthians to kill them, decided to just wait until the horse archers ran out of arrows. It was then that they noticed the Surena leading a column of a thousand camels onto the battlefield, each one carrying a pack bursting with ammunition.

Seeing no end to the relentless arrow storm in sight, the Roman cavalry, led by Crassus's son Publius, charged full on into the Parthian lines and were promptly skewered on the lances of the Surena's heavy cavalry like organic meat kabobs. The entire detachment was slaughtered, and Publius's head was put on a pike and paraded around in front of the Roman lines. When the sun mercifully began to set, the Surena informed Crassus that he had one night to mourn the loss of his son and consider this benevolent offer: surrender or die.

Crassus decided upon a bold new course of action to lead his army out of this desperate situation. As soon as the sun set, he bravely and resolutely ordered his men to break ranks and run for it. The next morning, the Parthians went after them, killing and capturing everyone they could find. Crassus was caught, killed, and beheaded, and molten gold was poured down his throat. Twenty thousand Romans were slain, ten thousand more were captured, and many others died in the desert trying to get home. Parthian casualties totaled like two guys with sunstroke and one archer who got a nasty blister on his index finger.

When the Surena returned home he led his troops in a parade down the streets of the capital, carrying around the heads of the defeated Romans, putting some of the POWs in dresses, and having his convoy of topless concubines sing offensive songs about how much of a pussy Crassus was. His success at the Battle of Carrhae made the Surena so popular and heroic a figure among his people that the king eventually got jealous and had him publicly executed. That's just how it goes sometimes—no matter how many times you bail a dude out, some jerks will screw you over at the drop of a hat.

The "Parthian shot" was when a horse archer was galloping at full speed away from you and somehow twisted his body completely around in the saddle and accurately fired an arrow backward from his horse without missing a step. Over the years, the phrase "Parthian shot" was bastardized to "parting shot," a term still used by jackass news media pundits across the country.

9

JULIA AGRIPPINA

(15–59 CE)

From this moment the country was transformed. Complete obedience was accorded to a woman—and not a woman like Messalina who toyed with national affairs to satisfy her appetites. This was a rigorous, almost masculine despotism.

—TACITUS, *ANNALS*

JULIA AGRIPPINA WAS "ROME'S SWEETHEART," KIND OF LIKE JULIA ROBERTS, ONLY IF INSTEAD OF ACTING IN CHARMING ROMANTIC COMEDIES SHE HACKED OSAMA BIN LADEN'S ARMS OFF WITH A CHAINSAW, NUKED NORTH KOREA, AND POISONED HALF OF THE HOUSE OF REPRESENTATIVES TO DEATH WITH CYANIDE CUPCAKES. She was a tyrannical, ultratough, take-no-prisoners woman who utterly destroyed anyone dumb enough to cross her and ruled Rome like a toga-wearing cross between Lady Macbeth and Martha Stewart's homicidal evil twin. She also had an extra set of canine teeth, which I guess is pretty cool if you're into that sort of thing.

In order to fully understand Agrippina's rise to power, we first need to take a look at her father, the stalwart Roman military commander Germanicus. The descendant of Augustus (by marriage) and Mark Antony (by birth), this guy was considered to be the pinnacle of Roman military ɹwess, beloved by his people and revered as one of the bravest and most noble men ever produced by the Imperium. Back in Augustus's time, a bunch of cantankerous German tribesmen ambushed some Roman legions, slaughtered tens of thousands of soldiers, nailed their skulls to tree trunks, sacrificed the survivors on the altar of their pagan gods, and carried three blood-drenched legion standards back to their ancestral homelands. As if that wasn't bad enough, the entire Roman army then went into a state of complete revolt soon after. Germanicus assumed command of whatever was left of the German legions, gave the troops a tongue-lashing so withering that it made R. Lee Ermey look like a talking cartoon dinosaur, and told his men that they were going to go restore their damn honor or die trying. The legions fell in line, executed the mutineers, marched into Germany, crushed the barbarian tribesmen, and recovered the captured standards. Germanicus was congratulated as the greatest hero of the Roman Empire and was loved by all, right up to the point that Emperor Tiberius surreptitiously poisoned him to death a few years later.

While Germanicus is considered one of Rome's greatest, most beloved, and most popular heroes, his offspring were some of the meanest, toughest, and most diabolical bastards to ever put on a toga for purposes other than convincing slutty sorority girls to get wasted on five-thousand-proof vodka and take their shirts off in front of a digital camcorder. Sure, Germanicus's life was cut tragically short, but this guy was famous for being in the revenge business, and when he went down he made sure his kids took the rest of imperial Rome down in flames with him.

While the psychotic emperor Caligula is the most infamous of Germanicus's issue, his daughter Julia Agrippina was the ultimate bad girl. She was beautiful, cunning, and diabolical, often planning intrigues and ruthlessly sabotaging her enemies for personal gain. She slept around on her husbands with members of powerful families, she used her station and her noble birth to get privileges otherwise unavailable to Roman women, and she utilized her father's position as a war hero to exert her influence over the army. When Tiberius finally keeled over and died, Agrippina's brother became the emperor Caligula, and Agrippina quickly became one of the most powerful women in Rome.

Caligula loved his sisters greatly (maybe a little *too much*, if you ask some historical sources), and Agrippina held a large amount of sway over her brother. Her image was placed on Roman coinage, she lived in the imperial palace, and she was awarded all the rights and privileges of the sacred Vestal Virgins (no matter how ironic that might seem), including front-row seats to the theater, all-you-can-eat shrimp, backstage passes to the Gladitorial Games at the Colosseum, and triple points on her frequent flier miles.

Once Caligula started getting really freaky and went nuts with those wild orgies and the arbitrary, wanton slaughter of his own citizenry, Agrippina plotted with one of her lovers to kill him and put her boyfriend on the throne. Unfortunately for our villainess, Caligula found out what was going on and had her exiled. All of her possessions were confiscated and she was shipped off to some island in the middle of nowhere, where she had to dive for sponges to make ends meet.

But it takes more than exile and not-so-subtle death threats to take out a ruthless social climber like Agrippina. Everybody in Rome eventually got sick of Caligula's attitude, and the Praetorian Guard stabbed him to death in 41 CE, placing Caligula's uncle Claudius on the throne. Claudius promptly recalled Agrippina back to the Eternal City, and she was pretty adept at parlaying her "unfortunate situation" into popularity and sympathy with the Roman people. Agrippina fell in love and married a wealthy senator, then immediately poisoned him to death and inherited his massive estate.

Agrippina's goal wasn't just wealth, however; it was the power that wealth brought. She had tasted the might of the emperor, and anything less than that was unacceptable. Her primary obstacle was Claudius's wife, Messalina, a woman whose primary claim to fame is that she was a total whore. It didn't take much effort for Agrippina to undermine the empress, defame her to the public, and subvert her to the point where the Praetorian Guard forced her to kill herself. With the emperor now suddenly single, the beautiful and seductive Agrippina did her thing. She married her uncle Claudius, which admittedly is kind of disgusting, but it's pretty much par for the course in ancient Rome. Seriously, take a look at the imperial family tree sometime; it looks like the diagram of a moderately complicated parallel circuit. No wonder the emperors were so crazy.

Now, Claudius was pretty much a spineless, sniveling pussy, and Agrippina was the balls of the empire during his reign. She wore a gold cloak, traveled in special carriages usually reserved for holy artifacts, and generally ran the show in imperial Rome. She got whatever she wanted, commanded limitless power, and cougared it up with virile young guys in her spare time. Life was good, the empire did well, and Agrippina commanded respect and power from the Roman people with an iron fist.

One of the great things about Agrippina was the way she worked the system for her own nefarious purposes. She took her foes out without being overt about it—realizing that she didn't need to use a chainsaw when should could just as easily manipulate others to do the dirty work for her. She eliminated her enemies in the government, the imperial family, the palace, and the Praetorian Guard, took out everybody from powerful senators to her own sister-in-law, and cemented her place at the top of the political food chain. She sometimes had people killed outright, but they were also exiled, poisoned, discredited, publicly condemned, arrested, demoted, forced to commit suicide, or simply transferred to political offices way the hell out on the outskirts of the empire. Nobody was safe from her wrath.

Her crowning achievement was when she convinced the weak-willed Claudius to announce her son as his successor over his own birth son

Britannicus. As soon as Claudius made this declaration official, she fed him some poisoned mushrooms, and that was the end of that. Her son became the emperor Nero, and we all know how well that worked out.

As Nero's mom, somehow Agrippina held even more power over the empire than she had as Claudius's wife. Nero allowed her to sit in on Senate meetings, silently surveying the situation from behind a curtain. She made the calls, ruled as emperor, and kept Nero in line. This worked out pretty well for a while, but Nero eventually started to grow a pair of nuts and tried to edge her out of her position. Well, nobody screwed with Agrippina that way. She tried to have him assassinated, but Nero figured out what was going on. First, he tried to poison her to death. This didn't work—in true badass fashion she had spent her entire life building up resistances to most poisons. Then he tried to crush her to death by collapsing the roof of a building on top of her, but she survived and crawled through the rubble to safety. Next, he sabotaged her yacht so that when she took it out on the lake it sank—she jumped overboard and swam to shore. Eventually he just had her stabbed to death by assassins, an act that earned him the hatred of the Senate and the citizenry alike. After she was no longer around to serve as a stabilizing force in her son's life, he went completely bat guano crazy, took up the fiddle, and burned Rome to the ground.

Though she may not have been the most virtuous woman this side of Mother Teresa, Agrippina was not a woman you stepped to if you enjoyed being alive. She was the daughter of a great commander and the only woman to ever be the wife, mother, and sister of emperors. She was the real might behind the throne of three all-powerful Roman rulers, worked tirelessly to build structures and improve the lives of citizens, and didn't think twice about slaughtering anybody stupid enough to attempt to take the crown from her. She destroyed emperors, deposed senators, and was exceedingly tough to kill. That, my friends, is a legacy to be proud of.

The Praetorian Guard was probably the worst outfit of bodyguards ever assembled. Sure, the soldiers who constituted the guard were elite fighters handpicked from Rome's mightiest legions, but more often than not when these guys drew their swords it wasn't for the purpose of cutting down a would-be assassin—it was because they were getting ready to run the emperor through themselves. During their long and storied career as the imperial royal guard, the Praetorians killed and/or deposed no fewer than ten different emperors.

Caligula tried to appoint his horse as consul once. It didn't work out so well. Consul is just one of those jobs that require opposable thumbs.

Julia Agrippina was named after her mother. To avoid confusion, Germanicus's wife is known as Agrippina the Elder, while our lady friend here is Agrippina the Younger.

AMAGE

While Julia Agrippina was a cunning, black-hearted mistress of deception and subtle manipulation, some classical-age women preferred to take a more direct approach to solving their issues.

Amage was the queen of the Sarmatians and an all-around kick-ass chick who eviscerated the ball sacks of anyone that tried to screw with her. Her husband, like many husbands both in antiquity and today, was completely and utterly useless in every way imaginable, spending all his time sitting around on the couch watching college football, ogling Hooters girls, and getting completely bombed on Miller High Life. With the king so completely vacuous that you could connect him to an EEG machine and have a physician pronounce him clinically deceased, Amage was left to run the country herself. And she did a pretty good job at it—she spent most of her time garrisoning fortresses, leading her armies against neighboring tribes, and presiding over disputes like a take-no-bullcrap judge on a trashy daytime courtroom TV show. In fact, she was so good at what she did that when her allies in the land of Cherson started getting dicked around by the neighboring Scythian Empire, they didn't even bother sending a letter to her worthless husband. They came directly to her.

The warlike Scythian king had been screwing with the Chersonians (or whatever the hell you call people from Cherson)—sending war parties to raid their refrigerators, watch their DVDs, and wrinkle their comic books—and pretty much everybody knew that Amage was the only person with the balls to do anything about it. She sent a letter to the Scythians telling them to leave her allies alone or suffer the consequences, but the Scythian king responded by faxing her a picture of his bare ass with the words "kiss this" written on his butt cheeks with a Magic Marker.

That was it.

Amage immediately summoned her elite royal guard—120 bloodthirsty cavalrymen handpicked for their peerless strength and unflinching bravery—and set out to teach that Scythian bastard a lesson in manners. This classical-age commando assault team went completely balls-out and traversed a distance of roughly 140 miles in under twenty-four hours, arriving unexpectedly in the middle of the night at the Scythian king's palace and storming the throne room. The warrior queen and her men killed the king, his guards, his family, his friends, his pets, people who owed him money, and pretty much everybody else they could get their hands on.

When the smoke cleared, the queen was standing triumphantly among a pile of dead warriors, her blade leveled at the throat of the young teenage prince of Scythia, who was the only member of his family not currently lying facedown in a pool of his own blood. In an icy, emotionless voice she informed him that he could stay alive and assume the throne so long as he took an oath never to defy her or screw with her allies. He quickly agreed, and Scythian armies never crossed the Sarmatians or any of their homies again.

2008

10

ALARIC THE BOLD

(370–410)

Corinth, Argos, Sparta, yielded without resistance to the arms of the Goths; and the most fortunate of the inhabitants were saved, by death, from beholding the slavery of their families and the conflagration of their cities.

—EDWARD GIBBON, *DECLINE AND FALL OF THE ROMAN EMPIRE*

THE STORY OF THE ROMAN EMPIRE HAS MANY PARALLELS TO THE EQUALLY TRAGIC LIFE OF MILLIONAIRE PLAYMATE/GOLD-DIGGER ANNA NICOLE SMITH. For a time, she was the sexiest gal out there, possessing near-limitless power, prestige, and wealth, and everybody either wanted her or wanted to be her. Then, over time, she got bloated, rich, bitchy, and pretentious, and spent way too much time drunk off her ass or wigged out on barbiturates. In the later years, Rome grew fat, drunk, and lazy as well. Its citizens were uptight stick-up-their-ass white people sitting on golden chaise lounges in togas and waving their hands nonchalantly while topless babes fed them grapes, they had more money than they knew what to do with, and they didn't give a crap about anything but themselves. Hell, they didn't even fight their own wars anymore—they had badasses like Alaric do it for them.

Alaric was a Goth. Now, when I talk about the Goths, it's important to understand that I'm not referring to those really skinny pale kids with smeared black mascara who live in their parents' basements and listen to terrible music. The long-haired European Visigoths were massively built, tough-ass Germans so hardcore they made the most black-hearted death metal enthusiast look like a beret-wearing French Renaissance painter, and their idea of a mosh pit involved cracking people in the back of the skull with an aluminum folding chair

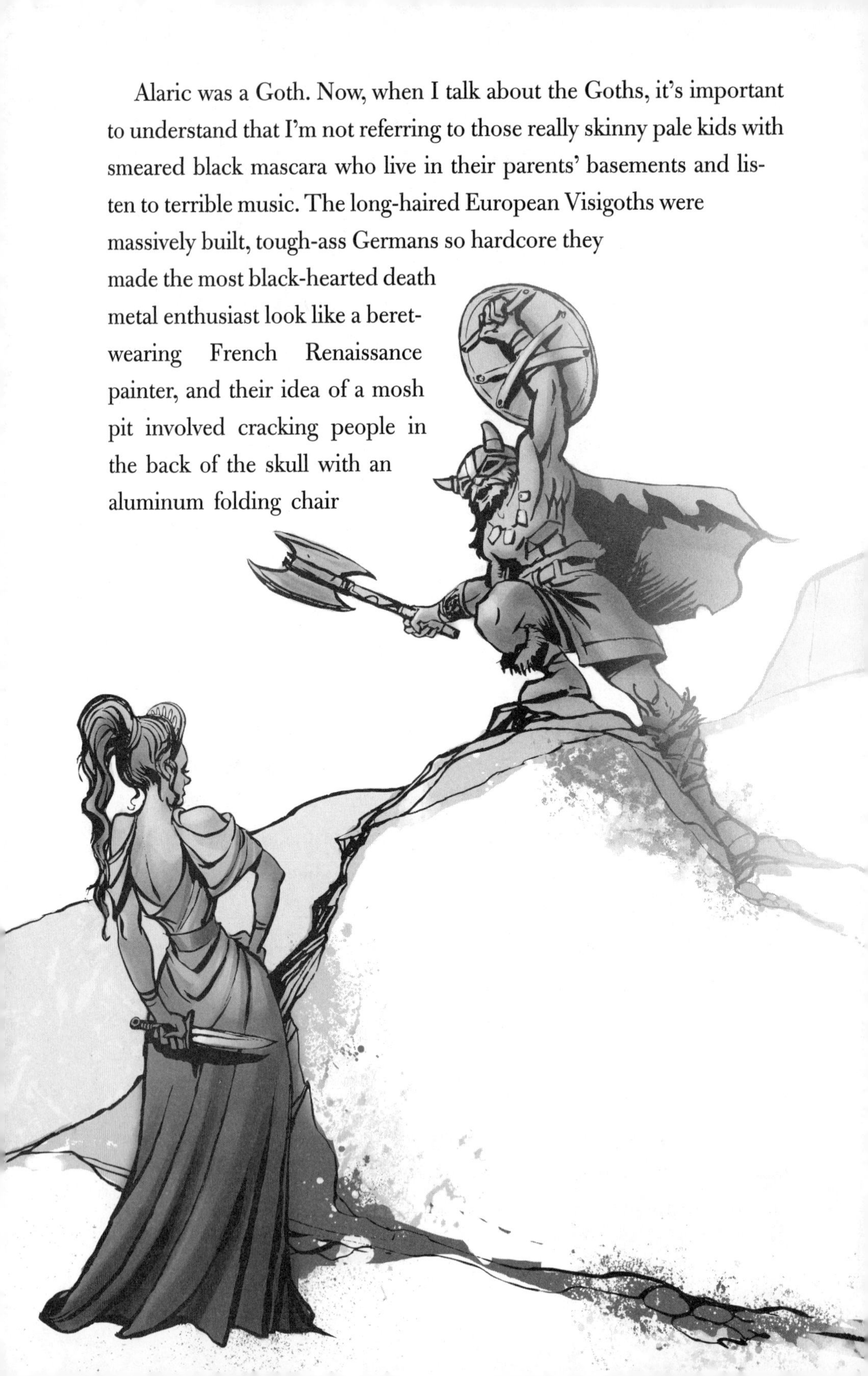

for no reason at all and then spitting blood on their unconscious bodies. These guys were known to drink an entire sixty-ounce flagon of mead in one gulp, smash the mug over your head, and then stab your friends to death with the broken shards of glass, all while listening to the subtle musical stylings of Yngwie Malmsteen. These brutal warriors went toe-to-toe with Rome's enemies in exchange for cash and prizes, and Alaric, being of noble Gothic birth, was a commander of these volatile auxiliary forces.

Unfortunately, fighting other people's wars for them wasn't as awesome as you might think. The Romans pretty much looked at the barbarians as expendable resources, and Alaric's kinsmen were usually utilized to spearhead Operation Human Shield—wave after wave of Gothic troops would be hurled into the fray, and then the Roman legions would climb over the mangled carcasses to achieve victory. This pretty much blew goats. After helping the Romans defeat the traitorous forces of the false emperor Eugenius, Alaric (along with any of his compatriots lucky enough to remain in one piece) was unceremoniously kicked to the curb. *Thanks for risking your life for us, now get the hell outta here.*

Well, fighting numerous battles and covering their blades in a demure shade of crimson really helped the Goths develop a taste for ultraviolence, so when they got back home they decided they were going to show the soft-ass Roman pussies who the toughest bastards in Europe really were. They proclaimed Alaric king of the Visigoths, raised him up on their shields in some kind of crazy Teutonic bar mitzvah ceremony, and immediately set about crushing all of Europe under their heel.

At the head of a screaming rabid horde of pissed-off bearded barbarians, Alaric the Bold made his way into Greece, capturing Macedonia and Thessaly without any resistance. He plundered the countryside, killing all men of military age and stealing their women, gold, and cattle. He allowed Athens to live in peace in exchange for a hefty ransom of gold and a nice hot shower, but Sparta, Corinth, and Argos weren't quite as lucky—their citizens were sold into slavery and their cities were ruthlessly plundered. In an effort to put an end to the relentless ass-beatings, the Eastern Roman emperor in Constantinople offered to appoint the barbarian ruler to the office of master general of Byzantium—the second-highest position in the empire next to the emperor himself—if Alaric would please stop slaughtering, pillaging, and enslaving people.

Alaric agreed to this sweet deal, but only because he had a nefarious plan. As master general, he ordered all the armories and smiths in Greece to forge top-of-the-line weapons and armor for the Visigoth army, essentially commanding them to create the instruments of their own destruction. This really takes being diabolically evil to the next level.

Now, if you couldn't afford the Oracle at Delphi, the next best thing in the classical age was to eat a bunch of shrooms, go to a place called a sacred grove, and stand around waiting for some random spirit to tell you something interesting. Alaric was pretty bored, so he went and did this a couple of times while his armies were reequipping with premium high-grade Grecian death implements. Eventually the grove said to him, "Away with delay, Alaric; boldly cross the Italian Alps and thou shalt reach the city." Alaric took this as a not-so-subtle hint that he was going to be able to capture Rome if he invaded immediately.

Unfortunately, the sacred grove was full of crap. The Goths crossed the treacherous mountains into Italy and besieged the emperor's summer home in Milan, but they were promptly counterattacked and defeated by the Roman general Stilicho. Alaric withdrew his forces back to Germany, and the Romans celebrated their victory by building a massive pillar signifying the utter and complete destruction of the Visigoth hordes forever.

Despite the fact that Stilicho bailed his ass out when his beach house was surrounded by bloodthirsty barbarians, Emperor Honorius of

Rome still got arbitrarily ticked off at his general for reasons I can't be bothered to go into right now. Honorius imprisoned Stilicho, his family, and his lieutenants, had them all executed, and then imprisoned the wives and children of all the Germanic troops serving in the Roman army. While the emperor thought this was a really goddamn brilliant way to exert his power over the Germans, it *amazingly* backfired—the troops all got pissed that their families had been locked up like criminals, ditched Rome, and flocked to Alaric with vengeance burning in their hearts. Thirty thousand soldiers rallied to the Visigoth king, and now that Rome's only semicompetent general had been taken out by his own emperor, the Goths crashed into Italy like an out-of-control cement truck with a beard. The countryside was sacked, stuff was on fire everywhere, and Alaric soon found himself standing outside the gates of Rome.

Now, as I said before, the Romans at this point were lazy-ass fat bastards who never worked a day in their entire miserable lives, yet still had everything they ever wanted. Alaric was a hardcore soldier, and he had no respect for people who didn't understand war. He surrounded the city, cut off access to food and communication, and proceeded to starve the Romans out. The gluttonous rich jerks of Rome tasted famine for the first time; men and women of the wealthiest families had to eat rat meat to survive, and most folks would have started violently murdering each other over a package of delicious chocolatey Swiss Cake Rolls. They begged Alaric for leniency, but he simply laughed in their faces. He told them he would agree to leave in exchange for 30,000 pounds of silver, 4,000 silk robes, 3,000 pounds of pepper, and 666 jelly donuts. They complied.

Being a man of his word, Alaric told the emperor that he would accept the ransom and leave Rome. He only asked one thing of the Roman ruler: he wanted a small plot of land in Venice where his tribe could live in peace. Emperor Honorius spat in the Visigoth emissary's face, saying, "The emperor of Rome will never submit to the demands of some dirty barbarian."

"Oh, really?"

On August 24, 410, Visigoth slaves living in Rome opened the gates in the middle of the night, and Alaric's warriors flooded the streets. The Gothic warrior king ordered that no holy places be destroyed, and no man or woman seeking refuge in a church should be killed, but other than that it was pretty much six days of pandemonium. Oppressed Visigoth slaves, tormented for years by their cruel and brutal Roman masters, finally got their revenge. Everything valuable was stolen. For the first time in 619 years, Rome was in the hands of a foreign invader. Alaric the Bold was in their base, killing their dudes.

After Alaric died the Visigoths got bored and migrated west, settling in Spain and western Gaul, where they lived peacefully until they got their asses wrecked by the Moors in 711. Rome would be sacked once again, this time by the Vandals, and the last Roman emperor was deposed by Germanic invaders in 476. The city has never really been the same since.

Alaric was a devout Arian Christian. Arians essentially believed that Jesus was divine, but that he was a separate entity created by God and wasn't actually God himself. Naturally, the Arians were declared heretics by the Roman Church and were hunted down, persecuted, and killed whenever possible.

Alaric is known as "Alaric the Bold," not just because he himself was bold, but because he was the leader of a barbarian tribe known as the Bolds. Furthermore, the name Alaric translates loosely to "king of all." So when you break his name down, it's "King of All, Ruler of the Bold People." I find this to be totally awesome.

Norway
Danes
England
London
Berlin
Saxons
Normandy
Paris
Frankish
Kingdom
Wallachia
Spain
Rome
Byzantine
Empire
Constantinop
Berbers
Mediterranean Sea
North Africa
Egypt
N

Section II
The Middle Ages

2008

11

KHALID BIN WALID

(592–642)

My sword is sharp and terrible. It is the mightiest of things when the pot of war boils fiercely. . . . I am the noble warrior, I am the Sword of Allah, I am Khalid bin Walid.

TRAINED FROM BIRTH IN THE HYPERMANLY ARTS OF HORSEMANSHIP, SWORD FIGHTING, WRESTLING, AND PUNCHING PEOPLE IN THE FACE SO HARD THAT THEIR BRAINS EXPLODE INTO TINY GRAY PARTICLES, THE GREAT MUSLIM WARLORD KHALID BIN WALID WAS BRED FOR ONE THING: KICKING SERIOUS ASS.

Born to the chieftain of the Quraysh tribe of Mecca, Khalid's life changed forever when the Prophet Muhammad came rolling into town in the year 625. At the Battle of Uhud, it was Khalid who led the Quraysh to victory against the invading army of the Prophet, inflicting the only defeat of Muhammad's well-documented military career. In the years following the battle, however, Muhammad and Khalid became homeboys, and Khalid eventually converted to Islam in 628. His penchant for slashing the face off anybody who crossed him and then suplexing their dead bodies over the side of a cliff led the Prophet to dub his mightiest warrior "the Sword of Allah."

Now, you can be pretty sure that Muhammad didn't give out totally dope nicknames like "the Sword of Allah" to just any idiot with a scimitar, and at the head of the Muslim army Khalid quickly became the most feared warrior in the Middle East. At the Battle of Mu'tah he flipped out and went into an insane battle rage when his force was surrounded and outnumbered by more than ten to one; during the maelstrom of ass-kicking he shattered nine different swords in his hand, probably by smashing them over people's heads with enough force to fracture the earth.

After Muhammad's death in 632 a bunch of jerkburgers decided that they were going to revolt and do their own thing, so the Prophet's successor, Caliph Abu Bakr, unleashed the Sword of Allah on those silly heathen nonbelievers. Khalid bitch-slapped the heretical tribes into submission, subdued rival chieftains, and ultimately reunited everybody under the banner of Islam through a subtle, delicate, refined mixture of diplomacy, negotiation, and relentlessly clubbing people in the face with the hilt of his scimitar until their teeth fell out and they forgot how to play the piano. It was also around this time that he got married to a woman said to be the hottest babe in Arabia—her husband had just unfortunately been accused of treason and was summarily beheaded on

the spot by Khalid, and she probably got so worked up watching the Sword of Islam do his thing that she pulled her burkha off and threw herself at him immediately. That's just how Khalid rolled, baby.

While in the process of littering the desert with the decaying corpses of traitors, heretics, and nonbelievers, Khalid came across a dude known as Muslaima the Liar. This guy was a total douche-canoe who told everybody he was a prophet of God, so of course Khalid had to go and personally tear him a brand-new asshole. Khalid showed up at Muslaima's crib with about thirteen thousand soldiers and found himself face-to-face with an army of nearly forty thousand ultrareligious zealot dumbasses. With both armies lined up across each other on the field of battle, Khalid took two steps forward, pounded his chest like Tarzan, and challenged the Liar to send forth his greatest champion. Some fool stepped up and didn't even have a chance to be pitied before he got his ass righteously smote by the Sword of Allah. After that, four more witless dickmeisters thought they wanted a piece of Khalid, and they all ended up being pummeled to death with bricks and run headfirst through an industrial-sized meat grinder. After watching this giant berserker waste his five greatest warriors in the span of about ten minutes, Muslaima the Liar dropped his sword and promptly ran screaming away from the battlefield like the bitch that he was. This didn't do a whole lot to bolster the fighting spirit of the warriors who believed Muslaima was the physical incarnation of God, and in the resulting battle the entire army of heretics had their heads cracked open like vinegar-soaked eggs. I'm not sure exactly what happened to the false prophet after Khalid caught up with him, but I can't imagine that it involved polite handshakes, trial by jury, or diplomatic immunity.

This incident should give you a pretty good indication that Khalid wasn't the sort of hands-off commander who was content to send his men into battle without trying to get a piece of the action for himself. He preferred to ride out at the head of his army, and before nearly every battle he would challenge the enemy commander to a mano-a-mano hell-in-a-cell ultimate-fighting death match. Taking Khalid up on his challenge usually resulted in a quick and painful death—there are no fewer than five recorded instances where Khalid jammed his sword through the abdomen of the enemy general before the battle even commenced, including one time in 634 when he decapitated the son-in-law of the Byzantine emperor and carried off the princess of Byzantium. Skipping the duel, while certainly a wise move, wasn't always a guarantee that you were safe from the terrible wrath of the Sword of Allah, either. During battle, Khalid always made of point of trying to fight his way to the enemy commander and stab him in the goddamned face as hard as he could. His theory was that it was much more difficult to command your troops when you've also got to worry about some bloodthirsty wild man trying to chop your brain in half with a broadsword. He was probably right.

So now, with the traitorous tribes either brought back into the fold or hacked into submission, Khalid went forth to spread the word of Allah to the godless heathens in the lands of Iraq, Syria, and Palestine. Against the mighty re-formed Persian Empire, Khalid cut down his enemies at the Battle of Walaja, overcame a force ten times larger than his own without even breaking a sweat in the Battle of Firaz, and during the Battle of Ullais, the Khasif River was said to have run red with the blood of his enemies. In the span of a mere eight months, Khalid and his small army of badasses somehow managed to completely cripple the Persian military and overrun their entire country.

With the Persians now pretty much totally boned, Khalid continued on his quest to head-butt all nonbelievers into submission with his bone-crunching Forehead of Death. He personally led his army through the treacherous Syrian desert toward Damascus, even though attempting to cross that uninhabitable wasteland was considered to be nothing short of suicidal. Khalid had crotches to kick, however, and didn't feel like wasting his time going around that bitch of a desert when he could just tear ass straight through it. To keep his men alive during the arduous journey, he took a bunch of camels with him, and halfway through the desert he had his men kill the camels, cut open their stomachs, and fill their canteens with nasty hump water. Sure, it's disgusting, and certainly not an act that would have been condoned by the medieval ASPCA (or FDA for that matter), but even the most patchouli-loving, biodiesel-brewing, vegetarian beatnik pacifist tree-hugger has to admit that it's also pretty damn hardcore.

Once in Syria, Khalid picked up right where he'd left off re: destroying all who opposed him in a cataclysm of gore. In 636, Khalid, now in charge of a combined force of twenty-five thousand Muslim warriors, drew up his battle lines against a massive army consisting of well over a hundred thousand soldiers from the all-powerful Byzantine Empire. Being the erudite tactician that he was, Khalid somehow managed to flank the enemy, donkey-punch them in the kidneys, and win a decisive victory, inflicting more than fifty thousand casualties on the enemy in just one day of fighting. This is an assload of kills, especially considering that the Muslims didn't exactly have access to assault rifles, tanks, and forty-foot-tall mechs with Gatling laser guns for arms and antipersonnel grenade launchers duct-taped to their heads. After dispatching the main body of the Byzantine army and piling up enough dead bodies to fill most Major League Baseball stadiums to capacity, the Muslims blitzed through the Middle East, capturing Jerusalem, Damascus, and Antioch in the span of just a few months.

For reasons nobody can really figure out, Khalid was eventually dismissed from the military by the caliph, despite the notable fact that it only took him about four years to defeat the two most powerful empires on earth and almost single-handedly morph the Muslim caliphate from a small regional power into one of the world's most dominant military forces. Being the honor-bound soldier he was, Khalid didn't complain or whine about it on his blog; he simply returned home, where he died an old man in 642. Because he was such a war-mongering hardass, with his last words he lamented the fact that he had not been killed on the battlefield: "I fought in so many battles seeking martyrdom that there is no place in my body but have a stabbing mark by a spear, a sword or a dagger, and yet here I am, dying on my bed like an old camel dies. May the eyes of cowards never sleep."

The towns and villages that Khalid came across were given three options: fight, convert to Islam, or agree to pay a tax known as the *jizya*. As long as people paid this tax on nonbelievers, they were free to continue practicing their religion and were exempt from having to serve in the Muslim military.

Khalid's tomb is located in an ornate mosque in Homs, Syria. His epitaph consists of an engraved list of the fifty major battles in which he commanded Muslim armies. He won all of them.

During the Crusades, the Muslim army featured specialized grenadier units known as *naffatun*. These pyromaniac foot soldiers wore fireproof suits and hurled pots full of burning pitch at their enemies, torching besieging armies and incinerating fortifications in a giant inferno of suck.

Another successful commander of the Islamic conquest was Tariq ibn Ziyad, also known as "Tariq the One-Eyed." This cycloptic Berber led the Moorish conquest of Spain, sailing across the Strait of Gibraltar in 711 with several thousand warriors eager to puncture the codpieces of Hispania's Visigoth defenders. When he landed his amphibious assault force on the southern coast of Spain, Tariq immediately torched all of his ships, telling his men that they had two options—victory or death. In the ensuing battle, the Muslims steamrollered the Goths, killing most of their nobility and establishing an Islamic presence that would flourish in Spain for nearly seven hundred years.

12

JUSTINIAN II

(669–711)

May I perish this instant—may the almighty overwhelm me in the waves—if I consent to spare a single head of my enemies.

EMPEROR JUSTINIAN II OF BYZANTIUM WASN'T A BRILLIANT MILITARY STRATEGIST, A CAPABLE RULER, A BENEVOLENT DICTATOR, OR EVEN A HALF-DECENT HUMAN BEING. He was a ruthless, merciless bastard who crushed all who opposed him, brutally eliminated his enemies, and let nothing stand in the way of his insane, over-the-top, possibly misguided mission to exterminate anyone ballsy enough to think they could screw with him for any reason. His entire existence was dedicated to one key tenet of badassitude: live for revenge.

Justinian inherited the throne of the Eastern Roman Empire in 685 at the age of sixteen, and immediately started going to war with everybody he could find. He quickly defeated the Muslim Umayyad caliphate in battle and negotiated a peace treaty that resulted in the caliph agreeing to pay yearly tribute to the almighty emperor (proving to everyone who had the hugest sack in the land), and then his army of crotch-stabbing warriors was dispatched to beat the loincloths off some jerkass barbarians that were causing trouble in Armenia and the Balkan Peninsula.

Even though his soldiers were doing an excellent job of turning wild hordes of rampaging savages into ground beef and the ruler of the most powerful nation in the Islamic world was sending him a fat welfare check every month, Justinian II was still pretty much utterly despised by the tightwad dickhead senators of the Byzantine Empire. First off, they didn't really dig Justinian's economic strategy, which basically involved taxing the ever-loving pants off the citizenry and then using that money to build incredibly huge buildings and massive statues of himself punching the Minotaur in the face or wrestling a fire-breathing three-headed dragon. On top of that, the populace was also a little upset that Justinian once tried to have the Pope arrested for disagreeing with him on religious matters. I suppose this is understandable, but I also think pretty much everyone can agree that signing an arrest warrant for the Pope because he doesn't agree with your interpretation of Christianity takes some seriously colossal steel testicles.

Unfortunately, the citizens of Constantinople didn't really have an appropriate appreciation for such flagrant displays of testicular fortitude, so the Senate convened an emergency session to do what senators do best—plot an underhanded coup d'état and depose the emperor. In 693, the Byzantine general Leontius, the Patriarch of Constantinople, and several senators busted into the imperial throne room and tackled Justinian like an overenthusiastic narcotics task force taking down a fleeing methhead on *Cops*. This group of usurpers roughed the emperor up, punched him in the stomach a couple of times, cut off part of his nose, slit his tongue down the middle, executed his closest advisors by burning them alive, and forcibly exiled Justinian to the craphole village of Cherson.

Well, not only did it suck that Justinian had just been humiliated and mutilated by a bunch of dillholes who were supposed to have pledged loyalty to him, but since the emperor was supposed to be flawless and perfect in every way, his new disfigurement meant that he was pretty much out of the running to ever regain his throne. But screw that. Justinian wasn't going to let something like a botched nose job stand in the way of his Palpatinian ambition. His first order of business was probably to get a custom-made gold plate to cover his hacked-up nose, which I imagine made him pretty much always look like a mix between Rip Hamilton and the Phantom of the Opera.

Years passed, but Justinian never forgot what happened to him. He just became more and more bitter. Every day for eight years he sharpened his sword, muttered under his breath, listened to pump-up music, and waited for his chance to strike.

Meanwhile, back in Constantinople, General Leontius was overthrown, exiled, and replaced by another usurper emperor named Tiberius. Tiberius correctly decided that it was too dangerous to have a ruthless, vengeful bastard like Justinian hanging around being not dead, so he sent some dudes to bring him in for a proper execution. Justinian figured out what was going on and was like, "Screw that"—he fled Cherson to go live with the Khazars, an unruly tribe of Jewish-Turkic nomads known for being hardcore all of the time and for eating (kosher) meat right off the bone. In the short time he was there, Justinian's bow-hunting skills, nunchuck skills, and bench-pressing ability impressed the Khazar tribal leader so much that he happily offered his own sister to Justinian in marriage. In 703, Justinian was wed to the Khazar princess, a woman named Theodora, and was starting to adapt to life amongst these tough warrior nomads. It should also be mentioned that they lived in the town of Phanagoria, a place so barbaric that the magazine *Fangoria* may well have been named after it.

Emperor Tiberius was still determined to turn Justinian into shark food, however, so he got in touch with the Khazar leader and together they conspired to put a hit out on him. Two goons busted into Justinian's bedroom in the middle of the night to kill him, but Justinian got the drop and choked them both to death with his bare hands. He then stole a fishing boat from the pier in the middle of the night and set out to seek his vengeance.

After crossing the treacherous Black Sea in a driving thunderstorm at the helm of a leaky wooden ship, Justinian arrived in the land of the

Bulgars, an even more vicious race of lawless, barbaric killmongers. Justinian made peace with the Bulgar khan and promised him truckloads of money and hookers in exchange for his help reclaiming the throne that was rightfully his, so the khan quickly assembled a well-trained, sufficiently frenzied force of bloodthirsty cavalrymen ready to kick serious ass. Together with his new allies, Justinian rode out for the gates of Constantinople. His force was too small to penetrate the massive walls of the heavily fortified city, but like any good diabolical madman hell-bent on the destruction of his enemies, Justinian had a plan. He knew about an old abandoned aqueduct that ran into the heart of downtown Constantinople, so in the middle of the night he and his men snuck into the city through a series of secret passages and immediately started hacking up disloyal soldiers, burning stuff, and generally just causing more havoc than a punch bowl of Red Bull at an eight-year-old's birthday party. The next morning, ten years after he had been deposed, Justinian once again took a seat on his blood-soaked throne.

Now the people who had messed with Justinian were humped, and by humped, I mean seriously humpty-humped. The senators and revolutionaries who had plotted against Justinian were sewn up into burlap sacks and thrown in the ocean. He arrested the false emperor Tiberius and sent his men to the farthest reaches of the earth to find that bastard General Leontius and drag him back to Constantinople in chains. Once he had both of these men firmly in his kung fu grip, Justinian slashed their noses and tongues just as they had done to him, had them bound and trussed, and then sat on his throne watching chariot races while using these men for footstools. When he got bored of resting his feet on the backs of his enemies, he had them publicly executed for treason. Justinian also tracked down the Patriarch who was responsible for his ordeal, stripped him of his rank, and put out his eyes with a really sharp number two pencil. Then he burned the town of Cherson to the ground and executed or enslaved everyone in the city, because it sucked being exiled there for like eight years.

Unfortunately, Justinian spent so much time exacting cruel retribution on everyone who had ever messed with him that he kind of lost track of what was going on in the empire. Towns revolted against him, foreign invasions threatened the borders, and he was eventually captured and executed by a bag of douches. His severed head was placed on display outside the city of Rome (which is actually kind of awesome when you think about it) and his infant son was murdered in an effort to erase this bastard's bloodline from history forever.

Greek fire was a badass version of medieval napalm used by the armies of Byzantium to turn their enemies into giant walking third-degree burns. This mysterious weapon, described only as "liquid fire," was generally deployed either in grenade-style bombs or by a flamethrower-like weapon attached to the front of a warship. The sulfurous fluid ignited on contact with the air, stuck to whatever it hit, and could not be extinguished even by complete submersion into water.

In the year 811 the Byzantine Empire invaded the land of the Bulgars and torched their capital to the ground. The Bulgar khan, a dude named Krum, got super pissed off and triggered a landslide that demolished most of the Eastern Roman army. Then he lopped off the head of the Byzantine emperor Nikephoros, scooped out his brains, and turned the emperor's skull into a decorative wine goblet.

2008

13

CHARLES MARTEL

(688–741)

The men of the North seemed like a sea that cannot be moved. Firmly they stood, one close to another, forming as it were a bulwark of ice; and with great blows of their swords they hewed down the Arabs. Drawn up in a band around their chief, the people of the Austrasians carried all before them. Their tireless hands drove their swords down to the breasts of the foe.

—ISIDORE OF BEJA'S *CHRONICLE*

BACK IN THE DARK AGES, THE KINGS OF THE FRANKS WERE COMPLETELY USELESS. Worthless, overweight, no-talent inbred sacks of solidified drunken apathy sitting on their giant gold-plated diamond thrones while skanky bimbettes fed them, these lazy bastards completely detached themselves from reality and generally just lived the vapid, mind-numbingly uninteresting lives of modern-day celebrity debutantes with more money than sense. During these times, the real power over the Frankish kingdom lay in the hands of an epic spine-breaking killmaster known as the Mayor of the Palace—the administrative mastermind responsible for running pretty much every aspect of the government and picking up all the slack while the syphilitic king was off lounging around on an inflatable pool float, sipping piña coladas, soiling himself, and complaining about the weather.

One such Mayor of the Palace was a dude named Pippin. Pippin's primary claim to fame is that he once impregnated some random peasant chick he hooked up with in a club one night, and his one-night-stand-gone-wrong ended up producing an illegitimate son named Charles. Despite the unfortunate situation surrounding his parentage, Charles was eventually accepted into Pippin's family and served as a captain in the Frankish army. He grew to be a mighty warrior known for his bravery and skill on the battlefield, and his uncanny ability to tenderize the faces of his enemies with a giant-ass mallet earned Charles the awesome nickname "Martellus," which is Latin for "the Hammer."

Pippin eventually beefed it in 714. Before his cadaver was room temperature, Pippin's bitchy wife seized control of the mayoralty and chucked her stepson Charles into prison like he was some kind of two-bit bastard son of a crackhead. He was shipped off to a maximum-security dungeon facility located deep in a remote part of the kingdom, a foul cesspool of wickedness and villainy known as the dread city of Paris. Well, hardcore ass-beaters with sick nicknames like the Hammer can't be contained by something as trivial and petty as a hellacious medieval torture chamber, and so the twenty-five-year-old Charles was able to bust out pretty much immediately by ripping the bars out of the wall with his teeth, shoving the warden face-first into a garbage disposal, and then head-butting ten guys so hard that their brains exploded out

the backs of their heads. He escaped to the countryside, put together an army of grim, vengeance-seeking warriors, and went off to show his stepmom who the baddest mother in town really was.

The warlike, head-splitting armies of Charles Martel met little resistance as they dominated faces across Gaul and Germany. Despite his father's dying wish—"Please, Hammer, don't hurt 'em"—Charles deposed his evil stepmother, regulated on a couple of rebellious Frankish provinces, and introduced several unruly bandit confederations to the true meaning of "Hammer Time." After securing his own borders, he launched campaigns against the pagan German barbarians to the east, pummeling them into giant heaping mounds of severed limbs and severely bludgeoned craniums and then sending St. Boniface out to baptize anything that happened to be left standing.

Despite being harder than volcanic rock and more than willing to take down all comers with a series of vicious running ball-knocks, Charles Martel was still quite concerned about the growing Muslim threat sweeping across the globe. Even as Charles consolidated his power in Europe by relentlessly pulverizing anybody who failed to recognize him as being totally awesome, the Muslims were blitzing into Spain, severing the heads of any Christian warriors they came across, and generally just pwning everything in their paths. Martel knew it wouldn't be long before a zerg rush of Moors would be kicking down the gates of his castle, and he wanted to make sure that they ran full throttle into a frothing-at-the-mouth, too-legit-to-quit horde of really pissed-off Germans waving ten-foot-long spears in their faces. He assembled a grizzled assortment of full-time veteran soldiers, organized them with rigorous drilling and training, and gave them valuable battle experience by campaigning against the barbarian tribes of the East.

In 732, the crimson tide of Islam came pouring over the Pyrenees on an avalanche of blood, trampling everything in front of it and tearing ass through western Gaul like a badass El Camino with a spoiler and a racing stripe. The mighty duke of Aquitaine marched out to face this massive invading army with a large force of Christian foot soldiers and ended up having his brain amputated by a razor-sharp scimitar. His regiments were smashed, and the Moors swept across the countryside, burning churches, looting, and capturing prisoners to sell into slavery. They easily sacked the Christian stronghold of Bordeaux and made their way toward the strategically critical city of Tours.

Charles was off in Germany sucker-punching godless pagans in the balls and smashing their heathen stone altars into dust with his forehead, but as soon as he heard that the duke of Aquitaine had just had his face exploded by the Muslims, the Hammer of Christendom slammed on the emergency brake, turned his army around, and burned rubber back home. Now, it's important to note that Tours was the home of the Basilica of St. Martin—the holiest place in the entire Frankish kingdom—and Charles would have rather passed a baseball-sized kidney stone made out of broken glass than allowed that blessed cathedral to be plundered and defiled by infidels. He crossed the entire length of Gaul, slowing down only to stop off at peasant villages and recruit volunteers to help him in his crusade, and somehow managed to take a defensive position outside the city before his enemies were able to reach it.

Now, the strength of the Muslim army was the Moorish heavy cavalry, a crotch-thumping unit of superpumped-up mounted warriors with great stats who had been trampling the crap out of the Christian knights in Spain and bringing pain and suffering to anybody misguided enough to face them. Nobody had yet been able to stand up to these fearsome warriors without having their gallbladders utterly flattened, but Charles Martel had a plan. He positioned large masses of heavy infantry along the forest at the top of a large hill, forcing the enemy to fight on terrain that favored the Frankish men-at-arms. He had his spearmen form up into defensive squares to protect themselves from being outflanked and lock their shields to create an unbreakable wall of unforgiving steel.

The Moors went lance-first into these formations several times but were unable to smash their way through this unyielding hedge of armor and spears. Once the enemy was worn down, Martel himself, uttering his battle cry of "Stop—Hammer Time!" led the decisive charge that shattered the Muslim army and left their commander coughing up his own prostate. The Saracens fled the field, leaving behind their plundered loot and prisoners.

Martel chased the Moors back into Spain before returning home and being honored by his subjects and his peers as the greatest champion and hero of Western Europe. He dedicated the rest of his life to securing his borders against the Muslims in the West and beating up and/or baptizing the godless pagan barbarian tribes in the East, and his actions paved the way for his grandson, the emperor Charlemagne, to bring the Frankish kingdom to prominence as the most powerful European civilization of the early Middle Ages.

After personally seeing Moorish heavy cavalry stomp bozaks on the field of battle, Charles Martel began to incorporate squadrons of well-armored mounted troops into his own army—these dudes would be the precursor to European knights.

The Frankish kingdom under Charles Martel was made up of present-day France, western Germany, Switzerland, Belgium, Holland, western Austria, Liechtenstein, and Luxembourg.

The Carolingian Dynasty really wasn't particularly inventive in their naming conventions. In the span of just a few generations they produced Charles the Hammer, Charles the Great, Charles the Fat, Charles the Bald, Louis the Pious, Louis the Second, Louis the Third, Louis the Child, Louis the German, Pippin of Heerstal, Pippin the Short, Pippin the Elder, and regular Pippin (the Nothing).

14

WOLF THE QUARRELSOME

(c. 1014 CE)

Wolf the Quarrelsome cut open Brodir's belly, and led him round and round the trunk of a tree, and so wound all his entrails out of him, and he did not die before they were all drawn out of him. Brodir's warriors were slain to a man.

—*THE STORY OF BURNT NJAL*

KNOWN AT THE TIME AS THE BIGGEST AND MOST CROTCH-CLUBBINGLY FEROCIOUS BARBARIAN ON THE PLANET, WOLF THE QUARRELSOME WAS AN ELEVENTH-CENTURY IRISH WARRIOR AND BROTHER OF THE LEGENDARY IRISH HIGH KING BRIAN BORU. Wolf's mother was killed by a Norse raiding party while he was still young, allowing him to cultivate an unending hatred for everything Viking-related, and while Wolf honed his ability to crack people's heads open with a gigantic face-cleaving axe and slam their hands shut in car doors, Brian made a name for himself by uniting all the Irish peoples under one banner and standing up to the combined forces of Viking jackasses across the island. You see, back in the day Ireland was divided into a bunch of puny little kingdoms, pointless city-states, and other such garbage, so Brian put together a giant army, kicked the snot out of a few dozen rival warlords, and unified the country—breaking the political hold the Scandinavian nations had over Ireland in the process.

Well, apparently not everyone realized how totally sweet it was to be ruled by Brian Boru, so some whisky-swilling turf cutters from the province of Leister decided to be complete dicks and revolt. In order to help them kick Irish ass they called in their BFFs, a horde of goddamned bloodthirsty Viking pillagers. Tens of thousands of Vikings, Irishmen, and other assorted Celtic and Gaelic warriors met at the Battle of Clontarf in 1014 and immediately proceeded to beat the crap out of each other with swords, hammers, axes, fists, tin pots, shields, stray cats, lead pipes, pitchforks, stun guns, shopping carts, bread, very small rocks, a duck, and whatever the hell else they managed to bring along with them. It was at this point in history that Wolf the Quarrelsome proved himself to be the hardest-core badass in an arena filled with hardcore badasses.

Now, in order to fully appreciate the importance of his actions, let's take a moment to examine Wolf the Quarrelsome from a historical perspective. First off, his name is Wolf. You don't get to be called Wolf by being a seventy-pound nerd who gives himself a hernia trying to pick up a box of file folders. Wolf is a serious name. In the Viking histories his first name is translated as Ulf, and as we all know Ulf is the sort of name that's reserved for guys who eat entire chickens in one sitting, drink their weight in beer, grow beards at the rate of one inch per hour, wail death metal on guitars shaped like lightning bolts, play professional ice hockey, and are so ripped that every time they flex their pecs their shirt explodes and flies off into the atmosphere. Ulf isn't a name; it's the guttural sound that your enemies make when you punch them in the stomach with enough force to make Rocky Balboa cough up blood. As if this isn't enough, his epithet is "the Quarrelsome," and you can be pretty damn sure that you don't get an epithet like "the Quarrelsome" by taking crap like an overworked fecal analysis technician. *Quarrelsome* by definition means that you completely destroy anyone who messes with you, so we can assume that this guy was so good at putting bitches in their place that his name became synonymous with beating the hell out of people for little to no reason. That's pretty epic. Since Wolf was champion of the Irish forces, you also have to assume that he was even more hardcore than the biggest, meanest, axe-swinging, Guinness-chugging, shillelagh-toting hooligan bastard rugby player you've ever seen. The guy probably drank whisky by the barrel and then went out into the woods to chop down trees with his crotch so he could whittle the ends into points with his teeth and hurl them at enemy castles.

Another thing that totally rocks about Wolf the Quarrelsome is that he only appears in history twice, and both times he's kicking ass. It's those folks that are shrouded in mystery who are often the most interesting, and Wolf is no exception. We never learn about his policy-making efforts. We don't know anything about his childhood, his girlfriend, his favorite color, or what he liked to do in his spare time. When you read a history of his life, you learn only one thing—he enjoyed smashing people in the face with an axe. That's it.

So when Brian Boru's army went up against the Vikings at Clontarf, you can rest assured that Wolf was right in the middle of the near-limitless carnage. The main thrust of the Viking offensive was personally led by an ill-tempered warrior named Brodir of Man, a legendary berserker so manly that it was his name. Brodir was one of those helmet-with-horns-on-it bastards with a giant long axe and an exceedingly bad attitude, and his force was really whipping Irish balls all over the place. Wolf the Quarrelsome got sick of that pretty fast, sought Brodir out on the battlefield, and engaged him in one-on-one combat. Brodir of Man took one shot at Wolf; Wolf sidestepped him and bashed him in the face with his axe, knocking him to the ground. Brodir tried to scramble to his feet, but Wolf smashed him with another mighty blow that sent him crumpling back to the earth. Brodir stumbled to his feet again, and this time Wolf kicked his ass down the side of a hill. By this point, the big bad Viking warlord decided he'd had enough of getting his face wrecked by an obviously superior warrior and ran off like a little girl skipping away from an anthill. With the Viking commander no longer leading his army, Wolf the Quarrelsome almost single-handedly cut a swath of destruction through the enemy ranks, severing countless limbs and adding a nice glossy crimson sheen to his axe blade as the Irish forces began to rout their Leister foes. By the end of the day six thousand Viking warriors had been slain and the political power the Viking aristocracy held over Ireland was forever broken.

However, it wasn't all unicorns, rainbows, butterflies, and giant piles of severed Viking heads for the Celtic warriors at Clontarf. You see, as Brodir of Man and his entourage of elite warriors was bravely running away from the serious ass-kicking Wolf the Quarrelsome had righteously laid upon them, by a sheer stroke of luck they came across the tent of Brian Boru. Now, while Brian Boru was a pretty strapping dude back in the day, at the time of the Battle of Clontarf he was like eighty years old. The Vikings busted into his tent, caught him in the middle of his prayers, chopped his head off, and ran off into the woods yelling about how awesome they were. About an hour later, Wolf the Quarrelsome returned to report victory and found the decapitated corpse of his older brother. This sent him into a completely insane rage, and he swore vengeance on the man who had killed his brother and his king. He immediately put together a force of tough-as-hell Celtic warriors and set out to jack Brodir up, because as you can probably guess, medieval badasses with names like Wolf the Quarrelsome don't screw around for one second when it comes to living for revenge. He and his men hunted the Viking raiders down and engaged them in the most brutal hand-to-hand combat this side of the original *Mortal Kombat* arcade game. All of Brodir's men were slain, and Wolf took down Brodir himself with a perfectly executed judo shoulder throw followed by a punch to the throat. Then he cut open Brodir's stomach with a huge battle-axe, pulled out all of his entrails, and tied them around a tree, causing Brodir to die a horrible and painful death. This is what happens when you mess with Wolf the Quarrelsome—you end up being strangled to death with your own intestines.

After destroying Brodir, scattering the Viking army, and breaking Norse control over Ireland forever, Wolf the Quarrelsome promptly vanished from history.

The Brian Boru Harp, currently housed at Trinity College in Dublin, is the national symbol of Ireland. This ancient instrument appears on the country's coat of arms and coinage, and also serves as the official logo of Guinness beer.

The Druids, an enigmatic group of mysterious priests known for human sacrifices, communicating telepathically with aliens, and moving giant rocks around with their minds, believed that when a person died his soul wasn't extinguished but rather was transferred to another living creature. The belief that death was merely a temporary setback inspired ancient Celtic and Irish warriors to go completely balls-out into combat without worrying about their own mortality.

Brian Boru came into prominence in a period following a series of devastating Viking invasions of Ireland. Through alliances, treaties, and wars, Brian was able to reunite most of the Irish counties, and as high king he used the money he earned from his campaigns to rebuild the monasteries and libraries that had been trashed by the Norsemen. He is remembered as one of Ireland's greatest heroes and military commanders.

Irish warriors fighting the French during the Hundred Years' War used to capture peasant children from small villages, strap them to cows, and then send the livestock out at the head of their battle formation. The astonished French archers refused to fire arrows at their own kids, thus saving the Irishmen from a pointy death. Isn't that jacked up?

Adaro

When most people think of mermen, they generally picture a bunch of wussy, effeminate metrosexual fish-people swimming around singing about how awesome life under the sea is and how much they love braiding each other's hair and getting together for intense underwater basket-weaving sessions. Well, in the mythology of the Solomon Islands, mermen are insane murderous bastards who would just as soon gut you like a trout and filet your carcass as shake your crazy unwebbed hand. The Adaro are a race of mermen who resemble humans with flippers, dorsal fins, and gills. These sociopathic extreme-sports aficionados travel through the air by surfing on rainbows and use their mad archery skills to shoot poisonous flying fish at sailors. The high-velocity aquatic cruise missiles come out of nowhere and stab you in the heart, killing you instantly and in a totally humiliating manner.

Chimera

The bitchin' chimera was a hate-filled demon from Greek mythology. This thing had the body of a lion, a tail like a lizard, and three heads—a

lion, a dragon, and an irate goat. As if it's not bad enough that this fiend could scratch your eyes out with its massive claws or head-butt the holy living god out of you with its crazy goat horns, it also breathed fire out of each of its angry heads. Honestly, is there anything more ridiculously awesome than a goddamned fire-breathing goat?

Fenrir

Fenrir is a gigantic angry wolf, kind of like Clifford the Big Red Dog if he got rabies and started biting the heads off everyone he saw. This massive beast is the offspring of the evil Norse god Loki, and when the great battle takes place at the end of the world, Fenrir will allegedly show up and chomp Odin in half. You know you're pretty baller when you can chow down on the king of the Norse gods like he's an oversized human-shaped bratwurst.

Kappa

The Kappa are a race of small bipedal reptilian river demons that infest the lakes and ponds of rural Japan. These monsters have two favorite foods: cucumbers and the blood of human children. To this day, some parents have been known to throw cucumbers into rivers before allowing their children to go swimming . . . just in case.

Unicorn

The unicorn is another malevolent mythical creature that gets a bad rap. While most people generally think of this one-horned equine creature as something out of a bad cartoon musical about princesses in frilly pink dresses carrying around tulips and belting out duets with anthropomorphic singing bunnies, many medieval bestiaries refer to the unicorn as a fearsome executioner capable of using its powerful magical horn to gore the hell out of everything from African elephants to grizzly bears. According to legend, the unicorn was an unstoppable killing machine that destroyed everything in front of it, and was unbeatable in single combat by even the bravest and most badass knight. The only way to tame this destructive, rampaging beast was for a beautiful maiden to take her shirt off—when unicorns saw topless babes they immediately stopped wantonly slaughtering everything they saw and became as docile as sedated newborn puppies. Personally, this kind of sounds like a ploy devised by some medieval naturalist to get a bunch of hot chicks to show their boobs, but who am I to argue with the primitive science of the Dark Ages?

15

WILLIAM THE CONQUEROR

(1027–1087)

King William came from the South unawares on them with a large army, and put them to flight, and slew on the spot those who could not escape; which were many hundred men; and plundered the town.

—*ANGLO-SAXON CHRONICLE*

THERE ISN'T MUCH KNOWN ABOUT THE MEDIEVAL WARLORD ROBERT THE DEVIL, BUT I CAN'T IMAGINE THAT HE WAS A SWEET-TEMPERED SOUL WHO COMPOSED ROMANTIC POETRY AND SPENT HIS WEEKENDS VOLUNTEERING AT THE LOCAL ORPHANAGE. In fact, I'd be willing to bet that with a name like Robert the Devil he was a lot more likely to be launching flaming arrows into the thatched roofs of small, disobedient European hamlets than pulling babies from the windows of burning buildings. What we do know about him definitively is that he was the duke of Normandy in 1027, a magical time when he became the proud father of a baby boy named William. Unfortunately, the mother of this tiny bundle of joy wasn't his wife, the duchess of Normandy—it was some young peasant woman that Bob just so happened to be boinking on the side.

Well, Robert mercifully went catapulting headfirst into a grave a few years later, but since he and the duchess never actually produced a human male child, young William—affectionately known among the Norman barons and nobles who completely hated his guts as William the Bastard—was suddenly tapped to succeed his father as ruler of Normandy. Of course, the tightwad jackass barons weren't super-omega pumped up about this turn of events, and they showed their displeasure by murdering the hell out of the first three men appointed to be William's legal guardian. For his own safety, William had to be hidden away in small villages and boarding schools until he was old enough to rule.

Life on the streets made William tougher than an over-the-top Spike Lee joint about ten-year-olds knifing each other in the kidneys with homemade shivs, and he ascended to the throne of Normandy in 1047 at the age of twenty. Pretty much immediately a large group of the aforementioned jackass nobles decided to revolt and overthrow the bastard, so Duke William raised an army and started beating the crap out of everyone just to prove to his people that he did in fact have the concrete testicles and creosote-soaked veins required of all professional medieval conquerors. He crushed the rebel army wherever he found it and eventually laid siege to the traitorous stronghold of Alecon, a fortress where the dumbass defenders thought it would be an incomprehensibly brilliant idea to taunt William by hanging a bunch of nasty animal skins from the castle walls (Will's mother was a tanner's daughter and that apparently was like some sort of reference to tanning or something).

That was a mistake.

Before we go any further, I'd just like to take a moment to point out that William the Bastard really, really, ridiculously hated it when you talked smack about his birth, his bastardship, his legitimacy, or his mother. I know a lot of wannabe hardasses out there are all like, "Hey, fool, what you say about my momma?" but Will really took it to the next level. After the display I just mentioned, William besieged the town, busted through the walls like an intoxicated Kool-Aid Man, pillaged the city, burned everything that was even remotely flammable, and cut off the hands and feet of everyone he could catch. Like I said, he took that sort of thing *very* personally. Of course, you can't necessarily say that the people of Alecon didn't get what was coming to them; I mean, what did they expect when they decided to taunt a guy whose father was known as Robert the Devil?

Another good example of William's deep-seated insecurity was when he courted Countess Matilda of Flanders, a highborn noblewoman who traced her family lineage directly to King Alfred the Great. Hearing of her great beauty, and wishing to further legitimize his position as a serious honest-to-God member of the nobility, William sent a messenger to ask for her hand in marriage. She responded by slapping the messenger in the face, spitting in his eye, and saying something to the effect of, "I would never stoop so low as to marry a bastard!" Then she kicked the dude in the junk with enough force to crack a coconut and body-slammed him through a table onto some thumbtacks.

Now, William had a temperament that made Bobby Knight's most assholish violent outbursts look like Mahatma Gandhi playing Nerf bas-

ketball with Martin Luther King Jr., so when the duke of Normandy heard about this affront to his manhood he immediately got on his horse, rode out to Matilda's castle, grabbed her long brunette braids, and threw her down on the ground by her hair (seriously). Amazingly, she pretty much immediately changed her mind and agreed to marry him. Even though the Pope himself protested the marriage (this was actually bonus points for William because, as I understand it, women really seem to dig forbidden love for some reason), they went ahead and got hitched, produced eleven children, and by all accounts had a very happy marriage, with neither one ever taking another lover.

Even though these two wacky newlyweds were having a grand old time constantly bitch-slapping each other in the face as hard as they could while telling the Pope to go hump himself violently with a chainsaw, some folks weren't really feeling the love—namely, King Henry I of France. Henry put an army together to try to bust up William's rapidly increasing base of power, but William responded by crushing Henry's prostate on two separate occasions. He then further strengthened his position as one of the top dogs in northern France thanks to a steady diet of the three A's of world domination—annexation, alliances, and ass-kickings. But consolidating his power over the Norman coast was just the beginning of William's tale.

In 1066, King Edward the Confessor of England died, and all of a sudden there was total anarchy in the UK. Harold Godwinson of the Saxons and the Viking ruler Harald Hardrada of Norway immediately started punching each other in the face trying to figure out who should be the next king of England, and our friend Will didn't want to miss out on an opportunity to get in on the sweet beat-down action.

Now, William didn't really have a superstrong claim to the throne, but he totally didn't give a crap either—he wanted the crown of England for himself, and damn it, he thought he deserved it. He put together a huge invasion force of roughly six hundred ships and seven thousand men, smashed full speed into the English coast, and immediately started marching toward London. Harold rode out to face William's invading Norman army at the Battle of Hastings on October 14, 1066, a brutal engagement that would change the face of Britain forever.

In the opening hours of the battle, things weren't looking so hot for William and his homies. The infantry on the Norman left broke and ran, hotly pursued by a horde of axe-swinging Anglo-Saxons. William had his horse moked out from under him during some particularly fierce hand-to-hand fighting, and everybody saw him bail out face-first into the turf and pretty much thought he was toast. However, just as things were starting to look bleak as hell, William sprang back onto his feet, took off his helmet to show everyone he was still breathing, and personally led a charge of heavy cavalry that chopped the enemy to shreds. For his trouble Harold Godwinson was shot in the damn eye with an arrow and died painfully on the battlefield.

You would think that capping the king in his ocular cavity with a goddamned bow and arrow would kind of cement your position as his successor, but this wasn't the case in England in 1066. The Anglo-Saxons coronated some other dumbass instead, saying that they didn't really want to be ruled over by some bastard from Normandy.

And there's that word again.

William immediately went to London, beat the pants off whatever pathetic resistance remained, and personally wrenched the crown from the hands of the punk-ass bitch the Anglo-Saxons had put on the throne. He was formally coronated William I, king of England, on Christmas Day 1066 in Westminster Abbey.

Pretty much immediately, the northern half of England revolted. Obviously Will wasn't going to stand for this crap, so he endeared himself to his new subjects by beating the rebellious territories into submission, burning everything in sight, killing bucketloads of people, and salting the earth so no crops would grow. This was pretty effective at deterring future rebellions, and by 1072 all of England was firmly in the palm of his ever-clenching iron fist. William ruled for another fifteen years, abolishing slavery, building castles, and bringing the feudal system to England. He died on September 9, 1087, when he was thrown from his horse while riding through the charred ruins of a rebellious town he had just finished razing to the ground. At least he died doing what he loved.

Before William came around, Matilda was madly in lust with some prissy nobleman named Bihtric, but when she confessed her undying love to him he told her to get bent. Matilda's first act as queen of England was to confiscate all of Bihtric's land and chuck his ass in prison, where he eventually died.

Many modern gangs such as the Crips and Bloods owe a lot to the Normans, who were the first group to hold their bows sideways just because it looked cooler. I think that's why they developed the crossbow. Many years later the bow has been replaced by the gat, but the premise basically remains the same.

William's story is masterfully illustrated in the Bayeux Tapestry; the medieval version of a badass graphic novel. This four-hundred-foot-long handwoven tapestry depicts the duke of Normandy doing awesome stuff like killing peasants with a sword, slapping Nazis in the face, doing keg stands, and ordering people around from a throne made out of human skulls.

2008

16

HARALD HARDRADA

(1015–1066)

Now when King Harald Sigurdson saw this, he went into the fray where the greatest crash of weapons was, and there was a sharp conflict, in which many people fell on both sides. King Harald then was in a rage, and ran out in front of the array, and hewed down with both hands; so that neither helmet nor armor could withstand him, and all who were nearest gave way before him.

—SNORI STURLUSON, *HEIMSKRINGLA*

HARALD SIGURDSON WAS THE LAST OF THE VIKINGS AND ONE OF THE MOST INSANELY BADASS ADVENTURERS TO EVER SAW A DUDE IN HALF FOR LOOKING AT HIM CROSS-EYED AND THEN DRIVE OVER HIS CORPSE WITH A RIDING LAWN MOWER. While his half brother, Olaf the Holy, is a Roman Catholic saint whose blood is said to have been able to cure blindness, Harald's story is less about the Holy Spirit manifesting itself in his hemoglobin and a lot more about lacerating the atria of his enemies and turning thousands of enemy soldiers into unwilling organ donors with a giant two-handed battle-axe.

St. Olaf was the king of Norway for a while, until one day some blue-balled dick-monkey named Knut the Great decided to show up, beat the hell out of Olaf, and pry the crown from his cold, dead fingers with a bloodstained crowbar. So at an age when most guys are worried about pimples and back hair the fifteen-year-old Harald was impaling Vikings with his bloodthirsty spear, fighting the Danish armies of Knut at the Battle of Stiklestad in 1030. During the bloodbath Harald was badly wounded by a goddamned broadsword-swinging sociopath, and the armies of Olaf the Holy were turned into the armies of Olaf the Holy Crap We Just Got Our Asses Kicked.

As soon as he was able to stand upright without passing out from the blinding pain associated with having a seven-foot-tall Norseman attempt to disembowel him, Harald and some of his followers left Norway for Russia. There they performed daring quests of heroic awesomeness for King Jaroslav: raiding dungeons, battling orcs, leveling up, and accumulating a vast stockpile of magical items and weapons. The exiled Viking also took the opportunity to hit on Jaroslav's hot daughter, Princess Elizabeth, whenever possible.

Eventually, Harald's adventures brought him south to stand before the towering spires and the golden-domed basilicas of the wealthiest and most magnificent city in the medieval world—Constantinople, the glittering capital of the Byzantine Empire. It was here that the Norse nobleman built up his wealth and prestige, particularly through his service in an infamous mercenary organization under the employ of the Byzantine Empire—a terrifying outfit of head-cleaving Viking warriors known as the Varangian Guard. The men of the guard, known alternatively as "the axe-bearing foreigners" and "the emperor's wine bags," faithfully served the Byzantine emperors for centuries, and were renowned for their ability to drink enough ale to drown a small army and then pummel their enemies to death with the empty kegs. Thanks to Harald's noble birth and his legendary skills as a face-demolishing ass-kicker, he quickly rose through the ranks to become the commander of this elite and colorful unit.

In the service of the emperor, Harald and the Varangian Guard crushed the enemies of Byzantium across the Mediterranean. They fought scurvy pirates off the coast of Greece, stormed castles in Sicily, and vanquished armies in North Africa. It was on the battlefield that Harald truly excelled, and his Viking warriors swept across the landscape plundering, looting, burninating, pillaging, and smashing people in the face with meat cleavers in the name of the Byzantine Empire. He tunneled under the walls of well-defended cities, sacked the treasuries of some of Europe's most imposing castles, and kicked in the gates of seemingly impenetrable fortresses.

One story claims that Harald faked his own death and then had his followers take his body to the gates of an impenetrable Sicilian stronghold. The Varangians offered the lord of the castle a large sum of money to allow them to give their leader a good Christian burial in the palace chapel. The lord agreed, and as soon as the pallbearers processed through the massive iron gates of the citadel, Harald punched through the lid of the sealed coffin like a reanimated zombie, leapt out of the pine box in full battle gear, and immediately started killing everyone he saw and eating their brains. The Vikings left Sicily with more wealth than they could fit into the cargo holds of their massive dragon-headed longships.

In 1040 the Bulgars decided to be total dicks and revolt against Byzantine rule. Under the command of a guy known as Peter Delyan they destroyed a bunch of Greek garrisons and told the emperor to go hump a donkey. Well, when that crap went down, the emperor knew who to call. The Varangian Guard parachuted into Bulgaria, knocked every trace of the rebellion face-first into the dirt, and then elbow-dropped them from the top rope like the "Macho Man" Randy Savage (ooh yeah). Harald personally performed some major elective surgery on Peter's face, and from that point on became known as the "Devastator of Bulgaria," which is a seriously harsh nickname.

After kicking ass in the Middle East, defeating brigands in Jerusalem, getting it on with the empress of Byzantium, and subsequently escaping from a Constantinople prison, Harald's next destination was the city of

Novgorod, on the Caspian Sea. There his mission was to hook up with Princess Elizabeth, the mega-hottie he had developed a massive crush on while he was chilling out in Russia. On the way out he composed an entire album of power ballads so face-meltingly awesome that when he wailed them out on his Flying V guitar her clothes just burst into flames on the spot. (I'm told his love for her was "like a truck.") The two were married, and with his adventures complete, Harald decided to head back to Norway to reclaim his throne. Along the way he sacked a bunch of towns on the coast of Sicily just to be a dick.

Harald and his Varangians landed in Norway, raised an army, and reclaimed the throne without encountering any significant resistance. Harald's over-the-top comic-book-style adventures serving three different Byzantine emperors and wrecking faces all across the known world had made him incredibly popular among the people of Norway, many of whom subscribed to the podcast of his voyages, and his people received their king with open arms. As King Harald III, he ruled for twenty years, earning the nickname Hardrada—which is the Norse word for "hard-ass." He built churches, founded the city of Oslo, defeated the Danes in several wars, ruled firmly but justly, and spent his summers loading up longboats and personally going out on raids.

When the aforementioned King Edward the Confessor died and everybody was running around all over the place trying to assert their claim to the throne of England, Harald decided that he was going to try to get in on all the action as well. He had even less of a claim to the throne than our friend William the Conqueror, but it wasn't like he really gave a flip. In 1066 he set out with three hundred ships loaded to the brim with ill-tempered Norsemen and sailed to the British Isles on a river of blood.

Initially, the forces of Harald Hardrada met with success, handily defeating the combined armies of two Saxon earls at the Battle of Fulford and ravaging the countryside like they did back in the good old days when you had to destroy your enemies by marching twenty miles through the snow (uphill both ways). However, the Saxon king Harold Godwinson launched a surprise attack on the Viking army at the Battle of Stamford Bridge, catching them with their loincloths down (figuratively, not literally). Many of Harald's men didn't even have time to get their armor strapped on before they were assaulted by pissed-off Saxons, but the Viking king didn't go and get addicted to Prozac just because a couple of Brits waved some spears in his face. He pulled out two swords, activated his blood-lust rune power, and waded through the enemy, dual-wielding death in a wrath-flavored manslaughter spree. The fifty-one-year-old sea king was finally killed in battle when some cowardly donkey-porker shot him in the throat with an arrow, going down in a blaze of glory and dying a death worthy of Valhalla.

It's kind of a funny story how the Vikings ended up discovering North America. First, Erik the Red's family was evicted from Norway because they killed a bunch of people. They fled west to Iceland, where Erik—whose nickname comes from the color of his hair and not from his penchant for killing everything with a pulse—was exiled for murdering several of his neighbors with a broadsword. Now banished from Norway and Iceland, Erik just got in his boat and sailed west, where he discovered Greenland. His son, Leif Eriksson, didn't have to go much farther west before he hit Canada, and the rest is history.

The Battle of Bravoll in 700 CE featured the greatest assortment of Viking names ever assembled. Among the combatants that fateful day were such warriors as Thorleif Goti the Overbearing, Hrolf the Woman-Loving, Odd the Wide-Traveling, Grette the Evil, Hothbrodd the Indomitable, Dag the Stout, Svein Reaper, Harald Wartooth, and Hadd the Hard.

THE DANISH AXE

Vikings were big dudes, and nothing allowed them to utilize their massive size better than the fearsome Danish war axe. This enormous, single-bladed weapon was wielded with two hands, and a frenzied Norseman was more than capable of striking with enough force to chop through steel helmets, shields, and armor. During the Viking age it was often used to perform amateur brain surgery on unsuspecting enemy foot soldiers.

At the Battle of Stamford Bridge in 1066, a lone Norse berserker with one of these man-slaughtering weapons single-handedly held a narrow bridge against an entire army of pissed-off Saxon warriors. This axe-swinging maniac killed more than forty of the enemy and wounded dozens more in a bloody, hate-fueled, murderous rampage. He was finally slain when a Saxon soldier drifted down the river in a barrel and thrust his spear up through the planks in the bridge, striking the battle-raging Viking in his lone weak point: the ball sack.

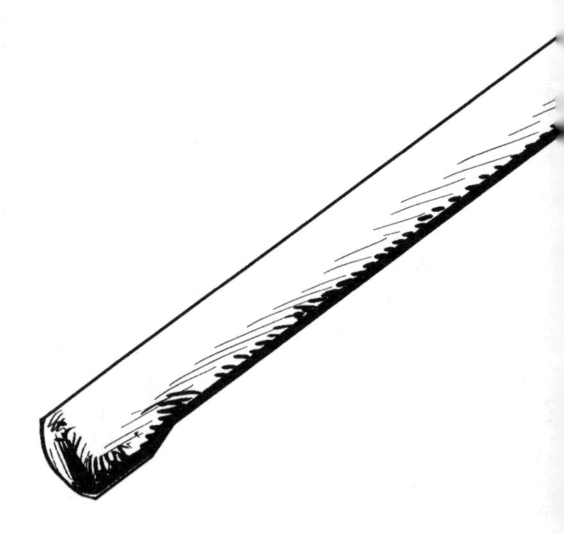

17

EL CID CAMPEADOR

(1040–1099)

Two with the lance and with the sword five of the foe he slew.
The Moors are very many. Around him close they drew,
They did not pierce his armor, though they laid on strokes of power.

—*THE LAY OF THE CID*

RODRIGO DÍAZ DE VIVAR WAS BORN IN THE SPANISH KINGDOM OF CASTILE IN THE EARLY ELEVENTH CENTURY. During his adventures dominating faces across the Iberian Peninsula he would come to be recognized as a peerless warrior, a ball-grabbingly tough military commander, and one of the most valiant and legendary knights to ever live.

Rodrigo's dad was a big dog under King Ferdinand the Great of Spain, and the two often spent their days together watching bullfights, drinking sangria, and trying to push the Moors out of Iberia in a series of excruciatingly bloody wars known as the Reconquista. When Ferdinand eventually kicked the bucket, instead of having one of his sons or daughters claim the throne of Spain, the Spanish king decided it would be an incredibly brilliant idea to divide the country into several different kingdoms, with each one ruled by one of his offspring. Obviously, Ferdinand's oldest son, Sancho, got the royal screw job (no pun intended) in this deal, and so of course the slighted prince immediately decided to reclaim all of Christian Spain for himself and rule the kingdom that he believed was rightfully his. His first acts as king were to appoint young Rodrigo as standard-bearer of his army and immediately declare war on all of his younger siblings at the same time.

The first time El Cid shows up in history in any meaningful capacity is during the Battle of Graus in 1063, when the army of King Sancho of Castile was trading face-kicks with the knights of Aragon. El Cid fought bravely, but really got a chance to display his badassery when the champion of the Aragonese army came forward to try to gank Cid's flag away from him. El Cid simply smashed this jerk knight in the sternum with the back end of his flagpole, whipped out his sword, executed a 360-degree jump-spinning maneuver known as the Whirlwind Slash, and sliced this supposedly hardcore warrior up like a band saw going through a can of Thanksgiving Day cranberry sauce. From that day forth, Rodrigo was known by his countrymen as "El Campeador," meaning "the champion." He was promoted to commander in chief of King Sancho's army, and would go on to lead Castilian troops to victory in battle time and time again.

As commander of the knights of Castile, Cid went up against seemingly impossible odds, and conquered the kingdoms of León, Galicia, and Toro. He also besieged and captured the stronghold of Zamora in 1072, but unfortunately, right as his men were seizing final victory from the hands of his much-hated siblings, King Sancho's cardiovascular system was seizing up as a result of multiple stab wounds to the back from a murderous assassin.

After Sancho died, the next heir to the Spanish throne was his brother Alfonso of León—a dude who'd already had his head caved in by Mr. El Cid and who had spent the past few years living in exile in Toledo (Spain, not Ohio, but still equally as boring). Alfonso returned to accept his coronation as the new king of Spain, but El Cid wasn't the sort of dude who was going to sit around and watch a potential injustice being committed; rumors had been circulating that Alfonso was behind the assassination of Sancho, and El Cid demanded to know the truth—he was too noble and honorable to kneel before a corrupt ruler. At a time when all the other sniveling spineless nobles lacked the *cojones* to stand up and say something, El Cid kicked down Alfonso's door, grabbed him by the arm, dragged him to the Burgos cathedral, and made him publicly swear on the Bible in front of statues of the saints and the Virgin Mary that he had nothing to do with Sancho's murder. Alfonso swore it, so El Cid decided to let him live and pledged his allegiance to him. And that, *mis amigos*, is how badasses handle things.

Well, you can pretty much guess that Alfonso wasn't a huge fan of being called out in front of all of his subjects. He also wasn't superfond of El Cid having shoved a sword up his ass and forced him into exile a few years earlier either, so it shouldn't come as an earth-shattering surprise that Cid was promptly replaced as commander in chief of the army and relegated to menial bitch-work throughout the kingdom.

On one such occasion in 1079, El Cid was sent to the Moorish kingdom of Seville to collect tribute from the emir. While Cid was in town, Seville was invaded by the kingdoms of Granada and Barcelona. Being the die-hard warrior that he was, El Cid took command of the heavily outnumbered army of Seville, went up against the combined might of two armies, and took them down like a back-alley knife fight between a rugby hooligan and a couple of third-graders. He humiliated the enemy generals, crushed their armies, captured their booty, and took some of Spain's greatest champions prisoner. Not long after this, the kingdom of Toledo started talking all kinds of smack to Cid, so he marched his troops out on a punitive expedition, plundered a couple of towns, and made off with a bunch of money and prisoners there as well.

Even though randomly inserting yourself into a couple of vicious blood feuds just for the sake of beating people up is damn awesome, King Alfonso pretty much blew a gasket anyway and sent Cid off into exile for going nuts and arbitrarily launching unauthorized attacks on neighboring kingdoms for no good reason. This sucked a bag of dicks, but it takes more than exile to keep a dude like El Cid down, so he decided to go around the country like a wandering Dungeons and Dragons–style adventurer, taking quests at the local heroes' guild, following up on leads he received from shady innkeepers, and rescuing damsels in distress from the clutches of two-headed ogres and magical fire-breathing red dragons. He eventually signed on as a mercenary working for the Moorish kingdom of Saragossa in 1081, where he defended the borders against hostile invasion, horsecocked the enemies of the emir up and down the Spanish countryside, and earned the nickname by which he is best known today: "El Cid" comes from the Arabic *al-sayyid,* meaning "chief" or "lord."

In 1086 Spain was invaded by a group of people called the Almoravids—hardcore Berber Muslim warriors from present-day Morocco. Out of nowhere, the Almoravids swept across Gibraltar and started kicking the holy living ass of everyone they came across. Our good friend King Alfonso went out to face them and wound up getting his entire army of armored knights killed in the span of a couple of hours. As he limped back home, he knew there was only one bastard in Spain who could lead the Christians to victory against the Almoravids, and that was El Cid Campeador. He immediately sent a messenger to get on his hands and knees and beg Cid to come back.

Cid had no love for Alfonso, but he realized this would be a good opportunity to restore his noble status and get in on some sweet, delicious ass-kickings in the process, so of course he was down for it. Serving Alfonso in name alone, El Cid led a huge army comprising Christians and Moors alike on campaign to conquer the incredibly wealthy Almoravid-controlled kingdom of Valencia in 1094. El Cid Campeador went head-to-head with the (until now) invincible Almoravid army, and despite being heavily outnumbered he managed to give them all Indian burns and steal their lunch money. This marked the first time the Spanish had been able to defeat the Almoravids, and the victory greatly boosted the confidence of Christian knights across the Iberian Peninsula. Three years later, the Almoravids tried to retake Valencia, but running into El Cid's army is like skateboarding at top speed into an unflinching brick wall and then having your now-boneless body catapulted into a black hole. The Almoravid invasion did not advance past Valencia as long as he was alive.

I should mention that El Cid was only alive for like another two years after that battle, passing away from natural causes in 1099. As soon as the Almoravids heard the news of his death, they immediately decided to launch another full-scale assault on Valencia in an effort to finally recapture it once and for all. When Mrs. El Cid saw an assload of enemy soldiers charging full speed toward the castle, she got her husband's dead body and tied it up to his horse *Weekend at Bernie's*–style, so it looked like he was still alive and well. She then sent the horse out into battle at the head of Cid's army. The Spaniards and Moors saw their commander riding beside them and were super-mega pumped up by the prospect of fighting alongside Zombie Cid, and as soon as the Almoravids saw their hated, recently deceased enemy trotting toward them, ready to cave in their faces from beyond the grave, they all crapped their collective pants and made a run for it. Even after he was dead, nobody could take El Cid in a fight, and a stupid thing like not being able to sustain basic life functions couldn't keep this valorous Spanish knight from driving his enemies before him.

El Cid was the man. Not only was he a fusion-powered juggernaut on the battlefield, but he had all the qualities that make him a true historical badass. He was just, honest, loved by the peasantry and nobility alike, and considered honorable and noble by everyone he met. He is now recognized as the national hero of Spain.

18

TOMOE GOZEN

(c. 1184 CE)

Tomoe had long black hair and a fair complexion, and her face was very lovely; moreover she was a fearless rider whom neither the fiercest horse nor the roughest ground could dismay. And so dexterously did she handle sword and bow that she was a match for a thousand warriors, and fit to meet either god or devil. Many times had she taken the field, armed at all points, and won matchless renown in encounters with the bravest captains. And so in this last fight, when all the others had been slain or had fled, among the last seven there rode Tomoe.

—*TALE OF THE HEIKE*

SAYING THAT THE WOMEN'S LIBERATION MOVEMENT HADN'T REALLY CAUGHT ON IN FEUDAL JAPAN WOULD BE KIND OF LIKE SAYING THAT HAVING ALL OF YOUR PUBIC HAIR REMOVED WITH SALAD TONGS WOULD BE MILDLY UNCOMFORTABLE. Though it wasn't entirely unheard of for women of this era to be trained to use a bladed poleax known as the *naginata*—the extralong reach of this weapon was a great way to neutralize the overpowering physical strength of an angry sword-swinging maniac, and often came in handy when rowdy neighbors needed to be slashed between the legs as hard as possible. Think of it as medieval pepper spray. Tomoe Gozen, however, took this sort of estrogen-fueled nut destruction to an entirely different elemental plane of face-stomping—she was one of history's only female samurai.

Lady Tomoe was a retainer of the Minamoto warlord Yoshinaka, whom she had served faithfully for many years as his foremost military general. Now, I'm going to go ahead and assume that you aren't an expert on medieval Japanese history and give you a little bit of background. Back in the twelfth century the Minamoto clan and the Taira clan were in the middle of a massive feud so bloody it made the Hatfields and the McCoys look like a bench-clearing brawl at a girls' under-ten church-league tee-ball game. Basically, these two families were beating the ever-loving bejesus out of each other with samurai swords, cattle prods, fireplace pokers, shovels, bullwhips, crotch bats, pitchforks, and anything else they could find lying around in an effort to flex their authority and get one of their kinsmen declared the barbarian-quelling overlord (shogun) of Japan. Yoshinaka was the commander of Minamoto forces in the northern part of Japan, and he and Tomoe were kicking more nut sack than an industrial-grade groin-kicking machine in a room full of men with elephantiasis of the balls.

Yoshinaka and Tomoe's victories were a great example of the time-honored axiom "Evil will always triumph because good is dumb." First, they defeated the Taira by having their soldiers carry red flags (the color of the Taira clan), march right up to a huge army of Taira soldiers, put down the red flags, put up their Minamoto-brand white flags, and immediately start killing everyone in sight. Another time they walked right up to the enemy's front lines and challenged them to a couple of duels. The Taira sent out their greatest warriors to fight brutal one-on-one death matches with a couple of hand-selected Minamoto swordsmen. This went on for a couple of hours, and then all of a sudden an entire army of Minamoto troops came up behind the Taira and slaughtered them while they were watching the gladiatorial combat. Basically, the Taira were dumbasses.

That's not to say that the bungling, Marx Brothers–grade ineptitude of her enemies should diminish the towering feats of heroism performed by Lady Tomoe—she was a kick-ass executioner who massacred the hell out of anyone who crossed her. As Yoshinaka's premier military commander, she always rode into battle at the head of the army, carrying a sturdy bow and a massive face-destroying samurai sword so awesome that its blade could catch on fire and slash through most types of composite tank armor. Her skill as a horsewoman was unmatched, and with a bow she could turn your eye socket into an erupting geyser of blood from two hundred yards away while riding at a full gallop. She was also superhot, but if you made any ungentlemanly advances toward her, you could probably expect to find out what it's like to be bludgeoned ruthlessly about the head and neck with your own severed dong. One story has Tomoe Gozen doing battle with a samurai warrior named Uchida Iyeyoshi, who had sought to capture her and take her as his concubine. This medieval date-rapist ripped the sleeve off her shirt while attempting to pull her from her horse, so she responded by decapitating the guy with one swing of her sword and kicking his headless corpse into an acid-filled ditch.

Thanks in no small part to Tomoe's uncanny ability to wreck the asses of opposing warriors with an unholy repertoire of strategic groin-slashing maneuvers, Yoshinaka's army destroyed the Taira presence in

northern Japan and marched into the capital city of Kyoto in 1184. The emperor conferred the title of Asahi Shogun upon Yoshinaka, and from that point on Yoshinaka pretty much became a total dick to everybody. He started drinking excessively, talking about how he was the goddamned coolest person to ever live, how he single-handedly kicked the asses of the Taira, blah blah blah, and everybody got sick of it pretty quickly. When Yoshinaka crossed the line and officially declared that the rest of his family were incompetent dickbrains, his kinsmen decided to put him in his place by slicing his face off with their *katana*s.

Yoshinaka, being the good samurai that he was, didn't even give two rats' nut sacks. He took his small bodyguard of horsemen up against a Minamoto army of more than ten thousand dudes and ordered his samurai to tear ass across the battlefield in a fearless suicide charge. Of course, no amount of bravery or swordsmanship is going to save you when you've got ten thousand assholes trying to disembowel you with super-pointy objects of metallic death, and by the time Yoshinaka's cavalry rode through the enemy lines and emerged on the other side, only seven warriors remained. One of them was Lady Tomoe, clutching the severed head of a slain foe, her face spattered with the blood of her enemies.

The samurai code compelled Yoshinaka to stand and die on the battlefield with honor, but he couldn't bear the thought of watching his greatest general get killed or taken prisoner. As the enemy prepared to launch their final charge, he told Tomoe Gozen to flee for her life. Being the badass samurai babe that she was, she obviously refused, saying that she was willing to fight to the end and take as many of those bastards with her as possible. Yoshinaka urged her to protect her honor and her life, and at last she reluctantly agreed to ride off toward safety. However, when she tried to break through the enemy lines, her path was blocked by a powerful samurai known as Onda Moroshige. Onda was an intimidating fighter from Musashi province known for his superb swordsmanship skills and his unrivaled strength, but Tomoe didn't even blink.

She rode right up beside his horse at a full gallop, pulled him out of his saddle in midstride, pinned him hard against her thigh, and—depending on the source—either sliced his head off with her dagger or twisted it off with her bare hands. She then threw the body down to the ground, held the head high in the air to show her liege that she was victorious once more, and rode off into the sunset, never to be heard from again.

The colors of the Minamoto and Taira clans—white and red—became the official colors of Japan and are represented today on the nation's flag and naval ensign.

The Mongols invaded Japan in 1274, landing three hundred assault craft loaded with vicious warriors on the southern tip of the island of Kyushu. However, that night a massive typhoon swept through the bay and this *kamikaze* (divine wind) utterly demolished the invasion fleet, sinking more than two-thirds of the Mongol ships. The vessels that weren't destroyed outright were boarded by the Japanese the following morning, and not even the toughest Mongol warrior stood a chance in close-quarters fighting against a fully armored, *katana*-swinging samurai.

The legendary sword Kusanagi-no-Tsurugi, part of the imperial regalia of Japan, represented the physical embodiment of valor and stood as a testament to the invincibility of the emperor. According to legend, the blade of the sun goddess Amaterasu had the power to control the wind, mow the lawn like a well-oiled John Deere (the name literally translates to "grass-cleaving sword"), and slay otherwise indestructible demons. The two-thousand-year-old weapon plummeted to the bottom of the Shimonoseki Strait along with the emperor at the end of the Genpei War in 1185, and neither has ever been recovered.

19

GENGHIS KHAN

(1162–1227)

The greatest happiness is to scatter your enemy, to drive him before you, to see his cities reduced to ashes, to see those who love him shrouded in tears, and to gather into your bosom his wives and daughters.

FIRST CAME THE REFUGEES. Throngs of wide-eyed, petrified peasants streamed in from the outlying villages with outlandish tales that sounded like something out of a low-budget horror flick. Crazy, impossible stories of bloodthirsty demons on horseback, riding forth from some intangible hell far beyond the eastern horizon, seemingly materializing from the fog without warning, and savagely laying waste to entire settlements. These invincible barbarian warriors committed acts of untold cruelty upon the unsuspecting citizenry, slaughtering all those before them in a frenzy of blood and fire and then drinking their chocolate milk *right out of the carton*.

The rumors had been circulating in the bustling city for nearly a month now, but most logical people believed them to be the nonsensical ramblings of rabble-rousers, fanboys, crazy conspiracy theorists, impressionable dumbasses, and doomsayers: stories of mysterious blood-drinking cannibals sent by God to exact His cruel vengeance upon the sinful, leaving nothing but death and ash in their wake, using foul black magic to turn the mightiest armies in the world into bloody handfuls of dust and sand. Some claimed to have seen the massive piles of sun-bleached skulls arranged into three morbid pyramids outside the doomed city of Nishapur—one stack for the men, one for the women, and one for the children. Reports claimed that more than two million people had been massacred by these heathens in the span of weeks, with thousands more carried off by savages to the darkest recesses of the earth, never to be heard from again.

Then came the devil's emissaries, strange-looking weirdos from a mysterious, undiscovered civilization bearing a simple, frightening message: submit or be destroyed. The high-ranking members of the city's aristocracy, pretentious, self-important tightwads unwilling to relinquish their near-absolute power over their subjects, responded by hanging the barbarians' heads from the walls of the city.

They chose . . . poorly.

Just as the peasants had warned, the devils came from nowhere, ghostly apparitions seemingly rising out of the sand itself. The thunderous din of stampeding hooves surrounded the terrified defenders on the city walls as an endless sea of horsemen descended upon them. The men on the ramparts watched in horror as they realized that the first wave of soldiers was actually comprised entirely of captured villagers from the outlying settlements—poor, imprisoned farmers forced under pain of death to push forward massive siege engines, catapults, and ballistae, assigned the cruel task of bringing destruction and mayhem to their own kinsmen. The soldiers reluctantly opened fire on these wretched saps, but even an endless stream of arrows couldn't stem the tide of heavy equipment being brought up to the massive moat surrounding the city. To their amazement, the defenders then saw the invading barbarians shoving their prisoners into the moat—using their bodies as a living bridge over which they rolled their infernal contraptions. The towering catapults were then loaded with large, foreign-looking clay pots, and when these projectiles smashed into the sturdy, seemingly impenetrable stone walls and guard towers of the city they exploded into giant showers of searing-hot flame, sparks, and smoke. Rock crumbled to dust and walls fell as though they were made of cardboard, utterly destroyed by this frightening evil magic conjured up from some nightmarish realm beyond the mortal world. With a bloodcurdling cry the demons charged forth, and hell followed with them.

The great khan smiled as his men prepared the helpless city for looting. He had come from nothing—an impoverished, illiterate outcast from a minor tribe of steppe nomads, he had spent his earliest years living off the rats and berries that his mother scavenged for him and thinking about how much his life sucked. Now the entire world was his for the taking.

Nearly sixty years old, the man known as Genghis Khan had spent his life clawing his way to the top despite seemingly impossible odds, scratching and fighting against any obstacles that stood in his way. When his enemies looted his family's small camp and kidnapped his beloved wife, he hunted them down, burned their tents, stole their possessions, rescued his queen, and annihilated every member of their tribe. When his own blood-brother betrayed him, Genghis Khan crushed his armies and united all the tribes of Mongolia under one banner for the first time in history. But this was just the beginning.

Then the emperor of northern China demanded that Genghis submit to his all-powerful might, so the great khan marched his army across the Gobi Desert, circumvented the formidable Great Wall, scaled the impregnable forty-foot walls of Beijing, and plundered the city for thirty days. Not long afterward, the sultan of the Khwarizmid Empire apparently didn't get the memo and beheaded an entire caravan of Mongol traders; Genghis's vengeance-seeking warriors cut a swath of near-limitless destruction through his territory, routing the sultan's armies, burning his cities, and killing millions of people across Central Asia.

But Genghis never believed himself to be a ruthless murderer or an unprovoked aggressor; he gave all of his enemies one opportunity to peaceably submit to his rule. If they defied him, they received only what they deserved. He had spared countless villages and cities that had wisely opened their doors to him, and to the people of those settlements he provided protection, freedom of religion, and access to the most lucrative and far-reaching trade routes in the world. Under his watchful eye, vast amounts of technology, information, medicine, and goods traveled freely between China, the Middle East, and Europe. He abolished torture, class systems, and aristocracies, promoted soldiers and civil officials based on their ability rather than their social rank, and commanded the unwavering loyalty of all Mongols. The rest of the world trembled and submitted out of fear and respect for his terrible might and fury, which was cool with Genghis.

At the head of an army of only a hundred thousand Mongols, he had single-handedly carved out an empire four times the size of Alexander the Great's and twice the size of what the Romans put together over the course of four hundred years. Now this once-destitute pariah ruled over a vast kingdom that stretched the entire length of the Central Asian steppe, encompassing nearly twelve million square miles—the largest contiguous land empire in human history.

He was the mighty Genghis Khan, and he had conquered all that was before him. His descendents would rule over southern China, do battle with Japanese samurai, and plunder Europe as far West as Germany. His men would stuff the most powerful man in the world—the mighty caliph of Baghdad—in a Persian rug and trample him to death with their horses, and eat dinner on top of the still-breathing bodies of Russian princes, slowly crushing them to death as they drank wine and watched dancing girls. He was the most successful conqueror in history, and even now, eight hundred years after his death, people across the world still equate the name Genghis Khan with one thing—ultimate badassitude.

> **I AM THE SCOURGE OF GOD. HAD YOU NOT CREATED GREAT SINS, GOD WOULD NOT HAVE SENT A PUNISHMENT LIKE ME UPON YOU.**
> **—GENGHIS KHAN**

For every civilization that Genghis Khan conquered, he took the most beautiful woman in that land to be his wife. The number of wives he accumulated in this manner must have been astronomical, because recent scientific studies have found that nearly sixteen million people—roughly 8 percent of the population of Asia—are genetically descended from the great khan.

Genghis Khan's great-granddaughter Khutulun was a crazy warrior chick who fought bravely in several Central Asian campaigns. In true badass fashion, this hot babe issued a challenge to all Mongols: she would marry the first man who defeated her in hand-to-hand combat. More than a hundred men answered the call, but when Marco Polo met the beautiful princess in 1280 she was still single.

Genghis Khan's birth name was Temujin, meaning "Iron Man." You know when your parents name you after a Black Sabbath song you're going to be trouble.

THINGS YOU CAN SHOOT OUT OF A CATAPULT

With massive castles and towering stone walls being all the rage back in the Middle Ages, invading armies needed to be able to punch through these defenses quickly if they wanted to get on with the looting, burning, and pillaging that everybody seemed to love so much. Nothing was more effective at this than the catapult, a time-honored method of flinging a multiflavored assortment of deadly objects at your unsuspecting enemies.

Very Large Rocks

Sometimes you have to stick with the basics, and you could do a whole hell of a lot worse than chucking a Volkswagen-sized boulder at your foes with enough velocity to crunch through brick and mortar and splatter foot soldiers across the battlements. There wasn't a whole lot the standard spearman could do to defend himself from some jerk lobbing an eight-foot rounded chunk of granite at his face, except of course get popped like a pimple, and even the most headstrong wall didn't stand much of a chance against a steady barrage of humongoid rocks. The only real pain in the ass was finding the ammunition and transporting it to the launch site.

Pots of Burning Pitch or Boiling Oil

Another medieval favorite was to load the catapult up with large clay pots filled with volatile materials and then wreak havoc on the enemy castle. Burning tar was a relatively common ingredient, since it did a pretty awesome job of catching the entire city on fire and burning the crap out of everything from hapless citizens to critical food supplies. Boiling oil was another effective way to express-mail third-degree burns, since the sticky substance adhered to human skin and usually resulted in unhappy peasants running around town screaming their heads off like maniacs.

Giant Bags of Crap

When artillery captains got sick of pitching endless waves of giant death-bringing rocks at their adversaries and wanted to spice things up a little, they would sometimes fire off biological materials designed to make the city inhabitants' lives miserable. Beehives and venomous snakes were a couple of choice payloads, but some commanders would just launch giant buckets of cow manure over the castle walls. Sure, lobbing big bags of crap at your enemies, while unhygienic, isn't exactly going to inflict copious amounts of death and carnage, but it is pretty goddamned degrading, and in the end, isn't the whole point of war to completely humiliate your opponent?

Dead Bodies

One of the earliest documented instances of biological warfare dates back to the fourteenth century, when the Mongols started using catapults to launch the dead bodies of plague victims over the walls of towns that didn't have the good sense to surrender to them. Not only is this diabolical, disgusting, and incredibly deadly, but it also had to be pretty damn demoralizing to see a lifeless corpse come flying toward you at high speed. I also came across some reports that our friend William the Conqueror had a nasty habit of loading his catapults up with the severed heads of slain enemy soldiers and then chucking those over the castle walls as a method of intimidating his opponents. It probably worked.

Prisoners

Of course, why settle for something as tame as dead bodies and severed heads when you could just load the catapult up with still-breathing prisoners of war and then use them as a weapon against their own people? Frederick Barbarossa captured the Italian city of Crema in 1160 by flinging live hostages, including children, nonstop day and night until the horrified inhabitants finally surrendered. He was a sweet guy.

20

VLAD THE IMPALER

(1431–1476)

Here begins a very cruel, frightening story about a wild bloodthirsty man: Prince Dracula. How he impaled people and roasted them and boiled their heads in a kettle and skinned people and hacked them to pieces like cabbage.

—EXCERPT FROM A FIFTEENTH-CENTURY PAMPHLET

FORGET VAMPIRES. Forget those irritating glow-stick techno raves where the repetitive bass-heavy house music makes you want to bash your face into a wall repeatedly until you die from it, forget the black-caped 1920s-era cheesy Nosferatus with bad European accents, slicked-back hair helmets, and pointy glow-in-the-dark fangs, and forget those effeminate Hollywood pretty boys who try to act all mysterious and sexy and evil but only come off as being trite ass-clowns who look like they just stepped out of a really freaky underwear commercial. Though his nickname—Dracula—may conjure up images of stiff-legged pale old men with overly developed canine teeth, a serious aversion to garlic bread, and a penchant for sleeping in old coffins, nobody ever said that Vlad III Tepes of Wallachia was a vampire—Dracula is really just the Romanian way of saying "son of the dragon" (or, alternatively, and perhaps more appropriately, "son of the devil") and was a way of differentiating young Vlad III from his father, Vlad II Dracul. The real Dracula wasn't an undead beast who spent his days hanging upside down from the ceiling in an unlit dungeon only to venture forth and suck the blood of wayward bimbos in the glow of the full moon—he was a complete wack job who made it his personal mission to take as many people as possible and stick them ass-first onto giant sharpened wooden stakes purely for his own amusement.

Born in Transylvania in 1431, Dracula had a pretty rough childhood. At the age of eleven he was captured by the sultan of the Ottoman Empire and shipped off to Adrianople, where he would spend the next six years growing up as a prisoner of the Turkish court. Being the total bastard that he was, Vlad was always causing trouble, bitch-slapping people and telling the Turks to go have sex with assorted varieties of farm animals, so as a result he spent much of this time being alternately whipped, beaten, or tortured for insolence. Meanwhile, back in Christian Europe, some turbo-douche named Vladislav seized the throne of Wallachia, and a bunch of disgruntled noblemen pulled Vlad Dracul's face off until he died from it. Dracula's older brother had his eyes burned out with a red-hot poker and was buried alive, which also sucked.

Eventually Vlad got his ass out of Turkey, raised an army, and marched determinedly into Wallachia with one thought on his mind—cruel, bloody, delicious vengeance. He crushed all resistance he faced, personally killed Vladislav in a sword fight, and seized the throne for himself in 1456. Dracula exacted his revenge on the nobility pretty much immediately, ramming them onto wooden stakes and conscripting their wives and children into forced-labor chain gangs tasked with building his evil castle, an undertaking that most of them did not survive. Saxon merchants living in Transylvania, who for some reason were deemed the enemies of the Romanian people, were dealt with just as harshly. Dracula's troops razed most of Transylvania to the ground, burned anything larger than a breadbasket, boiled people alive, looted, and dragged anyone stupid enough to surrender back to Wallachia so they could be impaled. He also went after the poor, the homeless, criminals, mimes, telemarketers, vagrants, graduate students, horses, and pretty much anybody else he deemed to be either utterly useless or a potential threat to his rule.

You see, Vlad the Impaler apparently got a charge out of running the kingdom of Wallachia with an iron fist and a wooden spike. Whenever anybody would cross him, he'd just jam them onto a large pointy object of some kind and call it a day. This was not only a sufficient way of keeping his subjects in line, it was also a highly effective crime deterrent and pretty much worked wonders for homeland security. Legend has it that crime dropped about 3,000 percent while he was in power, which is understandable.

Interestingly, Dracula is still fondly remembered by the people of Romania as a national hero who defended his people against the incursions of the Ottoman Turks (everybody else pretty much thinks he was a total nut job, but whatever). I have a hard time believing that being ruled by Muslims was a fate worse than having someone stick a kebab skewer so far up your ass that you cough up splinters, but who am I to judge? The fact remains that Wallachia was unconquered during Vlad's reign of blood, and his people were big fans of that arrangement.

Now, Vlad grew up in the same court as Sultan Mehmed the Conqueror, and these two guys seriously hated each other's guts. When Dracula seized control of the blood-soaked throne of Wallachia, he immediately stopped the age-old practice of paying tribute to the Turks. When Mehmed was like, "What the hell is your problem, dude?" Vlad responded by launching a massive campaign along the Danube River in 1461, burning everything in sight, destroying enemy garrisons, capturing forts, and mercilessly slaughtering tens of thousands of Turks. Mehmed sent two emissaries to see what was going on, but when the men refused to remove their turbans in the Wallachian prince's presence, Dracula had their headgear permanently hammered into their brains with huge-ass nails.

That was the last straw. Mehmed the Conqueror put together a force of a hundred thousand pissed-off Turkish warriors seeking vengeance. Vlad had no chance to survive with his small force of (at most) twenty thousand men, but he decided to see if he couldn't take some of the invaders with him anyway. After a month or so of fighting a losing battle, Vlad decided to launch a balls-out night raid on the sultan's camp. The Impaler and about seven thousand of his men disguised themselves as Turks (Dracula actually spoke fluent Turkish, having learned it while in captivity), snuck into the Ottoman camp in the middle of the night, and started setting everything on fire. In the confusion, the Wallachians were able to slay thousands of enemy soldiers, but were eventually beaten back before they could assassinate the sultan himself. This last-ditch effort, while daring, was ultimately unsuccessful in halting the Turkish advance on the Wallachian capital.

However, Dracula had one more trick up his sleeve, and holy cow, it was a foul one. As Mehmed's armies approached the grounds of Castle Dracula, they were greeted by the sight of twenty thousand Turkish prisoners of war impaled on stakes. The Turks were so freaked out by what they dubbed "the Forest of the Impaled" that they crapped themselves, turned around, and ran like frightened slasher-movie teenagers, screaming their heads off all the way back to Adrianople.

Even with his amazing, improbable victory over the Turks, Vlad's position as the all-powerful ruler of Romania still wasn't safe. Eventually everyone got sick of being stabbed in the ass and the people of Wallachia overthrew him. He was killed in battle with the Turks in 1476, and his head was brought back and put on a stake high above Istanbul to prove to the people of the Ottoman Empire that the vile Lord Impaler truly was no more.

Mehmed the Conqueror got his excellent epithet by capturing Constantinople in 1453. The twenty-one-year-old sultan besieged the fortified city for two months before assaulting the walls with endless waves of Turkish warriors. The outnumbered defenders were slain, the emperor was killed, the Byzantine Empire was destroyed, and the city was renamed Istanbul. I'm told that the reason behind this renaming is really nobody's business but the Turks.

Vlad campaigned against the Turks alongside the Hungarian lord Stephen Báthory, great-uncle of the infamous (and completely mental) "Blood Countess," Elizabeth Báthory. Elizabeth was a crazy lunatic who is widely believed to be the world's most prolific serial killer. This psycho hose beast lured hundreds of women to her castle, where she tortured them, killed them, and bathed in their blood, believing that this would somehow keep her looking youthful forever. She died by starving herself to death while under house arrest for her crimes, which is pretty hardcore.

Norway
Denmark
Great
Britain
London
Prussia
Berlin
Napoleonic
Empire
Paris
Vienna
Hungary
France
Austria
Rome
Portugal
Spain
Mediterranean Sea
Morocco
North Africa
Egypt
N

Section III
The Age of Gunpowder
Moscow

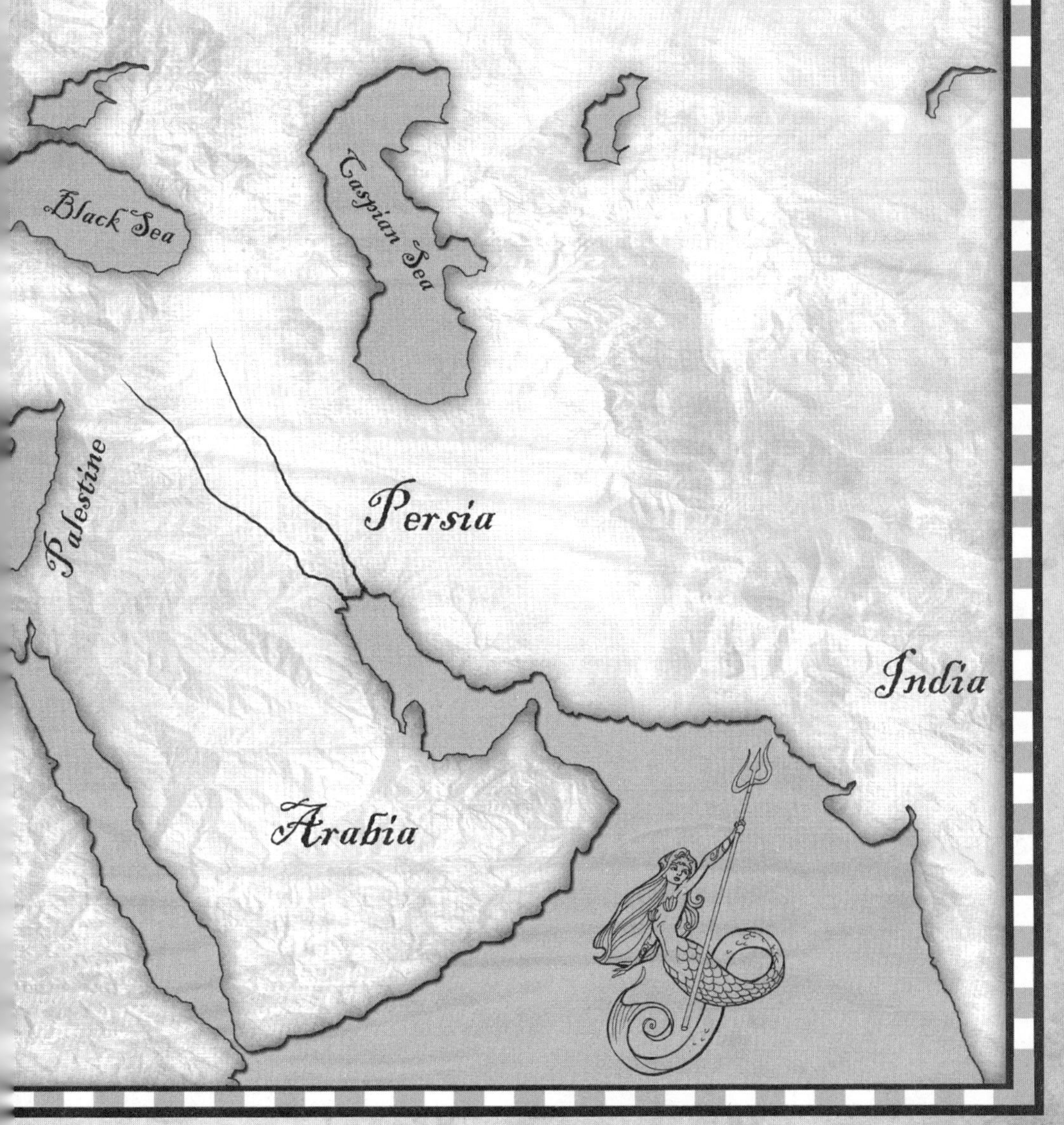
Russian Empire
Black Sea
Caspian Sea
Palestine
Persia
India
Arabia

21

MIYAMOTO MUSASHI

(1584–1645)

When you are even with an opponent, it is essential to keep thinking of stabbing him in the face with the tip of your sword in the intervals between the opponent's sword blows and your own sword blows. When you have the intention of stabbing your opponent in the face, he will try to get both his face and body out of the way. In the midst of battle, as soon as an opponent tries to get out of the way, you have already won.

THE JAPANESE WORD *KENSEI*, LITERALLY TRANSLATED, MEANS "SWORD SAINTS." The peerless warriors upon whom this honorific title was bestowed were such hardcore blade-swinging bastards that they were actually believed to have possessed otherworldly abilities with their weapon of choice. These fierce warriors were considered perfectly tuned fighting machines who had literally ascended to a plane where they had become one with the sword. Their movements were precise, their reactions instinctive, their form as flawless and graceful as it was deadly.

At the forefront of this pantheon of warrior-gods stands one legendary man: Miyamoto Musashi.

Musashi's life was like something out of a nitro-badass Clint Eastwood or Toshiro Mifune movie. This lone warrior would quietly roll into town, get involved in a bunch of crazy adventures, start trouble with the toughest dudes in town, slaughter everyone with a pulse, get a hot chick to fall in love with him, and then ride off into the sunset without stopping to say good-bye to the rotting piles of corpses he left in his wake. Musashi got his start early, killing his first man at age thirteen when he challenged some idiot samurai to a duel and bashed his brains in with a wooden sword *Legend of Zelda*–style. By the time he was thirty, he had won over sixty life-or-death duels, taught hundreds of students, and fought in six massive, epoch-defining battles that raged across the Japanese countryside.

At the age of sixteen, Musashi left his quiet home province to wander the land in search of pointy adventures. Despite the fact that he had received very little formal martial arts training of any kind, anyone who entered the dueling circle with this young doom-bringer could generally expect to find themselves face-planting a *katana* blade at high velocity. He won several fights against powerful martial arts adepts and slaughtered all who opposed him, but it was when a massive war broke out across Japan that Musashi really got the opportunity to hone his skill against a few hundred thousand worthy opponents. Serving in the army of the feudal lord Toyotomi Hideyoshi, Musashi fought on the front lines of several key engagements during Japan's ultra-brutal Warring States Period. Leading the charge in the vanguard during the epic, Kurosawa-esque battles of Fushimi, Gifu, and Sekigahara, Miyamoto Musashi was like Iron Chef Awesome slicing up the country's mightiest samurai like blowfish in the hands of an expert sushi master. When

Hideyoshi's armies were eventually defeated, Musashi didn't exactly go home crying or anything—he wandered off the battlefield, climbed the tallest mountain he could find, sharpened his sword while listening to eighties hair metal, and then got right back to the job of wandering the countryside in search of dumbasses who needed a tempered steel blade implanted in their abdominal cavities.

Now, Miyamoto Musashi wasn't your stereotypical neck-severing samurai death machine. First off, he had severe eczema on his face, which left him considerably scarred, disfigured, and more intimidating than the LSATs. He never cut his hair, seldom changed clothes, and bathed just infrequently enough for it to be disgusting (he was worried that he would be caught off guard while in the shower—he must have seen *Psycho* one too many times). He also didn't wear armor, and, even more interestingly, he rarely even fought with real swords! For many samurai this was unthinkable—the *katana* was the warrior caste's most prized possession, yet Musashi was perfectly content to just bludgeon his foes into submission with a *katana*-shaped hunk of hickory wood he'd carved from the mangled remains of a tree that was pissing him off.

When he wasn't slapping people around with his wood, Musashi dual-wielded swords in combat, a highly uncommon practice in the days of feudal Japan. While all semi-legitimate feudal samurai carried two swords—the long sword (*katana*) and the short sword (*wakizashi*)—they generally fought solely with the *katana*, preferring to hold it in two hands to maximize the weapon's speed and power. The *wakizashi* was primarily used to ritualistically disembowel yourself for failing your master and/or not adequately disassembling the face of every warrior who stood against you (a practice known as *seppuku*). Musashi had no real interest in severing his own abdominal aorta just because some self-righteous jackass in a silk robe told him to, and decided instead to just use both swords at the same time.

While the obvious benefit of using two blades is that you have an extra weapon to dice, mince, and puree the cerebral cortex of any man foolish enough to cross you, Musashi also used to just haul off and wing his short sword at people in the middle of a duel. I think we can all agree that this is pretty sweet. One time Miyamoto faced off against a master of a weapon known as the *kusari-gama*. A long chain with a razor-sharp sickle attached to one end, the *kusari-gama* was basically like the Grim Reaper's nunchucks. The battle-hardened warrior was swinging the chain around like crazy, whipping the sickle through the air in a series of lightning-quick maneuvers, but Musashi didn't even flinch. He pulled out his two swords and proceeded to chuck the short one right into his opponent's chest (he allegedly could hurl the thing with deadly accuracy at anyone or anything within ten feet of him, like a cross between Peyton Manning and a harpoon gun) while the dude was in the middle of his ridiculous pretentiousness. The guy stopped for a second, looked down at the giant-ass sword sticking out of his gut, and then glanced up just in time to see Musashi run up and slice him in half. The master's disciples, seeing that their leader had just gotten completely hosed, all jumped Musashi at once, but the blade-master fought them all off and escaped. During his adventures, Musashi also took on the masters of swords, lances, staves, and other crazy exotic weapons. No man could match him.

But that's not to say that people didn't try. For instance, during this time period, the most powerful assortment of swordsmen in Japan was the Yoshioka clan. This prestigious family of accomplished martial artists had served as the chief weapons instructors to the Ashikaga shogunate for generations and was considered by most people to be the deadliest assortment of fighters alive. Basically, these guys thought they were the most hardcore bastards around.

They were wrong.

Musashi challenged the patriarch of the Yoshioka clan to a duel and quickly TKOed the jerkass by thwacking him in the gourd repeatedly with his homemade wooden implement of brain-smashing insanity.

Yoshioka's younger brother showed up seeking revenge and assaulted Musashi with a six-foot-long iron rod, but Miyamoto just kicked the guy down, wrenched the weapon out of his hands, and pummeled him to death with it like a bitch. A few hours later, the rest of the clan ambushed Musashi all at once, and the Japanese sword fighter was suddenly surrounded by more than a dozen guys armed with bows, muskets, wooden spoons, bullwhips, folding chairs, blowtorches, and a gun that shot ninja stars. Musashi silently drew his blades, slaughtered all of his assailants in a thick spray of crimson mist, wiped the Yoshioka clan off the face of Japan, and quietly walked off toward the horizon in search of new adventures.

Musashi's most famous duel came against a numbnuts named Sasaki Kojiro, a master of the Ganryu style of fighting—a strength-first school also known as the "School of Rock" (seriously)—and an expert with the massive, Conan-esque two-handed sword known as the *no-dachi*. This guy was so confident he was a total sack-busting killbot that he refused to hear any talk about how Musashi was the real grandmaster of sword fighting. Obviously, Sasaki was in denial—kind of like how your girlfriend never seems to believe you when you tell her that all of her "best guy friends" really just want to sleep with her. Whatever the case, it was painfully obvious to everyone that the only rational method of settling the dispute was with a gruesome battle to the death on a remote deserted island off the coast of the Japanese mainland, because that's just the way total hardasses settle their differences. Especially in feudal Japan. Musashi showed up to the duel half an hour late (he believed that this was a good way of psyching out his opponents) and carrying an eight-foot-long wooden sword he'd whittled from a rowing oar on his boat ride out. He fought with his back to the east, forcing Sasaki to do battle with the blinding light of the rising sun directly in his eyes. Then, in the blink of an eye, Musashi and Sasaki both ran up and struck each other at the same time, like the heart-wrenching intro to *Ninja*

Gaiden on the old-school Nintendo. Sasaki dropped immediately. The wounded warrior attempted to slash upward at Musashi, but Miyamoto crushed his skull with one swing of the oar, walked back to his boat, and sailed off without saying a word.

After this incredible display of his giant tempered-steel balls, the thirty-year-old Musashi decided to settle down, stop violently killing people, and perfect his art. No longer needing to prove how tough he was, he opened a dojo, taught his fighting style, and made a name for himself as a talented artist, poet, calligrapher, sculptor, Zen master, strategist, and writer. When he got bored of that, he climbed a huge mountain, lived in a cave for a while, and composed the definitive treatise on the Zen of decapitation: the *Book of Five Rings*; a work that now functions essentially as a technical manual in the art of badassery. He died in 1645 at the age of sixty-one.

The *basan* is a nocturnal, fire-breathing ghost chicken from Japanese folklore that lives in the woods and comes into town at night to terrorize the populace. How awesome is that?

Iaijutsu was the art of quick-drawing swords. These duels were a lot like Old West gunfights, only pointier. Two dudes would stand face-to-face with their weapons in their scabbards, then pull their swords and strike in one fluid motion. The first guy to get cut in half was the loser.

One of Japan's greatest and most brilliant armorers, the mentally unstable Sengo Muramasa, produced powerful swords that could cut through even the thickest iron and steel with ease but were considered unlucky, violent, and incredibly bloodthirsty. These cursed blades hungered for death—if the weapon's owner failed to draw the blood of his enemies in a timely manner, the sword allegedly would drive him completely kill-crazy, forcing him to commit murder or suicide to appease the demonic spirits that haunted the weapon.

HATTORI HANZO

Hanzo Hattori was the grandmaster of the Iga ninja clan in sixteenth-century Japan and is considered by many to be the most badass ninja to ever live. His exploits have become legendary, and all who study the arts of ninjitsu and kicking ass look to Hanzo as the shining example of what it means to be totally awesome.

Hanzo began his training by climbing a mountain at the age of eight and seeking instruction from the most hardcore ninja master in all of Japan. He busted his nuts every single day for four years, practicing insane martial arts skills like jumping, flying, and stabbing, and was inducted into the ranks of the *shinobi* by age twelve. By the time he was sixteen, he had already proven himself as a remorseless head-slicing death-bringer, serving in countless battles for the Oda clan and earning the nicknames "Hanzo the Ghost" and "Devil Hanzo"—probably because he would sneak around undetected and then nail people in the face with a flying side kick when they least expected it. Then he'd drop a smoke bomb and vanish into the night, only to reappear moments later chopping off some jerk's head and doing backflips for no reason at all. When he wasn't exploding the faces of rival ninja masters with devastating 158-hit combos, he enjoyed climbing the highest mountains he could find and wailing bitchin' guitar solos so loud, flaming, and technically challenging that they set off explosions and fireworks in the sky above him.

Hanzo is reputed to have possessed otherworldly skills and supposedly could teleport, turn invisible, and make stuff explode just by swearing at it. He could also allegedly hold his breath underwater for two days straight, and his martial arts moves were so sweet that it made people barf all over their kimonos (in a good way). His ninja clan, the "Men of Iga," were recruited to battle the enemies of the Tokugawa shogunate and functioned as assassins, bodyguards, saboteurs, spies, and kidnappers. He had ninja operatives working undercover in the castles of many of Tokugawa's enemies, and his shadow warriors were more omnipresent than the CIA and the KGB smashed together into one giant Voltron of Secrecy.

Hanzo served the Tokugawa bravely for many years, dying valiantly in battle in 1590. The fifty-five-year-old warrior was chasing down the leader of a rival ninja clan when he ran into a trap and was burned to death by flaming oil, going out in a blaze of glory (nyuk nyuk) and probably looking awesome even in death.

22

PETER THE GREAT

(1672–1725)

Some notion of the boisterous high jinks that took place may be obtained from considering the damage done. They broke three hundred panes of glass. They had bust or prised open the brass locks of twelve doors. They had blown up the kitchen floor . . . they cut up the dressers and several doors. They covered the parlor floor with grease and ink; broke walnut tables and stands. They seem to have had wild games in the beds, tearing up the feather beds, ripping the sheets, tearing canopies to pieces and ruining precious silk counterpanes.

—STEPHEN GRAHAM, *LIFE OF PETER I OF RUSSIA*

PYOTR ALEXEYVITCH ROMANOV, TSAR PETER THE GREAT, FATHER OF HIS COUNTRY AND EMPEROR OF ALL THE RUSSIAS (THERE ARE MULTIPLE), WAS A TALL, THINLY BUILT TOWER OF A MAN. Standing six foot eight, this awe-inspiring autocrat transformed Russia from a second-class nation on the periphery of civilization into a mighty, three-billion-acre empire, a dominant Westernized power, and a major player in European politics for centuries to come.

But who cares about that crap? History is filled with dudes who took their underdeveloped countries and transformed them into mighty empires; what sets Peter the Great apart is the fact that he was the ultimate partier, rocking faces across the globe like a badass seventeenth-century Keith Richards. No matter how tough or awesome you think you are, Peter the Great would have drunk your ass under the table before your shot glass hit the bar, and then gone off to nail your girlfriend, burn your house down, conquer two tiny European nations, and hurl a dwarf a hundred feet in the air for no reason at all.

As a young man, Prince Peter hung out in the Foreign Quarter of Moscow, throwing wild parties with his Swiss buddy (and future grand admiral of the Russian navy), Francis Lefort. They would get wasted, spend thousands of rubles on strippers and booze, and then go drunkenly launch fireworks at two in the morning, pissing off their neighbors, causing massive explosions, melting stuff, and torching off their eyebrows. One time they even killed a Russian nobleman by busting him in the damn face with a bottle rocket, which is kind of hilarious in a weird way. Growing up, Peter also enjoyed archery, fencing, and musketry. Basically, if it had the potential to cause someone grievous bodily injury, Peter and his buddies would get so wasted that they couldn't see straight and then partake in these life-threatening hobbies. Once, drunk Peter slashed Lefort in the face with his sword when the dude wasn't even looking, then laughed so hard it broke every pane of glass within a hundred-foot radius.

Peter was appointed tsar in 1682, but it's not like a little thing as trivial as having near-limitless power to command the one hundred million citizens under his rule kept him from being totally awesome and irresponsible, and participating in stuff that no self-respecting aristocrat would be caught doing. Here is a brief list of the stuff Peter liked: ships, sailing, booze, women, bears, and midgets. Seriously. The guy had an insane amount of energy, so he would be out until like one in the morning every single night drinking enough booze to choke an army of donkeys, banging Russian babes, and screaming "Woo!" at passing oxcarts, and then he'd be up at five a.m. working at the dock and telling the imperial shipbuilders how awesome ships are. No kidding, the tsar of Russia would be on the wharf with a two-by-four and a hammer building boats by hand before dawn after a night of endless partying. No matter how much alcohol this guy consumed, he was almost never hung over, and he somehow sustained himself on about four hours of sleep a night and a diet about as nutritionally sound as eating tacks and chugging bleach-and-gasoline smoothies.

Peter loved his boats, but unfortunately the problem with Russia is that it's pretty much a desolate, inhospitable frozen wasteland that doesn't border a whole lot of water that isn't ridiculously freezing-ass cold all the time. So, to rectify that problem, Peter marched his armies against the Ottoman Empire for control of the Black Sea, which would provide the Russians access to the Mediterranean. After a couple of intense campaigns, the tsar wrenched power away from the Turks, captured land on the Black Sea, and set up the first permanent naval base in Russia's history.

Whaling on the Ottoman Empire with a garden rake was just the beginning, and Peter decided he was going to go around Europe trying to recruit help fighting the Turks. He lined up a badass European tour, known as the Grand Embassy, and visited England, Holland, Prussia, Austria, and Poland. The tsar tried to go incognito under the fake name Peter Mikhailov, but it's kind of difficult to conceal your secret identity when you're six foot eight and traveling with an entourage of dwarves, strippers, court jesters, and dancing bears. While the Embassy failed to recruit people to help fight the Turks, or really accomplish anything of value at all, Peter did get the opportunity to examine Western shipbuilding practices and party his ass off.

The Grand Embassy wasn't your typical diplomatic mission, and Peter wasn't your typical international ambassador. The Russian delegation, referred to as "baptized bears" by the Prussian baron de Blomberg (who remarked that he had never seen such hard drinkers before in his entire life), were like an unruly hard-partying rock band, smashing up every palace they stayed at and trashing more hotel rooms than the Sex Pistols. They utterly destroyed the house of Lord John Evelyn of England over the course of several nights of drunken insanity, and nearly every place that extended Peter hospitality eventually forbade him ever to return. Unfortunately, the party ended and Peter had to return home when there was a major revolt back in Moscow, organized and run by the tsar's wicked power-hungry stepsister.

If Peter the Great was a 1980s-style rock star, he would have been Ted Nugent or Glen Danzig because he partied hard, but didn't screw around when it came to busting people's heads open with a pipe wrench when he had to. He rode into Moscow, quelled the revolt, tortured and executed twelve hundred traitors, buried some people alive, and forced his bitchy stepsister to become a nun. Then he divorced his wife and forced her to become a nun, too (just for good measure).

Back in Moscow and with his base on the Black Sea firmly established, Peter then directed his attention to the Baltic Sea, going up against Charles XII of Sweden in the Great Northern War. He marched a massive force of thirty-seven thousand men into Sweden, and promptly had his army completely annihilated by just eighty-five hundred Swedes. Then Charles, who was an incredibly brilliant military genius, did a very unwise thing and attempted to invade Russia. You can't really blame him for embarking on this exercise in flaccid futility, however—he was one of the first people to try to march east toward Moscow and didn't yet realize that this was one of the stupidest things any human being could possibly attempt. Peter withdrew his army, avoiding direct combat, burning anything the Swedes could use, and massing his army for a counterattack—a solid strategy that would be reused time and time again by future Russian leaders to whip up on pretty much every militaristic megalomaniac dictator Europe has ever seen. The Russian army decisively defeated the Swedes at the Battle of Poltava, sent Charles packing, captured Sweden and Finland, and established a dominant presence on the Baltic Sea.

There was much rejoicing. Peter threw a huge party after his victory, and then every single year on the anniversary of the Battle of Poltava he hosted some of the biggest, most insane keggers in history. People would hang out in the courtyard of his massive palace, bears would serve people wine and beer on platters (and growl at people who didn't partake), and the Russian Imperial Guard would patrol the festivities and make sure everybody was getting appropriately wrecked. Anybody deemed too sober usually got punched in the face by the tsar (seriously).

Victory over the Swedes asserted Russia's dominance in Europe and started the rise of the mighty Russian Empire. Peter built up the navy, consolidated his power, and worked to modernize (read: Westernize) every aspect of the Russian people. Beards and arranged marriages were abolished, and the Orthodox Church was strongly encouraged to adopt more Roman-like practices.

While he made these moves as tsar, in his personal life Peter was much more interested in worshiping at the hedonistic altar of St. Trixie of the Sacred Thong. He created the Most Drunken Council of Fools and Jesters, a parody of the Holy Synod of the Orthodox Church, and held frequent meetings where everybody would get bombed and sing obscene parodies of well-known church hymns. Vodka was scattered from holy water sprinklers, topless babes carried drinks around on silver platters, and everybody would have wild parties and hurl in the Dumpster behind the local 7-Eleven. Every Christmas, the council would parade through the streets on sleighs pulled by bears and goats, stopping at the homes of prominent noblemen and singing profane Christmas carols at the top of their lungs. When they decided to elect a new "prince-Pope" for their council in 1718, the synod members pounded one shot of vodka every fifteen minutes for *eight days straight*. And you pussies think power hours are badass?

Peter the Great lived large, partied hard, and his urine, straight up, was at least sixty proof. He died of a gangrenous bladder (alcoholism is a nasty thing) in 1725 at the age of fifty-two, the ultimate rock star of imperial Russia and one of the most over-the-top world leaders to ever live. So, the next time someone asks you the trite "Which historical figure would you most want to have dinner with?" question, you'll know how to respond.

Even though his invasion of Russia went fubar, Charles XII was still badass because he was an emotionless automaton who didn't register physical pain, only spoke when threatening someone, and won every major battle he commanded (he was sick when the Swedes were defeated at Poltava). The guy was humorless, calculating, and super-omega tough. He brought Sweden to prominence as the most powerful nation in Europe, and when he went down he made sure the entire country went down in flames around him.

Under Empress Catherine the Great, vodka taxes and licenses accounted for roughly 25 percent of the Russian government's total revenue.

In 1812, Napoleon lost half a million men attempting to invade Russia. Hitler's 1941 expedition into the Motherland cost him twelve times as many troops.

Peter founded the city of St. Petersburg, and in 1710 put out a declaration encouraging all the dwarves in Russia to come live in his city. He liked to play practical jokes on his friends by bringing them giant cakes and then having naked midgets jump out of them.

AVVAKUM

Avvakum was a seventeenth-century archpriest in the Russian Orthodox Church and a rigid, inflexible orthodox traditionalist/crazy person. When the Church started moving toward a more Western approach he took it on himself to launch a one-man crusade against modernization. He basically just went around calling everyone heretics, harlots, devil worshipers, whores, dogs, heathens, sinners, etc. (you know how religious types can be)—placing curses and hexes on princes, assaulting street performers, accosting folks on the side of the road, trying to exorcise demons from random bystanders, breaking into churches and yelling at priests and congregations in the middle of Sunday services, telling everybody that the bubonic plague was the murderous embodiment of God's terrible wrath, and referring to the Patriarch and the tsar as unholy Satan worshipers who had sex with their relatives and made the baby Jesus cry.

Well, it turns out that Russians don't really appreciate that sort of thing. For his trouble, Avvakum was continually beaten up by the people he was harassing. He was knocked down, shot at, whipped, dragged behind horses, hit with axes, and thrown into a river. His house was burned down, and he was imprisoned for disorderly conduct and charged with treason. One time he angered a soldier so bad that the dude bit him. Another time a group of pissed-off women beat him with oven forks and shovels and threw him out a window. On yet another occasion he busted into a Patriarchal Council and called everyone godless Antichrists, so a group of high-ranking priests and Church officials beat him down with wooden rods and tossed him out into the snow.

Nothing could stop this crazy bastard, though. He was defrocked and banished to Siberia twice, but he just sat in his freezing cold studio apartment writing long, hate-filled letters to the Church and the tsar about how they were all going to rot in the fires of eternal hell for their sins. Eventually everyone got sick of his bull, and Avvakum was dragged back to Moscow, where he was burned at the stake for heresy and treason.

2008

23

BLACKBEARD

(1680–1718)

In time of action, he wore a sling over his shoulders with three brace of pistols hanging in holsters like bandoliers, and stuck lighted matches under his hat, which appearing on each side of his face, his eyes naturally looking fierce and wild, made him altogether such a figure that imagination cannot form an idea of a fury from Hell to look more frightful.

—DANIEL DEFOE, *A GENERAL HISTORY OF THE PYRATES*

THE ACRID STENCH OF SULFUR AND THE SCREAMS OF DYING MEN FILLED THE AIR AS A BRUTAL BATTLE RAGED ACROSS THE WATER-LOGGED WOODEN DECK. Through the thick black smoke and salty sea spray appeared the very vision of evil: a vile, bloodthirsty demon sent forth from the deepest recesses of hell itself to inflict pain and suffering on all those unlucky enough to gaze into his imposing and terrifying visage. This massive, six-foot-tall pirate captain, his physique resembling a hellish mix between a linebacker, an oak tree, and a grizzly bear, bellowed a blood-curdling laugh, and stormed through the fray, swinging his oversized, bloodstained cutlass like a wild man, hewing down all that stood before him like an angry lumberjack clear-cutting a rain forest. His appearance struck terror into the hearts of all he encountered. Cords of slow-burning hemp rope protruded from beneath his hat and were woven into his out-of-control, bristling black beard. These fuses were alight at the ends, leaving a trail of fire and smoke surrounding his face, unnaturally illuminating his wild eyes like white-hot orbs of searing flame. He drew one of the six fully loaded flintlock pistols he wore on bandoliers across his chest, violently jammed the muzzle flush into the chest of the French captain, and ended the brief but bloody engagement with a sickening muffled thud.

Edward Teach, better known by the incredibly sinister nickname Blackbeard, terrorized the seas during the golden age of piracy in the Caribbean and lives on as one of the most notorious and terrifying scalawags to ever hoist the black flag. Born in Bristol, England, Teach left home as a young man to seek awesome adventures on the high seas and club his enemies into submission with his raging kill-boner. When Queen Anne's War broke out in the waters of North America, Teach fell in with a British privateer outfit under the command of Captain Benjamin Hornigold, and together they raided and plundered French and Spanish galleons throughout the West Indies and the Spanish Main—breaking necks, cashing checks, and viciously thrusting their cutlasses into the faces of anybody who didn't own at least one clean pair of Union Jack boxer briefs.

When the war ended in 1713 and the queen declared that it was no longer "totally awesome" to go about indiscriminately killing Frenchmen and ganking loot from the cargo holds of half-destroyed Spanish vessels, Hornigold and Teach decided to put in a little off-the-books overtime. Together they became outlaw pirates: roving the seas, preying on shipping lanes, plundering more gold than they could carry, and drinking rum by the caskful.

One day the crew came across a massive French merchant ship called *Le Concorde.* Being the murderous pirates that they were, Hornigold's crew stormed the vessel and, after a brief battle, wrestled control of it. Hornigold was stoked about taking command of this huge ship but eventually decided that it was probably in his best interest to take advantage of the pirate amnesty that most European countries were offering at the time. Hornigold didn't feel like getting hanged by the neck like a chump, so he just up and retired from piracy like some kind of quitter. He left *Le Concorde* under the command of Blackbeard, who was, of course, the biggest badass in his crew, and the "Terrible Teach" immediately got busy crushing people's skulls into bone dust with the hilt of his cutlass.

Blackbeard decided that the three-hundred-ton ship wasn't as ultimate giga-mega-Xtreme as it could be, so he outfitted it with forty cannons, recruited a crew of three hundred toothless, foul-mouthed, hook-handed, peglegged, parrot-lovin', face-punchin', monkeycidal pirates to run it, and renamed the vessel *Queen Anne's Revenge* (this is a way more awesome name than *Le Concorde*, which quite honestly sounds like a luxury yacht full of beret-wearing, sweater-vested winos). Commanding this formidable pirate warship, Blackbeard impressed his buddies by winning naval duels against the British warships HMS *Scarborough* and HMS *Great Allen,* shouting "Yarr!" every time he got the chance, and generally just exerting his dominance over the Caribbean. Over the next couple of months, Blackbeard also captured several fast-moving sloops, added them to his fleet, terrorized the shipping lanes of the Atlantic, and plundered with impunity.

Now, despite what you may have heard, it should be noted that Blackbeard wasn't a totally heartless bastard. If he hoisted his Jolly Roger (no, that's not a euphemism for something dirty) and the other ship had the good sense to surrender without a fight, he would just sack the cargo hold, steal the passengers' jewelry, and let everybody go on about their business. If they were dumb enough to fire a broadside at him, Blackbeard would assault the ship, loot it, burn it, sink it, and kill every person on board. Of course, the latter didn't really happen all that often—Blackbeard was such a terrifying figure that most sailors regarded him as the devil incarnate and surrendered without a fight. This was usually a wise move.

Blackbeard was also seriously crazy, like out-of-his-mind psycho. One time, he went a couple of days without kicking any puppies or setting any Spanish sailors on fire, so one of his men foolishly doubted his meanness. Blackbeard simply shot his own first mate in the kneecap just to prove how nuts he was. Another time, he took his entire crew below deck and lit a huge sulfurous brimstone fire to see who was man enough to take the smoke the longest. Blackbeard won. Everyone else either ran off crying or asphyxiated.

Interestingly, this mentally unstable cutthroat buccaneer with a gigantic bristling beard was quite the ladies' man as well. Over the course of his tenure as pirate captain he married at least fourteen different women throughout the Caribbean, and allegedly fathered something like forty children. Despite his rampant polygamy, he was fiercely loyal to his wives and didn't particularly take well to being dissed. One story claims that one of Blackbeard's wives divorced him and gave her ring to some punk-ass sailor bitch, so Blackbeard hunted the guy's vessel down, sacked it, cut off the dude's hand (with ring still attached), and mailed it to his ex-wife in a box.

For much of his notorious career, Blackbeard did whatever he wanted to whomever he wanted at all times. He had a sweet arrangement where he sent the governor of North Carolina a portion of his treasure in exchange for a safe port (where he didn't have to worry about being imprisoned and violently executed for murder and piracy), and at one point his crew actually had the audacity to blockade the bustling colonial port city of Charleston, South Carolina, plunder the town, and pimp-slap the governor right in his stupid face. Blackbeard eventually became such a giant dick that the governor of Virginia put a massive bounty on his head and contracted a British navy lieutenant named Robert Maynard to take him out.

Maynard caught up with Blackbeard in the small cove known as Teach's Hole on November 22, 1718. The infamous pirate was on board the sloop *Adventure* when two British sloops-of-war sailed in toward him, but instead of getting nervous and blasting a load of grapeshot into his trousers, Blackbeard just cracked his knuckles, drew his pistols, and swore so heartily that it killed a dolphin. He waited until the enemy ships were almost on top of him and then fired a broadside right into their faces, crippling one of the British ships. Blackbeard immediately leapt onto the deck of the HMS *Ranger*, cutlass drawn, his full weight crashing into a large group of limey soldiers. The massive pirate captain was being attacked from all sides, but Blackbeard didn't pay any heed to their puny attempts to stop him—he just plowed ahead, knocking men to the deck and storming over to Maynard, his eyes varnished over with his trademark psychotic glaze. During the epic duel that followed, some chump Brit slashed Blackbeard in the neck when he wasn't looking, but it didn't even faze the towering monster. He just kept fighting, spilling sailors' guts all over the deck, until finally, completely surrounded and being attacked from all directions, the notorious pirate passed out from loss of blood, falling to his knees while pulling the hammer back on one of his pistols.

Later examinations of his body revealed that he had five bullets lodged in him and had been stabbed more than twenty times before he was finally brought down.

Maynard decapitated Blackbeard's lifeless corpse, threw the body overboard, and hung the captain's severed head from the bow of his ship, which is pretty cool, I guess. Legend has it that Blackbeard's body became possessed by Satan (and/or Michael Phelps) and swam three laps around Maynard's ship, but that seems a little hard to believe.

Port Royal, Jamaica, known affectionately as "the Sodom of the New World," was a pirate haven back in the seventeenth and early eighteenth centuries. This lawless British port was notoriously lax in its dealings with buccaneers and was a great place for the most dangerous men in the world to squander all of their hard-earned plunder on cheap booze and cheaper syphilitic prostitutes.

Scurvy was a nasty disease that proliferated during the age of sail and killed more seamen than cannons, cutlasses, white whales, and malaria combined. The Brits eventually figured out that this terrible affliction was brought on by a citrus deficiency, so they began issuing lemons and limes to their sailors to ward off the illness. From that point on, British sailors were known as limeys.

24

ANNE BONNY

(c. 1720)

The question isn't who is going to let me; it's who is going to stop me.

—AYN RAND

ANNE BONNY WAS A CRAZY-ASS PIRATE CHICK WHO SAILED ACROSS THE CARIBBEAN DESTROYING ANYBODY WHO LOOKED AT HER FUNNY AND GENERALLY BEING A VICIOUS, MAN-KILLING SCOURGE OF THE SEAS, MAKING A NAME FOR HERSELF BY HACKING THE ARMS OFF MERCHANT SAILORS, STEPPING ON THEIR NECKS, AND THEN SHOOTING THEM OUT OF A CANNON FACE-FIRST INTO A BRICK WALL. She was originally born in Ireland around the turn of the eighteenth century, but being that she was the illegitimate daughter of a wealthy lawyer named William Cormac and his maid, young Anne wasn't really all that well received when she came into the world. Mrs. Cormac took out an ad on the *Cook County Times* front page proclaiming William's adultery, and since that sort of thing was really frowned upon in Irish society back in those days, the Cormac family decided to relocate to Charleston, South Carolina, for a quiet life growing tobacco and watching a lot of college basketball.

At the age of fourteen Anne took over as the primary housekeeper for the estate and promptly got into a heated fight with a maid that resulted in Anne stabbing her in the gut with a steak knife. A year later some horndog asshat tried to rape her, so she beat the holy living hell out of him and bashed his unconscious body half a dozen times with a belaying pin. The dude was so badly messed up that he had to be hospitalized for months.

At sixteen she ran off, married a small-potatoes pirate named James Bonny, and moved to Nassau Island—a den of piracy that at the time was one of the seediest locales this side of Mos Eisley Spaceport. Things went okay for a while, but as you can probably guess, Anne wasn't the sort of badass babe who was going to be happy sitting around at home being a bored desperate housewife when she could have been out doing something epic. She also didn't really fit in with the locals very well: One legend has her going to a fancy-pants high society ball where she was introduced to the sister-in-law of the governor of Jamaica. That bitch made some catty remark about how Anne's shoes didn't match her purse or something, so Anne hauled off and slugged her right in her stupid face. The snooty debutante went down like the *Titanic* and lost two teeth for her trouble. Needless to say, this didn't get Anne invited to too many more parties. To further complicate Anne's misery, around this time James Bonny decided he was going to start selling out all of his pirate buddies to the governor of Nassau in exchange for cold hard cash. Since Anne really didn't want to be married to some slimy stool pigeon rat bastard, she started exploring other options.

It didn't take long before one presented itself. A relatively obscure pirate known as "Calico Jack" Rackham arrived on the island and immediately took a liking to Anne. At this point in time, Calico Jack was more renowned for his flamboyant wardrobe and inherent personal charm than he was for his tireless sword arm and ability to turn British merchantmen into giant flaming infernos, but Anne seized the opportunity to set sail for awesomeness. Jack and Anne hooked up at a keg party one night and the two fled the island on Jack's ship, the *Revenge*, and off they went on a perpetual honeymoon of nautical terrorism.

Since pirates weren't really the sort of folks who took too kindly to fighting alongside women, Anne initially disguised herself as a man in order to fit in with the crew. She quickly made a name for herself as a total hardass who didn't even bat an eye while hacking up sailors with her trusty cutlass or blasting dickbags in the mouth with one of the many pistols she carried on her belt at any given time. She didn't shy away from killing, she worked ship with the best of them, and she spewed forth enough profanity to make a marble statue of the Virgin Mary start crying tears of blood. She led boarding parties onto enemy vessels, made prisoners walk the plank, and was essentially considered the toughest pirate onboard.

After several months kicking ass at sea, finally one of her fellow crewmen caught on to the fact that she had boobs. At first this caused a clamor, but when everybody realized that she was probably one of the most dangerous and hardcore pirates onboard, they decided it was all good in the hood. Anne eventually took to wearing men's clothing when she went on raids and women's clothing when she was just hanging out around the ship, and everybody was cool with it. Later on in her high seas adventures, the *Revenge* would actually take on another female, a fellow face-breaking hellion named Mary Read, and with these two women onboard the crew enjoyed a period of unparalleled success, earning tons of gold and plunder from ports and merchant ships.

Unfortunately, we all know how most of these pirate stories turn out for our intrepid outlaws. In October 1720 the *Revenge* captured a Spanish galleon laden with gold and treasure, and everybody decided to get wasted to celebrate their victory. Well, right around the time the crew was on their second rendition of "What Shall We Do with a Drunken Sailor," a ship full of British marines pulled up, and all of a sudden the pirates found themselves about to get seriously wasted by the limeys. Anne and Mary were apparently the only crew members who could hold their liquor, so the two of them put up a valiant last stand against the onslaught of enemy soldiers. After holding off the Brits single-handedly for some time, the women were finally overwhelmed and the crew of the *Revenge* was captured. Anne was so pissed at the cowardice and uselessness of her fellow pirates that as she was being hauled off by the Brits she started firing her pistols at her own men. She was an angry drunk.

The crew of the *Revenge* were all thrown in prison and sentenced to death by hanging. Once it was revealed that Anne was pregnant with Calico Jack's baby, her sentence was commuted and she was released (a common practice for the times). Before she left jail, she stopped in to pay Jack a visit. She calmly walked up to the bars of his cell, looked him dead in the eye, and said, "I'm sorry, Jack, but if you had fought like a man, you would not now be about to die like a dog." Then she turned on her heel, strode out the front door, and completely vanished from history.

Some historians think that Anne Bonny and Mary Read were lesbian lovers and not just best friends and comrades-in-arms. These people need to stop watching so much porn.

Another tough Irish pirate chick was the notorious Grace O'Malley, the "Pirate Queen of Connacht," who terrorized the British coastline in the sixteenth century. This tough-ass seafarer commanded a small fleet of ships and led a crew of nearly two hundred pirates on daring raids against the merchant vessels of Queen Elizabeth.

BADASS PIRATES

Since being a pirate is one of the most hardcore professions in the history of the world, all students of badassitude should familiarize themselves with some of the masters of the craft.

Bartholomew Roberts

In terms of plunder and mad crazy bling, "Black Bart" was the single most successful pirate to ever live—he captured more than four hundred ships in the span of thirty months and terrorized the coasts of Africa, Brazil, and the Caribbean. At the helm of his forty-two-gun warship *Royal Fortune,* Roberts once captured a merchantman carrying forty thousand gold coins (not to mention a collection of custom jewelry handmade for the king of Portugal), plundered the city of Principe, and personally executed the governor of Martinique by hanging him from a yardarm. Roberts was eventually blown up by a broadside of grapeshot from a British warship.

François L'Olonnais

Once a slave of the Spanish Empire, L'Olonnais escaped to a life of piracy and dedicated his life to seeking brutal revenge on his former masters. He was notorious for viciously torturing and killing Spanish prisoners in exceedingly brutal ways, including one account where he pulled a dude's heart out, ate a piece of it, and threw it in the face of another prisoner. Somewhat ironically, L'Olonnais himself was later killed and eaten by cannibals.

Henry Morgan

This Welsh privateer led a pirate armada in the name of the British Empire, sacking dozens of South American towns, capturing the Panamanian silver train, and bludgeoning the entire Dutch navy to death in an hour and a half by swinging a two-ton ship cannon like a baseball bat. Then he ate a twenty-four-pound cannonball in one bite just to prove how awesome he was. Captain Morgan was eventually appointed lieutenant governor of Jamaica by Queen Elizabeth, retired to a life of luxury on a multimillion-dollar sugar plantation, and now has a popular brand of rum named after him.

Ching Shih

From an entry-level brothel girl to "the Dragon Lady of the South China Sea," she commanded a massive fleet of three hundred ships and forty thousand pirates operating off the coast of China in the nineteenth century. Not only did her "Red Fleet" sack innumerable towns and ships, but this chick actually went up against the Chinese navy and kicked its ass, sinking half the government's warships in a single battle. The only way the emperor could stop her from killing everything in sight was to give her full amnesty for her crimes and allow her to keep her amassed wealth. Ching agreed, and in 1810 she retired and opened up a wildly successful casino/brothel in Canton.

Hayreddin Barbarossa

The greatest and most feared of the Ottoman corsairs, Barbarossa carved out a privateer empire that dominated the Mediterranean for decades, sinking European shipping anywhere he could find it and wiping out scores of sword-swinging Christian knights in the name of the great Turkish sultan Suleiman the Magnificent. Barbarossa installed himself as governor of Algiers, served as grand admiral of the Turkish navy for over twenty years, won dozens of pitched battles, and established the naval supremacy of the Ottoman Empire.

Black Caesar

This massive, powerful African tribal chieftain led a revolt on the slave ship that was transporting him to the colonies, survived a brutal shipwreck, and settled into a career of piracy off the coast of Florida. He recruited a crew of like-minded swashbucklers, terrorized Caribbean

shipping, and had a harem of over a hundred women living at his base on Elliot Key. Caesar later joined up with Blackbeard and served as the infamous pirate's lieutenant right up until the grisly end.

Somali Pirates

The days when wooden warships ruled the sea are long gone, but piracy is still alive and well off the coast of Somalia. Zipping across the waves in fiberglass skiffs packed full of GPS systems, satellite phones, assault rifles, and rocket-propelled grenades, teams of crazy Somali pirates are making life miserable for any container vessels or cruise ships stupid enough to come within 250 miles of the African coast. In true pirate fashion, these guys swarm on board, overpower the crew, release the ship in exchange for a massive ransom, and go back home to live in giant mansions surrounded by scores of hot babes. Despite the best efforts of every civilized nation on earth to destroy these bazooka-toting buccaneers, Somali pirates are still believed to have collected roughly $50 million worth of ransom in 2008 alone.

25

PETER FRANCISCO

(1760–1831)

Without him we would have lost two crucial battles, perhaps the War, and with it our freedom. He was truly a one-man army.

—GEORGE WASHINGTON

ON A FOGGY NIGHT IN 1765, A FIVE-YEAR-OLD BOY WAS ABANDONED, MOSES-STYLE, ON A QUIET, LONELY VIRGINIA WHARF. Speaking no English and having little recollection of where he came from or how he arrived in the New World, this young man, much like the biblical figure whose origin story his own loosely mirrors, would grow to be a powerful hero who would deliver his people from the clutches of tyranny—and kill hundreds of people in the process.

Taken in by a wealthy judge and raised on a large Virginia farm, Peter Francisco grew to be a massive, Andre the Giant–style behemoth who easily dead-lifted Dodge Vipers, bench-pressed beer kegs with his eyelids, and did a bunch of other tremendous feats of manliness that you don't usually witness outside of those awesome strongman competitions on ESPN 8 at four in the morning. Standing six foot six and weighing over 280 pounds at a time when the average man stood about five-seven, Peter was like the Jolly Green Giant of colonial America, only instead of being jolly or green he was pissed off and more than willing to epically fracture your skull by relentlessly cracking you in the dome with the stock of his musket.

One day Peter went to go hear his adopted cousin—a dude named Patrick Henry—give a rousing pump-up speech to the Virginia legislature about how the English were being total wankers, and Peter quickly decided that he would dedicate all of his energy to punching British people in the dick and pulling out their vas deferens. So in 1776, when the Americans and the Brits threw down their leather jackets, whipped out their switchblades, and started snapping their fingers menacingly at each other, Peter Francisco immediately enlisted in the Continental Army and prepared to start whacking biznatches in the esophagus with a billy club.

In the early years of the war, Francisco fought on the front lines of a number of fierce battles, survived two gunshot wounds, and almost died from a terminal case of freezing his balls off at Valley Forge. His unrivaled strength and bravery on the battlefield soon became so legendary that George Washington himself awarded "the Virginia Hercules" with a special prize—a five-foot-long broadsword. With this badass weapon in hand, General George set him loose to smite some British ass-clowns and lacerate the carotid arteries of anybody who didn't think democracy totally kicked ass.

Peter got the perfect opportunity to put this ridiculous new sword to good use when he participated in a raid on the British garrison of Stony Point in 1779. At the head of a twenty-man suicide charge known as Operation Forlorn Hope, Francisco pulled his giant blade and charged balls-out toward the heavily defended fortifications. He avoided all the cannonballs and musket fire the Brits could fling at him (an impressive feat, considering the fact that a screaming, pissed-off, six-foot-six giant with a broadsword is probably a relatively high-priority target) and was the first man to hit the wall. Peter vaulted over the fortifications, cut three men down with his blade, cleared the enemy off the parapet, and breached into the fortress. Peter didn't stop there, though—this hell-hole of awesomeness plowed his way through the courtyard, killed a dozen soldiers, got slashed in the chest by a cavalry saber, and still managed to pull the British flag down from the battlements and signal the Colonial victory.

But pwning everyone in Capture the Flag was just the beginning. When the American lines crumbled at the Battle of Camden in 1780 and Peter Francisco found himself completely surrounded by dead Colonials and cranky Brits waving rifles in his face, he didn't even flinch. He just stabbed a cavalry soldier in the gallbladder with his bayonet, pulled the guy off his horse, jumped on, and rode to safety. When he reached American lines and found his commanding officer nearly dead from exhaustion, Francisco gave the horse to his commander and then—on foot—ran back to the battlefield to save an American cannon from falling into enemy hands, pulling the 1,100-pound gun from the field *by himself*. Then he probably body-slammed a horse through a concrete slab at Stonehenge and suplexed a 747 over the Grand Canyon.

Francisco had already earned a reputation as a one-man wrecking ball when his regiment marched into the critical Battle for Guilford Courthouse. This fight was one of the bloodiest battles of the American Revolution, thanks in a large part to the sword-swinging mayhem brought about by our boy Peter. When the carnage degenerated to close-quarters hand-to-hand combat, Francisco unsheathed his massive weapon and went nuts on anything wearing red, taking down thirteen British soldiers during the melee—including one guy who had his entire head sliced in half. Longways. When the redcoats saw this insane gigantic berserker freaking out and slaughtering everyone around him, they all decided to swarm him with bayonets, sabers, and rifles. Francisco was stabbed several times and finally passed out on the field from loss of blood. He was left for dead on the battlefield but somehow managed to regain consciousness and crawl to a nearby town, where he was found by a local farmer and nursed back to health.

Now, around this time a dashing young British cavalry colonel named Banastre Tarleton was raiding towns up and down the Virginia countryside. This famous commander, affectionately known in the colonies as "Butcher" Tarleton, was much loved by the citizens of England because of his expert skill in cutting down the filthy rebels, smoking out seditionists, and emotionlessly disposing of any traitor he got his hands on, usually with extreme prejudice all the way up your ass. While Tarleton's raiders were in the process of despoiling the countryside, plundering supply depots, and massacring unarmed prisoners of war, a small detachment of his men came across the colonial war hero known as "the Samson of the West." Our protagonist was alone—and still pretty severely wounded at this point—but it took more than a few gaping flesh wounds to keep Peter Francisco down, and for this guy merely brushing his teeth was a mass-casualty event. The British squadron commander approached the wounded veteran, ordering that he surrender immediately.

Peter said nothing.

The officer calmly approached, then looked down and noticed the silver buckles on Francisco's shoes. He demanded that the prisoner hand those over as well.

Peter told him that if he wanted the buckles, he would have to take them himself.

The British officer thought for a moment, then leaned down to remove the silver ornaments. As he did, Peter Francisco reached out, grabbed the redcoat's saber, drew the weapon from its sheath, and smashed the guy in the freakin' head with the pommel. The officer dropped to his knees, pulled his pistol, and shot Peter in the side. Peter responded by chopping the guy's hand off and then kicking him teeth-first into the gravel road. Another raider, hearing the commotion, rode up, jammed the muzzle of his rifle in Peter's face, and pulled the trigger.

Nothing.

Francisco grabbed the misfiring rifle with one hand, pulled the guy off his horse, and slashed him with the saber. Off in the distance, a group of about ten raiders hastily rode up toward the fray. Peter turned toward a nearby forest, cupped his hand over his mouth, and called out to an invisible army waiting in an imaginary ambush: "Now's your time, boys! We'll dispatch these few and then attack the main body!"

On hearing this, Tarleton's raiders screeched to a halt, turned tail, and fled as fast as they could. Peter Francisco leisurely trotted off with six riderless British horses and several captured weapons. He rejoined his unit, served valiantly with the Marquis de Lafayette during the decisive Yorktown campaign, and ultimately helped the United States win its independence from Great Britain. After the war, he went home, learned to read, became a successful blacksmith, and married three different women. When he wasn't reading Shakespeare, procreating, or knocking shoplifters unconscious by throwing anvils at their heads, he performed impressive acts of strongmanitude to impress the ladies.

Peter Francisco died in 1831 at the age of seventy-one, one of the great unsung heroes of the American Revolution.

THE MARQUIS DE LAFAYETTE

Americans love to talk smack about France and how we bailed their asses out after Germany kicked the holy living God out of them in World War II, but we tend to forget that if it wasn't for France—and particularly a dude known as the Marquis de Lafayette—we here in the States would all be speaking with unintelligible British accents, watching soccer on the telly, and eating a whole lot of spotted dick with our fish and chips.

Lafayette's dad was exploded by a cannonball while battling the English, so you can be pretty sure that the marquis of mayhem didn't have any love for the Brits. Eager to exact vengeance as soon as he possibly could, he enlisted in the French army on his sixteenth birthday. By nineteen, he was already a captain in the dragoons, one of the toughest cavalry units in the world at the time—and a pretty righteous ass-kicker.

It was around this time that the American Revolution broke out. Lafayette was so pumped up about rocking British faces and helping the oppressed colonists battle for their freedom that he immediately put together a company of soldiers to sail across the Atlantic and get busy with the ass-kickings. Unfortunately, the French were being total prudes at the beginning of the war, and Lafayette—being a member of French royalty—was officially forbidden from committing any of his soldiers to the American Revolution. Dudes were sent to arrest him and stop him from single-handedly dragging France into the Revolutionary War, but Lafayette and his men hopped a ship, evaded the British and French navies, and sailed two months across the Atlantic, landing on American soil in 1777.

It wasn't long before the marquis met up with fellow badass George Washington, and the two quickly became the Thelma and Louise of kicking British people in the junk until they barfed. When the Colonial government told Lafayette they didn't really have any money to pay him or his soldiers, Lafayette basically told them, "Screw it, dudes. I'm loaded already, and giving me the opportunity to jam my cavalry saber into English faces is all the payment I need!" He was promoted to major general, attached to General Washington's staff, and immediately set out to sever some aortas. At the Battle of Brandywine he was capped in the leg while leading his men on a bayonet charge, and at the Battle of Barren

Hill later that year Lafayette's forces managed to stop the British Army from capturing Valley Forge by incinerating them with a flamethrower.

Despite his tremendous ass-kicking prowess, Lafayette's greatest contribution to the American Revolution was his ability to get the French Crown off its ass and bail us out when we needed it most. Lafayette pretty much sent missives to the king every day demanding that he send cash and supplies to fund the war effort, and most of the time they gave in just to get him to shut the hell up about it. He rallied his crew, contributed $200,000 of his own money to the cause, and eventually convinced the French to join in on all the sweet face-melting action here in the U.S. of A. France officially declared war on England, and at only twenty-one years of age Lafayette participated in the Yorktown campaign and helped the United States achieve its autonomy from Great Britain.

After the war, Lafayette thought that sweet, delicious freedom was so damn awesome that he helped author the Declaration of the Rights of Man and of the Citizen—one of the documents that kicked off the French Revolution. During his own country's struggle for liberty, he was the commander of the French National Guard and advocated religious tolerance, popular representation, trial by jury, and freedom of the press—the same ideals he kicked ass for in the colonies. Unfortunately, things got out of hand pretty quickly when folks started chopping everyone's head off with the guillotine, and Lafayette was eventually arrested and thrown into an Austrian prison. He would sit for five years until finally being busted out by Napoleon, a man who knew a good badass when he saw one. Lafayette spent the final years of his life living in a gigantic mansion, where he would sometimes shelter refugees trying to escape execution at the hands of murderous revolutionaries. He died in 1834.

2008

26

HORATIO NELSON

(1758–1805)

First, you must always implicitly obey orders, without attempting to form any opinion of your own respecting their propriety. Secondly, you must consider every man your enemy who speaks ill of your king; and, thirdly, you must hate a Frenchman as you do the devil.

ADMIRAL LORD VISCOUNT HORATIO NELSON, ONCE REFERRED TO BY LORD BYRON AS "BRITANNIA'S GOD OF WAR," WAS THE MOST BALLS-OUT COMMANDER IN THE HISTORY OF THE ROYAL NAVY—AN ORGANIZATION THAT PRIDES ITSELF ON BEING THE DEADLIEST AND MOST INSANELY POWERFUL MILITARY FORCE CAPABLE OF AQUATIC FLOTATION. Throughout his long and illustrious career as a gallant and indomitable war hero who repeatedly demonstrated his astonishing ability to donkey-punch his enemies unconscious and then spit on their watery graves, Nelson's unorthodox tactics and ability to motivate his soldiers to kill the hell out of French people firmly established England's utter dominance over the high seas and frustrated Napoleon Bonaparte's expansionist ambitions.

The fifth of eleven children born to a small-town minister, young Nelson wasted no time, joining the navy as an apprentice at the age of twelve. By the time he was sixteen he had already served in patrol duty off the coast of India, crossed the Atlantic Ocean twice, and been attacked by a freaking polar bear while on a research expedition in the Arctic. My guess is that while the young cadet and his crew were in fact trying to find a mythical northern water route to India, their research actually ended up proving that it is a ridiculously bad idea to screw with a polar bear. According to the story, Nelson was in the process of trying to fight off the beast by swinging the butt of his rifle at it like some kind of half-demented Siberian mountain man when a volley of cannon fire from his ship scared it off. Of course, Nelson was young at this time—if this encounter had occurred ten years later, Horatio probably would have just slugged the beast right in the face without batting an eye.

Nelson was promoted to lieutenant at the age of sixteen, which is pretty awesome considering that during this time you had to be at least twenty to be made an officer in the British military. Obviously, Nelson was just so bitchin' that he transcended the petty rules of mortals.

Around this time, the colonies in the Americas got their panties in a wad about stamp acts and tea parties and other such ridiculous nonsense, so the British navy was dispatched to beat a little sense into them with an unending barrage of thirty-two-pound cannonballs. Of course, Horatio would rather have cut his own face in half with a chainsaw than missed out on an opportunity to dish out some righteous ass-whompings to traitorous American scumbags. He was stationed in the Caribbean, where he captured and/or destroyed Colonial blockade runners, privateers, and smugglers. When France and Spain joined in on the fun, Nelson greeted them with an enfilade of lead death, battling French warships and personally leading amphibious raids against Spanish fortresses in Central America.

After the American Revolution, Nelson took the fight against France back to the British side of the pond. The French Revolutionary War broke out in 1793, and Captain Nelson took command of the sixty-four-gun warship *Agamemnon*. He helped support the invasion of Calvi, captured Corsica, and lost the sight in his right eye when a goddamned cannonball exploded in his face. Nelson wasn't the sort of dude who needed two eyes to kick ass, as he proved in action against the Spanish at the Battle of Cape St. Vincent in 1797. When it appeared that the dirty Spaniards were escaping the battle, Nelson's ship came flying up unsupported from the rear of the British formation, plowed into the Spanish armada, and split the enemy formation in half. Nelson, acting on his own initiative and without any orders, single-handedly divided the enemy force, and even though his vessel took a beating from a half-dozen larger and more powerful warships, his move turned the tide of the battle. Instead of escaping, the entire Spanish navy was crushed. It was so awesome that Nelson broke a piece of the ship off with his teeth and then high-fived his first mate so hard that the guy's hand fell off.

But jamming up the works by voluntarily hurling himself into a meat grinder wasn't even the most badass thing he did in that particular battle—at one point two giant Spanish warships, the *San Nicholas* and the *San Jose,* crashed into each other and their rigging became entangled. Nelson pulled up alongside the nearest ship and personally led a boarding party onto the deck of the *San Nicholas*. After fierce hand-to-hand combat, Nelson captured the Spanish captain's sword and immediately had his men throw ropes over from the *San Nicholas* to the *San Jose*, climb on board, and continue fighting. For his daring actions in saving the battle and personally capturing two ships, Nelson was knighted by the king and promoted to the rank of admiral.

That pretty much sums up Nelson in a nutshell. He was courageous, brave, and fearless, and he always led from the front no matter how much stuff was exploding all around him. Seriously—while launching an amphibious assault on the fortress of Santa Cruz, a musket ball shattered every bone in his right arm. Nelson just went back aboard his flagship, had his arm amputated without anesthesia, and immediately returned to the battlefield. His strategy was just to go balls-out at all times, kicking it into overdrive and flying full speed toward the enemy.

Oh yeah, and he suffered from seasickness. You know you're a bitchin' naval commander when you can beat the holy living God out of your enemies with one eye, one arm, and stopping to hurl over the side of the deck every couple of minutes.

While all of the stuff up to this point is about as awesome as a ninja on fire riding a motorcycle, Nelson really showed the world what he was capable of when Napoleon Bonaparte started trying to flex his nuts in France. The French army landed in Egypt and was preparing to carve out an empire the likes of which the world hadn't seen since Alexander the Great, but Nelson had different plans. He set out in 1798 with a fleet of fourteen ships and went hunting for Napoleon's navy. After some searching, he came across a massed horde of warships and amphibious landing craft moored in Aboukir Bay at the mouth of the Nile. The Royal Navy launched a daring, quick-strike night attack, repositioning their fleet rapidly in the face of the enemy, and Nelson completely annihilated the entire French fleet—of the seventeen ships Napoleon dispatched to Egypt, only three made it out of the bay alive.

After effectively crushing Napoleon's lifelong dreams of an African empire in the span of a few hours, Nelson retired to Naples for a while, where he started banging Lady Emma Hamilton—a woman believed to have been pretty much the hottest babe in the British Empire. Sure, she was married to some other dude at the time (and Nelson also had a wife in the Caribbean), but neither of them really seemed to mind.

In 1801 the countries of Denmark, Sweden, Prussia, and Russia formed up into something called the League of Armed Neutrality. Nelson already hated neutrality and pretty much everything else that didn't involve gigantic explosions and/or having wild monkey sex with beautiful aristocrats, but when the league decided that France really wasn't all that bad after all, it was up to Nelson to sail into Copenhagen and smash all of their ships into driftwood until everyone was dead. During the battle, Nelson was given the signal to retreat, but he responded by giving his superior officer the finger, setting his phasers for disintegrate, and committing all of his ships to a full-scale attack. The League of Armed Pussies was destroyed, the city of Copenhagen was captured, and the king decided to make Nelson a Viscount of Ass-kickery.

Well, while Nelson was off pounding Swedes, Danes, Germans, Russians, and countesses, Napoleon rebuilt his navy and started getting his admirals psyched up about a possible invasion of the British Isles. Screw that. If the French were going to set foot on English soil, they were going to have to go through Admiral Horatio Nelson first.

But Nelson wasn't the sort of geezer who was going to sit around on his dick waiting for the French to make the first move when he could be out cracking people's skulls together, and on October 21, 1805, he tracked down Napoleon's navy off the coast of Trafalgar, Spain. In one of the largest and greatest naval battles ever fought, Nelson's twenty-seven ships went up against a combined armada of thirty-three Spanish and French vessels. Outnumbered and substantially outgunned (the allied fleet had roughly 250 more cannons than the British ships), Nelson resorted once again to his full-throttle tactics. Instead of approaching the enemy in an ordered line of battle, he aligned his fleet in a wedge formation, cut the enemy's line in two, and started laying pipe to the allied fleet. The superior training, gunnery, leadership, and morale of Nelson's men prevailed—12,000 enemy sailors and twenty-two ships were destroyed, while Nelson suffered just 449 dead and didn't lose a single vessel. Napoleon's ambition of taking down England—or anything else he couldn't walk to, for that matter—was crushed in a single day. From that point on, the emperor of France couldn't so much as wade knee-deep into a swimming pool without having a British frogman swim up and kick him in the ball sack with a flippered boot.

Sadly, it wasn't to be that England's greatest hero would go off drinking pints of Bass ale in a London tavern to celebrate his greatest accomplishment. While directing the battle from the quarterdeck of his flagship, HMS *Victory*, Lord Nelson was shot in the chest by an enemy sniper. He died shortly after receiving word that the French navy had been utterly destroyed. The British Empire, while elated that the immediate threat to her borders had been wiped off the face of the earth, went into a period of deep mourning for the loss of her greatest hero—a man who never gave less than 3,000 percent, who single-handedly established the superiority of his country's navy for centuries to come, and who boldly gave his life to defend his homeland, dying in the moment of his greatest victory.

Lord Nelson's full title is the Most Noble Lord Horatio Nelson, Viscount and Baron Nelson, of the Nile and of Burnham Thorpe in the County of Norfolk, Baron Nelson of the Nile and of Hilborough in the Said County, Knight of the Most Honourable Order of the Bath, Vice Admiral of the White Squadron of the Fleet, Commander in Chief of His Majesty's Ships and Vessels in the Mediterranean, Duke of Bronte in the Kingdom of the Two Sicilies, Knight Grand Cross of the Sicilian Order of St. Ferdinand and of Merit, Member of the Ottoman Order of the Crescent, Knight Grand Commander of the Order of St. Joachim.

Forest of Soignies
To Louvain
Wood of Ohain
1815
1000
Papelotte
La Haye
Chateau Hougoumont
JAQUINOT
From Nivelles

27

NAPOLEON BONAPARTE

(1769–1821)

Never interrupt your enemy while he is making a mistake.

IT'S SAFE TO SAY THAT NAPOLEON BONAPARTE WASN'T EXACTLY THE MOST POPULAR KID TO EVER LIVE. Born on Corsica, a tiny Mediterranean island nobody really gives a crap about, from the time he was sent off to military school at age nine, the young outcast was bullied, ostracized, and picked on by his jackass classmates because, as we all know, children are totally evil bastards. Well, Napoleon didn't let something as inconsequential as having no friends and being way too short to play on the basketball team get in the way of his dreams. He was determined to do something of consequence with his life, like grind all of Europe beneath his heel and train a legion of German shepherd attack dogs to ring the doorbells of his enemies and bite them in the scrotum when they opened the door. He buried himself in his studies, learned everything he possibly could about artillery, and secretly plotted his savage revenge against everyone who ever messed with him.

Bonaparte graduated and was commissioned a second lieutenant in the French army in 1785, and thus began a long and illustrious career of aerating faces with shotgun blasts of grapeshot and crunching mighty European kings in the nuts with a tack hammer. His hard work and training paid off, as Napoleon rapidly worked his way up through the ranks, and in 1793 the twenty-four-year-old major distinguished himself by shelling the mother hell out of the city of Toulon and playing an integral part in the French effort to recapture the city from the Brits. His most famous engagement as an artillery officer, however, came two years later, when he was serving with French forces stationed in Paris.

On October 5, 1795, a huge army of king-lovin' loyalist royalist dick-biters rose and threatened to wipe out the egalitarian republican government that had been set up during the French Revolution. Even though he wasn't even the ranking officer in the city, Napoleon rode to the rescue, seized control of the ragtag Paris militia, strategically positioned his cannons throughout the city, and shredded the royalist army with grapeshot. Despite outnumbering their Corsican foe six to one, Napoleon's enemies were obliterated in the span of just a few hours.

This improbable yet awesome victory made the young general a national hero almost overnight. He was immediately given command of all republican forces stationed in Italy, where he whipped a demoralized and undersupplied force into shape, and led a masterful campaign across the Alps like Hannibal (the Carthaginian, not the cannibal) and into the Italian countryside. Hopelessly outnumbered and without any chance of being reinforced or resupplied, Napoleon used his genius to lay down some righteous ass-kickings on the armies of Austria, Naples, Venice, Piedmont, and the Papal States. He fought sixty-seven actions, won eighteen pitched battles, and captured 150,000 prisoners, 540 cannons, and 170 regimental flags. He resupplied his army from captured enemy depots, and his unbelievable military conquests made him pretty much the most popular guy in all of France. Meanwhile, the captain of Bonaparte's high school football team probably plummeted into obscurity as an underemployed busboy doing bong hits in the broom closet during his lunch break.

After Italy was toast, Napoleon crossed the Mediterranean and landed a huge invasion force in Alexandria, Egypt. There he quickly went to work conquering more territory for the French Republic. In an insane battle that took place only a few miles from the pyramids, Napoleon crushed a force of more than sixty thousand Egyptians (probably by reprogramming the Great Pyramid to shoot lasers) and put an end to over seven hundred years of Mamluke dominance over the Nile. Then his men allegedly shot the Sphinx's nose off with a cannon, which I guess is cool if you're into defacing national landmarks.

Despite the fact that his unstoppable land armies were working like a well-oiled machine lubed up with greased pigs, Vaseline, and K-Y jelly, Napoleon eventually had to give up on his conquest of North Africa when our boy Nelson destroyed the French navy. But whatever, Napoleon didn't go off and start hyperventilating into a paper bag—he caught the first ride out of Egypt and snuck back into France. When he landed, Napoleon marched his troops into the legislature building and seized power for himself. Then he brought the Pope in to crown him emperor of the French in 1804, but right as the Pope was lowering the crown onto his head Napoleon was like, "Whatever," ganked the crown away from the Holy Father, and placed it on his own head. I find this hilarious for some reason.

Bonaparte's ultimate goal was to sail into England and drop-kick the king into the Baltic Sea, but once again our buddy Nelson threw a monkey wrench in the works with his previously mentioned shenanigans off the coast of Trafalgar. So Napoleon just had to content himself with crushing all of Europe instead. He raised a massive military force, marched east, and ran into the full might of the Austrian and Russian armies at the Battle of Austerlitz in the winter of 1805. Heavily outnumbered by the combined strength of two hostile nations, Napoleon beat them so hard that their teeth came out their urethras, with thirty thousand men killed or captured in a single battle. Those who didn't surrender on the spot foolishly attempted to flee across a large frozen pond, so Napoleon, being the master of disaster that he was, smashed the ice with his cannons and sent thousands of men to a freezing-cold watery death. The emperors of Europe's two most powerful military nations were forced to personally submit to his will, Austria was subjugated, the Holy Roman Empire was dissolved, and pretty much everybody recognized the fact that Napoleon was totally rad.

Well, everybody except the Prussians. They got all pissed off and mobilized their armies in a futile attempt to stem the tide of French people sweeping across Western Europe. Nineteen days after the Prussian military mustered in, Napoleon viciously backhanded them into their place, killing forty-six thousand men in the battles of Jena and Auerstedt and liquefying the Prussian army while losing about seven thousand of his own soldiers. He went on to cement his power in Europe, grind broken beer bottles into his enemies' faces, capture most of the Iberian Peninsula, kidnap the Pope, annex the Papal States, and marry the superhot archduchess of Austria. Not bad for a low-born Corsican who used to get atomic wedgies in middle school.

In 1812 Napoleon decided that the Russians were really pissing him off too, so he marched 450,000 men into the motherland to teach them a lesson in having their faces wrecked. Unfortunately for *l'empereur*, the Russians had no intention of fighting a pitched battle and subsequently being flogged mercilessly with their own small intestines, so instead they just kept retreating deeper and deeper into Russia, burning everything they came across to prevent the French from living off the land or capturing supplies (à la Peter the Great). When Napoleon arrived in Moscow and found the entire place torched to the ground, he was like, "Well, screw it," and turned around to head home. On the way back, relentless guerilla attacks, rampant desertion, a bitch of a Russian winter, and a lack of supplies dealt serious losses to the French—only about a tenth of the invasion force returned to Paris.

The European allies took advantage of Napoleon's temporary weakness, and he was defeated and exiled to the island of Elba in 1814. Just one year later, however, Napoleon busted out of his remote island prison and returned to the mainland of France. The reinstated French king, Louis XVIII, sent a regiment of troops to shoot Bonaparte, but he was such a badass that they decided to join their former commander and hop on the express train to awesometown instead. Napoleon chased the king out of Paris, reinstated himself as emperor, and immediately marched into Belgium to get his revenge.

You have to respect the fact that Napoleon's daring escape and subsequent full-scale assault was a balls-out gambit—roughly the political equivalent of cashing in your 401(k) retirement fund, going to Vegas, and betting it all on red. Unfortunately, Lady Luck is a sadistic, kinky bitch goddess who loves to bite you in the ass and steal your wallet when you least expect it. The French ran into the Duke of Wellington's British Army at Waterloo, and the two forces immediately started beating the hell out of each other. During the brutal fighting victory constantly hung by a single thread, but in the end Wellington's men stood strong and Napoleon suffered his final defeat. He was exiled again, this time to St. Helena, a tiny, desolate volcanic island in the middle of the Atlantic, where he wrote the definitive manual on nineteenth-century warfare and lived the life of a lonely, eccentric genius until his death in 1821 at the age of fifty-two. No matter how cool it was to live on a volcano like Sauron, with no more asses left to kick life was simply no longer worth living for this war-mongering hardass.

Napoleon's Imperial Guard was the world's most elite fighting force during this period. These fearless infantrymen, or artillerymen, and cavalry troopers, handpicked by the emperor to serve in his personal bodyguard, were the best-trained, best-equipped, and toughest troops in Napoleon's formidable army. All men in the unit had served the emperor from the beginning, and at the time of Waterloo many of these soldiers were ten- and twenty-year veterans. Their flawless tactical maneuvering and almost fanatical devotion made them feared and respected by armies across Europe.

Arthur Wellesley, the Duke of Wellington, was an awesome son of a bitch in his own right. Having served bravely for many years quelling native uprisings and rebellions in British India, the "Iron Duke" also managed to wrest control of the Iberian Peninsula from the French while Napoleon was off in Russia. It was his bravery and tenacity and that of his men that carried the day at Waterloo, an action that has made him a national hero of Britain.

Toussaint L'Ouverture was born into slavery on a plantation in Haiti in 1743. Realizing that slavery was a bullcrap enterprise that sucked his ass on fire, Toussaint led a slave rebellion, uniting all the oppressed blacks on the island and rising against the white aristocratic plantation owners in a struggle that went on for ten years. He overthrew the colonial regime, abolished slavery, rebuilt the economy, opened trade routes, and took control of the nation. Various European jackasses tried to screw with him, including world superpowers such as Britain, France, and Spain, but a combination of yellow fever, malaria, and relentless ass-beatings sent them all running home to their mamas. Napoleon eventually captured L'Ouverture and had him executed for treason, but France was never able to reclaim her old colony.

Most crazy people think that they are either Jesus or Napoleon. I have no idea why this is.

THE FRENCH FOREIGN LEGION

Formed shortly after the days of Napoleon, the French Foreign Legion is an insanely hardcore association of some of the most grizzled, dangerous, and fearsome men in the world, and a unit so ridiculously tough that its troops spend their R & R time wrestling bears and face-punching sticks of dynamite.

Created in 1831 as a mercenary force attached to the French army, the Legion was famous for allowing pretty much anybody and everybody into their ranks. Enlistment procedures involved no background checks, no paperwork, and no questions asked. Hell, you didn't even have to give them your real name—you told them what you wanted to be called, and they spent your entire tenure referring to you as Corporal Maxminster Overdrive Awesometown. Basically, as long as you were willing to carry a rifle and suffer a gory and horrific death in the name of France, you were good to go.

Well, the problem with having a regiment full of men seeking to preserve their anonymity is that they were generally doing so in order to escape a particularly sketchy past. As a result, the Foreign Legion ended up being more or less an entire regiment of some of Europe's most violent criminals—ruthless, bloodthirsty men seeking to escape imprisonment and/or execution for crimes like murder, mass murder, and super-murder. While these bloodthirsty lunatics with nothing to lose were highly effective when they had an outlet for their uncontrollable rage, in times of peace they became somewhat of a liability. In fact, Legionnaires were pretty notorious for their unquenchable thirst for looting, drinking, and getting arrested for looting and drinking. One time, an entire company of the Polish Battalion got drunk and beat up all of their officers. Another time, a full battalion of men pawned all of their weapons and equipment in exchange for booze money. Not surprisingly, there was a law stating that no member of the French Foreign Legion was ever allowed to set foot in France.

Eventually, the French decided that the best way to keep these scoundrels and ruffians from running amok all over the place was through ruthless discipline, a brutal training regimen, corporal punishment, and near-constant warfare. Operating out of their home base in Algiers—all of their training and drills took place in the middle of the damned Sahara Desert—the Legion fought across Africa, Europe, Central America, and Asia. They also rode camels occasionally, which is pretty sweet.

While the Legionnaires were mostly foreigners (generally Poles, Germans, Swiss, Spanish, Belgians, Italians, and Dutch), the officers were all French, and all commands and orders were issued in French. After performing their tour of duty in the Legion, soldiers were made full citizens of France and issued an official passport in the name of their choosing. Sure, life in the regiment was hard, and the odds were not exactly stacked in your favor in terms of survival, but escaping to the Legion offered thousands of European thugs the unique opportunity to receive a blank slate, a new identity, and a fresh lease on life—and to legally kill a lot of people in the process. It also provided the French army with a fearsome assortment of the world's most dangerous men, an unstoppable force of blood-mongering psychos who were more than eager to rip France's enemies into tiny shreds just because they loved violence and, honestly, because they really had nothing better to do.

2008

28

AGUSTINA OF ARAGON

(1786–1857)

Oh those base invaders of my country, those oppressors of the best of its patriots; Should the fate of war place any of them within my power, I will instantly deliver up their throats with my knife.

THE BEAUTIFUL NORTHERN SPANISH CITY OF SARAGOSSA HAD ENJOYED OVER SEVEN HUNDRED YEARS OF PEACE, LOVE, AND HIPPIE TREE-HUGGER PROSPERITY STRETCHING FROM THE TIME OF EL CID UP UNTIL THE FATEFUL YEAR 1808, WHEN HER WALLS WERE THREATENED BY THE MARAUDING ARMIES OF NAPOLEON BONAPARTE'S EVER-EXPANDING FRENCH EMPIRE. Napoleon, perhaps suffering from the psychiatric complex that bears his name, had this crazy hard-on to conquer all of Europe, and one of his primary goals was to force all of Spain and Portugal under whichever one of his thumbs wasn't currently shoved inside his coat pocket. Obviously, the Spanish weren't too psyched about capitulating to the French (and who can blame them?), so the two nations became embroiled in an incredibly bloody and brutal campaign that would come to be known as the Peninsular War.

The point here is that in 1808 the quiet city of Saragossa was completely surrounded by arbitrarily pissed-off Frenchmen with thin, waxed curlicue moustaches and berets, all eager and willing to slaughter some Spaniards for no good reason at all. The town had been cut off from supplies and ammunition for weeks, and the beleaguered defenders of the city were constantly being pounded by artillery and musket fire as the French commander tried to break their will like an Entenmann's spokesperson at a Weight Watchers meeting. Finally, after sixty days of the siege, the French launched a full-on balls-to-the-wall invasion of the city. At this point the town was only defended by a small, heavily outnumbered force of volunteer soldiers, and before long the massive horde of Perrier-swigging, wine-connoisseuring Frenchies broke through the city gates and started flipping out on everyone.

The imperial army fell on the artillery positions located just inside the gates, and many of the front-line Spanish defenders either ran for their lives or got some up-close-and-personal hard-hitting interviews with the pointy end of a bayonet. Within minutes it appeared that the defensive lines had broken, and it was beginning to look more and more like the citizens of Saragossa were going to need to start developing a taste for frog's legs, moldy cheese, and Jerry Lewis.

However, all was not as screwed up as it seemed. Amid all the confusion, smoke, gunfire, and epically graphic strings of Spanish profanity stood a woman known as Agustina Zaragoza Doménech. During the initial fighting she had been up on the battlements, passing out apples, PowerBars, and Gatorade to the men to help sustain their fighting spirit and replenish their electrolytes, doing her part to help defend her city. However, when she saw all these dudes running away with their panties in a wad shrieking like grade-school girls just because a couple of French dudes were waving knives in their faces, she did what any badass worthy of that moniker would have done—she got really pissed and started bashing people's heads together like B. A. Baracus from *The*

A-Team. When one of the Spanish cannon crews dropped their gear and ran screaming away from the rampaging French invaders, Agustina of Aragon charged full speed toward the abandoned gun. With an entire company of angry, screaming soldiers only a few hundred feet away and rapidly closing in her position, she shoved a canister of black powder and grapeshot into the muzzle and packed it down with the ramrod. Then, right as the French troops were preparing to lunge at her with their bayonets and skewer her like a meatsicle, she coolly took a long drag from a cigarette, said something insanely witty, and flicked the lit cigarette into the hatch, sending forth a massive shotgun blast of metallic death into the enemy from point-blank range. When the smoke cleared, the bloodthirsty, stab-happy French troops had been reduced to a smoking crater of dead-ass bitches.

Having effectively proven that she had the biggest, brassiest balls of anyone in the town (or is *ovarian fortitude* the correct terminology here?), Agustina turned and looked over her shoulder at the Spanish soldiers behind her. The men were all like, "Damn, if this chick can kick so much ass all by herself, what the Molly Ringwald are we doing standing around here with our hands in our pockets?" They immediately rushed back to their positions and began pouring artillery and small-arms fire into the invaders. Agustina's inspiring actions pumped up the Spanish, and the soldiers were able to not only push the French back out of the city but also launch a counterattack that would force the enemy to lift the siege of Saragossa.

Unfortunately, this wasn't the last the Spanish would hear of Napoleon. The French returned a few months later, and after several weeks of hardcore house-to-house back-alley street fighting, the city's hopelessly outnumbered defenders were forced to capitulate. Agustina was taken as a prisoner of war (she was working as part of an artillery crew during the battle, because after showing off her ability to vaporize organic meatbags the Spanish couldn't possibly have ignored her bravery or mastery with a heavy weapon) and thrown in prison, but promptly led a daring Conan the Barbarian–style prison break from a maximum-security prison camp. Once free, Agustina joined up with the underground Spanish guerilla movement, where she participated in daring raids against French supply depots and military bases, doing her part to try to liberate her people.

After a few years of bitter fighting, the Spanish, along with their British and Portuguese allies, began to break the Grande Armée's double-reverse choke hold on Spain. Agustina's *guerrilleros* were absorbed into the Free Spanish regular army serving under the command of a fellow badass, the Duke of Wellington, and during the campaign to liberate Spain she was placed in command of an artillery battery in Murillo's division. At the Battle of Vitoria in 1813, Agustina de Aragon and her men fought bravely as Wellington's forces defeated the French army and drove them from Spain once and for all. She returned home a hero, was awarded a medal for bravery by King Ferdinand, and was officially commissioned a lieutenant in the Spanish Artillery Corps. She earned an officer's pension for life, and the "Maid of Saragossa" was often seen striding through the streets of the city she loved, proudly wearing her Spanish military officer's saber and jacket with a long petticoat.

FUN FACT:
Shrapnel is named after the man who invented it—General Henry Shrapnel!

HISTORY'S LEAST BADASS PEOPLE

KING JOHN

King John of England went by two equally un-badass nicknames: "Lackland," because he received no inheritance from his father, and "Softsword," because his skill as a military commander vaguely resembled a flaccid penis. The younger brother of King Richard the Lionhearted, John took over when Richard was imprisoned in Austria and promptly started bungling everything up all over the place. He lost several wars, let Normandy be overrun by the French, and allowed himself to be voluntarily and publicly humiliated by the Pope. He also tried to have sex with the wives of a bunch of prominent barons. The nobility weren't huge fans of this, and they hated the guy so much that they refused to serve him, repeatedly deserted him on the battlefield, and eventually forced him (under extreme duress) to sign the Magna Carta—a legal document that drastically limited the power of the king forever. Nowadays, King John is best known as the guy who gets repeatedly crotch-punched into submission in every single iteration of the Robin Hood story.

PHILIP THE FAIR

King Philip IV of France was what we like to refer to as a "mimbo"—a male bimbo. He was a handsome, charming fellow who enjoyed smooth jazz, long walks on the beach, persecuting the Jews, and leading several wildly unsuccessful military campaigns against England, but there really wasn't a whole lot going on upstairs (if you know what I mean). When the Church excommunicated Philip for adultery, he responded by sending a group of thugs to beat up and arrest the Pope. When the prisoner Pope died, Philip appointed a new one, moved the papacy to France, and then posthumously convicted the old (dead) Pope of sodomy, heresy, sorcery, puppy-kickery, and hockery of giant loogies onto the cross. Next, he rounded up the Knights Templar—the legendary holy order of warrior-monks—and had them all brutally tortured and burned at the stake without a trial. Then he stole all their money and turned their headquarters into his summer home.

Jack McCall

"Coward" Jack McCall is hatefully remembered as the gutless bastard who shot Wild Bill Hickok in the back of the head for no reason at all. This slimy cattle rustler randomly walked up to the famous lawman and gunfighter one day while he was playing poker and busted a cap in his brain just to be a dickhead. McCall was tried for the murder by the city of Deadwood and somehow miraculously acquitted in 1876. Believing that he had just gotten away with cold-blooded murder, McCall moved to South Dakota and started talking smack about how awesome he was at gunfighting, but everybody quickly got sick of this loser and arrested him, retried him, and then hanged his stupid ass from the gallows.

Vidkun Quisling

This one-time defense minister of Norway cravenly sold out his own country for the sake of aiding the Nazis. Despite the fact that the Norwegians were more than eager to defend their homeland from Hitler's Fascist storm troopers, Quisling collaborated with the Germans, gave them valuable intelligence, subverted his own country's coastal defenses, and ordered his military commanders not to resist the invasion. Norway quickly capitulated, and Quisling was made prime minister of a puppet Nazi-run government. Vidkun promptly bent over and took it from Hitler, allowing the Reich full access to all the money and raw materials they needed for their wars, and then he put together a Fascist secret police force to beat up his citizens and discourage the rampant dissent that was spreading across his country. Norway's national debt tripled, its finances were pillaged, and Quisling's name became synonymous with miserable treasonous scumbags. He was unceremoniously executed by firing squad in 1945 and is now hatefully remembered by people across Europe.

Canister shot was a particularly nasty type of artillery ammunition. A tin cylinder packed full of small metal balls that spread out in every direction when fired, canister fire (much like grapeshot) basically morphed the cannon into a massive shotgun capable of liquefying any organic matter foolish enough to be standing within a few hundred yards of the barrel.

In 1805 a small company of eighty-eight Polish light cavalrymen under Napoleon went on a ferocious charge up a mountain pass into a battalion of sixteen Spanish cannons. In an unbelievable display of brass nuts, the Poles, riding through a dense fog and a hail of grapeshot, somehow managed to hack the defenders to death with their sabers, force them off the ridge, and capture the guns. The ranking officer, Lieutenant Niegolewski, was later found pinned underneath his horse with nine bayonet wounds and two gunshot wounds to the head. He survived, received the Legion of Honor, and lived to his sixties.

During the Battle of Gettysburg, U.S. general Daniel Sickles's right leg was blown off by cannon fire. Sickles recovered the leg, as well as the cannonball that destroyed it, and donated both items to a museum; they are currently on display at the National Museum of Health and Medicine in Washington, D.C.

U.S.
MARSHAL
2008

29

BASS REEVES

(1838–1910)

He stepped out into the open, 500 yards away, and commenced shooting with his Winchester rifle . . . his first bullet cut a button off my coat, and [the] second cut my bridle rein in two. I shifted my six-shooter and grabbed my Winchester and shot twice. He dropped, and when I picked him up I found that my two bullets had hit within a half inch of each other.

A LONE RIDER CAME TO A LEISURELY HALT ALONG THE SIDE OF THE DUSTY TRAIL. Standing in his path were three of the deadliest outlaws in the Indian Territory—the notorious Brunter brothers. These infamous murderers and thieves were the sort of cop-killing fugitive bastards who would just as soon have immolated you with a blowtorch as urinated on your burning corpse. The men, all looking like they'd just stepped off the set of the movie *Tombstone*, pointed a multiflavored assortment of shotguns and revolvers at the interloper, gesturing for him to dismount from his horse. The rider complied.

Bass Reeves calmly took three steps toward the Brunter brothers, his grim face registering neither fear nor respect for these punk-ass bitches. He was an intimidating, serious-looking man, standing over six feet tall and solidly built. His clothes and equipment were nondescript, covered with the dust from several thousand miles of hard riding, hard fighting, and hard drinking. His beaten-up black hat and long black coat sported a variety of bullet holes and bloodstains. The brass star proudly displayed on his lapel was tarnished with age.

"What the hell are you doing out here, lawman?" the eldest Brunter brother demanded.

Bass spat. "Well, I've come to arrest you," he said in the sort of nonchalant, matter-of-fact way that an evil mechanic tells you that you need

a new transmission. "Got the warrant right here." He reached into his coat pocket, produced a worn, folded-up piece of paper, and casually handed it to the eldest brother.

The Brunters all looked at each other in disbelief. They couldn't believe the stupidity of the man standing before them to have admitted this fact as plainly as he had. Sure, they respected the fact he possessed what obviously must have been solid brass balls, but they were still definitely going to have to kill his ass.

The eldest brother unfolded the warrant and jokingly showed his brothers the lengthy list of serious charges leveled against them. The moment their collective eyes looked down toward the page, Reeves's right hand twitched ever so slightly. Then, in a flash, he closed his fingers around the handle of the .45-caliber Colt Peacemaker strapped to his thigh, drew his weapon, and fired two shots from the hip in rapid succession. Both bullets hit home, sending two Brunters spinning into a dance of death. The eldest brother pointed his gun at the lawman's head, but before he could fire it Bass Reeves was on him. Reeves grabbed the man's revolver with one hand, redirected the weapon so it was pointing up into the air, and then proceeded to pistol-whip the dude unconscious with his free hand. In the span of about twenty seconds, the toughest U.S. marshal west of the Mississippi had just taken out three of the Indian Territory's deadliest criminals.

Starting his life out as a young, illiterate slave belonging to Confederate colonel George Reeves, Bass was an unlikely candidate to become one of the most insane, over-the-top, jerky-chomping ass-kickers in the American West. Sure, he was big, tough, and strong, but for a lot of black slaves living in 1860s Texas there really wasn't a whole lot available in the way of social mobility. Growing up, all Bass really had to look forward to was a lifetime of servitude and bullcrap menial labor.

Well, screw that. One day, Bass and Colonel Reeves were playing a nice friendly game of cards when all of a sudden things became a little less than friendly. The colonel was being a ten-gallon jackoff, so Bass leaned back and cold-cocked the dude in the chops with a lights-out roundhouse punch. Colonel Reeves hit the deck like a sack of lead potatoes, TKOed by a solid George Foreman–esque right hook.

Realizing that he'd basically just signed his own death warrant, Bass decided it was time to get the hell out of Dodge. He fled the plantation and traveled several miles north, crossing the Red River into Indian Territory (present-day Oklahoma). The law of the white man had no sway there, and Bass was soon taken in by the Seminole Indian tribe of Oklahoma.

While living with the Seminoles, Bass learned how to speak the languages of the Five Civilized Tribes, and trained himself in the arts of sweet badassitude. He enthusiastically took up shooting, becoming a deadly marksman with a rifle and developing an incredibly fast draw with pistols. He was ambidextrous, firing equally well with both hands, and dual-wielding pistols Chow Yun Fat–style. He even became such a crack shot with a rifle that that he was actually forbidden from participating in all competitive turkey shoots in the Indian Territories.

After the Thirteenth Amendment made the South a little less sucktastic for black people, Bass Reeves left his adoptive home with the Indians, bought a house in Arkansas, got married, had like ten kids, and lived for a while as a farmer and a horse breeder. That was cool and all, but Bass Reeves was the kind of guy who was always looking to serve up a nice warm knuckle sandwich to anything capable of feeling pain, and he wasn't happy living the boring life of a successful rancher. So when the infamous hardass "hanging judge" Isaac Parker put out a call for U.S. marshals in 1875, Bass was one of the first volunteers ready and willing to bring lethal hordes of armed-and-dangerous felons to justice. Thanks to his mammoth physical strength, tracking skills, intimate knowledge of the terrain, and language proficiency, he easily earned a spot on the force.

Now, back in the 1870s the Indian Territory was a sick murderous nightmare from hell. The vast uncharted expanse—nearly seventy-five thousand square miles of lawless terrain—was infested with fugitives, criminals, and escaped convicts, and was a horrible bitch that feasted on the broken dreams of wayward travelers and drank the blood of anyone foolhardy enough to cross her. It was up to guys like Bass Reeves and other U.S. marshals to go into the dangerous territory, hunt down murderers, rapists, bank robbers, bootleggers, legbooters, and cattle rustlers, and bring some of the West's most dangerous outlaws in for some cowboy-style justice. Bass quickly proved that he was more than up to the task.

Going out on lone-wolf-style missions deep into unknown territory, Reeves relied on his toughness and his wits to survive and bring his men to justice. He used tactics he had learned from the Seminoles to traverse vast distances quickly and leave no trace of his trail. He tracked his foes down, never backed away from a job no matter how many bounties or death threats were leveled at him, and never blinked in the face of extreme danger. In thirty years of service, Bass Reeves arrested more than three thousand fugitives—including one trip to Comanche country when he single-handedly captured and brought in seventeen prisoners. He was also the man who took out the notorious bank robber and murderer Bob Dozier. Dozier had eluded capture from posses and lawmen for several years, but he wasn't quite as adept at eluding a gunshot wound to the brain from Bass effing Reeves.

Another famous Reeves arrest was Belle Starr, the "Bandit Queen of Dallas," who was a hard-drinkin', hard-ridin', hard-swearin', gunfightin' hardass who enjoyed gambling, wearing over-the-top outfits, sleeping around, and raking in cash hand over fist through an organized racket of horse thievery and stagecoach robbery. During her sixteen-year career as an outlaw, Bass Reeves was the only lawman to ever successfully apprehend her.

Despite the fact that he spent much of his life drilling folks in the head with bullets, Reeves's service record was utterly stainless. He killed fourteen men in gunfights—more than Wyatt Earp, Doc Holliday, Billy the Kid, and Wild Bill Hickok—and wounded dozens more, but was never once convicted of unlawful use of force, murder, police brutality, or any of that stupid crap. He couldn't be bribed or paid off, and was so devoted to administering justice that one time he even hunted down and arrested his own son when the kid murdered Bass's daughter-in-law. Unbelievably, Bass Reeves was also apparently more bulletproof than a Steven Seagal movie, seeing as how he was never wounded once during his time on the force. He had his belt shot in two, his hat brim shot away, a button on his coat shot off, and his bridle reins cut in half by bullets, but never felt the sting of a gunshot to any part of his body.

Bass Reeves served valiantly for three decades, and when his branch of the marshals was disbanded in 1907, the seventy-year-old lawman took a job as a police officer with the Muskogee Police Department, walking the beat with a cane and a revolver. He retired two years later and died in 1910, one of the most badass and obscure heroes of the American West and a man whose story is so over-the-top awesome that it pretty much generates its own gravitational field.

BADASS REVOLVERS

Bass Reeves was known to carry a couple of well-worn **Colt Model 1873 Army** revolvers (A) on him at all times. The famous "gun that won the West," this .45-caliber single-action cartridge revolver was the most popular weapon among cowboys, cavalrymen, outlaws, gunfighters, and lawmen of the American frontier. Its nickname, "Peacemaker," should be a good indication that it wasn't a weapon to be screwed around with. Here are some other revolvers you should be aware of.

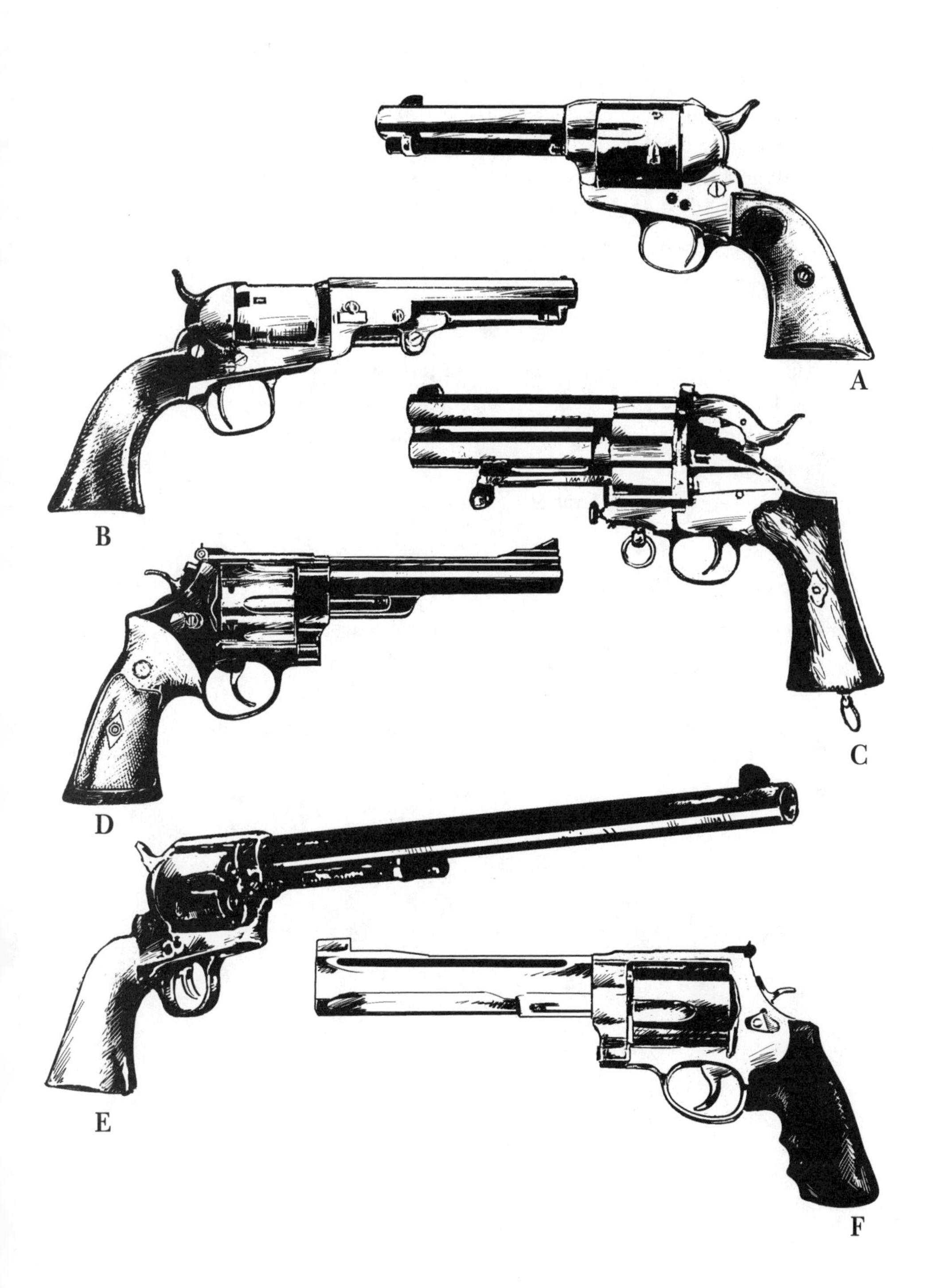
A
B
C
D
E
F

Colt 1851 Navy (B)

This six-round, cap-and-ball .36-caliber pistol was popular among officers and cavalrymen on both sides of the American Civil War of Northern Aggression Between the States, and was also the preferred sidearm of the legendary gunfighter Wild Bill Hickok, Confederate general Robert E. Lee, and globe-trotting British adventurer Sir Richard Francis Burton. This durable and reliable weapon remained popular well after the war, and many Western cowboys later had their trusty revolvers converted to accept cartridge rounds.

Le Mat (C)

The Le Mat was a ridiculously sweet nine-shot cap-and-ball revolver with a short, 16-gauge shotgun barrel mounted just below the main firing chamber. In the hands of guys like the swashbuckling Civil War cavalry commander J. E. B. Stuart, this weapon—half pistol, half sawn-off shotgun—was utterly devastating at close range.

Smith and Wesson Model 29 (D)

The original .44 Magnum, this urination-inducing double-action weapon has been making punks feel unlucky for decades. Popularized by the immortal Dirty Harry Callahan, who characterized it in no uncertain terms as "the most powerful gun in the world," this gun is as intimidating as a Viking helmet and can punch a quarter-sized hole in anything you point it at. And seriously, if it's good enough for Clint Eastwood, it's good enough for everyone.

Buntline Special (E)

Wild West legend has it that Wyatt Earp used to pistol-whip the hell out of varmints, rustlers, and hoodlums with a custom-made Peacemaker with a twelve-inch-long barrel. This massive weapon, known as the Buntline Special, had an attachable walnut wood shoulder stock, giving it the accuracy and range of a rifle while retaining the badassitude of a .45-caliber revolver.

Smith and Wesson Model 500 (F)

The largest revolver out there today, this beast is fifteen inches long and weighs six pounds when empty, so when you inevitably run out of bullets you can easily just bludgeon any surviving bad guys to death with it. It holds five of the biggest bullets ever created for a pistol, the behemoth Smith and Wesson .500 Magnum round, which is about the size of a AA battery and has the stopping power of a Civil War–era smoothbore cannon. Merely pointing this weapon at someone is enough to cause incontinence. Sure, actually shooting it might break your wrist, but at least you can rest assured that this weapon compensates not only for your own penis but also for every single penis in the tristate area.

30

NIKOLA TESLA

(1856–1943)

By scientific application we can project destructive energy in thread-like beams as far as a telescope can discern an object. The range of the beams is only limited by the curvature of the earth. Should you launch an attack in an area covered by these beams, should you, say, send in 10,000 planes or an army of a million, the planes would be brought down instantly and the army destroyed.

PRETTY MUCH EVERYBODY EVEN REMOTELY ASSOCIATED WITH STRATEGY VIDEO GAMES HAS HEARD THE NAME TESLA—THE SERBIAN GOD OF LIGHTNING'S OMNIPRESENT, EVER-ZAPPING COILS HAVE BEEN RUINING THE LIVES OF DIGITAL SOLDIERS AND GIBBING U.S. WAR MACHINES INTO SPARE PARTS SINCE THE RELEASE OF COMMAND AND CONQUER: RED ALERT IN 1996—BUT SURPRISINGLY FEW PEOPLE THESE DAYS ARE FAMILIAR WITH THE LIFE AND TIMES OF ONE OF HUMANKIND'S MOST ECCENTRIC, BADASS, AND VOLUMETRICALLY INSANE SCIENTIFIC SUPERFREAKS.

First off, Nikola Tesla was brilliant. And not just like Ken Jennings trivia master brilliant, either—I mean like "Holy jeebus, my head just exploded from all the awesome" brilliant. The Croatian-born engineer spoke eight languages, almost single-handedly developed technology that harnessed the power of electricity for household use, and invented things like electrical generators, FM radio, remote control, robots, spark plugs, fluorescent lights, and giant-ass machines that shoot enormous, brain-frying lightning bolts all over the place. He had an unyielding, steel-trap photographic memory and an innate ability to visualize even the most complex pieces of machinery—the guy did advanced calculus and physics equations in his freaking head, memorized entire books at a time, and successfully pulled off scientific experiments that modern-day technology *still* can't replicate. For instance, in 2007 a group of lesser geniuses at MIT got all pumped up out of their minds because they wirelessly transmitted energy a distance of seven feet through the air. Nikola Tesla once lit two hundred lightbulbs from a power source twenty-six miles away, and he did it in 1899 with a machine he built from spare parts in the middle of a godforsaken wasteland of a mountain range. To this day, nobody can really figure out how the hell he pulled that crap off, because two-thirds of the schematics existed only in the darkest recesses of Tesla's all-powerful brain.

Of course, much like many other eccentric giga-geniuses and diabolical masterminds, Tesla was also completely insane. He was prone to nervous breakdowns, claimed to receive weird visions in the middle of the night, spoke to pigeons, and occasionally thought he was receiving electromagnetic signals from extraterrestrials on Mars. He was also obsessive-compulsive and hated round objects, human hair, jewelry, and anything that wasn't divisible by three. He slept just two to three hours per night and remained celibate for his entire life. Basically, Nikola Tesla was the ultimate mad scientist, which is seriously rad.

Another sweet thing about Tesla is that he conducted the sort of crazy experiments that generally result in hordes of angry villages breaking down the door to your lab with torches and pitchforks. One time, while he was working on magnetic resonance, he discovered the resonant frequency of the earth and caused an earthquake so powerful that it almost obliterated the building on Fifth Avenue in New York that housed his Frankenstein castle of a laboratory. Stuff was flying off the walls, the drywall was breaking apart, the cops were coming after him, and Tesla had to smash his device with a sledgehammer to keep it from demolishing an entire city block. Later, he boasted that he could have built a device powerful enough to split the earth in two. Nobody dared him to prove it.

Tesla also ordered the construction of the Wardenclyffe Tower or Tesla Tower, a giant building shaped like an erect penis to house the largest Tesla coil ever built. The massive structure, ostensibly designed to wirelessly transmit power, has been cited as a potential cause of the mysterious 1908 Tunguska event—a ten-megaton blast that detonated in the wastelands above central Russia, completely deforested everything unlucky enough to be located within 830 square miles of the blast site, and left an eerie glow that could be seen in the skies above Europe for several days. While nothing has ever successfully proven Tesla's involvement in the ass-destroyingly huge explosion, it's pretty awesome that this guy could potentially have detonated a weapon a thousand times more powerful than the nuclear bomb that destroyed Hiroshima, and have done it back before they'd even invented the submachine gun.

During his adventures blinding half of the world with science, Nikola Tesla harnessed the power of Niagara Falls into the first hydroelectric power plant, constructed a bath designed to cleanse the human body of germs using nothing but electricity, and created a 130-foot-long bolt of lightning from one of his massive coils (a feat that to this day remains the world record for man-made lightning), but perhaps his most badass invention was his face-melting, tank-destroying, supersecret atomic death ray. In the 1920s he claimed to be working on a tower that could potentially have spewed forth a gigantic beam of ionized particles capable of disintegrating aircraft from two hundred miles away and blinking most people out of existence like something out of a Flash Gordon or Buck Rogers comic. His weapon, known as the teleforce beam, allegedly shot ball lightning at sixty million volts, liquefying its targets with enough voltage to vaporize steel, and while it could shoot farther than

two hundred miles, its effectiveness beyond that range was limited by the curvature of the earth. Luckily for all humans, this crazy crap never came to fruition—most of the schematics and plans existed only in Tesla's head, and when he died of heart failure in 1943, little hard data on the project existed. Still, J. Edgar Hoover and the FBI confiscated all his personal effects and locked them away anyway, just to be safe.

Despite being incredibly popular during his day, now Tesla remains largely overlooked among lists of the greatest inventors and scientists of all time. Thomas Edison gets all the glory for discovering the lightbulb, but it was his onetime assistant and lifelong archnemesis, Nikola Tesla, who made the breakthroughs in alternating-current technology

that allowed people to use electricity to cheaply power appliances and lighting in their homes. They constantly fought about whether to use alternating or direct current (their bitter blood feud resulted in both men being snubbed by the Nobel Prize committee), but ultimately Tesla was the one who delivered the fatal kick to the crotch that ended the battle: at the 1893 World's Fair in Chicago, his AC generators illuminated the entire experience, marking the first time that an event of that magnitude had ever taken place under the glow of artificial light. He also demonstrated how safe AC power was by running two hundred thousand volts of electricity through his own body just to be awesome. Today, all homes and appliances run on Tesla's AC current.

Nikola Tesla was an incredible supergenius whose intellect placed him dangerously on the precipice between great scientific mind and utter madness. He held seven hundred patents at the time of his death, made groundbreaking discoveries in the fields of physics, robotics, steam turbine engineering, and magnetism, and once melted one of his assistants' hands by overloading it with X-rays—which isn't really scientific but is still pretty cool. And honestly, if there was one man on this planet who was ever capable of single-handedly destroying the earth through his insane scientific discoveries, it was Tesla. That alone should qualify him as a pretty righteous badass.

Thomas Edison spent much of his life engineering a massive mud-slinging propaganda campaign aimed at slandering Tesla's good name, as well as his alternating-current method of bringing electricity into homes. Edison's most brazen display of the dangers of AC power was when he invented the world's first working electric chair, demonstrating it on August 6, 1890, by electrocuting an axe murderer named William Kemmler. One reporter described the event as "an awful spectacle, far worse than hanging."

Norway
Estonia
Scotland
Latvia
Lithuania
Denmark
Netherlands
Ireland
Belarus
Poland
England
Berlin
Germany
London
Belgium
Axis
Czech
Ukr
Paris
France
Austria
Hungary
Switzerland
Romania
Italy
Yugoslavia
Bulgaria
Rome
Spain
Portugal
Greece
Turkey
Tunisia
Algeria
Mediterranean Sea
Morocco
Egypt
N

Section IV
The Modern Era
Moscow
Russia
Black Sea
Caspian Sea
Iraq
Iran
Lebanon
Israel
Afghanistan
Pakistan
Saudi
Arabia

2008

31

MANFRED VON RICHTHOFEN

(1892–1918)

I no longer know any mercy. For that reason I attacked him a second time, whereupon the aeroplane fell apart in my stream of bullets. The wings fell away like pieces of paper and the fuselage went raring down like a stone on fire.

DOGFIGHTING ISN'T WHAT IT USED TO BE. Sure, there's something to be said for doing insane barrel rolls, hurtling through the atmosphere at Mach Five Million, flipping on the afterburners, and taking it right into the danger zone, but at the end of the day most modern fighter pilots are really just launching missiles at the giant green blobs on their heads-up displays. Back in the day of the Great War, however, when fighter planes were little more than flying metallic deathtraps with large-caliber machine guns strapped to their wings, dogfighting was a much more up-close-and-personal affair. Taking down an airplane from a range of only a couple of hundred feet with nothing more than a few hundred bullets isn't exactly like shooting hippies in the face with a water cannon—it takes steel nerves, the lightning-quick reaction time of a schizophrenic cat, and the ability to accurately use the iron sights of a 7.92 mm machine gun from a standing position while deftly maneuvering a barely airworthy flying contraption so that it evades enemy bullets and doesn't crash nose-first into a mountain and explode into flaming shrapnel.

Alternately known to cowering Allied pilots by the dope nicknames "the Red Baron," "the Bloody Baron," and "that goddamned Richthofen," Manfred von Richthofen was undisputedly the most balls-out and successful airplane-destroying maniac to ever hop into the cockpit of a piece-of-crap triplane and send dozens of enemy fighter planes spiraling down in flames. He kicked ass in the skies above France in a blood-red death plane that was seemingly impervious to gunfire, and to most British, Canadian, French, and American pilots the mere mention of his name was more frightening than the thought of being woken in the middle of the night by the sound of a chainsaw revving up.

An accomplished rifle marksman and an avid hunter from an early age, Manfred always had a rather keen and moderately unhealthy interest in shooting things with firearms until they were dead. He was also a damn good horseman, a tack-eating hardass, and an unyielding competitor who thought that anything less than the best was a felony. One time in cadet school he participated in a horse race, and the jackass horse had the audacity to throw Manfred into the mud. Richthofen face-planted the turf and broke his collarbone, but this only served to make

him pissed off—he got up, dragon-punched the horse, jumped back in the saddle, and rode the final forty-five miles with a goddamned broken clavicle. Oh yeah, and he won the race.

Richthofen enlisted in the cavalry when he finished cadet school. Of course, developments such as barbed wire, trenches, hand grenades, and machine guns made most cavalry about as useful as a bachelor's degree in liberal arts, so Richthofen spent his first days on the Western Front shoveling horse manure, sleeping in ankle-deep mud, and fantasizing about the day when he would finally get to impale Frenchmen with his sharpened, gleaming saber. But Richthofen wasn't the sort of bastard who was going to be content sitting around with his thumb up his rectum when he could be out there turning British people into giant bloody conflagrations, so despite the fact that he'd never even so much as flown in an airplane before, he applied for a transfer to the German air service. He received a little bit of training (pull back on the stick to go higher, don't crash into any mountains, shoot as many people as you can, etc.) and was shipped out to the front.

It wasn't long before he got the opportunity to start putting his soon-to-be-infamous airplane-smashing skills to use. He scored his first kill on September 17, 1916, blowing the ass out of a French scout plane and igniting a ravenous thirst for human blood so intense that it makes the Vampire Lestat look like a triage nurse at St. Jude's. In under a month Richthofen took out five planes, officially earning the title of fighter ace. Soon afterward he destroyed a rogue bomber that had been secretly dispatched to strafe the headquarters of a prominent Austrian duke. The rescued nobleman was so pumped up about this daring display of awesomeness that he personally pinned a one-of-a-kind Medal of Duke-Saving +1 on Richthofen's chest.

About a month later, the baron found himself squaring off against notable British hardass Lanoe Hawker, a nine-kill ace, winner of the Victoria Cross, and the most famous and successful aviator in His

Majesty's service. Well, the baron didn't give a flying fornication in the direction of a rolling donut about this dude's reputation—he capped Hawker in the face and sent his corpse careening nose-first into the ground, where it exploded into tiny pieces of shrapnel (which subsequently exploded again). By January of 1917, the twenty-five-year-old Richthofen had shot down sixteen bogeys and was awarded the prestigious Blue Max—a great old Atari game, and the ultimate award for military badassitude offered by the German Empire, a place that was pretty much universally known for its military badasses.

Next, Manfred von Richthofen transformed his squadron, Jasta 11, into the foremost fighting unit in Europe. The cocky, swashbuckling aviator's prestige allowed him to recruit the best pilots and top-scoring aces in the empire to his crew, and with Richthofen flying at the head of the formation, Jasta 11 became the ultimate dream team from hell. Never was this more painfully obvious than during the carnage of April 1917, a time better known to the British as "Bloody April." The Royal

Air Force lost a third of their pilots—912 men—in the span of thirty days, with Richthofen accounting for twenty-one of those kills personally. By the end of the month, he was the war's ace of aces, having added fifty-two fiery infernos to his scorecard. That's like wiping out an entire professional football team, and MVR did it back in the days before heat-seeking missiles, photon torpedoes, and multibarreled rotary autocannons that shot giant silver hollow-point bullets filled with C-4, chlorine gas, and sulfuric acid.

The famous I-dare-you-to-screw-with-me red paint job was symbolic of the Red Baron's fighting style. He wanted to be seen by friend and foe alike and go completely balls-out, full throttle, guns blazing all the damn time. He didn't have some prissy flyboy piloting style, either. He forbade his pilots from doing barrel rolls, loop-de-loops, and other such acrobatic garbage nonsense, requiring them instead to train relentlessly in machine gun marksmanship and ambush tactics. In fact, by most accounts, Richthofen was only marginally capable as a pilot. He would simply lie in wait for his enemies and then launch his plane full speed in steep dives with the sun at his back, pouncing on Allied pilots like a head-cleaving ninja getting the drop on an unsuspecting feudal lord. Not only did his unique fighting style help him score more kills than any other pilot in the war, but his leadership abilities and tactical skill melded the entire squadron into a formidable assortment of highly trained, über-efficient plane-killers.

Jasta 11 shot down one hundred Allied planes in just three months, and Richthofen was then made commander of Jagdgeschwader 1, a fighter wing consisting of four squadrons and ten consonants. He led JG1 until he was hospitalized in July 1917 when a damned aircraft machine gun bullet capped him in the skull. He was totally hardcore, though: he spent his time off hunting in the forests, getting wicked headaches, and thinking about how awesome it was going to be when he finally got back into the air. The German government asked him to retire, knowing that if he were to die it would be a serious blow to imperial morale, but he was like, "Dude, do I look like some kind of pussy?" and hopped right back in the cockpit. A mere forty days after taking a gunshot wound to the damn brain Richthofen got right back to the business of machine gunning Brits and Frenchmen to death like it was his job (which it was).

The Red Baron was never really the same after returning from his head injury, which is kind of understandable because no matter how hardcore you are, you're probably still going to be a little screwed up when a machine gun bullet splinters your skull. His kill total plateaued, and on April 21, 1918, the twenty-six-year-old pilot was shot down simultaneously by a massive horde of British, Australian, Canadian, and Scottish fighter planes, machine guns, zeppelins, large-caliber handguns, tanks, slingshots, water balloons, Stinger missiles, and antiaircraft artillery. The Allies recovered his body and gave him a full military burial with honors; they knew they had to do this worthy adversary justice, especially since he had rocked their asses so hard.

Manfred von Richthofen ended his career with a brain-destroyingly astonishing total of eighty kills, and there were a couple of other adequately jacked-up aircraft that were never officially confirmed. He was undisputedly the top fighter pilot of the war, a twenty-time ace, and one of the biggest ass-kickers to ever put on a leather jacket and a pair of flight goggles and leave a trail of scrap metal and fireballs in his engine wash.

Voytek the Soldier Bear

A Syrian brown bear cub taken in by a Polish artillery regiment, Voytek morphed into a massive ass-kicking soldier who enjoyed three things—smoking cigarettes, drinking beer, and Greco-Roman wrestling. This alcoholic, Nazi-killing bear was enlisted as a private in the Polish military,

marched on his hind legs alongside the troops, and actually (seriously, no kidding) carried artillery shells to the front lines during the Battle of Monte Cassino in southern Italy. He also once thwarted a spy by cornering the dude in a bathhouse and growling at the terrified saboteur until the dumbass cried out for help and surrendered. Voytek served with the Poles throughout the war, then lived out the rest of his life in the Edinburgh Zoo, where his old comrades often used to visit him—throwing smokes down into his waiting hands or jumping into the enclosure to wrestle with him for old times' sake. Voytek still appears on the official unit insignia of the Polish 22nd Transport Artillery Company.

Cher Ami

This brave carrier pigeon from the United States Signal Corps's 1st Pigeon Division carried vital information between commanders throughout World War I, making trips in excess of nineteen miles in just about twenty minutes of flight time. When the American "Lost Battalion" was stranded in the Argonne Forest and started getting seriously jacked up by their own artillery, Cher Ami was dispatched to stop the barrage. During his dangerous flight, the bird lost an eye and a leg, but still delivered the message in time to save the Marines from complete destruction. This avian hero's incredible effort earned him a wooden leg, a retirement pension, and the French Croix de Guerre. Cher Ami survived the war, and his taxidermied corpse is currently on display at the Smithsonian.

Peruna

The official mascot of Southern Methodist University, this three-foot-tall Shetland pony might not look like the second coming of the nightmarish, fire-breathing black steed that relentlessly carried the Headless Horseman after Ichabod Crane, but he does hold the badass distinction of being the only live mascot to ever kill another live mascot in the middle of an athletics contest. On the sidelines of a football game in 1936, the Fordham ram got a little too close for comfort, so Peruna kicked it in the head, killing it instantly. Peruna, who is named after an old-school Prohibition-era alcoholic beverage, also knocked down the University of Texas longhorn with a back kick and tried to hump Texas Tech University's horse mascot in his mad rampage of carnage.

Sinbad the Sea Dog

This homeless mutt was adopted by the men of the Coast Guard cutter *George W. Campbell* in 1937 and sailed on many dangerous missions throughout the North Atlantic during World War II. As "chief dog" on the *Campbell*, Petty Officer Sinbad served the Coast Guard for fourteen years, crossing the ocean dozens of times and hitting the bars with the men at every stop along the way. He loved whisky, beer, and harassing sheep—a practice that earned him a permanent ban from ever setting paw in the country of Greenland. On one particularly ass-tastic mission in 1943, the *Campbell* was attacked by five German U-boats, suffering torpedo damage to her hull but somehow emerging victorious. Sinbad stayed on board and did what he could to cheer up the survivors, all of whom appreciated the friendly companionship of their best bud. Today, a bronze statue of the sea dog sits in the mess hall of the *Campbell*.

The highest-scoring fighter ace of all time was the German pilot Erich Hartmann. Fighting the Soviet Union in World War II, Hartmann recorded an unbelievable 352 aerial victories over the span of 1,400 combat missions, and survived having nineteen different planes shot out from under him. Fittingly, after the war he commanded a West German fighter wing named after Richthofen.

World War I pitted the armies of the Central Powers—the German Empire, Austria-Hungary, and the Ottoman Empire—against the Entente Alliance of France, Russia, Britain, Italy, and the United States. Seeing as how none of the Central Powers currently exists today, I'll let you go ahead and guess who won.

2008

32

HENRY LINCOLN JOHNSON

(1897–1929)

No, I ain't scared. I came over here to do my bit, and I'll do it. I was just letting you know there's liable to be some tall scrappin' around this post tonight.

IN EARLY 1918, HENRY LINCOLN JOHNSON WAS WORKING AS A HUMBLE REDCAP IN THE NEW YORK CITY SUBWAY SYSTEM, WHICH BASICALLY MEANS THAT HIS JOB REVOLVED AROUND PICKING UP INCREDIBLY HEAVY THINGS AND PUTTING THEM WHEREVER THE MAN TOLD HIM TO. As you can probably imagine, this type of work sucks serious donkey tits. So when the United States decided it was sick of Germany's bad attitude and joined in the twenty-four-hour all-night European booze-and-babes fiesta known as World War I, Johnson knew that this was a perfect opportunity to quit his stupid job, go to France, and do something epically awesome. He enlisted in the New York National Guard and was shipped out to Europe as a member of the all-black 369th Infantry Division, a formidable unit of soldiers better known as the Harlem Hellfighters.

Unfortunately, early on in the campaign the Hellfighters really didn't have the opportunity to dole out these much-needed ass-beatings because American High Command decided to give the African American regiment every single bullcrap job on the Western Front. They unloaded cargo vessels, dug ditches, and did all sorts of lame menial tasks, the extent of which fell somewhere between janitorial work and dishwashing on the Badassery Scale. Finally, after weeks of this with no end in sight, the French generals were like, "Well, if you won't let these guys get in there and start busting heads, then we will," and they decided to see whether or not "Harlem Hellfighters" was more than just a clever name. The 369th and Johnson were transferred to the French military command and were immediately pressed into service in the Argonne Forest.

The Hellfighters didn't disappoint. They saw 191 consecutive days of combat across the Western Front—more than any other American unit in the war—and were the first Allied regiment to cross the Rhine River into Germany. Despite being underequipped and woefully undersupplied (they usually only had one wool blanket available for every four men in the unit), the two thousand officers and men of the 369th won over a hundred medals for bravery from the French government, and came to be fearfully known by the German soldiers as "the bloodthirsty black men." Despite all of their battlefield successes, perhaps the greatest and most notable display of Harlem Hellfighter badassitude came on the night of May 14, 1918, in a thermonuclear bloodbath that would come to be known only as the Battle of Henry Johnson.

Sergeant Johnson and his buddy Needham Roberts were put on the graveyard shift of guard duty, and while on watch an entire platoon of about thirty German infantrymen rushed their position. Johnson fought bravely, but was hit with a grenade, stabbed, and shot in the chest twice with a revolver, while Roberts was drilled with a shotgun and knocked to the floor like a sack of potatoes that had just been blasted at close range with a well-packed charge of double-aught buckshot. The Germans rushed in, grabbed Roberts, and started to haul him away as a prisoner.

Well, Henry Lincoln Johnson wasn't about to let that fly. This card-carrying Hellfighter managed to somehow stagger to his feet and charge after the Germans, firing his rifle and chucking grenades like a madman. When he finally caught the poor bastards, his gun jammed, so he beat the snot out of them with the rifle butt. When he broke his rifle over some jerk's head, he then whipped out the ferocious twelve-inch Jason Voorhees–style bolo knife he always kept strapped to his belt.

Now try to picture this for a minute. You've got a dude who's already been wounded *twenty-one damn times* with everything from rifles to hand grenades, armed only with a bloody machete, in the midst of about twenty German soldiers, and he's going off like a crazy-ass samurai hacking these bastards to pieces while they stand around like the evil black-clad ninjas from a bad 1970s kung fu flick. Despite massive injuries, Johnson slashed, stabbed, bobbed, weaved, and hacked at anything that moved. Every time he was knocked down he got back up, and at one point a dude jumped on his back and tried to choke him out, so Johnson judo-flipped the guy over his shoulder and stuck him in the ribs with his blade. In his intense battle rage Johnson killed four men, including the German platoon commander, critically wounded an additional twelve, and drove the remainder of the enemy back into the woods. When the coast was clear, Johnson strode over the huge steaming pile of dismembered corpses and dragged Needham Roberts back to his foxhole. The next morning, when reinforcements arrived, they found the two seriously wounded men sitting together singing jazz songs around a blazing campfire.

For his heroic stand in the Argonne Forest, Johnson became the first American to ever receive the Croix de Guerre, the highest award for bravery offered by the French government. Just in case you think "the highest award for bravery offered by the French Government" is an oxymoron, I should mention that he also received the U.S. Distinguished Service Cross and was nominated for the Congressional Medal of Honor. His one-man frenzy against dozens of enemy troops made him a hero in the States almost overnight, and the soft-spoken sergeant's hospital bed was soon flooded with a deluge of letters from admirers back home. Despite the fact that he was pretty much covered from head to toe in incredibly painful, life-threatening injuries, Johnson passed up the opportunity to take a free ride home, refusing to be separated from the men in his unit. He remained on the Hellfighters' muster roll until the end of the war, at which point he and the rest of his comrades returned home as heroes, receiving a ticker-tape parade down Fifth Avenue in New York City. Johnson became a public speaker, had a son who went on to be one of the Tuskegee Airmen (no small feat of awesomeness in and of itself), and is now remembered as one of the toughest American heroes of World War I.

The pilots of the 332nd Fighter Group, better known as the "Tuskegee Airmen," made a name for themselves by blowing the hell out of anything and everything over the skies of Germany, Italy, and North Africa during World War II. Fighting the Nazis wherever and whenever the opportunity presented itself, these daring African American pilots flew 15,000 missions, won 111 aerial victories, destroyed hundreds of planes on the ground, derailed 57 trains, and flew over 200 consecutive escort missions without losing a single bomber.

A bolo is an extra-long, single-edged mix between a knife and a machete. Originally designed in the Philippines and ranging from nine inches to three feet in length, it was generally used by peasants to hack through dense underbrush and harvest sugarcane. Despite the bolo's seemingly innocuous agricultural roots, badass Filipino berserkers did manage to use these terrifying melee weapons rather effectively in their numerous wars against the Spanish and the Americans.

Archduke Franz Ferdinand hated the sight of creases or wrinkles, so any time he appeared in public he demanded to be sewn into his suit. Unfortunately, this ended up being his downfall—after he was shot by a Serbian assassin in Sarajevo, he was unable to receive prompt medical attention because the medics couldn't get his jacket off without cutting the entire suit apart.

BELLEDIN

33

ELIOT NESS

(1903–1957)

We were a rugged-looking crew, I suppose, to a man unaccustomed to violence.

CHICAGO, **1929.** An American war zone. A once-proud city now dominated by a seamy underbelly of remorseless gangsters, machine-gun-toting bootleggers, angry street prostitutes dancing the Charleston, and crooked jackass cops on the take from the mob. An intricate web of lies, corruption, and murder kept the terrified citizenry firmly wedged between the fat, ever-clenching fingers of the steel-plated, gonad-mashing iron fist of one man—the notorious criminal kingpin "Scarface Al" Capone, a guy so tough that the mere mention of his name caused grown men to go into respiratory failure and reach for their inhalers. An uncompromising, dangerous murderer who had violently clawed and scratched his way up from the ranks of Mafia enforcer and built his vast criminal empire one bullet-riddled corpse at a time, Capone would just as soon have pumped you in the face with a clip of .45-caliber ammunition and beaten your family to death with the empty gun as spit on your mother's corpse. The far-reaching tendrils of his all-powerful syndicate cast a Mecha-Godzilla-sized shadow over the city; no one was safe from his terrible and often misguided wrath, his overpowering garlic breath, or his obscenely foul temper. Rival gangs, cops, innocent douchebags, and even federal prosecutors fell victim to his uncontrollable 'roid rage as this brazen tyrant ran his brutal regime through a steady diet of fear, bribery, and delicious freshly baked lasagnas. Those who refused to play ball on Capone's recreational-league softball team of murder, blackmail, and extortion quickly found themselves on the wrong end of a Louisville Slugger—and even though Scarface's swing wasn't exactly the second coming of the Great Bambino, trust me when I say that you didn't want to have this guy playing home run derby with your skull.

Only one man had the gigantic titanium nut sack to stand up to this madman and his army of fedora-wearing gangster hoodlums: federal agent Eliot Ness. Ness was an out-of-control freight train of justice who slugged punks in the jaw with brass knuckles and saved the questions for the AP American history exam, and he alone had the guts to tell the toughest mob boss in U.S. history to go to hell—and fornicate with livestock once he got there.

The twenty-eight-year-old Ness had served on the Treasury Department's Prohibition Bureau for a couple of years, compiling an impressive list of arrests despite the notable setback that pretty much every other bastard in his outfit was on Al Capone's payroll. Totally bitter that this large, unwieldy force was roughly as impotent as a eunuch with acute radiation poisoning, Eliot decided to put together his own crew—ten men, hand-selected for their detective skills, toughness, and loyalty to the cause of pistol-whipping Mafia thugs unconscious with their boners and confiscating all their beer.

The year before, Al Capone's massive criminal syndicate had raked in

$75 million in illicit bootlegging operations. Ness's moderately suicidal mission was to demolish this obscenely lucrative racket at its source by locating Capone's supersecret beer-manufacturing plants and using a hatchet to violently annihilate everything in his wheelhouse. Eliot figured that if he could put the breweries out of commission by repeatedly bashing homemade stills, beer barrels, and Mafia brewmasters with a gigantic axe, Capone would run out of money—and once he could no longer afford to buy off corrupt cops and politicians, his entire criminal empire would collapse around him.

Of course, the Mafia is pretty good at concealing things they don't want the feds to find, and Capone's breweries were certainly no

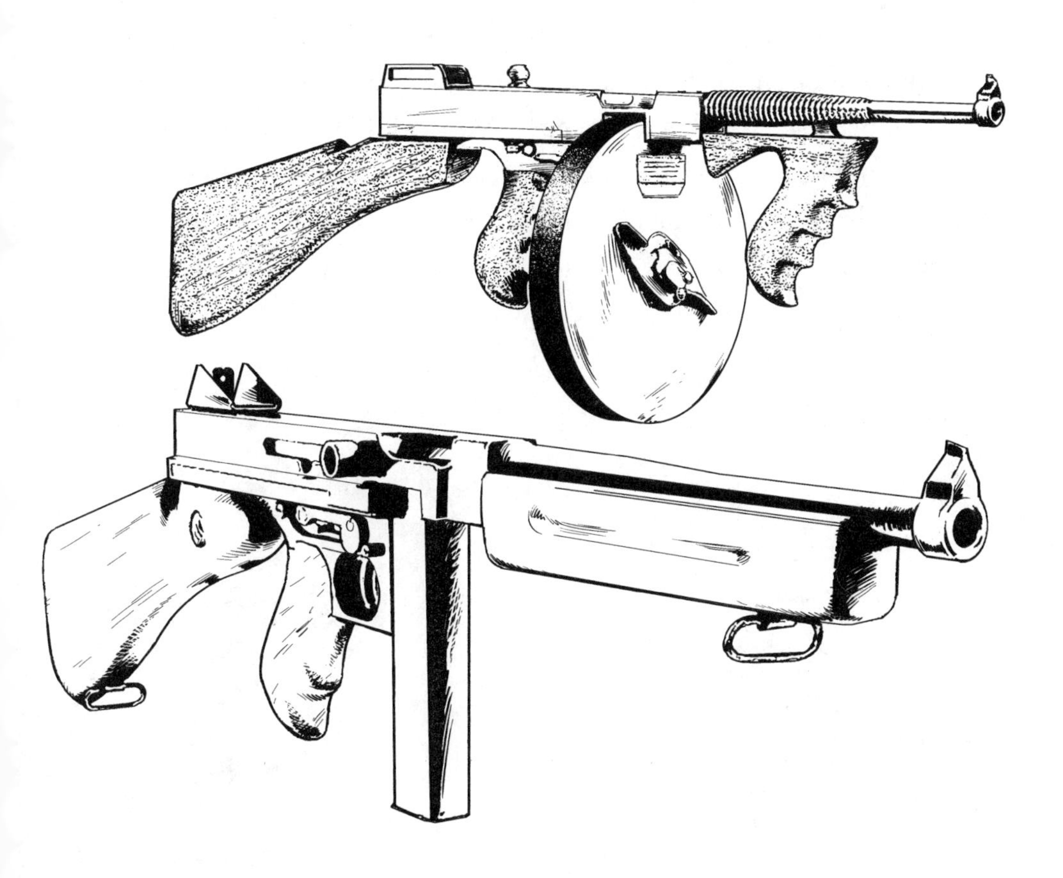

exception. It took some badass, hard-boiled 1920s pulp-fiction-style detective work to track these hideouts down, but Eliot Ness was more than up to the task. Ness and his men tailed delivery trucks, went on stakeouts in seedy motels, and set up clandestine wiretaps on Mafia phone lines. Since this was back in the days before the government could just shoot you in the face with a satellite beam and download the entire contents of your brain onto a DVD, Ness's men needed to personally access the phone lines and cross the wires by hand. As you can probably imagine, plugging into the Capone brothers' private business line (an act Ness accomplished) was not a task undertaken by men who were testosterone-challenged.

Once Ness and his crew tracked down the locations of the syndicate's secret breweries, his plan for assaulting these fortified installations was just as straightforward as he was. He simply drove up outside the building in a completely insane ten-ton flatbed death truck fitted with a gigantic custom-built steel bumper that looked like a cross between a medieval torture device and the cowcatcher on a nineteenth-century locomotive, revved the engine, and plowed right through the front door of the building at top speed. The 1920s version of the A-Team van

would obliterate the brewery doors in a giant cloud of twisted iron and splintered wood, and before any stupefied mob thugs had any damn clue what the cake-eating whomp-ass was going on, Ness would leap out of the still-moving vehicle, train his sawed-off shotgun on the nearest gangster, and dare somebody to make a move.

Eliot Ness was basically like a head-smashing mix between Sherlock Holmes, Batman, and a cinder block. While leading a one-man war against the nation's most dangerous criminal organization, Eliot Ness crashed through the sixth-story windows of a warehouse to get the drop on some punks, chased down a fugitive while hanging on to the running board of a speeding cop car, sweet-talked hot babe secretaries for information, and leapt onto the tailgate of a truck full of murderous cop-killing gangsters to try to bring them down. One time, Ness, who was trained in jujitsu, actually took a thug out by judo-chopping him in the throat. Seriously, he just kung-fued the ass out of the dude with a Captain James T. Kirk–style knife hand to the goddamned neck. Another time, a Mafia enforcer thought it would be a catastrophically brilliant idea to tear up a federal warrant and throw it in Eliot's face. Ness stared at the hulking goon for a moment, his expression as grim as a funeral, and then, out of nowhere, belted the dude unconscious with one punch.

Now, here in America there are two things you really aren't supposed to mess with—Texas and the Italian Mafia. First, Capone generously offered Ness a cash bribe of $2,000 a week. Ness, whose yearly salary amounted to $2,800 (before taxes), responded by having the local paper photograph him giving Capone the finger and quote him as saying, "Big Al can eat a giant bowl of my dick"—an act of defiance that led the press to anoint his squad with the sweet nickname "the Untouchables." When it became obvious that Ness wasn't going to be bought off, the syndicate decided it would be cheaper (and easier) to just bust a cap in his ass and leave him in a ditch somewhere. They broke into his office, tried to run him down in the street, planted a car bomb under his hood . . . hell, they even dispatched a hardcore Mafia hit man to whack him, but Ness discovered the plot, ambushed his would-be assassin, and pummeled the guy unconscious with the butt of his service revolver.

Not even the ever-constant fear of being splattered across the streets of Chicago by cheesed-off mobsters could stop Ness from his mad desire to annihilate Al Capone's bootlegging operations. The Untouchables closed thirty breweries, each capable of producing hundreds of barrels of booze a day, seized forty-five delivery trucks, and destroyed millions of dollars' worth of liquor, beer, and brewing equipment. They successfully dried up all illicit booze operations in Chicago, put Capone's mob in dire financial straits, and captured stacks of critical evidence that would eventually be used by the Treasury Department to nail Scarface for tax evasion. When Al Capone was arrested, convicted, and sentenced to eleven years in federal pound-me-in-the-ass prison in 1931, it was Special Agent Eliot Ness who personally escorted the handcuffed mob boss to the train station for his trip to the pen.

But that's not even the end of Ness's story. After bringing down the Capone mob, he was sent to Kentucky, Tennessee, and Ohio to purge the mountains of renegade moonshiners while hillbillies took potshots at him with their varmint-huntin' rifles and played "Dueling Banjos" with their amps cranked all the way up. Later, as the director of public safety for the city of Cleveland, he eliminated corruption in the police department, declared war on the Mafia, established the city's first police academy, and guillotined the aristocracy. He also went on to win the Navy's Meritorious Service Citation for smashing prostitution rackets on military bases across the East Coast during World War II (probably much to the dismay of many sailors). He died of heart failure in 1957.

The Thompson submachine gun, developed in 1916 by U.S. Army colonel John Thompson (no relation), accepted two different magazines of .45-caliber ammunition. The straight, twenty-round clip was popular among American GIs serving in World War II, while the circular, fifty-round drum was employed in the arguably more serious business of drive-by shootings and crazy 1920s gangland warfare.

2008

34

JACK CHURCHILL

(1912–1996)

In my opinion, sir, any officer who goes into battle without his sword is improperly dressed.

JACK MALCOLM THORPE FLEMING CHURCHILL WAS IN THE MIDST OF HIS SECOND TOUR OF DUTY WITH THE BRITISH ARMY WHEN WORLD WAR II BROKE OUT IN EUROPE. In his first hitch in the queen's service he spent most of his time learning to play the bagpipes, riding his motorcycle across the entire Indian subcontinent, and representing England in the 1939 World Archery Championship, but he really hadn't had the opportunity to prove to the world that he was an officer, a gentlemen, and a righteously awesome destroyer of Nazi asses who eagerly undertook obscenely dangerous missions with an almost fanatical zeal for adventure. This time, things would be different.

Churchill went to France in 1940 to assist the rest of the British Expeditionary Force in their mission to reinforce the Maginot Line, but when Hitler decided to send his goose-stepping legions to break all the toys in France, the Brits found themselves right in the middle of a gigantic crapstorm. The Nazi blitzkrieg ripped through France like a maelstrom of heavily armored steel death as elite SS panzer regiments obliterated the French army and occupied the country in the span of just a few weeks. This put the Brits in a particularly nasty spot—they quickly found themselves surrounded, backed up against the sea by the unstoppable onslaught, and doing whatever they could to stall the Germans' seemingly inexorable advance.

It was up to men like "Fighting Jack" Churchill to buy the British Expeditionary Force time to load up their transports and escape, only instead of flying snowspeeders over the desolate wastes of some remote ice planet, Jack had an even more balls-out plan. Riding his trusty motorcycle and armed with an English longbow, he got medieval on the Germans' asses, launching raids on enemy supply depots and shooting Nazis in the heart with a quiver full of steel-tipped arrows. As if that isn't insane enough, Churchill also carried a Scottish claybeg broadsword with him at all times, and you've really got to love a guy who didn't have a problem battling machine-gun-toting Nazi storm troopers with a pair of weapons that have been obsolete since the fifteenth century.

Despite being shot in the neck by a goddamned Nazi machine gun, "Mad Jack" Churchill battled throughout the French countryside, at one point winning the Military Cross for bravery by rescuing a wounded officer from a German ambush and pulling him to safety. He probably popped a couple of totally sweet wheelies on his motorcycle while doing so.

After the British evacuation at Dunkirk, Jack returned to England and promptly signed up to be a member of a new supersecret organization known as the Commandos. At the time he signed the paperwork Churchill wasn't actually even sure what a Commando was, but he was excited about the prospect of kicking German asses, and he knew the work would be insanely dangerous, so he just couldn't resist. He was promptly put through the grueling training regimen of the British Special Forces, and loved every minute of it.

The newly commissioned Commandos' first mission was an amphibious night raid on German shipping and war matériel operations along the coast of Norway. Churchill's small squadron was assigned the unenviable task of assaulting the fortress on Maaloy Island, taking out four fortified coastal artillery positions, and clearing the way for the main body of the Commando force to land. While this highly dangerous suicide operation would have had left pussier men crippled by a severe case of vaginitis, Mad Jack spent the entire trip out there playing "The March of the Cameron Men" on the bagpipes to pump his soldiers up. When the assault ramp of their amphibious transport dropped into the knee-deep water off the coast of Maaloy Island and the covert operation was ready to roll, Jack unsheathed his broadsword, held the well-polished blade aloft, and led his men charging toward their objective, screaming battle cries like a host of somewhat misguided medieval knights with automatic weapons. Twenty minutes later, the commanding officer of the British operation received the following telegram:

MAALOY BATTERY AND ISLAND CAPTURED. CASUALTIES SLIGHT. DEMOLITIONS IN PROGRESS. CHURCHILL.

Awesome.

Churchill won another medal for leading Number 2 Commando in a daring amphibious assault against entrenched German positions at the

Italian port city of Salerno. His men went ashore in the middle of the night, ambushed a panzer crew before they could get to their tank, and captured the enemy positions with relative ease. When the Germans finally got their crap together the next morning and launched a full-on counterattack on the Commandos, Jack stood on the roof of his headquarters building (in full view of the enemy) with a pair of binoculars, calling out coordinates and directing mortar fire down onto Nazi heavy weapons teams.

The following day, Churchill's squad was charged with sneaking into the town of Pigoletti and taking out an artillery battery that was zeroing in on the landing operations. So in the middle of the night, Jack had his small group charge the town from all sides, screaming *"Coommaaannnn-dooo!"* as loudly as possible the entire time. The Germans couldn't figure out what in the mother hell was going on, so, thinking they were under attack by a far superior force, they mounted a half-hearted defense and promptly surrendered. The fifty men of Number 2 Commando took 136 prisoners and inflicted an unknown number of casualties.

Amazingly, that wasn't even the most balls-out, borderline insane thing Mad Jack did on the campaign. One night, he single-handedly took forty-two German prisoners and captured a mortar crew using only his broadsword and his giant nut sack. He simply took a patrolling guard as a human shield and went around from sentry post to sentry post, sneaking up on the guards and then shoving his sword in their faces and yelling at them until they surrendered. His response when asked about how he was able to capture so many soldiers so easily:

I MAINTAIN THAT, AS LONG AS YOU TELL A GERMAN LOUDLY AND CLEARLY WHAT TO DO, IF YOU ARE SENIOR

TO HIM HE WILL CRY "*JAWOHL*" [YES SIR] AND GET ON WITH IT ENTHUSIASTICALLY AND EFFICIENTLY WHATEVER THE SITUATION.

Personally, I think it's just human nature to surrender when a damned crazy person is holding a three-foot blade to your throat, but maybe that's just me.

Churchill continued to lead his men in action against the German forces in Yugoslavia, but was eventually captured by the enemy while fighting for Point 622 on the island of Brac in the Adriatic Sea, when every man in his Commando team was killed or wounded and he ran out of ammunition for his pistol. Knowing that he was not going to escape, and having no further means of killing Nazis, Jack started playing sad songs on his bagpipes until he was finally fragged by a grenade and hauled off to the concentration camp at Sachsenhausen.

But not even something as formidable as a goddamned Nazi prison camp stood a chance against Mad Jack. When he arrived, Churchill met up with veterans from the famous Great Escape and joined them in an attempt to dig a secret passage out of the camp. Churchill spent several hours a day tunneling through rock and soil with little more than a broken spork he ganked from the mess hall, eventually carving out a huge cavern leading under the walls of the prison and up through the ground like a spastic gopher. Fighting Jack made a break for it, eluded enemy patrols, and evaded capture for fourteen days, but was eventually tracked down by the Gestapo and shipped back to Sachsenhausen.

Not long afterward, word came down that the prisoners were going to be relocated to the Nazi death camp at Dachau. Churchill didn't want to get in on that rodeo, so he escaped by breaking free from his bindings, jumping out of a moving prison truck, and sprinting into the woods. He spent seven days living off the land and traveling through the enemy-infested wilderness before crossing Allied lines, meeting up with an American armored unit, and hitching a ride back to Britain.

The war was pretty much over by that point, but Jack's adventures weren't quite finished yet. At the age of forty, Churchill completed jump school and qualified as a paratrooper. He went on to serve in action in Palestine, where he earned fame for defending a Jewish medical convoy from an Arab ambush by carjacking an armored personnel carrier, calling in an artillery strike, and providing small-arms fire while wearing his full military dress uniform. And then another time, he helped evacuate a hospital filled with Israeli medical personnel when they came under attack by Arab rockets.

After Palestine, Fighting Jack Churchill went on to serve as an instructor at land-air warfare school in Australia and become a hardcore surfer. He retired from the army in 1959, one of the most awesome and badass heroes in the long and storied career of the British Army, and a man who exemplified everything that it means to go completely balls to the wall in the service of king and country.

After the war, Jack went to Hollywood and played a bit part as an archer in the 1952 film *Ivanhoe*, starring Elizabeth Taylor. Taylor was in the film *Rhapsody* with Vittorio Gassman, who was in *Sleepers* with Kevin Bacon.

The Great Escape occurred on March 24, 1944, when seventy-six inmates of the German POW camp Stalag Luft III escaped through a three-hundred-foot-long tunnel dug, by hand, thirty feet below the ground. Of the escapees, only three soldiers successfully made it back to Allied lines. The others were recaptured, and fifty of them were summarily executed by the SS. The Nazis were dicks.

2008

35

IRINA SEBROVA

(1914–2000)

We slept in anything we could find—holes in the ground, tents, caves—but the Germans had to have their barracks, you know. They are very precise. So their barracks were built, all in a neat row, and we would come at night, after they were asleep, and bomb them. Of course, they would run out into the night in their underwear, and they are probably saying, "Oh, those night witches!" Or maybe they called us something worse. We, of course, would have preferred to have been called "night beauties," but, whichever, we did our job.

—LIEUTENANT GALINA BROK-BELTSOVA

THE WEST LOVES TO TALK ABOUT HOW IT SINGLE-HANDEDLY WON WORLD WAR II BY FACE-KICKING THE BEACHES AT NORMANDY AND THEN SMASHING HITLER IN THE BICAMERAL LEGISLATURE WITH A TACK HAMMER, BUT THEY OFTEN CONVENIENTLY TEND TO FORGET ABOUT HOW IT WAS THE SOVIET UNION THAT DID MOST OF THE HEAVY LIFTING FROM 1941 TO 1945. The Russkies took it kind of personal when Adolf broke a nonaggression pact, invaded their country, killed twenty million of their people, and rolled his panzers within a hundred miles of Moscow, and as such, they dedicated their entire lives to ruining Nazi asses. In fact, they were so epically cheesed off about the whole thing that they don't even refer to the conflict as World War II—they call it the Great Patriotic War.

So when things started getting seriously nuts in Russia, it was up to every red-blooded Communist worthy of their manifesto to get their asses out there and start serving up knuckle sandwich cockpunches to the Fascists courtesy of Uncle Joe Stalin. Men and women alike participated in the massive war effort, desperately trying to prove to the Nazis that any attempt to follow in Napoleon's Russia-invading footsteps was going to result in a similar degree of ball-searing agony.

Now, when I say that women were getting in on the ass-kickings, I mean that the chicks in the Soviet Union were out there on the front lines pulling the trigger and showing the Krauts what it was like to have bullets forcibly injected into their frontal lobes. This sisterhood of unstoppable ass-beatings was never better exemplified than by Irina Sebrova and the 588th Night Bomber Regiment—an ultra-hardcore unit of women aviators, pilots, mechanics, armorers, and all-around Nazi-hating sack-kickers.

Irina was a humble Russian peasant girl who had clawed her way up from extreme poverty, learned to pilot an aircraft, and was working as a flight instructor when Hitler's minions decided it would be really incomprehensibly brilliant to launch a massive invasion of the Russian motherland. When Sebrova heard that the Red Army was looking for a few daring chicks to undertake insanely dangerous missions and vaporize hordes of kill-hungry Nazis with C-4 and dynamite, she was one of the first ones to sign the liability waiver on the dotted line.

Sebrova's first stop was a brutal basic training regimen designed to smash three years' worth of air combat instruction into six months of non-stop drilling with a giant proletariat-powered jackhammer. These chicks studied the fine art of aeronautical mayhem eighteen hours a day, every day, and the ruthless commandant had a nasty habit of waking the cadets up at midnight to simulate air raids and then marching the girls barefoot around the tarmac wearing nothing but their petticoats in the frigid, sub-zero temperatures of the Russian winter (it's not as sexy as it sounds).

The 588th finally got in on the Fascist-killing action in 1942, fighting the Nazis as part of the exceedingly bloody Stalingrad campaign. These borderline-insane women would fly out to the German positions in the middle of the night, drop bombs on their targets, and haul ass back to Allied lines as quickly as possible. From the cockpits of their Polikarpov Po-2 night bombers, these hardcore chicks blew the hell out of everything from barracks and supply depots to bridges and enemy tank concentrations, destroying the Fascist war machine with giant bombs painted with pictures of Stalin giving Hitler the finger, and generally just making it a horrible time for the German troops to be alive.

Now, the Po-2 bomber was like the aeronautical equivalent of a 1978 AMC Gremlin with bald tires, faulty brakes, and a nasty habit of spontaneously combusting every time it got within two hundred yards of an open flame. For starters, these crap-tastic propeller-powered biplanes were originally designed in 1927 to serve as civilian crop dusters, so they weren't exactly flying death fortresses capable of glassing entire continents with their limitless firepower. Already fifteen years old and technologically obsolete when the war began, these unwieldy machines were made entirely out of wood and canvas, meaning that basically anything more serious than lighting a match in the cockpit was going to send this Wright brothers reject down in flames. Seriously, a friggin' German soldier standing on the ground firing his submachine gun wildly into the air was a very real danger to these pilots, to say nothing of the antiaircraft flak cannons the Nazis conveniently stationed around every moderately interesting ground target larger than a portable toilet.

The Po-2 had a crew of two—a pilot and a navigator. It didn't have a radio, carried one machine gun, and mounted five hundred pounds of bombs on the wings. Of course, the bombs had a particularly lovely habit of not deploying when the pilot flipped the drop-bombs switch, meaning that it wasn't uncommon for the navigator to have to *climb out onto the wing of the moving plane in midflight* and detach the bombs by hand. Seriously, read that last sentence again and give the utter insanity of that statement a moment to sink in. The vehicle boasted a top speed of 90 miles per hour, which is about 30 mph slower than the top speed of most modern automobiles. Meanwhile, German Bf-109 fighter planes cruised at a combat speed of 348 mph.

You'd think that having an engine roughly half as powerful as a solar-powered calculator would at least mean that the aircraft was quiet, but this wasn't the case either. In fact, the cacophonous thumping of the Po-2's engines was so excruciatingly loud that the women of the 588th actually shut the engine completely off when they were about a mile out and silently glided through the night air toward their objectives. They released their bombs over the target, and the moment the explosions started the engines were switched on and the pilots slammed the throttle open and took off out of there as quickly as possible. These unnerving, completely silent nocturnal raids resulted in the angry, sleep-deprived Germans referring to these mysterious female daredevils as the *Nachthexen*, "night witches."

As a wing commander in the 588th, Senior Lieutenant Irina Sebrova was always the first woman off the tarmac every night and the last one to land in the morning. During her Kraut-smashing adventures in the skies above Russia, the Ukraine, and Germany, she flew a ridiculous 1,008 night missions and 92 day missions—more than any of the other Night Witches. Seriously, consider this crap—if an American bomber pilot successfully survived twenty-five missions over Europe, he was considered to have fulfilled his duty to the Allied cause and was given an honorable discharge from the military. To put this balls-out (not the right phrase, but *tits-out* just doesn't carry the same connotation) hard-ass's crotch-rupturingly awesome accomplishments into perspective, if she had been flying for the United States, she would have successfully completed forty-four tours of duty.

Sebrova also survived being shot down twice, which is kind of a big deal considering that the Night Witches weren't issued extraneous equipment such as, um, parachutes. Most of the time the Witches didn't mind, since it was probably better to go down in flames than be captured by the Germans, but you'd have to think that they would have at least liked to have had the *option* of not careening hundreds of feet down to a gruesome death.

Anyways, the first time Sebrova was shot down she ditched in a dark field, pulled her wounded navigator out of the cockpit, and traveled on foot toward enemy lines. At one point the two Soviet aviatrixes were riding on a ferry across a large waterway when a Nazi dive-bomber swooped down and blew the ass out of their boat, but the women somehow managed to swim to safety and successfully make it back to Russian lines unscathed.

The second time, Sebrova was coming back from bombing Danzig (the city, not the band) when antiaircraft fire cut her oil line. She killed the engines and glided for a while, finally putting down in an unlit area deep behind enemy lines. Irina and her navigator drew their pistols and worked their way back toward Allied lines, traveling away from the sounds of gunfire, desperately trying to avoid being discovered. They covered ten kilometers, in the snow, in the middle of the pitch-black, potentially grue-infested night, successfully evading several German patrols and finally reaching friendly lines. When Sebrova got back to base, she sat in her tent, put her head in her hands, and felt utterly depressed—not because she had just been hunted down like a dog, but because she had been shot down on her first sortie of the night and wouldn't get to go on any more bombing raids until the next day. Like I said, this chick was utterly hardcore.

For her daring raids over the skies of Russia, Poland, Germany, and the Ukraine, Irina Sebrova was awarded the title Heroine of the Soviet Union—the highest award for military bravery offered by the USSR. After the war she stayed on with the Soviet air force and worked as a test pilot, flying recently repaired, structurally unsafe planes and making sure that they didn't explode in midflight. After miraculously walking away from a particularly nasty plane wreck in 1948, she decided that she'd tested the Grim Reaper's patience one too many times, and ended an illustrious career as one of the most underappreciated badasses in the history of military aviation. Not bad for a poor peasant girl from Moscow.

Bf-109 vs. Po-2

Designation:	Messerschmitt Bf-109E-3	Polikarpov Po-2
Role:	Fighter/interceptor	Night bomber
Crew:	One	Two (pilot, navigator)
Length:	28 feet 4.5 inches	26 feet 9 inches
Weight:	5,875 pounds	2,167 pounds
Top Speed:	348 mph	93 mph
Horsepower:	1,175	125
Range:	410 miles	329 miles
Ceiling:	34,450 feet	13,125 feet
Rate of Climb:	3,100 feet per minute	546 feet per minute
Armament:	Two twin-linked 20 mm cannons Two twin-linked 7.92 mm machine guns	One 7.62 mm machine gun

In 1942 the Nazis unveiled "Heavy Gustav"—the largest artillery piece ever built. This massive cannon weighed 1,344 tons, could only be transported by train, and required a crew of five hundred men to operate. Gustav's 31.5-inch barrel fired a Volkswagen-sized 10,500-pound artillery shell a distance of more than twenty miles. Because of how impractically massive the weapon was, it was only fired forty-eight times during the entire war.

2008

36

BHANBHAGTA GURUNG

(1921–2008)

In the absence of orders, find something and kill it.

—ERWIN ROMMEL

THE GURKHAS ARE SUBTERRANEAN CRAZY. These take-no-prisoners Hindu hardasses from the Himalayan Mountains of Nepal have served the British Army with distinction since 1816, winning thirteen Victoria Crosses and fighting in every major British military action from India to Iraq. Over their long and storied career, courageous Gurkha troops have forcibly pacified rebellious Punjabi princes, fought two world wars, wrenched Baghdad from the hands of the Ottoman Empire, tracked elusive guerillas through the canopy jungle of Vietnam, spearheaded the assault on the Falkland Islands, and castrated terrorists in the mountains of Afghanistan. These brave soldiers' impeccable service record and remarkable talent in the fine badass fields of melee combat, excessive profanity, alcohol consumption, and general hell-raising have earned them the respect of their allies and the deep-seated terror of anyone unlucky enough to wind up on the business end of a well-sharpened Gurkha knife.

Bhanbhagta Gurung was a corporal in the 3rd Battalion of the 2nd King Edward VII's Own Gurkha Rifles when World War II went off and turned the entire surface of the planet earth into one giant explosion. In 1943, the men of the 2nd Gurkha were sent to Burma (present-day Myanmar), where the imperial Japanese army was pushing through the dense jungles of Southeast Asia, preparing to strike a deadly blow into the heart of British-controlled India. Gurung saw action during the Chindit expedition, when the British general Ordo Wingate (doesn't that sound like the name of a *Star Wars* character?) led a small force deep behind enemy lines to sabotage railway stations, torch supply depots, and clandestinely disrupt the enemy's operations by basically blowing up and/or incinerating everything they came across. Gurung participated in several brutal engagements against battle-hardened Japanese infantry and was commended for bravery when he saved a critically wounded comrade's life by pulling the guy out of a raging firefight and carrying him three miles to the nearest field hospital.

On March 5, 1945, Gurung led his ten-man rifle squad on a patrol toward the top of a strategically important hill known as Snowdon East—a heavily fortified ridge where just a few days earlier a small force of Gurkha troops had been violently dislodged by a horde of livid Japanese soldiers with samurai swords, welding torches, and submachine guns. As Gurung's patrol approached the web of bunkers and machine gun nests near the top of the hill, a Japanese sniper opened fire on them from his concealed position in a nearby tree, wounding a couple of guys and sending the rest of the squad diving for cover. Almost immediately, heavy weapons and mortars started pasting their position, and the Gurkhas soon found themselves hopelessly outgunned and pinned down by heavy fire.

Well, all the Gurkhas except Bhanbhagta Gurung. For him, it was on like Donkey Kong. This crazy bastard heard these bullets ricocheting all over the place, the heavy thumping of gunfire, and the pained cries of wounded soldiers and just got really insanely pissed out of his mind. He clenched his teeth, swore loudly, drew himself up to his full height, and carefully aimed his standard-issue service rifle at that son of a bitch who was sniping his buddies. With bullets zipping past his head and chopping up the vegetation around him, Gurung calmly drew a bead on the gunman and popped him in the medulla oblongata, sending the sharpshooter flying backward out of the tree and crashing to the ground below.

Gurung, now totally berserk, decided, "Screw these dicks," and single-handedly went completely nuts on those Japanese bastards like a velociraptor at an all-you-can-eat superbuffet. He firmly gripped his rifle and sprinted twenty yards uphill toward a fully operational machine gun position, where imperial gunners were desperately trying to mow him down. Gurung somehow reached their position in one piece, pulled two grenades off his belt, and lobbed them into the gun port, gibbing the machine gun team into bite-sized morsels. With the heavy weapon rather efficiently neutralized, this kill-crazy Gurkha warrior then sprinted toward a nearby foxhole, where two Japanese soldiers were foolishly trying to shoot him in the neck. Gurung dropped feet-first into the bunker, rifle at the ready, and promptly gutted the now-terrified defenders with his gruesome three-foot-long bayonet. As if this wasn't enough destruction, Gurung then charged a *second* foxhole, clearing it

out with a well-placed hand grenade, and then immediately proceeded to yet another enemy position, where he disposed of the horrified Japanese defenders with his rifle and bayonet.

At this point, it's safe to assume that pretty much every Japanese weapon on the hill was pointed in the direction of this ultra-stabby samurai-killer who was impaling dudes all over the flipping place, but Gurung couldn't have cared less about the constant stream of deadly bullets constantly buzzing around his head if you'd paid him to. When a heavy machine gun team from a nearby pillbox had the nerve to direct its fire toward the Gurkha infantryman, it succeeded only in making him even angrier. He commando-rolled out of his foxhole and ran full speed toward the concrete bunker, avoiding bullets all the way, and vaulted himself up onto the roof of the fortified position with one jump. Though he was completely out of bullets and frag grenades, Gurung pulled the only armament he had left—two phosphorous smoke grenades—and chucked them through the window of the bunker. The grenades went off in a flash of white smoke and superheated liquid, and when two burning Japanese soldiers came running out of the entrance to the bunker, engulfed in flames and screaming like madmen, Gurung eviscerated them with his totally awesome Gurkha knife. He then ran into the pillbox, where he found a wounded machine gunner still attempting to operate his weapon. Unable to swing his knife in such tight quarters, Gurung simply grabbed a gigantic rock and bashed the dude's head in with it.

Even though he had just single-handedly eliminated a dozen soldiers with little more than brute force and a healthy disrespect for his own safety, Bhanbhagta Gurung's work *still* wasn't finished. He ran outside the now-empty bunker, signaled for the rest of his squad to advance, set up a heavy machine gun in the pillbox, and manned the position against a desperate Japanese counterattack. By the time the smoke cleared at the end of the day, Snowdon East was firmly in Gurkha hands, and the bodies of sixty-six Japanese soldiers were strewn along the hilltop.

For his incredible actions in the battle for Snowdon East, Bhanbhagta Gurung won the Victoria Cross—the highest award for bravery offered by the British Government—and his unit was issued a battle honor for valor in combat. Gurung returned home after the war, took care of his sick mother, nailed his hot wife, and raised three sons who also went on to become Gurkhas. Despite having an impossible to spell name featuring no fewer than eleven consonants, he now has a wing of the Gurkha training facility named after him and is remembered as a testament to how tough these Nepalese warriors can be.

A Sikh soldier named Nand Singh performed a similar feat of awesomeness in 1944, when he single-handedly assaulted a heavily fortified Japanese trench network armed only with a bayonet and a handful of grenades. Despite being wounded six times, he annihilated four imperial bunkers and fragged thirty-seven of the forty men garrisoning the position.

The Gurkhas have an elephant polo team. I would assume that these guys win the World Series of Elephant Polo pretty much every single year, since I have a hard time believing that anybody else in the world is hardcore enough to tear ass at full speed around a football field on the back of a giant pachyderm waving a giant stick around like a crazy person (or take on the Gurkhas at any kind of physical competition, for that matter), but maybe that's just me.

When Prince Harry went off to serve in Afghanistan he was stationed with the Gurkhas for a very good reason—the Taliban are terrified of them. Some Afghan fighters believe that these Nepalese warriors are living demons who slaughter men and eat captured soldiers alive, so they generally just refuse to fight against them. The Gurkhas, for their part, do nothing to dissuade these notions.

37

GEORGE S. PATTON

(1885–1945)

We're not going to just shoot the sons of bitches, we're going to rip out their living goddamned guts and use them to grease the treads of our tanks. . . . War is a bloody, killing business. You've got to spill their blood, or they will spill yours.

AS A YOUNG MAN GROWING UP IN SAN GABRIEL, CALIFORNIA, GEORGE SMITH PATTON JR. CULTIVATED A LOVE FOR ALL THINGS AWESOME. He studied the great works of classical badassery, read any military history book he could get his hands on, and spent long evenings listening to his father's buddies swap tales about shooting people's faces off in the American Civil War (six of Patton's great-uncles were Confederate officers). Basically, Georgie pretty much knew he wanted to be the second coming of Hannibal before he was out of short pants.

At the 1912 Olympics in Stockholm, Patton represented the United States in an event known as the modern pentathlon. This event was basically a combination of all the major badass food groups: fencing, shooting, horseback riding, swimming, and running. Patton performed well in every single event and ended up finishing fifth in the final standings. However, there is some controversy regarding this final score, because during the handgun accuracy portion of the competition Patton was ruled by the official scorers as having completely missed the target on his final shot. Patton argued that the bullet didn't miss the target but instead passed through the bullet hole from the shot before—the modern-day equivalent of Robin Hood splitting the arrow at the archery competition—but instead of being hailed as the greatest and most accurate shooter in history, Patton was completely hosed out of a chance at winning the gold medal in badassitude.

Patton also receives further points in my book because while the Olympic standard for the shooting competition was a .22 caliber round, Patton rejected that pussy ass bullcrap and used his .38 instead, because what good is handgun accuracy if your bullets lack adequate stopping power?

Patton spent one year at the Virginia Military Institute before transferring to West Point, where he graduated and was commissioned a second lieutenant in the United States Cavalry. After graduation he continued his study of cavalry tactics, horsemanship, and fencing, and eventually was certified as the army's first Master of the Sword. I'm not really sure what a Master of the Sword actually is, but I picture it having something to do with raising your saber over your head and shouting,

"By the power of Grayskull!" while a bunch of stuff explodes around you. He was actually such a skilled sword fighter that the army asked him to help design the Model 1913 cavalry saber, a design known today as the Patton Saber.

But even though he knew he was totally dope, George was still dying to test out his skills on the battlefield. He finally got the opportunity to do so while serving under the famous hardass American general "Black Jack" Pershing. Patton went into Mexico as part of the Punitive Expedition to try to hunt down Pancho Villa, and while the mission itself was pretty much a complete bungling clusterhump of an operation, Patton did manage to track down and kill two high-ranking bodyguards in Villa's army, capping them in the head with his custom-made ivory-handled, nickel-plated Colt .45 Peacemaker revolvers during an epic John Woo-esque shootout in an old abandoned Spanish mission. Patton returned to camp with the dead Villistas' bodies tied to the hood of his Jeep.

Pershing was duly impressed with Patton's pistol skills and his kill-'em-all attitude, so he took the young officer to France to fight in World War I as commander of the newly commissioned United States Tank Corps. Patton quickly rose through the ranks, earning a battlefield promotion to colonel, winning a Distinguished Service Cross, and getting shot in the thigh by a machine gun during the Battle of St. Mihiel. After the war, he would often get drunk, drop his pants, and tell everyone he was the "half-assed general," which is kind of cool, I guess.

Between the world wars, Patton became an advocate for armored warfare and went to work designing, organizing, and training the next generation of American tank forces. By the time the Germans needed their butts whipped once again in 1942, Patton was already a major general in command of the U.S. 2nd Armored Division, a unit lovingly known as "Hell on Wheels."

It wasn't long before "Old Blood and Guts" would get his chance to prove his mad over-the-top generaling skills. Early in the North Africa campaign, the U.S. 2nd Corps was under the command of some dude named Lloyd Fredenhall, who was basically an incompetent moron. For the first couple of months of Operation Torch, Fredenhall was getting his ass whomped up and down the northern coast of Africa by the notorious German general Erwin Rommel, a guy who was pretty much in the business of making the Allies his bitch all over the place. Eventually General Dwight D. Eisenhower got sick of hearing about how the Allies were getting kicked in the sack every day, so he yanked command away from Fredenhall and gave it to Patton, who, as we've seen, was an original gangsta of tank warfare. Together with the British Eighth Army under General Bernard Montgomery, the Allies were able to face-kick Rommel and push the Nazis out of Africa. After Africa, Patton invaded Sicily in 1943, where his

rapid assault and relentless attacks helped the Americans capture the strategic strongholds of Palermo and Messina. Then it was off to England to gear up for D-Day: the big-ass Allied invasion of Normandy.

By this time, Patton's epic, profanity-riddled, blood-and-guts speeches and his no-screwing-around attitude had already earned him quite a colorful reputation among his soldiers and the American public, but it was Patton's success at the helm of the U.S. Third Army in Europe that would cement his legend as one of the twentieth century's most hardcore military commanders.

During the Normandy campaign, Patton burned rubber through the French countryside like a six-legged robotic ass-kicking machine with the kick-ass dial cranked up to maximum firepower. He covered nearly sixty miles in the span of about two weeks, encircled and outflanked the German defenders, and liberated most of northern France from Nazi control. He knew that his armor wasn't going to be able to slug it out with the heavier and more powerful German Tiger tanks, so he preferred to use the Allied forces' superior mobility and speed to its fullest extent. He outmaneuvered the enemy, surrounded them, and pretty much disregarded all classical and traditional military tactics in favor of full-on, balls-out attacks. The only thing that was able to slow down the Third Army in Normandy was when they ran out of gas, and even that was just a temporary setback.

Patton's full-throttle "kick them in the crotch repeatedly until they die from it and then continue kicking them a couple more times just for good measure" leadership strategy was a good representation of the man himself. He was headstrong, cocky, stubborn, and ambitious, and he didn't tolerate anything less than victory. He did his best to drill a sense of discipline and toughness into his soldiers through strict rules of conduct and rousing speeches, and he once got in deep trouble for slapping a man in the face because he was being a pussy and bitching about being shell-shocked. For the most part, Patton was largely unpopular with his soldiers, but even so, his confidence rubbed off on them and deep down they all trusted him to get the job done and get them home alive. He didn't let them down.

While he pounded the Hun up and down the hedgerows of Normandy, Patton is perhaps best known for his actions in the Ardennes Forest during the Battle of the Bulge in 1944. In this particularly brutal campaign, Hitler's elite SS panzer units made a last-ditch mad dash toward Antwerp in an effort to break through the Allied lines, and a large portion of the U.S. 101st Airborne Division was besieged in the town of Bastogne. Patton's Third Army disengaged the enemy they were fighting and blitzed north at top speed several hundred miles in the middle of a damn snowstorm to bust through the German lines and end the offensive. Afterward, they marched east, liberated the Buchenwald concentration camp, and were already in Prague by the time the war ended. When Hitler finally capped himself in the dome and the rest of Germany was like, "Whatever, okay, you guys win—just please stop hitting us already," Patton wanted to keep marching east and fight the Soviet Union "while the bayonets were still sharpened." Luckily for the Russkies, he never got the chance to stick it to those Commie bastards—he died on December 21, 1945, as a result of injuries sustained in a car accident a few days earlier.

George S. Patton is one of the most hardcore bastards the United States has to offer and one of the most widely recognized military hardasses to ever live. No legitimate discussion of badassitude is complete without him.

I don't want to get any messages saying, "I am holding my position." We are not holding a goddamned thing. Let the Germans do that. We are advancing constantly and we are not interested in holding onto anything, except the enemy's balls. We are going to twist his balls and kick the living shit out of him all the time. Our basic plan of operation is to advance and to keep on advancing regardless of whether we have to go over, under, or through the enemy.

The first all-black armored unit in U.S. history, the 761st Tank Battalion, served in Patton's Third Army throughout the war. The baddest man in the 761st was a guy named Warren Crecy—a soft-spoken, mild-mannered dude who became a crazy Nazicidal maniac on the battlefield. Crecy won the Silver Star for climbing out of his broken-down tank and using the roof-mounted machine gun to single-handedly take out a couple of German machine gun nests, a bazooka team, and two full companies of regular infantry. During the war he is believed to have killed more than three hundred enemy soldiers.

While marching toward Berlin, the men of the Third Army captured a thoroughbred racehorse intended as a gift from Adolf Hitler to the Japanese emperor, Hirohito. Patton kept the steed for himself, and was occasionally seen riding it through the streets of liberated European villages.

MALEY
2008

38

CARLOS HATHCOCK

(1942–1999)

He's dead, sir. They just flop around a lot when you shoot them in the head.

SNIPERS ARE SOME OF THE DEADLIEST SOLDIERS IN THE HISTORY OF WARFARE. Sitting motionless in their cleverly concealed hiding spots, lying in wait for anyone stupid enough to stroll into the crosshairs of their telescopic sights, and controlling their breathing and heart rate to ensure the steadiness of their aim, these insane sharpshooters are more than capable of blowing your face off with a well-placed round from hundreds of yards away. By the time the sound of the gunshot reaches you, you're already dead. In this demanding, ultra-high-stress job, one that requires superhuman mental and physical fortitude, one man stands out as being the toughest and most hardcore individual to ever peer through a scope and calmly squeeze the trigger—United States Marine Corps supersniper Carlos Hathcock.

Standing five-ten and weighing all of 150 pounds soaking wet and with a ten-pound barbell hidden underneath his jacket, Hathcock didn't exactly look like the sort of dude who could snuff out a man's existence with the same ease that most people rip a giant fart. Well, this guy knew how to work a rifle before most kids know how to work a toilet, using a bolt-action .22 to hunt for food in the woods behind his tiny Arkansas farm as a young child. At seventeen, Hathcock enlisted in the United States Marine Corps, earned a stripe on his sleeve, and then promptly had it cut off when he slugged his commanding officer in the face during a rowdy bar fight. Sure, that kind of sucked, but seriously, if you're going to get demoted, cracking your boss in the face is probably the most badass way of accomplishing the task.

When he wasn't beating the hell out of his superiors, grilling up delicious burgers, or tying a bunch of awesome knots, Carlos served on the Marine Corps Rifle Team. This dedicated killaholic put in thousands of hours on the firing range and was such a stone-cold gunslinger that he won the 1965 National American High-Powered Rifle Marksmanship Shooting Accuracy Competition Contest Challenge of America—the most prestigious shooting competition in the United States. He beat out two thousand elite sharpshooters for the prize, including a bunch of other U.S. servicemen and some of the top members of the National Rifle Association (and you know those NRA dudes can really shoot their asses off).

As cool as it is to be pretty much universally recognized as the most bananas marksman in the U.S. of A., Carlos Hathcock had bigger fish to sauté—namely, the entire country of North Vietnam. When those crazy Commies started their wacky hijinks in 1966, Hathcock was immediately shipped out to the South Pacific in a giant radioactive overseas freight container labeled "Whup-Ass" and unleashed on the unsuspecting enemy hordes.

I probably don't need to tell you that hunting down guerillas deep in the canopy jungle of Vietnam isn't like bull's-eyeing womp rats in your T-16 back home. As a death-dealing Marine Corps sniper, Hathcock constantly found himself alone, unsupported, and surrounded by hostile Vietnamese people actively seeking to wedge large chunks of lead into his torso at incredibly high velocities. But Hathcock wasn't exactly going to go AWOL and swim across the Pacific Ocean on the back of a magical dolphin just because some dumbass with a rifle wanted to take a few potshots in his general direction. Quite the opposite, in fact. Wearing a camouflaged boonie hat with a single white feather stuck in the hatband and using a Winchester Model 70 sniper rifle—an old throwback weapon from World War II—Hathcock soon made a name for himself as a legend in the Marine Corps. In one of his first missions he busted a .30-06 cap in the infamous Vietnamese sniper known as "Apache Woman," a vicious manslayer who commanded a Viet Cong sniper platoon and was notorious for publicly torturing American POWs to death in such horrific ways that it made the Spanish Inquisition look like the animatronic party time jug band at Chuck E. Cheese's.

Another time, Hathcock and his spotter pinned down an entire North Vietnamese Army (NVA) rifle company—well over a hundred men—in the middle of an open valley for five straight days. Five freaking days! Hiding in a concealed perch on the side of a rolling hill, Hathcock waited and dished out head shots while his spotter sat there and yelled things like, "Killing spree!" "He's on fire!" and "Is it the shoes?" On two separate occasions the NVA soldiers attempted to escape under cover of darkness, but both times Hathcock inflicted so many kills that they were forced to run and cower behind a two-foot-high mound of dirt. Eventually, when all of the unit's commanders had been killed and Hathcock got bored of groin-shotting fools in the nards, he allowed them to flee to a nearby abandoned village. Then he obliterated the village by radioing in and having the entire site dusted with napalm.

Working alone, planning his own missions, and patrolling deep in the unforgiving jungle, Carlos Hathcock terrorized NVA soldiers, killed their leaders, and unsettled the enemy worse than a bank teller wearing a ski mask in the middle of July. During one of his mad sniper rampages, he set the record for the longest kill shot in history, popping a dude's head off from 2,500 yards out with a jury-rigged .50-caliber machine gun fitted with an 8× scope. Honestly, I'm not sure whether it's more interesting that he made such an incredible shot or that they actually keep records for that sort of thing.

Hathcock's reputation for being a completely nails hardass also earned him the opportunity to go on some of the most critically important and ludicrously dangerous missions his commanders could think up. One night he was airlifted deep behind enemy lines, where he traveled five kilometers undetected through absolute pitch darkness and set up an ambush for a French interrogator working with the NVA. This dude was like a supersadistic Commie-Nazi pinko hippie Fascist pie-hating terrorist pedophile en route to kick some puppies and ruthlessly torture a couple of captured American pilots, so Hathcock put a bullet in that dumbass's left ventricle from five hundred yards out and sprinted back to the landing zone while being shot at by more assault rifles than the Texas State Gun Show. Another time, Hathcock spent four days crawling undetected, Solid Snake–style, through a wide open field toward a heavily defended fortress compound deep behind enemy lines. Once he got within range, Hathcock assassinated a high-ranking NVA general with a single pull of the trigger, then avoided frantic enemy patrols and made it back to American lines safely. Did I mention that this guy was crazy?

Well, Charlie certainly thought so—Carlos became so infamous that Ho Chi Minh put a bounty out on "Long Tra'ng"—the American devil known only to the Vietnamese as "White Feather." At a time when most NVA bounties were in the $5–$8 range, the price on Hathcock's head was five figures. The North Vietnamese even trained an entire sniper platoon for the express purpose of hunting this guy down like a dog. Hathcock heard about this unit, tracked them down, and killed the unit's commander by *shooting him through the scope of his rifle*, instant-messaging a bullet directly into the dude's eye socket and then ganking the busted scope as a war trophy.

Gunnery Sergeant Carlos Hathcock recorded eighty kills in six months, with a total of ninety-three confirmed during his career—though the actual (albeit unofficial) number is believed to be somewhere in the range of three hundred to four hundred. He went on to provide dozens of aspiring Marine snipers with some serious on-the-job battlefield training, molding them into an efficient fighting force, and personally commanding the Marine sniper platoon in combat. His men notched seventy-two kills in the month of July 1969 alone and were one of the only platoon-sized units in history to receive the highly prestigious Presidential Unit Citation from the commander in chief.

But being a marauding, belligerent, stone-cold sniper isn't the only reason why Carlos Hathcock was a badass dude. One day, while he was heading out to a dangerous mission to assassinate a giant Marine-eating gorilla, the armored vehicle Hathcock was riding in drove over an antitank mine and promptly exploded all over the place. Things were blowing up everywhere, the entire truck was engulfed in flames, and everyone and everything was basically on fire. Well, instead of keeling over and succumbing to complete immolation of his entire body like a wuss, Carlos Hathcock pulled himself up, mustered what little strength he had left, and somehow dragged six unconscious Marines out of the fiery wreckage. The inferno left 40 percent of his body covered by second- and third-degree burns, and Hathcock required thirteen skin grafts to repair his horrific injuries, but all six Marines survived.

In case there was any doubt as to how tough this man was, just five months after almost becoming a human-sized lump of charcoal Carlos Hathcock was back out on the gun range coaching the Marine Corps Rifle Team for an upcoming competition. In 1977, he helped establish the USMC Sniper School, developed the curriculum, and trained the first class of Marine snipers to go out into the bush and tear the enemies of democracy some new bungholes. Hathcock retired after nearly twenty years in the service, his ballsy reputation as an unerring sharpshooter so firmly cemented in Marine Corps mythos that the USMC's highest award for marksmanship is now named after him. Appropriately, Hathcock spent the later, quieter years of his life hunting one of the few things on this earth deadlier than humans—he spent his weekends fishing for gigantic three-hundred-pound man-eating lemon sharks in the choppy waters of the Atlantic Ocean.

Anything less life-threatening would have been too boring.

Over the course of a thousand yards, a bullet's trajectory is dramatically affected by factors such as wind and gravity. While the exact numbers vary from weapon to weapon and bullet to bullet, in order to hit a target a thousand yards away in a 10 mph left-to-right crosswind, you would generally need to aim for a spot roughly twenty-five feet above your target and seven feet to the left.

BADASS MARINES

WE'VE BEEN LOOKING FOR THE ENEMY FOR SOME TIME NOW. WE'VE FINALLY FOUND HIM. WE'RE SURROUNDED. THAT SIMPLIFIES OUR PROBLEM OF GETTING TO THESE PEOPLE AND KILLING THEM.

—CHESTY PULLER

Dan Daly

A permanently pissed, rawhide-gnawing Marine's Marine, Sergeant Dan Daly won the Congressional Medal of Honor twice—once for single-handedly defending the American Embassy in Beijing from a throng of armed peasants during China's Boxer Rebellion with nothing more than a machine gun and his combat knife, and once for leading thirty-five Marines to victory against more than four hundred ambushing militia troops in Haiti. Despite all of that, he's probably best known for his brave actions during the Battle of Belleau Wood in World War I. When his platoon was pinned down by heavy German machine gun fire, Daly stood up in full view of his men and angrily yelled, "Come on, you sons of bitches, do you want to live forever?" before charging balls-out toward the enemy positions. His inspired Marines overran the entrenched German positions and carried the day.

Lou Diamond

A hardass veteran of World War I, "Mr. Leatherneck" was a fifty-two-year-old master sergeant when he hit the beaches of Guadalcanal in 1942. One of the toughest and most colorful men the Corps ever produced, as well as a deadly marksman with an 81 mm mortar, legend has it that he once single-handedly destroyed an offshore Japanese cruiser by dropping a round down its smokestack from several hundred yards away. Lou was famous for his long white beard, his complete disregard for USMC dress code, and his standing orders—every morning, without exception, one of his privates was to go down to the beach, pick up a case of beer from the quartermaster, and bring it to Lou. Actor Lou Diamond Phillips is named after this guy, which is pretty cool as well.

Gregory Boyington

A champion collegiate wrestler who, like Hathcock, was once reprimanded for face-punching his commanding officer in a barroom brawl, "Pappy" Boyington was the Corps's top fighter ace in World War II. He destroyed twenty-eight Japanese fighters, first as a member of the Flying Tigers, and later as the commander of the famous Black Sheep Squadron. Eventually shot down while leading a combat patrol over enemy territory, Boyington spent twenty months in harsh captivity before returning to the States and personally receiving the Medal of Honor that had already (incorrectly) been issued to him posthumously.

Peter Julien Ortiz

A former reconnaissance officer in the French Foreign Legion, Ortiz enlisted in the Corps after escaping from a Nazi prison camp in 1940. He immediately parachuted into France, where he helped coordinate the French Resistance and rescue downed Allied pilots. One time, he was hanging out in a French nightclub and heard a bunch of Nazi officers talking smack about the Marines. Ortiz went into the club's bathroom, changed into his USMC dress uniform, walked up to the officers' table, unholstered his pistol, and ordered them to drink a toast to President Roosevelt and the United States Marine Corps. They did.

Chesty Puller

In thirty-seven years of service to the Corps, Lewis B. Puller rose through the ranks from private to general and won the Navy Cross five times—more than any other Marine or sailor in history. He fought well-armed rebels in Haiti and Nicaragua, commandeered a U.S. Navy destroyer during Guadalcanal (despite having absolutely no authority to do so) and used it to rescue a group of stranded Marines from an overrun beachhead, and led the epic USMC breakout from the Chosin Reservoir during the Korean War. He earned a reputation as a ten-gallon hardass who tolerated nothing less than ultimate badassitude from his men and offered nothing more than a giant boot up the ass to anybody who stood in his way. To this day, Marines in basic training at Parris Island end their day by shouting, "Good night, Chesty Puller, wherever you are!"

John Ripley

Captain Ripley was an advisor to a small, underequipped garrison in South Vietnam when he heard a report that a massive column consisting of thirty thousand soldiers and two hundred tanks was converging on his position. Ripley sprang into action. He ran to the bridge at Dong Ha—the only crossing point over the Cam Lo River for miles—hooked himself to the underside of the structure, and began single-handedly laying explosives. Pulling himself along, hand over hand, while NVA soldiers fired AK-47s at him, Ripley set several explosive charges and blew the bridge up before the column could cross. Then he called down artillery on the traffic jam his demolitions had created.

2008

39

BRUCE LEE

(1940–1973)

If I were to be completely realistic in my films, you would call me a violent, bloody man. I would simply destroy my opponent by tearing his guts out. I wouldn't do it so artistically.

IT SEEMS LIKE YOU CAN'T BUY A CHEESEBURGER IN A UNIVERSITY STUDENT UNION WITHOUT TRIPPING AND BEEFING IT FACE-FIRST INTO A CRAPPY, MAKESHIFT STOREFRONT WHERE SOME OLD EX-HIPPIE IS HOCKING OVERPRICED BLACKLIGHT POSTERS OF BRUCE LEE. While I'm not exactly against blacklight posters (or ex-hippies, for that matter), it's still a little ridiculous that a man like Lee, who was once widely regarded as the pinnacle of human skill and physical conditioning, is now relegated to the same overcommercialized fate that has Che Guevara twirling in his grave like a cordless drill cranked up to maximum torque.

Of course, the current belief that Bruce Lee is pretty much the most badass human being to have ever lived certainly has a solid foundation in fact. Not only was this guy a pioneer who single-handedly brought face-smashing martial arts films to relevance in the United States and served as the idol of pretty much every Chinese kung fu action star since the 1970s, but he also was a throat-crushing brawler who dedicated his life to honing his body into the ultimate killing machine.

Born in the Hour of the Dragon (7 a.m.–9 a.m.) in the Year of the Dragon (1940), Bruce Lee was a natural actor (and, apparently, dragon). He appeared in his first film at three months old, and had been in almost twenty movies by his eighteenth birthday. Growing up on the mean streets of Hong Kong, Bruce Lee studied Wing Chun kung fu, joined a street gang called the Tigers of Junction Street, got into a bunch of no-holds-barred back-alley street fights, and beat up anyone who screwed with him. Interestingly, he and some chick won the 1958 all–Hong Kong cha-cha dance competition as well, representing the ultimate duality of Bruce's badassery. He also won the 1957 Hong Kong boxing championship, defeating a three-time champion, taking three consecutive boxers down with first-round knockouts, and making the toughest fighters in China look like a bunch of Glass Joes, Don Flamencos, and King Hippos.

After proving that he rocked the pants off Hong Kong in every possible way, Bruce moved to the United States and started making a name for himself here. He quickly became well known for his legendary feats of awesomeness—the most famous of which was the almost-mythical one-inch punch. Basically, Bruce Lee would make a fist and put it 2.54 centimeters from your midsection, and then he would generate so much velocity in that small span that he could punch a hole directly through your torso and rip out your still-beating heart. If he was feeling particularly generous, he would spare you the vicious internal dismemberment and would just send you flying across the room, planting you ass-first into a chair strategically positioned six feet behind you.

Of course, Bruce didn't locate some crazy Ring of Strength and magically acquire the power to tear a hole in the space-time continuum with his bare hands; generating twenty-seven tons of force by moving his fist the length of his pinky finger was something that he developed through rigorous training and discipline. The dude routinely busted out sets of 50 one-armed chin-ups, did dozens of push-ups using just the thumb and forefinger of *one hand*, could break boards ten inches thick with a single kick, and was known to be able to throw a three-inch-thick board into the air, kick it in midflight, and split it in half. He toughened up his knuckles by punching rock-hard heavy bags filled with gravel or metal shavings, and then when he was done working the bag for the day he emptied the contents into a bowl, added a little whole milk, and ate it with a spoon. Then he ate the spoon.

Bruce also had a supersecret technique known as the unstoppable punch, a move he demonstrated at the 1967 International Karate Tournament in Long Beach, California. First, he stood about six feet away

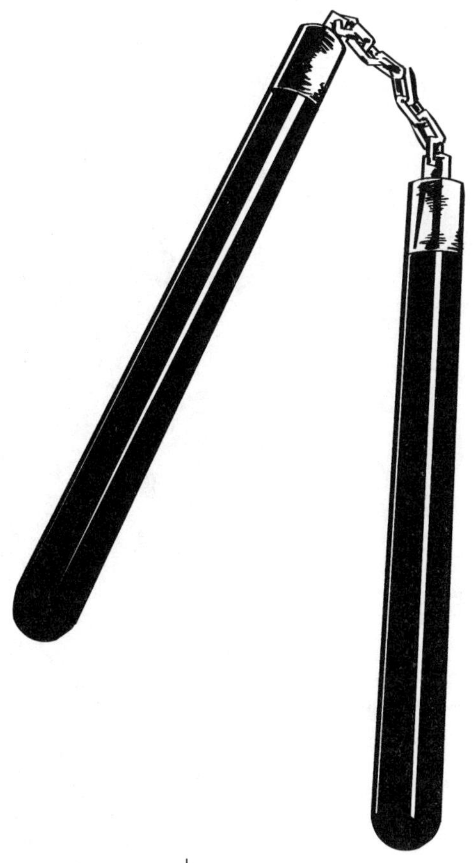

from world karate champion Vic Moore, a dude who had won the tournament the year before by completely dismantling the greatest martial artists in the world (except of course for Bruce, who didn't participate in these things because the sparring wasn't full contact and he wasn't interested in any "pussy fighting" that didn't involve pulling out a guy's spinal column through his urethra). Bruce said something to the effect of "Okay, I'm going to punch you in the face. Don't let me." Then he glided across the floor, covering six feet in about two-tenths of a second, and before anybody knew what the hell was going on Bruce Lee was holding his fist about half an inch away from Vic Moore's face. Moore demanded a second opportunity to block the unstoppable punch. Bruce Lee gave him seven chances. Every attempt provided the same results.

But what good is an arsenal of totally flipping sweet moves if you can't back it up in an actual battle? Well, when you're Bruce Lee you get a lot of opportunities to show people how massive your balls are. One time, some dude named Wong Jak Man got all worked up because Bruce was teaching kung fu to non-Asians, so he challenged him to a fight. Bruce defeated the dude (who allegedly turned and ran away after getting his ass seriously handed to him by a flurry of rock-hard fists) but was ultimately disappointed with his performance, simply because ruthlessly pummeling this guy for three minutes straight left him slightly out of breath. Bruce looked on this overwhelming physical victory as a moral defeat and rededicated himself to relentless training and practice. Wong eventually recovered from this crotch punch to his ego to train guys who compete on the Ultimate Fighting Championship circuit.

One of Bruce's most famous street fights came on the set of *Enter the Dragon* in 1973, when some wannabe thug poser decided he was going to try to expose Lee as a fraud. This guy was huge and jacked, and started hurling endless multitudes of vicious "your momma" jokes at Bruce until the movie star could take it no longer. According to some of the guys on the set who witnessed the fight, Bruce dodged an oafish attempt at a haymaker punch, slammed the dude up against a wall, swept the leg Cobra Kai–style, shoved his knee in the kid's neck, and busted him ruthlessly in the face and head until the guy tapped out and cried like a bitch.

What Bruce Lee is probably most famous for, however, is his unparalleled contribution to martial arts cinema. In addition to breaking pretty much every single box office record in Hong Kong and single-handedly bringing about the rise of kung fu movies in the United States, he's also famous for face-kicking a dude with a bear claw attached to his hand and introducing the world to such over-the-top action movie heroes as Black Belt Jones and Chuck Norris. He also rejected all that wacky, high-flying wire-fu stuff, instead preferring to portray his fights as straight-up, no-frills martial arts death matches between two guys actively seeking to pummel one another so hard that they throw a clot in their brains and forget how to tie their shoelaces. I respect this.

Bruce was pretty much innovative in everything he did. In addition to teaching kung fu to notable hardasses such as Steve McQueen, Bruce also developed a fighting system known as Jeet Kune Do, or "the Way of the Intercepting Fist." Basically, this martial art is known as the "style of no style," meaning that the fighter needs to constantly adapt his tactics to fit the situation and not constrain himself to any individual style. JKD has grown to be an incredibly popular martial art, well known for its badassitude, which is probably why pretty much every poser on the Internet claims to be a master of it.

In 1973 Bruce Lee died suddenly and unexpectedly when he suffered an adverse reaction to a prescription medication. As is the case with many badasses, Bruce Lee had become too awesome for his own good and suffered from an early passing at the age of thirty-two. In his short life he established himself as the biggest name in martial arts cinema history and one of the most complete and total King Fu masters (or dick-breakers) to ever walk the planet. His legacy still lives on.

Mas Oyama was a Korean-Japanese martial arts master who was famous for killing bulls by punching them in the face. He trained alone in the mountains, hardening his knuckles by smashing pine trees with his bare hands and strengthening his fists to the point where he could break twenty-pound rocks by whacking them with a single punch. If you're interested, there are a couple of kung fu movies based on his life: *Champion of Death* and *Karate Bear Fighter*.

Bruce Lee's given name was Li Zhen Fan. His family name utilizes the same Chinese character as that of Jet Li, even though the Americanized versions of their names are spelled differently. The character—李 (pinyin: lǐ)—literally translates to "plum" or "plum tree."

Nunchucks, like medieval flails, were originally farming tools designed for threshing grains such as rice, wheat, and corn. Much like the modern-day chainsaw, these implements were eventually adapted into weapons by civilians who didn't have access to high-tech gear such as swords, spears, or pump-action shotguns.

Bruce's favorite trick was to have you hold a dime in your open palm. He would stand about three feet from you and tell you not to let him take the dime from you. Then, in a quick flash of awesomeness, he'd swoop in and snatch the coin from your hand before you could close your fist. When you reopened your palm, you'd find that he'd left you a penny.

MHALEY
2008

40

JONATHAN NETANYAHU

(1946–1976)

To kill at such very close range isn't like aiming a gun from a hundred yards away and pulling the trigger—that's something I had already done when I was young. I've learned since how to kill at close range, too—to the point of pressing the muzzle against the flesh and pulling the trigger for a single bullet to be released and kill accurately, the body muffling the sound of the shot. It adds a whole dimension of sadness to a man's being.

IF I WAS GOING TO MAKE A LIST OF ORGANIZATIONS I DON'T WANT TO SCREW AROUND WITH FOR ANY REASON, THE ISRAELI SPECIAL FORCES WOULD BE VERY CLOSE TO THE TOP—PROBABLY SOMEWHERE BETWEEN POST-APOCALYPTIC SUPERMUTANTS AND BEAR CAVALRY ON THE SCALE OF "GROUPS THAT COULD SNAP YOUR NECK IN HALF AND DETONATE YOUR ENTIRE BODY LIKE A GIANT MAN-SIZED BEEF GRENADE WITHOUT UTILIZING THEIR OPPOSABLE THUMBS." The face-smashing commandos of the elite counterterrorist unit Sayeret Maktal are the sort of hardcore bastards who eat Uranium isotopes for breakfast and crap out nuclear warheads, and their over-the-top method of brutally and efficiently taking down terrorists is kind of like going deep-sea fishing with intercontinental ballistic missiles.

It's pretty safe to say that the Israelis and the Arabs pretty much hate each other's faces off with the realness. They're up there with Greeks-Turks, Hutus-Tutsis, and Yankees–Red Sox in terms of vicious, undying blood feuds that can apparently only be solved by excessive violence, hit-batsmen, and Don Zimmer face-plants, and as a member of the Israeli paratroopers, Netanyahu was right in the middle of that endless violence on several occasions—during the Six-Day War he combat-dropped behind Egyptian lines in Sinai, destroyed their fortified positions from the rear, and faxed their commanding officer a message saying, "All your base are belong to me." When Syrian paratrooper commandos assaulted an Israeli headquarters building during the Yom Kippur War, Jonathan escaped a carefully laid ambush and single-handedly annihilated a twelve-man Arab Special Forces team with nothing more than an Uzi and his giant ball sack. He also won a medal for infiltrating deep behind enemy lines in the middle of the night and rescuing a wounded Israeli officer from certain capture and death while successfully evading and fighting off a convoy of Arab tanks in the process.

Basically, this guy was like a crazy Jewish ninja, and not a traditional ninja in the black pajamas—a badass, Snake Eyes–style flying death machine with twin Uzis and twelve-inch combat knives who somersaulted over spiked pits, shot red barrels that exploded into giant towering spires of burning oil, and chopped rhinos in half with a booted roundhouse kick. When he had his entire arm smashed by AK-47 fire in the Golan Heights, he army-crawled two miles across the war-torn battlefield on a shattered elbow with explosions, artillery shells, and bullets zipping past his face. He took a few months off to study at Harvard, and as soon as he regained feeling in his fingertips he went right back and reenlisted in the Israel Defense Forces to continue busting terrorist nut sacks.

As a field officer in the Israeli counterterrorism unit Sayeret Matkal, the kosher Jack Bauer was responsible for keeping insurgents out of Israel, prematurely exploding suicide bombers before they reached their intended targets, and assaulting secret terrorist training camps in Syria and Lebanon. This tough government assassin also took part in

Operation Spring of Youth, when he was sent to personally inform the masterminds behind the tragic massacre at the 1972 Munich Olympics that it wasn't cool (or very smart) to screw with Jewish athletes. His team accomplished this unenviable task by amphibiously landing on the shores of Lebanon in the middle of the night in an inflatable raft, driving to the apartment building where the terrorist leaders were living, blowing the doors off their hinges with plastic explosives, and filling the room with a salvo of 9 mm automatic weapons fire. After gunning down their targets, Jonathan and his men took the local SWAT team on a high-speed car chase through the streets of Beirut, smashed through a couple of police barricades, traded fire with the Lebanese army, and somehow escaped back to Israel in one piece.

Now, all of this is seriously wicked, but, somewhat amazingly, it's not even the primary reason why all students of badassitude should be aware of Jonathan Netanyahu. It was after he assumed command of Sayeret Matkal that he organized, planned, and executed one of the most daring and balls-out operations in the history of counterterrorism—the raid on Entebbe.

On June 27, 1976, Air France flight 139 was hijacked by jackasses on its way from Tel Aviv to Paris. Palestinian and East German terrorists armed with pistols and grenades fought their way into the cockpit, took over the plane, and forced it to land in the Ugandan city of Entebbe for some reason. The men, women, and children on board were then herded into the main terminal, where Ugandan government soldiers armed with assault rifles separated the Jews from the Gentiles. The non-Jews were allowed to leave unharmed, but the others were kept as hostages. The hijackers demanded the release of several known terrorists held in Israeli prisons. Failure to comply would result in a pretty spectacular bloodbath.

Well, Israel has a pretty inflexible position when it comes to hostage situations. They don't negotiate with terrorists—they destroy them.

Sayeret Matkal commander Jonathan Netanyahu was selected to lead the rescue operation, and this dude certainly wasn't going to miss out on an opportunity to take out Palestinians, Germans, and Communists all at the same time—I mean seriously, if you threw in the Philistines, you'd have had the superfecta of traditional Jewish archnemeses. So on the night of July 4, 1976, a small group of C-130 transport planes landed on the runway at the Entebbe airport. Out of the lead vehicle, a convoy of black Land Rovers bearing Ugandan flags rolled off the loading ramp and slowly made its way toward the main terminal. When the urban assault SUVs reached a guard post manned by battle-hardened Ugandan troops, the heavily tinted windows rolled down and Jonathan Netanyahu opened fire, dropping the startled defenders with a surprise Uzi-gram.

Thirty-eight IDF commandos bailed out of the vans and sprinted the last thirty yards toward the doors of the main terminal. Netanyahu was the first man inside, flying side-kicking through the doors and blasting the ass out of anything that moved. The commandos charged through the terminal, wasted more tangos than a Tom Clancy novel, eliminated all the terrorists, and reached the hostages within three minutes of the beginning of the gunfire. The terrified yet relieved passengers were quickly escorted from the building, loaded into a C-130 outfitted with medical supplies, and took off for home.

Unfortunately, Jonathan Netanyahu didn't survive to be recognized for his daring actions in the service of his people—as he was loading hostages onto the plane he was hit by a sniper round fired from the airport control tower and died of his wounds en route back to Israel. The mission, however, was an epic success. The final tally of the raid (later dubbed Operation Jonathan in honor of the fallen commander): six terrorists dead, over a hundred Ugandan military casualties, 103 hostages rescued, one IDF operative killed in action.

Jonathan's younger brother, Benjamin Netanyahu, was the prime minister of Israel from 1996 to 1999, and was reelected again in 2009. In honor of his brother, Benjamin established the Jonathan Institute, a government-sponsored think tank dedicated to the study and prevention of international terrorism.

KRAV MAGA

Krav Maga is a neck-breaking close-quarters fighting system developed by a fearless Hungarian martial artist named Imi Lichtenfeld. Imi was a world champion boxer, wrestler, and gymnast, but when the Nazis rolled into town during World War II he quickly realized that his training hadn't adequately prepared him for a no-holds-barred street fight against hate-filled Teutonic thug dumbasses. So Imi developed Krav Maga—a merciless self-defense style that combines back-alley street fighting with ruthless testicular trauma, and includes numerous techniques to defend against knives, pistols, shotguns, assault rifles, and hostage situations.

Krav Maga operates under the assumption of no quarter, meaning that you have to expect that every encounter will be fought to the death. Your objective is to control the situation, neutralize your enemy by kicking him in the balls until he coughs up his prostate, break every major joint on his body, steal his weapon, kill him repeatedly with it, and escape. There are no dojos, no multicolored belts, no uniforms, no holds barred, no illegal strikes, and no such thing as excessive force. Your only objectives are to survive and to kick this guy's ass so hard that his grandchildren are born without functioning colons.

Lichtenfeld used his home-brewed fighting system to defend the Jews from roving gangs of anti-Semitic Fascist thugs on the streets of his hometown. After successfully escaping the Nazis, he served in the Israeli military and dedicated over thirty years of his life to training the people of Israel in the fine art of thumping their enemies unconscious by smashing them in the back of the head with a skateboard and then doing a kickflip over their half-dead carcasses. His techniques are still taught to every new recruit in the Israel Defense Forces and are currently employed on a regular basis by elite Special Forces, police, and counter-terrorist organizations across the globe.

BIBLIOGRAPHY

Anybody can make history. Only a great man can write it.
—Oscar Wilde

Abbot, Jacob. *William the Conqueror*. Harper and Brothers, 1877.

——. *Xerxes*. Brunswick, 1917.

Abdul-Jabbar, Kareem, and Alan Steinberg. *Black Profiles in Courage*. HarperCollins, 2000.

Abernathy, Francis Edward. *Legendary Ladies of Texas*. University of North Texas Press, 1994.

Adi, Hakim, and Marika Sherwood. *Pan-African History*. Routledge, 2003.

Adkin, Mark. *The Waterloo Companion*. Stackpole, 2001.

Akram, A. I. *The Sword of Allah: Khalid bin al-Waleed*. National Publishing House, 1970.

Alsop, Joseph W. "Beam to Kill Army at 200 Miles, Tesla's Claim on 78th Birthday." *New York Herald Tribune*, July 11, 1934.

Anderson, M. S. *Peter the Great*. Ames and Hudson, 1978.

Anglo-Saxon Chronicle. Trans. James Ingram. Everyman Press, 1912.

Arnold, James R. *US Commanders of World War II*. Osprey, 2002.

Arthur, Max. *Forgotten Voices of World War II*. Globe Pequot, 2004.

Asher, Jerry, and Eric M. Hammel. *Duel for the Golan*. William Morrow, 1987.

Ashkenazi, Michael. *Handbook of Japanese Mythology*. ABC-CLIO, 2003.

Asiatic Journal and Monthly Register for British and Foreign India, China, and Australia. Parbury, Allen, and Co., May-August 1835.

Axelrod, Alan. *Miracle at Belleau Wood*. Globe Pequot, 2007.

Axelrod, Alan, and Charles Phillips. *What Every American Should Know About American History*. Adams Media, 2007.

Backman, Clifford R. *The Worlds of Medieval Europe*. Oxford University Press, 2003.

Badke, David. "The Unicorn." *The Medieval Bestiary*. http://bestiary.ca, 2008.

Baird, W. David, and Danney Goble. *The Story of Oklahoma*. University of Oklahoma Press, 1994.

Barrett, Anthony. *Agrippina: Sex, Power, and Politics in the Early Empire*. Yale University Press, 1996.

Barton, Simon, and Richard Fletcher. *The World of El Cid*. Manchester University Press, 2000.

Bell, J. *Travels from St. Petersburg into Russia to Diverse Parts of Asia*. 2 vols. Glasgow, 1763.

Bennett, G. *The Battle of Trafalgar*. Barnsley, 2004.

Bergreen, Laurence. *Over the Edge of the World*. HarperCollins, 2004.

Bhargava, Purushottam. *Chandragupta Maurya*. Read Books, 2007.

Boardman, et al. John. *The Cambridge Ancient History*. Cambridge University Press, 1988.

Boese, Alex. *Hippo Eats Dwarf*. Harcourt Trade, 2006.

Bogoslovsky, M. M. *Peter the First*. 5 vols. Leningrad, 1940–48.

Bonaparte, Napoleon. *The Military Maxims of Napoleon*. Ed. David G. Chandler and William E. Cairnes. Da Capo, 1995.

Bonds, Ray, and David Miller. *Illustrated Directory of Special Forces*. Zenith, 2002.

Booth, Charlotte. *The Ancient Egyptians for Dummies*. Dummies, 2007.

Bown, Stephen R. *A Most Damnable Invention*. Macmillan, 2005.

Boyne, Walter J., and Philip Handleman. *Brassey's Air Combat Reader*. Brassey's, 1999.

Bradford, Ernle. *Thermopylae*. Da Capo, 2004.

Brayley, Martin. *World War II Allied Women's Services*. Osprey, 2001.

Brody, Seymour. *Jewish Heroes and Heroines of America*. Lifetime, 1996.

Brown, Carl. *The Law and Martial Arts*. Black Belt Communications, 2001.

Brown, Dee Alexander. *Bury My Heart at Wounded Knee*. Macmillan, 2001.

Bucholtz, Chris. *332nd Fighter Group*. Osprey, 2007.

Bunch, James C. *Coast Guard Combat*. Turner, 1997.

Burgess, Alan. *The Longest Tunnel*. Naval Institute Press, 2004.

Burton, Arthur T. *Black Gun, Silver Star*. University of Nebraska Press, 2006.

Butterworth, Alex. *Pompeii*. Macmillan, 2006.

Bury, John Bagnell. *A History of Greece to the Death of Alexander the Great*. Macmillan, 1913.

Bury, John Bagnell, et al. *The Cambridge Medieval History*. Macmillan, 1913.

Caner, Ergun Mehmet, and Emir Fethi Caner. *Christian Jihad*. Kregel, 2004.

Catchpole, Heather, Vanessa Woods, and Mic Looby. *It's True! Pirates Ate Rats*. Allen and Unwin, 2008.

Chapel, Charles Edward. *Guns of the Old West*. Courier Dover, 2002.

Chartrand, Rene, and Richard Hook. *American War of Independence Commanders*. Osprey, 2003.

Chenoweth, H. Avery. *Semper Fi*. Sterling, 2005.

Cheney, Margaret. *Tesla: Man out of Time*. Simon and Schuster, 2001.

Cheney, Margaret, Robert Uth, and Phylis Gellar. *Tesla: Master of Lightning*. http://www.pbs.org/tesla. New Voyage Communications, 2000.

Chlapowski, Dezydery. *Memoirs of a Polish Lancer*. Emperor's Press, 1992.

Clark, William M. *Tales of the Wars*. Oxford University Press, 1836.

Clarke, Henry Butler. *The Cid Campeador*. G. P. Putnam, 1897.
Claudian. *The Gothic War*. Trans. Maurice Platnauer. Harvard University Press, 1972.
Cohen, William A. *Secrets of Special Ops Leadership*. AMACOM, 2005.
Collins, Larry, and Dominique Lapierre. *O Jerusalem!* Simon and Schuster, 1988.
Comnena, Anna. *Alexiad*. Trans. Elizabeth A. Dawes. Routledge, Kegan, Paul,1928.
Cook, Bernard. *Women and War*. ABC-CLIO, 2006.
Cordingly, David. "Bonny, Anne." *Oxford Dictionary of National Biography*. Oxford University Press, 2004.
Cottam, Kazimiera Janina, and Galina Markova. *Soviet Airwomen in Combat in World War II*. Military Affairs, 1983.
Craig, James F. *Famous Aircraft*. Arco, 1968.
Crody, Eric, et al. *Chemical and Biological Warfare*. Springer, 2002.
Cummins, Joseph. *History's Great Untold Stories*. Murdoch, 2006.
Cuppy, Will. *The Decline and Fall of Practically Everybody*. David R. Godine, 1998.
Curtis, John, Nigel Tallis, and Beatrice Andre-Salvini. *Forgotten Empire*. University of California Press, 2005.
Dahl, Hans Frederik, and Anne-Marie Stanton-Ife. *Quisling*. Cambridge University Press, 1999.
Davis, William Stearns. *Readings in Ancient History*. Allyn and Bacon, 1912.
D'Este, Carlo. *Patton*. HarperCollins, 1996.
DeFoe, Daniel. *A General History of the Pyrates*. Ed. Manuel Schonhorn. Courier Dover, 1999.
DeGrout, Gerald J., and C. M. Peniston-Bird. *A Soldier and a Woman*. Longman, 2000.
DePau, Linda Grant. *Battle Cries and Lullabies*. University of Oklahoma, 2000.
Desjardins, Chris. *Outlaw Masters of Japanese Film*. I. B. Tauris, 2005.
Dewald, Carolyn, and John Marincola. *The Cambridge Companion to Herodotus*. Cambridge University Press, 2006.
Druett, Joan. *Sea Captains: Heroines and Hellions of the Sea*. Simon and Schuster, 2000.
Du Chaillu, Paul Belloni. *The Viking Age*. C. Scribner's Sons, 1890.
Duffy, Eamon. *Saints and Sinners: A History of the Popes*. Yale University Press, 2002.
Durham, Philip, and Everett L. Jones. *The Negro Cowboys*. University of Nebraska Press, 1983.
Edgerton, Robert B. *Hidden Heroism*. Westview, 2002.
Emerton, Ephraim. *The Beginnings of Modern Europe*. Ginn, 1917.
Evangelista, Nick, and William M. Gaugler. *Encyclopedia of the Sword*. Greenwood, 1994.
Farrokh, Kaveh. *Shadows in the Desert: Ancient Persia at War*. Osprey, 2007.
Farwell, Byron. *Over There*. W. W. Norton, 1999.
——. *The Gurkhas*. W. W. Norton, 1984.
Finlay, George. *Greece Under the Romans*. J. M. Dent, 1907.
Fletcher, R. A. *The Quest for El Cid*. Oxford University Press, 1991.

Florescu, Radu R., and Raymond T. McNally. *Dracula: Prince of Many Faces.* Back Bay Books, 1989.

Foss, Clive. *The Tyrants.* Quercus, 2006.

Fraser, David. *Knight's Cross.* HarperCollins, 1995.

Freeman-Mitford, Algernon Bertram. *Tales of Old Japan.* BiblioBazaar, 2005.

Fremont-Barnes, Gregory, and Christa Hook. *Trafalgar 1805.* Osprey, 2005.

Fu, Poshek. *Passivity, Resistance, and Collaboration.* Stanford University Press, 1996.

Fuentes, Ventura. "El Cid." *The Catholic Encyclopedia.* Vol 3. Robert Appleton, 1908.

Furneaux, Rupert. *Invasion: 1066.* Prentice-Hall, 1966.

Gabriel, Richard A. *The Culture of War.* Greenwood, 1990.

——. *The Great Armies of Antiquity.* Greenwood, 2002.

Genji and Heike. Trans. Helen Craig McCullough. Stanford University Press, 1994.

Gershevitch, Ilya, and William Bayne Fisher. *The Cambridge History of Iran.* Cambridge University Press, 1985.

Gibbon, Edward. *Decline and Fall of the Roman Empire.* Macmillan, 1914.

Gjerset, Knut. *History of the Norwegian People.* Macmillan, 1915.

Glete, Jan. *Warfare at Sea, 1500–1650.* Routledge, 2000.

Gokhale, Balkrishna Govind. *Ancient India.* Popular Prakashan, 1995.

Gottschalk, Louis. *Lafayette Comes to America.* Read, 2007.

Graham, Stephen. *Peter the Great.* Ernest Benn, 1929.

Greenwood, Alice Drayton. *Empire and Papacy in the Middle Ages.* S. Sonnenschein, 1892.

Grey, Ian. *Peter the Great.* J. B. Lippincott, 1960.

Grousset, Rene. *The Rise and Splendour of the Chinese Empire.* University of California Press, 1953.

Guilaine, Jean, and Jean Zammit. *The Origins of War.* Blackwell, 2005.

Gurstelle, William. *Art of the Catapult.* Chicago Review Press, 2004.

Hack, Karl, and Tobias Rettig. *Colonial Armies in Southeast Asia.* Routledge, 2006.

Hagedorn, Ann. *Savage Peace.* Simon and Schuster, 2007.

Hakim, Joy. *The New Nation.* Oxford University Press, 1993.

Hale, Beth. "The Hero Bear Who Went to War." *Daily Mail.* January 25, 2008.

Hall, John Whitney, and Peter Duss. *The Cambridge History of Japan.* Cambridge University Press, 1988.

Hamilton, J. R. *Alexander the Great.* University of Pittsburgh Press, 1974.

Hamburger, Robert. *Real Ultimate Power.* Citadel, 2004.

Hardy, Grant, and Anna Behnke Kinney. *Establishment of the Han Dynasty.* Greenwood, 2005.

Hawley, Samuel Jay. *The Imjin War.* University of California Press, 2005.

Hayes, Stephen K. *The Ninja and Their Secret Fighting Art.* Tuttle, 1990.

Heath, Ian, and Angus McBride. *The Vikings.* Osprey Publishing, 1985.

Heckel, Waldemar, and John Yardley. *Alexander the Great: Historical Texts in Translation.* Blackwell, 2004.

Henderson, Charles. *Marine Sniper.* Berkeley, 2002.

Herlihy, Patricia. *The Alcoholic Empire.* Oxford University Press, 2002.

Herodotus. *The Histories.* Trans. G. C. Macaulay. Spark, 2004.

Hesiod. *Theogany.* Trans. Glenn W. Most. Harvard University Press, 2006.

Hill, Robert. *World of Martial Arts.* Lulu, 2008.

Hinds, Katherine. *Life in Ancient Egypt.* Marshall Cavendish, 2006.

Hobbes, Nicholas. *Essential Militaria.* Grove Press, 2004.

Holbrook, Sabra. *Lafayette.* Athenum, 1977.

Hollister, Edward Payson. *The Life and Services of Major-General the Marquis de Lafayette.* Beadle, 1861.

Holmes, Tony. *Spitfire vs. Bf-109.* Osprey, 2007.

Homer. *The Iliad.* Trans. Richmond Lattimore. University of Chicago Press, 1951.

——. *The Odyssey.* Trans. Richmond Lattimore. HarperCollins, 1967.

"Honour Sought for Hero Bear." BBC News. January 25, 2008.

Hoxie, Frederick E. *Encyclopedia of North American Indians.* Houghton Mifflin, 1996.

Hulbert, Homer B., and Clarence Norwood Weems. *History of Korea.* Routledge, 1999.

Hull, Michael D. "Peter Francisco: American Revolutionary War Hero." *Military History Magazine.* July/August 2006.

Ireland, William Henry. *The Life of Napoleon Bonaparte.* J. Cumberland, 1828.

Isidore of Seville. *Etymologies.* Trans. Stephen A. Barney. Cambridge University Press, 2006.

James, T. G. H. *Ramses II.* Friedman/Fairfax, 2002.

Jensen, Joseph. *God's Word to Israel.* Liturgical Press, 1990.

Johnson, Joseph. *Brave Women.* Gall and Inglis, 1875.

Johnson, Loch K. *Strategic Intelligence.* Greenwood, 2007.

Jones, Archer. *The Art of War in the Western World.* University of Illinois Press, 2000.

Jones, David E. *Woman Warriors.* Brassey's, 2001.

Jones, H.G., K. Randell Jones, and Caitilin D. Jones. *Scoundrels, Rogues, and Heroes of the Old North State.* History Press, 2005.

Jordan, David. *The History of the French Foreign Legion.* Globe Pequot, 2005.

Jordanes. *The Origin and Deeds of the Goths.* Trans. Charles Mierow. Princeton University Press, 1908.

Katz, Samuel. *Against All Odds.* Twenty-First Century Books, 2004.

———. *Targeting Terror.* Twenty-First Century Books, 2004.

Keay, John. *India: A History.* HarperCollins, 2001.

Keller, Scott. *Marine Pride.* Citadel, 2004.

Kendrick, T. G. *A History of the Vikings.* Courier Dover, 2004.

Kennedy, Hugh. *The Great Arab Conquests.* Da Capo, 2008.

Kilduff, Peter. *Richtofen: Beyond the Legend of the Red Baron.* Arms and Armour Press, 1993.

——. *Red Baron.* David and Charles, 2007.

Kinard, Jeff. *Pistols.* ABC-CLIO, 2004.

Kitchen, Kenneth Anderson. *Ramesside Inscriptions.* Blackwell, 1999.

Kliuchevsky, Vasili. *Peter the Great.* St. Martin's, 1958.

Knight, Ian. *Rorke's Drift 1879.* Osprey, 1996.

Knight, Roger. *The Pursuit of Victory.* Westview Press, 2007.

Konstam, Angus. *Blackbeard.* John Wiley and Sons, 2006.

Kilduff, Peter. *Red Baron.* David and Charles, 2007.

Koburger, Charles W. *Pacific Turning Point.* Greenwood, 1995.

Konstam, Angus. *Blackbeard.* John Wiley and Sons, 2006.

Konstam, Angus, and Tony Bryan. *Pirate Ship 1660–1730.* Osprey, 2003.

Konstam, Angus, and Roger Michael Kean. *Pirates: Predators of the Sea.* Skyhorse, 2007.

Laplander, Robert. *Finding the Lost Battalion.* Lulu, 2006.

Laughton, John Knox. *Nelson and His Companions in Arms.* Kessinger, 2006.

Lay of the Cid. Trans. Robert Selden Rose and Leonard Bacon. University of California Press, 1919.

Lazarus, Edward. *Black Hills, White Justice.* University of Nebraska Press, 1999.

Lee, Robert. *Blackbeard the Pirate.* John F. Blair, 1990.

Lehr, Peter. *Violence at Sea.* Routledge, 2006.

Leonard, Jonathan Norton. *Early Japan.* Time-Life Books, 1968.

Lewis, Bernard. *The Arabs in History.* London: Hutchison University Library, 1950.

Lewis, David Levering. *God's Crucible.* W. W. Norton, 2008.

Lewis, Jon E. *The Mammoth Book of Special Forces.* Carroll and Graf, 2004.

Lewis, Mark Edward. *The Early Chinese Empires.* Harvard University Press, 2007.

Little, John. *Bruce Lee.* Tuttle, 2000.

——. *Words of the Dragon.* Tuttle, 1997.

Little, John, and Bruce Lee. *The Art of Expressing the Human Body.* Tuttle, 1998.

Livy. *History of Rome.* Trans. B. O. Foster. Loeb Classical Library, 1919.

Lord, Walter. *The Miracle of Dunkirk.* Wordsworth, 1998.

MacDonald, John. *Great Battlefields of the World.* Wiley, 1988.

Martinez, Laura Lara, and Maria Lara Martinez. *La Guerra de la Independencia a Traves de sus Protaganistas.* Liceus, 2008.

Mathes, Mildred S. "The Story of Peter Francisco." *American Monthly Magazine.* July-December 1895.

Matthew, D. J. A. *The Norman Conquest.* London: William Clowes and Sons, 1966.

McCarthy, Kevin. *Twenty Florida Pirates.* Pineapple Press, 1994.

McLachlan, Sean. *Byzantium*. Hippocrene, 2004.

McLynn, Frank. *Napoleon*. Pimlico, 1998.

——. *Richard and John*. Da Capo, 2008.

Meaney, Rick. "Tesla Proven Right as Technology Is Transmitted Wirelessly." *RINF Alternative News*. June 8, 2007.

Miller, David. *The Illustrated Directory of 20th Century Guns*. Zenith, 2003.

Miller, Donald. *Masters of the Air*. Simon and Schuster, 2006.

Miller, Thomas. *History of the Anglo-Saxons*. H. G. Bohn, 1856.

Miyamoto Musashi. *The Book of Five Rings*. Trans. Victor Harris. Overlook, 1974.

Monstrelet, Enguerrand de. *The Chronicles of Enguerrand de Monstrelet*. Trans. Thomas Jones. Routledge, 1840.

Moreman, Timothy Robert. *British Commandos 1940–1946*. Osprey, 2006.

Moreman, T. R. *The Jungle, the Japanese, and the British Commonwealth Armies at War*. Routledge, 2005.

Ness, Eliot, and Oscar Fraley. *The Untouchables*. Simon and Schuster, 1947.

Netanyahu, Jonathan. *Self-Portrait of a Hero: The Letters of Jonathan Netanyahu*. Random House, 1980.

Nicolle, David, and Angus McBride. *El Cid and the Reconquista 1050–1492*. Osprey, 1988.

Njal's Saga. Trans. George W. DaSent. London, 1861.

Noggle, Ann, and Christine White. *A Dance with Death*. Texas A&M University Press, 2002.

Oakeshott, R. Ewart. *The Archaeology of Weapons*. Courier Dover, 1996.

Oman, Charles. *The Dark Ages*. Rivingtons, 1908.

O'Neal, Bill. *Encyclopedia of Western Gunfighters*. University of Oklahoma Press, 1991.

Pan Ku. *The History of the Former Han Dynasty*. Vol. 1. Trans. Homer H. Dubs. Waverly Press, 1938.

Parker, Geoffrey. *The Cambridge Illustrated History of Warfare*. Cambridge University Press, 1995.

Patton, George S., and Paul Donal Harkins. *War As I Knew It*. Houghton Mifflin, 1947.

Pawley, Ronald, and Patrice Courcelle. *Napoleon's Polish Lancers of the Imperial Guard*. Osprey, 2007.

Pegler, Martin. *Out of Nowhere*. Osprey, 2006.

Pennell, C. R. *Bandits at Sea*. New York University Press, 2000.

Perl, Lila, and Erika Weihs. *Mummies, Tombs, and Treasure*. Clarion, 1990.

Perry, Dan. *Blackbeard*. Thunder's Mouth Press, 2006.

"Peter Francisco: Remarkable American Revolutionary War Soldier." *American History Magazine*. October 1998.

Pham, John Peter. *Heirs of the Fisherman*. Oxford, 2004.

Pliny the Elder. *Naturalis Historia*. Trans. John Bostock and H. T. Riley. Bohn's Classical Library, 1855.

Plutarch. *Fall of the Roman Republic*. Trans. Rex Warner. Penguin, 1958.

———. *Lives*. Trans. W. Heinemann. Loeb Classical Library, 1988.

Polo, Marco. *The Travels of Marco Polo*. Cosimo, 2007.

Polyaenus. *Stratagems of War*. Trans. R. Shepherd. London, 1793.

Porter, Roy. *The Greatest Benefit to Mankind*. W. W. Norton, 1997.

Pringle, Patrick. *Jolly Roger*. Courier Dover, 2001.

Pryor, Alton. *The Lawmen*. Stagecoach, 2006.

Rabinovich, Abraham. "Shattered Heights." *Jerusalem Post*. September 25, 1998.

Rasenberger, Jim. *America, 1908*. Simon and Schuster, 2007.

Ratti, Oscar, and Adele Westbrook. *Secrets of the Samurai*. Tuttle, 1991.

Rausch, David A., and Blair Schlepp. *Native American Voices*. Deutsche Wirtschaft, 1994.

Regan, Geoffrey. *The Brassey's Book of Military Blunders*. Brassey's, 2000.

Reynolds, Patrick, and Brett Tjaden. *The Oracle of Bacon*. http://oracleofbacon.org/, 2008.

Richthofen, Manfred von. *The Red Battle Flyer*. Trans. J. Ellis Barker. R. M. McBride, 1918.

Riha, Thomas. *Readings in Russian Civilization*. University of Chicago Press, 1969.

Roberts, Craig, and Charles W. Sasser. *Crosshairs on the Killzone*. Simon and Schuster, 2004.

Rosa, Joseph A. *They Called Him Wild Bill*. University of Oklahoma Press, 1974.

Rose, Carol. *Giants, Monsters, and Dragons*. W. W. Norton, 2001.

Rossabi, Morris. *Kublai Khan*. University of California Press, 1989.

Sakaida, Henry, and Christa Hook. *Heroines of the Soviet Union 1941–45*. Osprey, 2003.

Saga of Erik the Red. Trans. J. Sephton. 1880.

Santamaria, Jason A., Vincent Martino, and Eric K. Clemons. *The Marine Corps Way*. McGraw-Hill, 2005.

Saxo, Grammaticus. *The Danish History*. Trans. Oliver Elton et al. Norroena Society, 1906.

Schom, Alan. *Napoleon Bonaparte*. Harper, 1998.

Scriptores Historiae Augustae. Trans. David Magie, Susan Helen Ballou, and Ainsworth O'Brien-Moore. Harvard University Press, 2000.

Seifer, Marc J. *Wizard: The Life and Times of Nikola Tesla*. Citadel, 1999.

Sharma, Gautam. *Valour and Sacrifice*. Allied, 1990.

Shaw, Karl. *Book of Oddballs and Eccentrics*. Book Sales, 2004.

Shaw, Stanford J., and Ezel Kural Shaw. *History of the Ottoman Empire and Modern Turkey*. Cambridge University Press, 1976.

Sima Qian. *Records of the Grand Historian*. Trans. Burton Watson. Columbia University Press, 1993.

Sjoholm, Barbara. *The Pirate Queen*. Seal Press, 2004.

Smith, Robert Barr. "Fighting Jack Churchill Survived a Wartime Odyssey Beyond Compare." *WWII History Magazine*. July 2005.

"Somali Pirates Free Arms Ship." BBC News. February 5, 2009.

Southern, Pat. *The Roman Army*. Oxford University Press, 2007.

Southey, Robert, and Charles Michael Wolseley. *History of the Peninsular War*. J. Murray, 1837.

Southey, Robert. *The Life of Admiral Horatio Nelson*. Perkins, 1902.

Stackpole, Michael, et al. *Wasteland*. Electronic Arts, 1988.

Strebe, Amy Goodpaster. *Flying for Her Country*. Greenwood, 2007.

Sturluson, Snorri. *Heimskringla*. Trans. Erling Monson and Albert Hugh Smith. Courier Dover, 1990.

Suetonius. *The Lives of the Twelve Caesars*. Trans. Alexander Thomson and Thomas Forrester. G. Bell and Sons, 1911.

Tabari, Abu Ja'far. *The History of al-Tabari*. Trans. Michael Fishbein. State University of New York Press, 1997.

Tacitus. *The Annals of Imperial Rome*. Trans. Michael Grant. Penguin, 1956.

Tesla, Nikola. *My Inventions*. Filquarian, 2006.

Thomas, Bruce. *Bruce Lee*. Frog, 1994.

Thomas, Hugh M. *Norman Conquest*. Rowman and Littlefield, 2008.

Thomas, Susanna. *Rameses II*. Rosen, 2003.

Thucydides. *History of the Peloponnesian War*. Trans. C. F. Smith. Loeb Classical Library, 1923.

Timm, Annette, and Joshua A. Sanborn. *Gender, Sex, and the Shaping of Modern Europe*. Berg, 2007.

Tokitsu, Kenji. *Miyamoto Musashi: His Life and Writings*. Trans. Sherab Chodzen Kohn. Weatherhill, 2005.

Torres, Jake. "Peruna Is the Real Deal." *SMU Daily Campus*. October 29, 2008.

Tucker, Spencer, Laura Wood, and Justin D. Murphy. *European Powers in the First World War*. Taylor and Francis, 1996.

Turnbull, Stephen. *The Lone Samurai and the Martial Arts*. Arms and Armour, 1990.

——. *Samurai Swordsman*. Tuttle, 2008.

Turnbull, Stephen, and Wayne Reynolds. *Ninja AD 1460–1650*. Osprey, 2003.

Tyldesley, Joyce. *Ramesses: Egypt's Greatest Pharaoh*. Penguin, 2000.

Tyrrell, William Blake. *The Smell of Sweat*. Bolchazy-Carducci, 2004.

Van der Vat, Dan. "Bhanubhakta Gurung VC." *Guardian*. April 22, 2008.

Vaughn, Jack, and Mike Lee. *The Legendary Bruce Lee*. Black Belt Communications, 1986.

Wallace, Martin. *100 Irish Lives*. Rowman and Littlefield, 1983.

Warry, John. *Warfare in the Classical World*. Salamander, 1980.

Weatherford, Jack. *Genghis Khan and the Making of the Modern World*. New York: Three Rivers Press, 2004.

Widrow, Martin. *French Foreign Legion*. Osprey, 1971.

Whitelaw, Ian. *A Measure of All Things*. Macmillan, 2007.

Williamson, Gordon. *Knight's Cross with Diamond Recipients*. Osprey, 2006.

Wilson, Joe. *The 761st "Black Panther" Tank Battalion in World War II*. McFarland, 1999.

Wilson, William Scott. *The Lone Samurai*. Kodansha, 2004.

Wise, James E., and Scott Baron. *The Navy Cross*. Naval Institute Press, 2007.

Wolpert, Stanley. *A New History of India*. 6th ed. Oxford University Press, 2000.

Wood, W. J., and John S. D. Eisenhower. *Battles of the Revolutionary War*. Da Capo Press, 2003.

Woodbury, George, and Woodes Rogers. *The Great Days of Piracy in the West Indies*. Norton, 1951.

Wright, David Curtis. *The History of China*. Greenwood, 2001.

Xenophon. *The Anabasis*. Trans. Edward Spellman and Maurice Ashley Cooper. Harper and Bros., 1867.

——. *The Persian Expedition*. Trans. Rex Warner. Penguin, 1949.

Yi Sun-sin. *Nanjung Ilgi*. Trans. Ha Tae-hung. Yonsei University Press, 1980.

Yong, Charlotte. *Cameos in English History: From Rollo to Edward II*. Kessinger, 2004.

Zabecki, David T. "Heavy Gustav." *World War II: A Student Encyclopedia*. ABC-CLIO, 2005.

Zerjal, Tatiana, et al. "The Genetic History of the Mongols." *American Journal of Human Genetics* 72, 3 (March 2003): 717–21.

ACKNOWLEDGMENTS

Don't do anything by half. If you love someone, love them with all your soul.
When you go to work, work your ass off. When you hate someone,
hate them until it hurts.

—Henry Rollins

My sincerest gratitude goes out to the following people who aided me on my epic quest:

First and foremost to my wife, the illustrious Hot Andrea. I could never have done this without her constant support and endless patience. Even on my most hopeless days I always know that I can count on her for a good laugh, a word of encouragement, and as a second player in all my favorite video games.

To my brother Clay, for helping me in every stage of the process and talking me through some of the most difficult creative and stylistic decisions I had to make. From article selection to proofreading, he put in countless hours of reading, rereading, re-rereading, and editing to help me ensure that the final product was the best it could possibly be.

To my family—my dad for getting me interested in history from an early age, my mom for always convincing me that I can achieve anything, my grandmother for always being supportive of all my endeavors, and my brother John, who is the biggest badass I know in real life. To J. Matt for all the hard work he put in helping me edit and improve the book, and to all my friends who gave me encouragement along the way: Matt, Andrew,

Jess, Rick, Bill, Tom, Chris, BLT, Mike, Evan, Sarah, Brian, Maria, and John; my in-laws Manoli, Suella, James, and Sophia; the Classical Studies faculty at Boston University; the SMU Sports Information Office and Meadows School Dean's Office; the UWSOM Dean's office; and everyone else who assisted me throughout this process. To Sir Lucius et Algerion Diamond, First of His Name and Champion of Righteousness, aka Michael Roy. He didn't get a chance to see this book published, but his memory will continue to live on in the hearts of those who knew him.

To my agent, Farley Chase of the Waxman Agency, for believing in this project from the beginning; to my editor, Matthew Benjamin at HarperCollins, for advocating on my behalf, guiding me through the entire process, and letting me know when my crazy run-on sentences and obscure 1990s pop culture references were getting way too over the top; to Jessica Deputato of HarperCollins, for warning me when my off-color remarks might cause an international incident; to my copy chief, Amy Vreeland, for fixing my terrible grammar; to designer Lorie Pagnozzi, for making the finished product look appropriately badass; and to Lance Rosen, Bob Woody, and Sandy Mallenbaum, for helping me sort out all of the appropriate legal issues.

To my illustrators, Thomas Denmark, Miguel Coimbra, Matt Haley and Steven Belledin, all of whom produced amazing work. Their art makes these characters come alive in a way that words could never do, and I am sincerely in awe of their incredible talent.

To Whitney, Rose, and the rest of the staff at the Marriott Residence Inn in Seattle, for finding the flash drive containing the only electronic copy of this book *both* times I lost it in the hotel computer lab.

And last but certainly not least, to all of the fans of the website, not only those who have e-mailed me suggestions and kind words but also all those who simply gave their silent approval by visiting the page each and every week. Without you, none of this would have been possible.

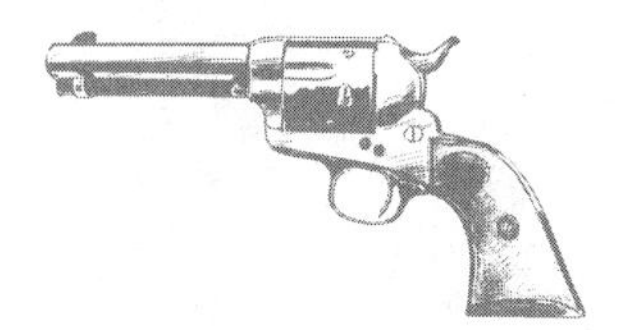

ILLUSTRATION CREDITS

Steven Belledin (www.stevenbelledin.com): Cover art, Alexander, William, Vlad, Bonny, Francisco, Ness.

Miguel Coimbra (www.miguelcoimbra.com): Caesar, Surena, El Cid, Tomoe, Genghis Khan.

Thomas Denmark (www.studiodenmark.com): Leonidas, Liu Ji, Justinian, Peter the Great, section maps, and the warrior battles along the bottoms of the pages.

Matt Haley (www.matthaley.com): Ramses, Chandragupta, Agrippina, Alaric, Khalid, Martel, Wolf, Harald, Musashi, Blackbeard, Nelson, Agustina, Reeves, Tesla, Richthofen, Johnson, Churchill, Sebrova, Gurung, Patton, Hathcock, Lee, Netanyahu, and everything else.

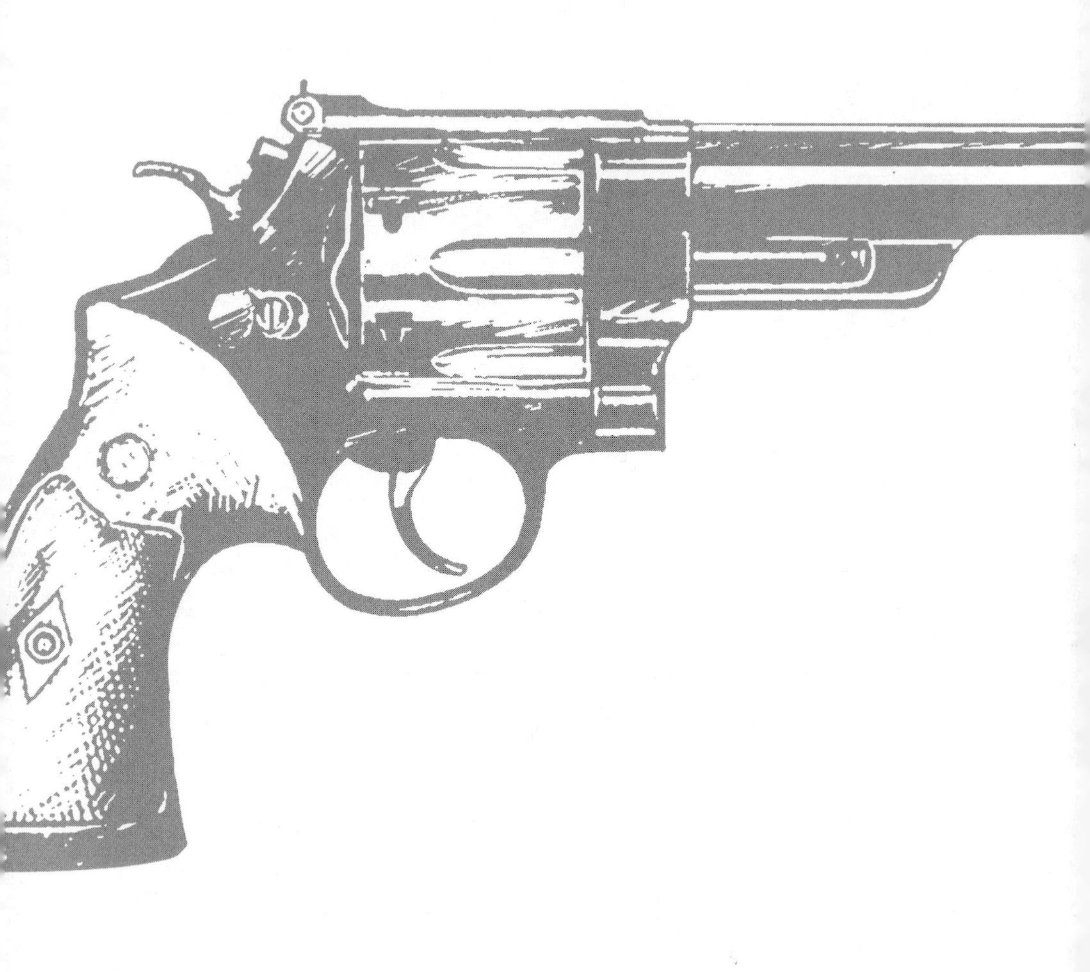

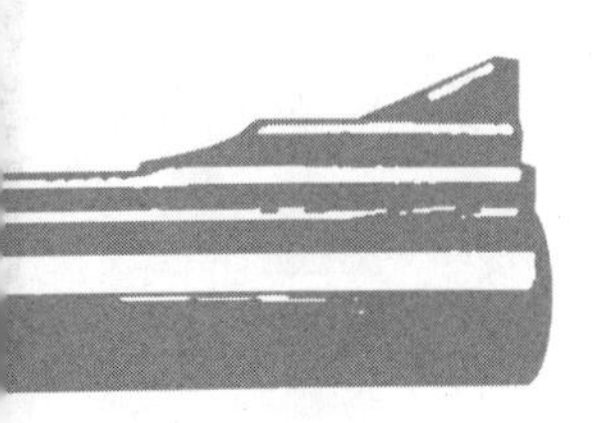

BEN THOMPSON: Badass Expert, +5 Charisma

Thompson is a lifelong student of history. After graduating from the honors program at Florida State University with degrees in history and political science, Thompson realized he needed a real job. He has spent the last seven years working as a full-time corporate wage slave, and spends his free time researching and writing about great badasses in history. He runs the highly successful website badass oftheweek.com and currently lives in Seattle with his wife.